RIGHT THROUGH ME

a novel

by Shannon McKenna

For information contact:
http://shannonmckenna.com

Edited by Hilary Sares
Cover design by Wax Creative

Paperback ISBN: 978-0-9977941-1-3
Digital ISBN: 978-0-9977941-0-6

First Edition: July 2016
10 9 8 7 6 5 4 3 2 1

Dedication

... for Hilary Sares, my editor, for making me spit nails and spill ink.

... and for Lisa Marie Rice, for the hand-holding and the ass-kicking.

Also by Shannon McKenna

PRAISE for the novels of Shannon McKenna . . .

"Blends an intensely terrifying psychic thriller with a mind-blowing erotic romance."
—Library Journal, on *Fade To Midnight*

"Blasts readers with a highly charged, action-adventure romance . . . extra steamy."
—Booklist

"Pulse-pounding . . . with searing sex and raw emotions."
—Romantic Times, 4 ½ stars

"Shannon McKenna makes the pulse pound."
—Bookpage

"Shannon McKenna introduces us to fleshed-out characters in a tailspin plot that culminates in an explosive ending."
—Fresh Fiction

"An erotic romance in a suspense vehicle on overdrive. . . sizzles!"
—RT Book Reviews

"McKenna expertly stokes the fires of romantic tension."
—Publishers Weekly

"McKenna strikes gold again."
—Publishers Weekly

"Her books will take readers on a nonstop thrill ride and leave them begging for more when the last pages are devoured."
—Maya Banks, *New York Times* bestselling author

"Full of turbocharged sex scenes, this action-packed novel is sure to be a crowd pleaser."
—Publishers Weekly on *Edge Of Midnight*

"Highly creative. . . erotic sex and constant danger."
—Romantic Times on *Hot Night* (4 ½-star review and a Top Pick)

"Aims for the heart with scorching precision."
—Publishers Weekly on Ultimate Weapon

Chapter 1

SOMEONE JUST CUT the lights. What the hell?

Noah Gallagher put down his pen and looked around, startled, as drums began to thump from the hidden sound system of the penthouse conference room. Some exotic instrument joined in, throbbing and wailing.

The door to the conference room opened to a shimmery jingling sound, then a flash of fluttering purple. Everyone at the table was staring and murmuring.

Oh, Christ. Not possible. Noah rose to his feet, but the belly dancer was already halfway through the door, her hands weaving in a hypnotic pattern. Wide, light-catching green eyes laughed at him brazenly as she shimmied straight toward him, leading with one pulsing hip.

Her eyes caught him . . . and held him.

The world narrowed down. Whatever he was going to say or do stopped. Words were gone. Air was gone. Air didn't matter. Nothing moved while she moved.

She had commandeered all movement. With that smile. Those eyes.

He was sitting again, with no memory of deciding to do so. His mind had gone blank. The woman was like a walking, breathing stun code, personally keyed to him. He'd always wondered how it would feel to be one of the unlucky chosen few at Midlands who'd gotten stun and kill codes embedded in their minds. His own brain implants had been bad enough. Stun and kill codes were worse.

But this dancer wasn't a goddamn stun code. She was just a random woman, shaking her stuff. When her act was done, he'd pull it together. Exert the fucking authority he was entitled to as the CEO of Angel Enterprises.

He had exactly until the music stopped to get control of himself.

Simple enough to figure out who'd dreamed up this unwanted birthday present. His younger sister Hannah lurked by the door. The wide-angle enhancement of his sight made it possible to see the gleam in Hannah's eyes without looking away from the belly dancer for a single second.

Not that he could have looked away.

He saw his fiancée Simone's face with his peripheral vision. She'd chosen to sit at his side for this important meeting. It was painfully obvious from her tight, expectant smile that she was waiting for him to turn to her, to smile and laugh and make light of this stupid situation. Not just for her. For everyone in the room.

He couldn't do it.

Try. Do an analog dive. Grab a hook. Concentrate.

A spotlight from somewhere gilded the dancer's body, highlighting every perfect detail. Silver anklets that jingled over her small, bare feet. Golden toenails. Shapely legs flashed between purple veils that floated from a low-slung, glittering belt. The belt and top were swagged with shining chains and dangling beadwork. Still more chains, draped from an ornate headdress, dangled over her forehead and under her chin, creating a constant soft shimmer of sound.

High, full breasts quivered, lovingly presented in the spangle-studded velvet bra. She arched back, floating a purple veil edged with spangles high in the air above herself and swishing her thick fall of of glossy black hair around.

Had to be fake hair, falling to well below her ass. It brushed the curve of her hips. Fanned out as she twirled.

Everything he'd monitored in his peripheral vision was gone now. He no longer saw Hannah, or Simone, or anything else. His inner vision was too busy with the vivid fantasy of that woman straddling him. Imagining her bold, sensual smile as she swayed over him, teased him. Running her fingers through her hair, lifting it, tossing it. Coiling it around her waist like a slave rope.

He wanted to rip away all the filmy veils and all the goddamn beads and chains. See her bare-assed. Bare-breasted. Yeah.

The deep curve of her waist was perfectly shaped for his fingers to grip. The curves and hollows of her belly and her hips looked so soft. Touchable.

His hands shook with the urge to reach, stroke. Seize.

The rush of erotic images ramped up his advanced visual processor into screaming overdrive. Even with eyes shielded from eighty percent of the ambient light, even using a double layer of custom-designed shield specs, his AVP combat program was off and running, scrolling a thick column of data analysis past his inner eye.

And even that couldn't distract him from her show. Not for one instant.

His heightened senses reached out, so greedy for more that he found himself actually taking off the back-up shield specs. He'd have popped out the contacts, too, but his AVP was already going nuts at the lower protection level. Combine that with adrenaline, and a huge blast of sexual arousal—*fuck*.

The light level in this room could zap him into a stress flashback if he didn't protect his eyes. Not only that. The dark shield strength contact lenses hid the animal flash of amber luminosity caused by his visual implants. Outsiders couldn't be allowed to see that. The room was packed with outsiders. He wanted them gone.

Especially Simone. Which made him a total asshole. He tried hard, really hard, to feel guilty. Not so much as a twinge. His conscious mind had been almost totally hijacked by the dancer.

He wanted to throw everyone else out and lock the door. Study that woman with his naked eyes, dancing under the spotlight. But only for him. He wanted to gulp in the whole data flow. It was being filtered out in real time and lost to him forever, and it drove him . . . fucking . . . *nuts*.

And he couldn't do a thing. Not with an audience. His fists clenched in fury.

Heart racing, temperature spiking. Sweating profusely. No way to hide it. It was an AVP stress dump. A massive dose of fight-and-conquer energy, channeling straight into his dick, which strained desperately against his pants.

He struggled to grab onto the analog hooks that he'd established. His hooks were emergency mental shortcuts, activating an instant, deep withdrawal into the ice caves of his subconscious mind when the AVP got out of control. Best way he could devise to calm his stress reactions and stay on top of himself.

Not a hook to be had. Couldn't find them, couldn't feel them. Couldn't use his highly developed power of visualization at all, after years of grueling practice. All gone.

He was fully occupied imagining that woman naked and writhing beneath him.

His intense reaction to this spectacle made no sense. He'd seen belly dancing before and been unmoved. He did not have complicated fantasies or fetishes. He didn't even get the fun factor. He wasn't known for his sense of humor. In fact, he had no imagination at all, unless you counted biotech engineering designs, or plotting ways to grow his business, or scheming to keep his chosen family alive, secret, and safe.

That demanding enterprise left no bandwidth for fun and games.

He wasn't playful about sex, either. He was tireless, focused. Relentless in making sure that his partners were satisfied. To the point of exhaustion, even. Theirs, not his. They would tell him he was the hottest lover ever and then call him cold.

So? Noah didn't do emotions. Cold was safer for everyone concerned.

Not that he could explain that to whoever happened to be in bed with him.

He couldn't change his nature. He saw to it that his lovers had many orgasms to his one, to compensate for those mysterious intangibles. Whatever the fuck else they wanted from him, it just wasn't there. He didn't even know where to look for it.

The dancer's arms lifted, swayed. He inhaled the scent of her dewy skin as she spun closer. Fresh, sweet, hot. Sun on the flowers. Rain on the grass. His mouth watered.

Since what happened at Midlands, his senses were sharper than normal by many orders of magnitude. He had ways to blunt the overload, but not this time. He was catching a full data load now, shields and all. Tripping out on her undulating hand movements.

He was reading her energy signature, right through the shield lenses. A cloud of hot, brilliant colors surrounded her. Her floating purple veils blended with trailing clouds of her body's energy, to which his AVP overstimulated brain assigned all the colors of the spectrum and more besides. Colors not visible to anyone but him.

Along with it a strange sensation was growing. Tension, anticipation. Dread.

He was used to being alone in an insulated bubble. Other people's drama raged outside that protective barrier and left him completely untouched. He needed it that way to stay in control. Maintaining isolation required constant effort and vigilance.

Now, suddenly, he wasn't alone. The girl had danced through his force field. Invaded his inner space. It was messy and crowded in there now.

She took up room. Confused him with her colors, her scents. Her smile was so unforced and sensual. She was bonelessly flexible, yet still regal in her diaphanous veils.

It made him jittery to have someone so close. The intimacy felt awkward. Ticklish.

He felt hot, red. No control over his face. Stuck here, sitting among colleagues and family, right next to his fiancée. Any one of them could watch him watch her. At least the massive conference table concealed his colossal hard-on.

He had not felt this helpless since Midlands.

Her luminous green eyes met his and then flicked away, but the electric buzz of that split instant of intimacy jolted him to depths he'd never felt before.

He knew he'd never seen this woman before, and yet he recognized her.

* * *

Caro narrowly missed slamming her hip into the table. For the third time.

Look away from the guy, for God's sake. Get a grip. It's just a dance.

But her gaze kept getting sucked back to Noah Gallagher, the birthday boy. Ultra-powerful CEO of the oh-so-myserious Angel Enterprises, cutting-edge biotech firm.

The man was gorgeous. Barrel chested. A dense slab of muscle. Short hair showed off the sharp planes and angles of his face, a wide, strong jaw. He wore shaded glasses, but he'd taken them off a few seconds into her dance. It was incredibly hard to stay focused on the music and remember her moves while being examined with such blazing intensity. It wiped her mind blank. Made her lose the thread.

To say nothing of her physical balance.

Holy flipping *wow*. They said he was turning thirty-two today, but he seemed older, or maybe it was just his expression. Each time she twirled, she snagged a new yummy detail. The shape of his ears. Thick, straight dark brows. Sexy grooves framing a stern but still sensual mouth. Sharp cheekbones. His face was a taut mask of tension, as if he were suppressing strong emotion. But it was his eyes that really got to her.

His scorching laser focus made her temperature rise. She'd always been sensitive to the quality of a person's energy. Noah Gallagher's energy dominated the room. He looked like he'd tear you to pieces if you gave him any trouble, despite the elegant suit that sat just right on his huge shoulders. He didn't laugh or look embarrassed like most men did when surprised by a belly dancer. He just sat there, with the charged stillness of a predator poised to spring. Radiating danger.

Her smile faltered as she shimmied and spun. Suddenly, she was hyper-conscious of the erotic allure of the dance. His silent, very male sexual energy made it feel deadly serious. As if they were alone, and she'd been summoned for a private, uninhibited performance designed to drive him crazy.

Oh my. What a stimulating scenario.

She was actually getting aroused. For the love of God. Rising panic began to shred the sensation. Enough of this ridiculous crap. She had to get out of here, and fast.

Finish the dance. You need the cash. He's only a hot guy, not a celestial being. You're freaking yourself out. Chill. Usually she spread the wealth, bestowing flirtatious smiles on everyone. Not tonight. They weren't feeling it. Young men were usually always enthusiastic, and there were several of them here, but no one made a sound. Tension was thick in the air. No laughter, no snickering, no whistles.

Who cared. Her mind was fully occupied with the task of not gaping at Noah Gallagher's godlike hotness. Being aware of every inch of skin she displayed to him.

Her gaze bounced across the blond woman who sat next to him. A little younger, but not a colleague or an assistant. They sat too close together for that. The woman's mouth looked tight and miserable. Next to her sat a flushed, heavy older man who stared fixedly at Caro's beaded bra, nostrils flared.

Rise up, cupcake. Take back the power. This was a tough crowd, maybe, but everything was relative. The people in this room weren't trying to frame her for murder, kidnap her or kill her. And she certainly had the birthday boy's full attention.

So she'd play with it. What the fucking hell. That man needed to be humbled. To worship at the feet of her divine awesomeness. She'd dance like she'd never danced before, blow his mind, and melt away, forever nameless. Leaving him to ache and writhe.

That's right, big boy. Prepare to suffer.

But Noah Gallagher's fierce, unwavering gaze was having a strange effect on her. Ever since she'd gone into hiding, she'd had a sick, heavy lump in her belly. For months it had been sitting there, like a chunk of dirty ice that would not melt. But when she looked at him, that pinched coldness eased. It turned soft and warm and alive.

It felt amazingly good. Dancing for him, she could actually breathe again.

For as long it lasted.

The dance was ending. Caro sank to her knees, arching back in a pose of abandoned sensual ecstasy as the music reached its climax, luxurious fake hair brushing the ground in her grand finale. Dancing had never made her feel so naked before. She was stretched before him like a sacrificial virgin on an altar.

Take me.

The pose felt obscene, but only because there were other people in the room. If there hadn't been, it would have felt right. It would have felt . . . *hot.*

The sound of one person frantically clapping broke the silence. Hannah Gallagher, the girl who had hired her. Noah Gallagher's younger sister, from the looks of her. Caro rose slowly to her feet. Noah Gallagher didn't applaud. He just stared at her, as if he wanted to leap over that table and pin her down.

Tension built like an electrical charge. The other people in the room looked up, down, anywhere but at her. Caro smiled brightly. Held her head as high as possible.

Not fair, to throw a paid performer into the middle of someone else's big fat faux pas and make her swim in it. Bastards.

"That was fabulous!" Hannah's voice was a little too high. "Thanks for a gorgeous dance, Shamira! Happy birthday, Noah! Wasn't she awesome, everyone?"

Not one yes. There was only dead silence, downcast eyes, awkward looks exchanged all around. And still, Noah Gallagher's devouring eyes.

So what. She'd stay dignified. While running for her life, fighting the powers of darkness, scrambling for money. Even if it involved putting on a scanty costume and shaking her booty for rude or indifferent strangers.

Or, in this case, one single intense, lustful, smoldering stranger.

She took a slow, deliberate bow, as if she were in front of an adoring crowd. Taking her own sweet time. Rubbing their faces in it.

Take that, you rude shitheads. Like it would kill you to clap.

She didn't need any validation from these self-important bio-tech-nerd idiots. Just her fee, which she would get whether they liked her performance or not.

Fuck 'em. She had things to do. Important things. After one more hungry peek at the mouthwatering godking. Lord, he was fine.

She flash-memorized him in one breathless instant, whipping her gaze away from his face before eye contact could start the inevitable sexual mind-melt reaction. Then she swept out of the room, chin up, shoulders back. A regal sweep of purple veils.

That was it. She would never see him again. She wasn't going to feel that hot rush of opening in her chest, ever again.

Suck it up. Ignore the lust buzz. Sport sex is reserved for normal people. Fugitives do without. And don't whine.

Hannah followed her out of the room, and slammed the door harder than was necessary. "You were gorgeous," she said fervently. "You're so talented. I'm so sorry they didn't clap or anything. I'm going to tell them all off. Noah will kill me, but I'm used to it."

"I'll rather not watch that," Caro said hastily. "I'll just be on my way."

"Oh no! Stay just a minute! You have to at least say hi to Noah. No matter what he says to me, he certainly enjoyed your dance. I'm the villain here. You're just an innocent bystander. Noah's very fair that way. And I'm sure he'll want to meet you!"

In your dreams, honey. "Let me, ah, change first," Caro said, backing away.

"You remember the way to the office? Come back after. I'll introduce you."

The door flew open. A man strode out, not the birthday boy. This one was tall, blue eyed and very built, his thick dark blond hair hanging down to his shoulders. His eyes flicked over her with controlled curiosity and then turned back to Hannah.

"What the *hell* were you thinking?" he asked.

Definitely her cue. Caro took off, hurrying back toward the nondescript office that'd served as a dressing room. She didn't even want to know what Hannah's answer might be. Not her family, not her fight.

Once inside the empty office, she could still hear them arguing from behind the door. Other people had gotten into the mix. Voices were being raised. Her heart pounded as she peeled off her costume and packed it up. She pulled on her shapeless street clothing, trying not to overhear. She had her own problems. Big nasty ones. Time to cruise discreetly away and let them get on with theirs.

Makeup pads got most of the paint off. She rolled the expensive dancing wig into its carrying bag, and put on her street wig, a thick brown bob with heavy bangs and wisps curling in around her face to conceal its shape. When she arrived, she hadn't worn the mouth prosthesis, which puffed out her cheeks and distorted her jawline. She'd figured that the coat and hat were enough weirdness for the client to swallow. But the job was done, and she hoped to God she could slink out unnoticed, so in went the mouth thing. Big tinted glasses finished the look, topped off by her hat with LED lights in the brim, ordered off the Internet to foil facial recognition software her pursuers might use to find her on social media.

Who knew if it really worked. At least the wide brim kept the Seattle drizzle off.

Her hands still shook as she pulled on her oversized black wool coat. The foam lining she'd sewn in bulked up her shoulders and hips. She looked sixty pounds heavier, and slightly humped.

At first, she'd tried changing the way she moved as part of her disguise, but after all the bodywork she'd done in college, she decided that the psychological toll of slumping and shuffling was dangerous to her soul. Inside her frumpy cocoon of foam and wool, she still had her pride and attitude. Hidden, maybe, but structurally intact.

When she exited the office, she looked like a sketch that had been blurred on purpose. Noah Gallagher would stare right through her even if she were inches away.

That thought was so depressing, she could barely stand to think it.

Chin up. She'd had her fun, turning him on. Time for the disappearing act. Eat your heart out, Laser Eyes.

But disappearing didn't feel powerful to her. It just felt flat. Empty and sad.

The route back to the elevators took her right past the conference room.

Hannah Gallagher and several others were still arguing outside it. If she kept her head down, turned the corner and cut swiftly across the open space, she'd only be in their line of vision for a few seconds. Then it was a straight shot to the elevator.

One, two . . . *go.*

When she was squarely in the danger spot, Noah Gallagher came out the door.

That was her undoing. She slowed down. Not consciously, but simply unable to resist the temptation to steal one last look at him before fleeing.

His gaze snapped onto her, like a powerful magnet coupling.

Oh, God. Oh, no. He strode through the center of the group, scattering them, and followed her. Even with her back to him, his eyes burned through her layered, ugly disguise, a focused point of heat against her concealed skin. She stabbed the elevator button. He was twenty yards away. Fifteen, and closing. Picking up speed.

He couldn't have recognized her. In this dreary get-up, she couldn't be more different from Shamira the sexy dancing girl. She barely recognized herself dressed like this. The door slid open. She lunged inside. No other riders, thank God.

"Hold the door!" Gallagher called, loping for the elevator.

Asfuckingif. She punched the close button, and the mechanism engaged.

Their eyes locked, as the doors shut in his face.

Her heart was thudding, as if she'd done something wrong and had almost gotten caught. Maybe he was just wondering who the scruffy stranger was. Dressed like that, she stuck out like a sore thumb in the muted corporate elegance of Angel Enterprises.

She hurried through the lavish front lobby. Outside, a cab was letting a passenger out. She bolted for it, waving it down.

Noah Gallagher emerged from the entrance just as her cab pulled away. His eyes locked onto hers again instantly. Even shadowed by the hat, obscured by the dark glasses, through the back window of a cab that was already a half a block away.

He started running after her. Right out onto the street. Eyes still locked. The contact felt like a wire, pulling tighter and tighter. Then the taxi turned a corner and he was lost to sight. It hurt. As if something vital had been snipped with bolt-cutters.

Her fizz of excitement died away. The cold lump of fear was back in place.

She was so sick of feeling this way. She wanted to yell at the driver to circle the block, just on the off chance of catching one last glimpse of Noah Gallagher. To feel something different than that cold, heavy ache in her core. Just for a second or two.

But she could not have this. Not even a stolen taste of it. She could not let lust trash her good judgment. She had to stay murderously sharp. Constantly on the defensive. Without rest.

Sexual frustration wouldn't kill her.

But there were other things out there that definitely could.

SHANNON MCKENNA

Chapter 2

SHE WAS GONE. He told himself to stop running. *Stop, goddamnit.*

Noah forced himself to stop sprinting and slow to a walk. He stood there in the street, panting. Vibrating with the near-uncontrollable urge to keep pursuing her.

Breathe. Breathe it down.

Cars swerved around him, horns blatting. He was making a spectacle of himself, standing out in the middle of city traffic. Like he gave a shit about the noise and shouted insults. He just kept staring, trying to follow her taxi with his gaze even after it turned the corner. But even his enhanced vision couldn't bend light rays.

The dancer's bulky disguise—it had to be a disguise—couldn't fool him, not now that he'd seen her energy signature. Unique to her. Invisible to anyone but him. Unless, of course, that person used cutting-edge visual imaging, similar to the micro-tech implanted in his own eyes and brain to support his AVP combat programming.

Her energy sig was the most beautiful he'd ever seen. A vivid bloom of color, floating in the air and superimposed over her drab coat. It struck him as intensely feminine, though he'd never assigned any gender attributes to energy sigs before. His hands clenched as he tried to shut down his raging frustration.

At the speed that cab had been going, he could have outrun it without breaking a sweat. Like a panther taking down an antelope. He wouldn't even need AVP to access his emergency fuel stores. He could have wrenched the door right off the vehicle, flung it away and claimed his prize, then and there. Nobody on earth could have stopped him.

He wanted to howl like a wild animal.

Just his luck that she'd gotten away. She'd saved him from police involvement, legal action, media buzz. Viral fucking videos circulating on the Internet, filmed with the phones of whoever was passing by. And somebody was always passing by.

The Obsidian Group was lurking out there, watching and listening for them even years after rebellion day. Ready to come down on him, above all, like a ton of bricks. Behaving the way Obsidian had programmed him to behave would put everything and everyone he cared about in danger.

He would . . . not . . . do it. *No.*

Breathe, dick-for-brains. Grab a hook. Go sit in the freezer until you're capable of at least pretending to be a normal human being.

A car horn blared long and loud, zapping his combat program into furious play again. He whipped his head around. Fixed the offending driver with a lethal stare.

The guy flinched, lifting his hands off the horn. He quickly swerved into the opposing lane of traffic to stay well clear of Noah's highly effective Look of Death, tires squealing as he accelerated away. The other cars stopped well short of him and waited as he strode across the roadway and back onto the sidewalk.

The combat program was in full swing, measuring and analyzing everything his enhanced eyes perceived, pumping him full of corrosive stress hormones. Everyone he saw was was an enemy, automatically assessed for threat level. The program churned out an instantaneous bare-hands kill plan for each one, urging him to act, move, take them out fast, kill them, kill them now, now, *now* . . .

No. Those people are not enemies. They're ordinary citizens of Seattle going about their usual afternoon business. Step back.

He would not follow their program. He was his own man. He was who he chose to be. Not Obsidian's rabid hound lunging on a chain. Fuck that. *Fuck* them.

Grab the hook. Grab it!

He swiftly descended into his most efficient analog, an arctic glacier, a maze of ice caves, blue-tinted and deep. All senses engaged with the biting cold to chill him . . . the fuck . . . *out.*

The red haze retreated. The constant scroll of data down his field of vision began to slow down, as did his thudding heartbeat. He was still generating kill plans, but the urge to violently follow through on them was ebbing. Slowly.

He'd trained himself over the years to function normally in the outside world while simultaneously analog diving. It created a double vision effect, but he was used to it, to the point where he could even conduct a coherent business conversation like that.

He chilled in his ice cave while he made his way back into the office building. Ignoring people's puzzled stares in the same way that he ignored the combat program's helpful, detailed suggestions as to how to most efficiently tear them all into small, bloody pieces.

Yeah. Thanks. Not today.

He hadn't had a stress event this severe in over ten years. And right in the middle of an important meeting. Seconds away from signing key documents.

Hannah's timing was a balls-on disaster. Everyone in that room, including his fiancée and her stepfather, had seen him chasing a party entertainer out of the building in much the way that a big predator chased down its lunch.

That was going to be tough to explain. He couldn't even explain it to himself. He faked normal pretty well these days, for the most part. He did all the normal things. He'd even gotten engaged to Simone Brightman, the perfect woman.

He had his shit together, or so he thought. He was on top of the bad stuff in his past. He'd left it behind, had not allowed it to define him. Heading down the straight and narrow path to marriage, kids, a house in the suburbs. What could be more normal than that?

So his reasoning had gone. But he'd obviously been fooling himself. If a pretty dancing girl could knock him right off his rails and get him running AVP hot, right out of fucking nowhere . . . that was bad.

He was still deep in the shit. Deeper than he'd thought. He groped for the shades in his jacket pocket. Put them on. The extra light shield helped a little.

He should have talked to Simone about this, but what could he say? He couldn't tell her the truth about Midlands and what happened there. He couldn't come clean about his modifications.

His phone buzzed in his pocket as he waited for the elevator. He pulled it out. An encrypted message on his private line.

Heads up. yr future father-in-law Batello has dealings with Mayburg Group, a subsidiary of Obsidian. Don't sign. Asa

The text message was followed by a series of links.

He realized some time later that he was blocking the entrance to the elevator. People were sidling awkwardly around him, shooting him nervous glances. They sensed the buzzing bad energy he was giving off. There was once again a personalized kill plan glowing on his inner screen for every single person in his line of vision.

Batello? How could Noah and his team have missed a connection between Batello and Obsidian, with all their due diligence? And how the *fuck* did his brother Asa know about it?

How did Asa know anything about them at all, after thirteen years without contact?

His mind reeled. His focus was blasted all to shit. *Asa?*

As soon as he could move at all, he followed the first directive in his own damage control checklist. *Isolate yourself ASAP.*

Stairwell. He went for it.

Twenty-four flights of stairs at a dead sprint would drain off some excess energy.

So would randomly killing someone. Whatever happened first.

*   *   *

It was hard to sit still. The bus lumbered through the University District. Not her first choice for a getaway vehicle, but it had been stopped near the taxi when Caro jumped out. She perched on the plastic seat, vibrating with urgency. She wanted to jump up, run, yell, do something, anything. Whenever she closed her eyes, she saw Noah Gallagher staring after her cab as he sprinted down the middle of a busy street, as if the honking cars swerving around him were not even a relevant consideration.

She almost wished he'd caught up with her. So strange and sexy, to be seen like that. So deeply. Delicious and toe-curling, that a man like him wanted her attention so much he'd run out into traffic to try and catch her.

It was more fun to think about her fantasy lover than to dwell on the terrifying real issues of her life. But please. She had to stay focused. A psycho killer was after her ass. No one was going to save that ass but her. She was almost certainly being followed, which meant Mark probably knew where she was. She couldn't swoon off into romantic daydreams. Much less full-on sexual fantasies.

The suspicion that she was being tailed began yesterday after she'd seen Bea. By now it was as big and heavy as a rock in her throat. There was no one in the bus to inspire mortal dread, just a Goth girl rocking out to headphones and an old lady opposite her. A plaid purse on her lap held a yappy little dog. The dog stuck its head out and eyed Caro balefully, as if it knew something that Caro didn't.

She'd seen the guy twice yesterday. Big, tall. Black ponytail, hawk nose, strolling casually about a block or so behind her. He hadn't looked directly at her, but that meant nothing. The competent ones never seemed to be looking.

Then she'd spotted him again at the Stray Cat after that stupid bachelor party gig. That clinched it. More than once was once too often. He'd filmed her on his phone. There were no coincidences. If something seemed sinister, it *was* sinister. Count on it.

She craned her neck until it ached, squinting through the rainspotted window at headlights and taillights. She didn't dare draw any more unhealthy attention to Bea, who had problems of her own. It was wrong to pull anyone into the toxic mess of her life.

Like she'd done to Tim.

She shoved that thought away fast, before it could swallow her.

She'd been on the bus since that bizarre belly dancing gig, just riding the loop and hoping to keep Ponytail off her trail until she pinned Bea down one last time.

Sexual fantasies were a huge improvement over her usual thought patterns, at least. Noah Gallagher was going to haunt her dreams, and her dreams were already haunted. His smoldering gaze was a mindblowing distraction.

One she didn't need. Not when she had to fight for her very existence.

Her eyes stung from lack of sleep. Lashes were gummy from old mascara. She rubbed them, and when she opened them, her stomach dropped into a bottomless hole.

Her hands were wet, crimson. Slippery with blood. She held a boxcutter in her shaking hand. It dripped with hot gore.

She looked up, in dread. The big guy who had been with Mark Olund on the night of the attack at Dex's office stood before her. The one who had held her down on the worktable while Mark murdered Dex.

She'd killed him. Almost by accident. She'd grabbed the boxcutter at random with her scrabbling hand, and gotten in a wild lucky jab right to his neck. He'd cut her too, in the brief struggle that took place afterwards. She'd barely noticed at the time.

The ghost man stared at her with pale, accusing eyes. His bloody fingers pressed against the hole she'd punched into his throat. Slowly, tauntingly, he lifted his hand—and hot pulsing spurts of blood pumped out, drenching her.

He grinned, with bloody teeth, and toppled slowly toward her.

She jumped up to evade his falling body with a cry—

He was gone. So was the blood, the boxcutter. Of course. It was just the old lady on the plastic bench, peering up with a suspicious frown. Her tiny dog stuck its head out of the purse and bared its sharp yellow teeth, growling low in its throat.

The bus was dead silent. Everyone was giving her the Look. Shrinking away as far as they could get from a crazy passenger who yelled at things no one else could see.

It made her cringe to be that girl again. With her overdeveloped capacity to visualize, combined with extreme stress, hallucinations could happen out of nowhere. The first time was when she was little, after Mom died. Since then . . . she'd had others.

She knew the difference between fantasy and reality. And it wasn't all bad. Her freakish visual ability had given her art, masks, costume design. It had brought her to the attention of Dex Boyd of GodsEye Biometrics. Which had transformed her life.

Her body clenched instinctively when she thought about Dex. His murder had happened only eight months ago. Still a raw wound in her mind.

The bus lurched to a standstill. It was one stop too soon, but she had to get away from the sidelong glances. She grabbed the bag that held her dancing costume and headed for the exit as the door opened.

The vehicle hissed and groaned and lumbered away, leaving her in near darkness with raw wind gusting around her. Her knees still wobbled from the shock of the ugly hallucination. And now she had twelve extra blocks to walk. Great.

She was chilled to the bone when she found Bea's boyfriend's house. She tucked her glasses into her bag, spat out the jaw prosthesis, peeled off the wig, raking a hand through her flattened hair. She felt horribly exposed without her disguise.

She spun around. No one seemed to be lurking. So far, so good.

The house was a weatherbeaten green, the sparse lawn fenced with chain-link. She went up onto the sagging porch and pressed the doorbell.

The curtains twitched to the side. A man peered out. Her heart sank. She'd been hoping desperately to talk to Bea alone. The door opened, stopped short by a clanking security chain. A stocky, bearded guy peered out. She knew who he was. Todd Blount, originally from Chelan, Washington, a special ed teacher in elementary school.

"Can I help you?" he asked.

"I hope so. I want to speak to Marika." The name Bea used in her new life.

He looked at her suspiciously, but not like he was afraid of her. Caro concluded that he knew diddly about his girlfriend's secrets.

"What's it about?" Todd demanded.

"I knew her back in college," Caro improvised.

"Is she expecting you?"

"Tell her it's Caroline," she said. "We spoke briefly yesterday."

He looked her over. Caro self-consciously smoothed her hair.

"Wait here." The door closed and the chain rattled. Todd wasn't taking chances. Deadbolt was next.

She was debating ringing the bell again when the door opened again. Bea's big blue eyes were red-rimmed. Her formerly ash blond hair had been dyed a dull black that made her look pale and ghoulish.

"I told you no," she whispered fiercely. "How did you find me here?"

"Bea," Caro said softly. "Listen—"

"Don't call me that. I'm Marika, please. And I'm not interested."

"Who's this person, babe?" Todd appeared behind her. He flung an arm over Bea's shoulders.

Bea flinched at the contact and gave him a tight smile. "Just someone I used to know."

The phone began to ring in the room behind them. They all just stood there in an awkward silence, listening to it ring, and ring.

"Uh, would you get that?" Bea asked him. "Let me talk to her. I'll be fine."

The phone rang two more times before Todd grunted in reluctant assent and lifted his possessive arm off Bea's shoulder. "Be right back," he said, still scowling.

Caro leaned forward as soon as he was out of earshot. "Did you look me up online?" she whispered. "New York City? Caroline Bishop?"

Bea's hunted gaze caught hers and slid away.

"I see you did," Caro said. "It's true, what I said yesterday. I'm not out to get you. We could help each other. We both have a problem, and I think it's the same problem. We should join forces."

"You're going to get me killed." Bea's voice was a strangled whisper.

Caro could not argue with that in all good conscience, so she just moved on. "You saw the news stories about me? Because I read the ones about your boyfriend."

"I don't want to talk about Luke," Bea hissed fiercely. "None of your business."

"Mark Olund caught Luke Ryan in the same trap he used for me," Caro's voice was low and insistent. "It was Mark Olund who killed Luke's client and took all that money and jewelry last year. Luke took the blame, but he's innocent, like I am. And you must know something, or you wouldn't be Marika instead of Bea, and selling sandwiches out of a truck instead of finishing your graduate degree at the U of Chicago. Am I right?"

"Keep your voice down." Bea glanced back. "I don't know anything. And how do you know the guy who hurt Luke is this Mark Olund? How can you be so sure?"

"Mark has art pieces that they say Luke Ryan stole. A famous sapphire brooch. I saw it in his apartment. Mark also murdered my boss and set it up to look like I did it. Sound familiar?"

Bea just kept shaking her head until Caro wanted to smack her.

"Luke Ryan didn't rob or kill anybody and neither did I," Caro went on. "I've been looking for you for months." She reached through the crack in the door, and seized the other woman's clammy hand. "Seriously? Do you want to live this way forever?"

Bea tried to jerk her hand back, but Caro's grip was relentless. "I just want to keep living."

"I understand," Caro said. "But we could testify against him. If you have any proof of what Mark did to Luke—"

"Let go." Bea finally jerked her hand away. "Anyone could see you out there."

"So invite me inside," Caro suggested. "It's raining."

"Todd would hear." Bea's eyes darted to the side. "We can't talk here."

Caro's heart sank. "Please, Marika. Please. Help me."

"Tomorrow." Bea's voice was a rushed whisper. "There's a coffee shop off Pioneer Square. Luciano's. I'll meet you there tomorrow morning. Around eight thirty."

"Do you have any evidence?" Caro persisted. "Did you see anything at all?"

Bea's lips flattened. "Not personally. But Luke videoed his meeting with this guy. I retrieved it after Luke disappeared. I was going to give it to the cops, but when I saw it, I just ran. Cops can't protect me from that guy. No one can."

Caro's heart thudded heavily. "A video?" she said. "Of Mark, doing something to Luke Ryan? Holy shit, Bea. What the hell are you waiting for?"

"You don't understand." Bea whispered. "You can't just go after that guy, Mark, or whatever his name is, if we're talking about the same guy. He's like . . . a monster."

Caro flashed on a memory that her mind still struggled to comprehend. Mark Olund, clutching Dex's frail, paralyzed body from behind as his mouth fastened onto the crown of Dex's head. As if kissing it, or somehow . . . sucking on it.

Of course, that was disgusting and crazy. She'd concluded that it was a stress induced hallucination, but Dex had died. That was real.

So was being accused of killing him.

"I've seen him," she said. "I know he's terrifying. But exactly what did Mark do to him?"

"Who's Mark?"

The loud male voice made them both start. Bea spun. "Huh?"

"Is this woman bothering you, baby?" Todd's beefy arms folded over his chest.

"Ah, no," Bea faltered. "No, she's just, ah . . ."

Caro met Bea's eyes. *Does he know?* Bea gave her a desperate head shake. *No.*

"Who's this Mark guy?" Todd persisted, advancing on her.

"Um . . . I'm just doing Step Nine," Caro blurted. "It's part of my recovery."

Bea and Todd looked at her blankly. "Part of your *what*?" Todd said.

"Recovery. I'm in Narc Anon," she improvised. "I just got out of rehab. Cocaine. This is one of the Twelve Steps. You contact anyone that you hurt while you were using and make amends. Unless by so doing you'd hurt them worse, which I hope isn't the case. Back in my snowbunny days, I, um . . . got really high, and, uh, slept with her boyfriend."

"That would be this Mark?" Todd said.

"Yeah. Him." Caro let defensiveness creep into her tone. "So, like, whatever. I'm sorry. It was a slutty thing to do, and it hurt you, and I'm really sorry."

Todd waited for more. Caro just stood there trying to look shamefaced. Easy enough after all that time lurking in the shadows.

"All done?" Todd's tone was cold. "OK then. Good. You're sorry. Go now and sin no more. Have a nice life."

Caro searched Bea's desperate eyes. "Please, Marika?" she asked. "I'm trying so hard to get my life together. Maybe this could help both of us."

"How about you just leave right now, lady?" Todd suggested forcefully.

"I was hoping you'd forgive me," she said to Bea.

"It was always about you, you, you," Bea whined. "And now you're like, what, repenting? And to hell with anyone you leave bleeding on the side of the road."

Caro sighed. "Look, if you want to talk, find me. Please, Marika. Find me."

"I don't know. I'll think about it, but don't hold your breath."

The door shut. Caro descended the porch steps, legs rubbery.

Maybe there was hope after all. As in an actual video to show the Feds that proved Mark had framed another innocent person for theft and murder.

Which made it more credible that he could have done the same to her.

She saw a bus approaching and ran for it, splashing through puddles. City buses were her refuge today, a dry place where she could keep on moving. She couldn't go to her apartment if she was being followed.

Her former life seemed like a dream of crazy luxury. Her nice little New York studio apartment in SoHo, with that beautiful arched window. She'd loved that place. Her gig at GodsEye Biometrics, coaching people into seeing like she did. Or thinking that they could. Whatever. She wasn't a miracle worker.

But oh God, how she'd loved having money for things she needed. Enjoying friends, food. Making art. Being able to go to bed and just sleep. No hellish nightmares. No cold sucking hole inside her as she lay in bed watching what Mark had done to Dex looping over and over in her mind. She couldn't seem to stop that endless replay.

The driver had seen and waited for her, bless him. The bus door opened as she pounded toward it, trying to unthink that random thought about Dex as she scrambled up into the bus. Thinking of Dex was a trigger, and she couldn't afford to—

Oh no. Oh *fuck*. She stared in horror at the bus driver.

His eyes had been torn out just like Tim's. Blood streaked down his face and soaked the front of his uniform. Caro froze, a shriek of horror trapped in her throat.

She shut her eyes, teetering on the edge of screaming panic. *Not real. Not real.*

Noah Gallagher. She seized onto the image of him. His intense gaze as he sprinted after her through the car-clogged street. Searching for her.

The image radiated heat through her.

Air came into her lungs. Slowly, she dared to open her eyes.

". . . gettin' on this bus or not, miss? Come on! I don't got all night!"

The driver had his eyes again. Blue, frowning at her in puzzlement. His uniform was clean, blood free, his buttons straining over a heavy gut. Just a middle-aged man with beard scruff and heavy jowls. He looked tired and annoyed.

A few passengers put in their two cents, rudely.

She mumbled an incoherent apology, scrambled the rest of the way in and found an empty seat, winded. She'd gotten through that so quickly. No nausea. No lingering aura.

Just a vision she couldn't shake of a man like no other. And there wasn't a damn thing she could do to get Noah Gallahger out of her head.

Not that she wanted to.

Chapter 3

NOAH FELT STRANGLED by his own clothing when he got upstairs. He unbuttoned his collar and loosened his tie with an angry tug as he strode through Angel Enterprises. His employees scrambled frantically out of his path. He must look ferocious.

He felt ferocious. He'd been on the verge of acquiring Rand Batello's biomed company. Batello's stepdaughter, the brilliant Simone Brightman, had just recently agreed to marry him. Batello's company seemed a perfect match for Angel Enterprises, just as Simone had seemed perfect for him personally. She was elegant, intelligent, beautiful.

And the safest possible choice for a partner. He would have seen the signs, if Simone were mixed up with Obsidian. He hadn't run AVP on her, since she knew nothing about his past, but even through the contacts and the shield specs, there was no way he could have missed that.

He'd never liked her stepdad Rand, but an annoying in-law was a walking cliché. Noah welcomed anything that added apparent normalcy to his life. Even if it bugged the shit out of him.

But Asa's warning cast Batello in a new light.

It could be a coincidence. Obsidian had its tentacles everywhere. If Obsidian had found them, it wouldn't waste time or resources on infiltration.

It would eat them alive and spit out their bones.

Several of his team, including Hannah, were still crowded around the conference room door when he approached. She called something out to him as he passed, her tone sharp and defensive. He couldn't be bothered to listen or respond.

He had more pressing problems at the moment.

Simone turned to him as he walked into the room. No smile. Her lipstick looked startlingly red against her pale skin.

As always, she was impeccably put together. Understated jewelry, slender figure set off by a silver gray designer suit. Her hair was swept up, invisibly pinned. Pure class. Total sophistication. The absolute opposite of a hired exotic dancer bedecked with dollar-store trinkets and twirling veils.

Simone held herself ramrod straight, looking him right in the eyes.

He wasn't used to that. He realized that he'd never seen her angry before.

"What's going on?" Rand Batello demanded. "Where did you run off to? That belly dancer have anything to do with it?" Rand's fleshy face was even redder and more congested looking than usual.

"No." Noah exhaled before he allowed himself to answer, and the words that came out surprised him. "Things have changed. The deal's off."

There was a breathless moment in the room, just enough time to reflect upon how crazy it was to make a decision this big based on an unsolicited text message.

From Asa. Who he hadn't seen or spoken to in thirteen years and whose agenda was a mystery. But it didn't matter. When Noah made a decision, it stayed made.

Batello shot an accusatory glance at Simone, and then looked at the documentation laid out across the table where Noah had been sitting. "What the fuck? This was a done deal. What the hell happened?"

Obsidian happened. Your secret partner. My family's mortal enemies.

"I can't discuss the details," Noah said.

"The hell you say," Batello sputtered. "You can't back out with no explanation!"

"I just did," Noah replied.

"At least explain why you've changed your mind." Simone's voice was strained.

"Like I just said, I can't. Sorry."

"Sorry?" The pitch of Simone's voice climbed. "You throw this in my face, in front of a room full of people, and then you tell me that you're *sorry?*"

"Yes. I am."

Sisko, his right hand man, caught his eye, sending a silent message. *Good luck with that, my friend.*

Simone crossed her arms over her chest. "This is about us, isn't it?"

"This has nothing to do with us," Noah assured her.

Simone's red lips curled. "Like hell it doesn't."

"Simone, this is not the time or place!" Batello growled.

"Actually it is." Her voice had a bell-like clarity. "I'm entitled to know why he stopped wanting me."

Chairs scraped and the table rattled as all present scrambled to get the hell out of there. Batello alone stood his ground, breathing heavily. "Don't waste words on this son of a bitch," he said. "We'll let our lawyers deal with him."

"Give us a minute, Rand." Simone didn't even turn to look at him.

Batello snarled an obscenity and stumped out of the room.

The door shut behind him and a freshly awful silence fell.

"So?" Simone said. "Do you have anything to say to me worth hearing?"

He didn't.

"Like I thought." Her voice was soft and bitter. "You've got nothing."

Jesus, this was heading right off a cliff, and he couldn't think fast enough to head off the inevitable nosedive. "Listen. Simone. I'm sorry that—"

"Just tell me one thing, Noah. Were you even aware that I was sitting next to you while that girl was shaking her tits in your face?"

He closed his eyes, took a moment. "I knew you were there," he said.

Some answer. Simone was just warming up.

"I'm thinking you did me a favor," she hissed. "First during the dance when you forgot that I existed and went off into your porno fantasyland right in front of everyone. Then just now when you broke the deal. I don't like being blindsided, Noah."

"It wasn't intentional."

"Just . . . shut . . . *up*. I'm not interested in your bullshit." Her voice snapped like a whip. "I'm not sorry this happened, Noah. Better now than after ten years and two kids. Much better now."

Listening to her was like holding a live electrical wire. All he could do was hang on, letting the charge buzz until his teeth rattled and his hair stood on end. The pain in her eyes was very real. The raw anguish in her eyes said it all. He'd thought that she was cool by nature and he'd liked her coolness, hoping it would mesh with his own preference for control. Hoping she might not need the intimacy all the other women he had sex with always wanted.

He'd bought a ring. Proposed. Entered into an actual engagement. He'd promised something that he didn't actually have to give.

He cleared his throat. "I didn't mean to hurt you. Asking you to marry me is the biggest compliment I could pay a woman. I admire you. You're brilliant, accomplished, beautiful. And I . . ." He searched for more. Found nothing to say.

"And you thought that was enough," Simone finished. "Until you didn't."

He didn't dare reply. He was in over his head.

She turned away so all he could see was the sharp line of her jaw, the small gold drop earrings. "You know what, Noah? I really thought you were different."

He had no idea where she was going with this. Certainly nowhere good.

"How?" he asked.

"All that old-fashioned courtship. You, telling me you were happy waiting to have sex. I thought, aw, how sweet. How quirky and unusual and romantic. I thought you must have hidden depths. And that there would be so much more to discover. Hah."

"Simone—"

"But it's all a front. You have no hidden depths. There's nobody home in there. I'm glad I never had sex with you." She tugged her finger, pulling off the square-cut diamond he'd given her. "Take this back."

He held up his hands. "Wait. Simone, can't we talk first?"

"Take it, or I'll flush it in the ladies." She grabbed his hand, and closed his fingers forcibly over the ring. "Do you think I want to remember this feeling? Oh joy and fucking rapture. You want some advice, Noah?"

He wanted advice from her about the way he wanted a fractured skull, but he had no right to show her any attitude. He clenched his teeth and gestured for her to have at. Stick it to him.

"Give yourself a birthday treat." She flung the words at him. "Celebrate your freedom. Play out your pathetic sexual fantasy right here on the conference room table if you want. Better her than me."

She walked out, her elegant back very straight.

Noah stared at the door. The diamond ring dug deep into his palm. He breathed slower, slower . . . until Simone's kill plan winked off his inner screen in the absence of visual stimuli. He was glad when it did.

He'd held back on sex with Simone, and he finally understood why. Because he was afraid of that inevitable moment afterwards. When she'd cuddle up to him with a hopeful, expectant look on her face, and there he'd be, like he always was. Wondering what the fuck to do with her now. And how soon could she leave.

He pressed his hand against the table. The sensual grain of wood made him think of the dancer's hair. That sexy fanning flare it did as she dipped and spun.

Play out your pathetic fantasy right here on the conference room table if you want. Simone's words unleashed vividly erotic images. Lust shocked his unstable AVP into action again. Enough. He'd never analog dived to stall a sexual fantasy before, but there was a first time for everything.

When he had himself more or less together, he stepped out of the conference room and into an unnatural silence. Everyone in the place who had an office with a door that closed was behind it. The ones assigned to cubicles hunkered down and made themselves small while he stalked through the place.

Hannah stood in the corridor by his office door, obviously worried.

"Noah?" she asked.

He shook his head and went into his office. Tossed Simone's ring on his desk. He looked out the floor to ceiling glass window at Mount Rainier, towering in the distance. Barely visible in the fading light of the afternoon.

His office door opened silently. He turned to find Hannah gazing at the ring on his desk. "If a four minute belly dance could break your engagement, then it really needed to be broken," she said flatly.

"Thanks for the advice. Like you know what you're talking about. Your last relationship was over in less than a week."

"So?"

He ignored her mulish look. "So what the *fuck* did you think you were doing? Was this your idea of a joke?"

"Oh. Well, actually, no," Hannah admitted. "We had a very good reason for calling her. The belly dancer was one of Mark Olund's mistresses. Maybe."

Noah stood there, speechless. He couldn't process that info. The warm, vivid woman he'd just seen. The ice cold killer Mark Olund, formerly of his rebel Midlander group. Those two didn't go together in the same breath. Or even the same thought.

"What the fuck are you talking about?" he demanded.

Hannah sighed. "Remember a couple years ago when you told Zade to keep track of all the women Mark hooked up with?"

"Of course I remember," he snapped.

"Well, Zade did. He has bots tracking them, using facial recog," Hannah said. "And the belly dancer was one of them. Zade called me this morning and told me one of Mark's girlfriends was cruising around Seattle within a mile of Angel Enterprises. So we decided to check her out more closely." Hannah shrugged. "I suppose we should have told you. But we thought it would be more interesting this way."

Mark had once been one of them, years ago. He'd undergone the same Midlands brain stim program as Noah. He and Noah were the only two of the Eyes Guys to survive the rebellion.

They had parted ways years ago, when Mark chose another path. A darker one.

"I can think of a lot of reasons why not," Noah said. "And not one good reason to keep me in the dark about it."

"I wanted you to look at her, preferably with AVP," Hannah said. "But she ran away too fast. Skittish. Not that I blame her, if she's had anything to do with Mark. Did you catch up with her outside?"

"No. She was already leaving." He shot Sisko an accusing look.

Sisko threw up his hands. "No clue," he said hastily. "Not my idea."

"This girl showed up on the surveillance vidcam that Zade planted on Bea McDougal's sandwich truck," Hannah told him. "Zade tailed her. Saw her do a belly dancing gig last night. We thought, great. Your birthday was all the excuse we needed."

"Without clearing it with me."

"Clearing it my ass." Hannah's voice was defiant. "We knew exactly what you would say. Grit your teeth. Wait and see. Be patient. Fuck that, Noah. We need leads to find Luke. If Mark sent her to spy on us then she already knows who we are. And you'd know a lot about her right away if you just AVP scanned her."

"You know that I can't take off my shield specs in front of outsiders."

"Outsiders?" Hannah snorted. "Oh, you mean, like, the woman you were about to marry? *That* outsider? The one who can never be allowed to see your real irises?"

"Hannah," Noah warned. "Don't push me."

"We have to start somewhere. You could've organized to see her—"

"In front of my fiancée. Yeah, I can see it. Hey, girl, loved your sexy dance. What do you say we meet for coffee after you put your clothes back on, just us two? Sounds like a genius move, Hannah."

"I was trying to speed things up," Hannah said, annoyed.

"Don't," he said. "It was stupid. And it puts us all in danger."

"You think everything puts us in danger. You have to relax."

"Really?" He laughed harshly. "After a stunt like this?"

"Well, it got weird really fast, when you tore out of the room," Hannah admitted. "And why on earth did you kill the Batello deal? Without even giving us a heads-up?"

Noah pulled Asa's message up on his display, and handed the phone to Hannah.

Her face went white. The dusting of freckles on her face came into sharp focus.

Asa had been Hannah's favorite big brother. Noah was doomed to be the pain-in-the-ass eldest, forever trying to take the place of their absent parents. That left Asa free to be the fun brother, the cool brother. The one Hannah admired and adored. The one who never annoyed or lectured or pestered her. The one who "understood her."

She'd blamed Noah when Asa left. She'd cried for weeks afterwards.

And in exchange for her favorite brother, Noah had given her the Midlands horror show. What a trade-off. He usually managed not to think about that.

Just not when her eyes had that look.

"He tracked you down?" Sisko's eyes widened. "Figured out your identities? Shit. He's good."

"Damn right," Noah said. "He encrypted my message using your private code."

Sisko lunged for the phone, outraged. "What the fuck? He's an unmod. No one cracks my code. Not even Zade."

Noah turned away from him to check out Hannah, who was unnaturally silent. Her eyes had taken on that blank Midlands stare. Her lips had gone blue. Blood pressure drop. His bar had a small espresso machine, so he slid in the coffee capsule and brewed a cup. He sugared up the resulting beverage, and pressed it into Hannah's hand.

"Drink that," he directed. "You're fading."

Hannah's attitude revived enough for her to roll her eyes. She sipped, grimacing.

Noah hit the switch on the wall that engaged the window shades. It was made of the same material he used for shield specs, to filter out all the frequencies that disturbed him and left just enough light to function. The motor hummed as the shades descended.

Sisko sighed as darkness engulfed them. "Great," he muttered. "This again."

"Now?" Hannah asked plaintively. "Really?"

Noah ignored them and popped out the contacts. He could only do a bare-eyes scan in near darkness, and he needed to scan Hannah right now.

Sisko and Hannah exchanged resigned glances. Every time he called a meeting of the Midland rebels, he scanned them. Made sure everyone was chilled. Dangerous secrets hidden. Identities intact. No erratic thought patterns or chemical imbalances.

Everything smooth, normal. Move along, folks, nothing to see here.

He'd lost too many of them already. Some during the Midlands research trials, some in in the rebellion day battle. Some after, lost to traumatic stress, depression and suicide. He'd been the one to persuade them to rebel, at Midlands. But they'd had no real choice. They'd been fighting for their lives.

Obsidian would pay someday. But in the meantime, he would keep an AVP enhanced eagle eye on the ones left, and the very second that one of his people skipped a beat, he'd be all over his or her ass. He'd be damned if he'd lose another one.

Hannah checked out, more or less. Coffee helped. The shock was passing. She was burning too hot with excitement in some places, and too patchy in others, but he'd seen her worse. Sisko looked worried but otherwise normal.

It was his Midlands legacy. All of them had one. Together, they were a circus freakshow, but Noah's hounding kept their weirder stuff under the radar. Mostly.

Hannah gave him a resigned eye-roll. She was the only one who could meet his eyes when he used AVP. The rest of his group avoided his gaze, which took on a luminous, reflective amber glow like a night predator. It made their skins crawl.

He didn't give a shit. They'd survive skin crawl. He was all about survival.

Sisko stared out the shielded window, bored and stoic. Humoring him.

"Let's call him," Hannah said suddenly. "Instead of just sitting here, wondering about him. Call him, right now. Ask him where the hell he's been for thirteen years."

"No," Noah said.

Her mouth tightened. "But if there's such a big hole in our security—"

"He knows too much about us."

"His message doesn't sound like he wishes us any harm," Hannah argued. "Why warn us about Batello and Obsidian if he wanted to hurt us?"

"We don't know anything about him," he snarled.

"That's bullshit. I know him. He's my brother, goddamnit. And I'm not asking for your fucking permission." Hannah spun and marched for the door.

"Stop!" Noah punched all the force of his will into the word. Hannah froze with her back to him, her hand on the door handle. Her slim shoulders vibrated with tension.

"Ease off, Noah." Sisko had a worried frown between his dark brows.

"Do not contact him," Noah said to Hannah, enunciating with harsh clarity. "Do nothing, unless we talk it through first. Do you understand?"

"Oh, yes. I understand perfectly. You were jealous and competetive with him before, and surprise, surprise . . . you still are. Happy birthday, Noah. Fuck you, too."

She slammed the door after herself.

"What the hell is wrong with you?" Sisko demanded. "You having trouble with your combat programming again?"

"I'm fine." Noah handed his phone to Sisko. "Take this number. Find out everything you can about Asa. And follow Hannah. Make sure she doesn't do anything stupid. Thirteen years is a long time. I have no idea who this guy is now."

"I'm on it." Sisko gave the big block of data a swift glance and handed it back. They all had the photographic memory mod, but Sisko's talent for data-gulping and ferreting out information was uncanny even by Midlander standards.

"Find Zade, too. Tell him to get his ass in here to talk to me," Noah said. "But be careful on the phone. We've definitely been hacked."

Sisko gave him one final worried stare before the door fell closed.

Finally, he could just sit alone in the dark and try to chill. These massive back-to-back adrenaline dumps were going to take a long time to metabolize. Good thing he didn't actually need sleep.

Or at least, not what an unmod would call sleep.

There were several episodes in his life that he made a point of not remembering. The one in his mind now made the short list. That day he woke up after Dad's death and found Mom gone. He'd been seventeen. Asa, fifteen. Hannah, nine.

She never came back. CPS had been farming them out to foster homes when Noah took his younger brother and sister and ran away.

He'd kept them going for quite a while. Scrounging, stealing and scamming was all he knew how to do at the time, so he'd clenched his teeth and done it. They had to eat.

He and Asa were both skilled, having learned the craft from Mom and Dad. Places to stay were more complicated, but they managed, sleeping in flophouses, or on the streets. They might have gone on like that indefinitely but for a run of bad luck. Hannah had pneumonia when the Midlands recruiter found them. Asa was being surly and secretive, sneaking out at night. All of them were hungry, dirty and cold.

The recruiter overdid his promo spiel. The way he told it, Midlands was an elite school for magical superkids. Like any elite, desirable place would be free, ever. The guy said Midlands would give them powers, abilities that would make them special.

Riiiight. It sounded like a big fucking fairy tale to him, but he figured, why not go with it for now? Get some hot food, a shower, antibiotics for Hannah. As soon as they were on their feet again, they'd pick a lock and breeze on out of there.

Asa had disagreed violently. Fuck, no, he said. Don't get near the place. Those scumbags would shackle them and eat their livers.

Noah lost it. Told Asa to fuck off. Big fist fight. And Asa had fucked off.

Permanently.

His brother never did get to gloat about being right. Midlands had been worse than he'd ever imagined. And Noah had led his baby sister in there by the hand.

He shoved that thought down into the dark where it belonged. Or tried to. Despite his best efforts, he could still feel its cold dead weight inside him. He needed to leave that stuff behind. He had problems enough to deal with right now.

Like Asa's mysterious message. Aside from its content, the message implied other alarming things. Asa knew Sisko's codes, Noah's cell private number, the secret Batello deal. He knew about Noah's engagement, which had never been announced.

Most of all, he knew about the Obsidian Group, the investors who had funded the Midlands research facility. But how?

He put on the contacts and shield specs again, and raised the shield shades so he could stare at Mount Rainier again. To an unmod the mountain would be completely hidden in the gathering dusk. He could see it just fine even through shield specs.

He'd chosen this office for that mountain. The view chilled him like an analog hook. He'd climbed it many times. Even from a distance, he could

could almost smell the snow, feel icy air burn his nose and the jagged black rock scraping his fingertips.

He pictured huge, cold spaces around him, vast and empty. Big enough even for him to breathe, to move. To fully exist without crashing into anything.

He wondered if he'd screwed them all, with this one impulsive, stupid move.

Asa could be lying about Batello, of course. But why would he? Asa had his faults, sure, but dishonesty was not one of them.

Only death could be more honest than thirteen years of silence

Chapter 4

THE DOOR BURST open. Noah blocked his eyes, but not before the light flooding in gave his head a sharp, rattling zing. *Shit.*

Stupid, not to lock the door while his shield specs were off. He was getting sloppy.

Zade Ryan entered, the door shut, and the light dropped back to manageable levels.

"You could knock," Noah said.

"I don't believe in giving advance warning," Zade replied.

"This isn't a surprise attack." Noah rubbed his throbbing forehead. "I hope."

"Relax, Noah. Sisko told me that I was summoned into your exalted presence, so here I am. I've been out there, doing your bidding."

"Yeah? What bidding was that? Refresh my memory."

"Keeping tabs on Mark Olund's girlfriends, among other things," Zade said. "Did you like your dance? Sisko said the chick made a big impression on you. Sorry I missed it, but I couldn't let her see me, since I'm the one who's been tailing her."

Noah's jaw ached from tension. "You had your heads up your asses to bring her in here without telling me."

Zade looked unrepentant. "She might know something about Luke. Look at this." He tapped at his phone.

Noah turned his AVP on Zade as he established the data connection to do a quick scan. Nothing unusual. Zade looked the same as always, outwardly, which made Noah's teeth grind. He urged his people to blend in visually, with varying levels of success. But Zade took his rejection of Noah's advice to a whole new level. The guy was six-four and two-thirty, and more good-looking than was good for him, though even Noah couldn't fault him for that. But the rest was over the top. The black mane, the earring, the tattoos, and the studded leather jacket, distressed not by a fashion machine but for real after getting scraped a quarter mile over a rough road when Zade wiped out on his motorcycle. Another accident he'd survived somehow. He took chances.

"Is Mark here in town with her?" Noah asked.

"Can't say," Zade said. "I haven't seen any signs of him. Just her. Look. Check this out."

A photo popped up on the wall monitor. Noah narrowed his eyes against the light as a photo of a beautiful girl appeared on the monitor. Long dark curly hair. Pale skin. Light green eyes. She looked younger, more vulnerable, somehow, without the dancer's makeup.

"Hot, right?"

"Yeah." Noah took a moment to ensure that his voice was even. "So what's her story?"

"Creative type. You know, a freelancer. But she used to have a real job. High level tech."

Noah wasn't sure he'd heard right. "Yeah? Doing what exactly?"

"Consulting. Or something like that. But there's a twist. Her boss was murdered last year."

"What?" Noah looked away from the photo, startled. "Murdered how?"

"Shot at close range. She's a person of interest. The investigation turned up evidence that she stole industrial secrets from her boss and sold them."

"Is that all?" The comment was meant to be wry, but Zade didn't get it.

"No. Another man was stabbed to death at the scene. Caroline Bishop hasn't been seen since. But Mark was parading her around like a girlfriend for a little while before the murders, which is why she's in my database. I tagged her photo file with my fave facial-recog program and yesterday I got a ping from the microcam I stuck onto Bea McDougal's sandwich truck. Ran right over and spotted her just in time to start a tail."

Noah studied the monitor. "She didn't kill anyone."

Zade gave a quick nod of agreement. "Which made me think that she was probably framed. Like Luke. She might know something. We should talk to her."

Zade's voice vibrated with suppressed emotion.

Zade's twin brother Luke Ryan was another Midlands veteran of rebellion day.

As of last year, Luke had been chief of security for a Chicago billionaire—until the man was found with two bullets from Luke's gun in his head. Luke himself had vanished, along with eighty million dollars in bearer bonds and a hoard of priceless antique jewelry. A manhunt was launched. Luke stayed lost. So did the loot.

Luke's girlfriend Bea McDougal had changed her name and her appearance, then gone into hiding for reasons still unclear. Noah and his people kept track of her for Luke's sake. Bea aka Marika now sold sandwiches from a food truck, never staying long in any one place. For the past few months she'd been in Seattle.

The Midlanders knew things about Luke that the police, Interpol and the FBI didn't. Most importantly: that Luke was not a killer or a thief. It would never even occur to him to hurt someone innocent or rip someone off.

And he had to be alive. They just didn't know where. Only an all-out psychopath with a full arsenal of augmentations and enhancements could have taken out a warrior like Luke.

Someone like, say, Mark Olund. Who hated them all ferociously.

But they had no proof, and they couldn't reveal their suspicions without giving themselves away. Or so Noah constantly repeated to his restless crew.

"I'll show you her conversation with Bea," Zade said, thumbing his phone. "The microcam was slapped up under the awning."

The still photo on the monitor was replaced by footage of lined-up people peering into a food truck window. "Caroline Bishop is third in line. Big black coat," Zade said. "See her?"

Noah's heart thudded heavily. The woman Zade had indicated was hunched and nondescript. The fisheye lens of the microcam fastened to the truck distorted faces. But he recognized hers when she looked up. The swift glimpse of wide, shadowy eyes was startling. She seemed much thinner and paler than in the photo. She reached for her sandwich, and asked Bea a question.

"No audio?" Noah asked.

"Conked out," Zade said.

Bea flapped her hands in a gesture that was clearly meant to get Caroline Bishop to go away.

She didn't. She appeared to be pleading.

Bea jerked back into the truck and slammed the window shut. The people behind Bishop in line protested. One man knocked on the window. The feed began to blur as the truck pulled away.

Caroline was left behind, standing on the street.

"That's all. Didn't look like Bishop was threatening her, did it?" Zade said.

"More like she was asking her for something," Noah said. "Or begging her."

"What I was thinking myself."

Did you keep tailing her?" Noah asked.

"Yeah." Zade held up his phone. "With this for a backup camera. They went to the hospital. Look." He thumbed the phone again.

This clip showed a slim form in a fuzzy rainbow wig, a big red nose and a baggy patchwork suit. A huge rubber stethoscope hung around her neck.

"She's a clown," Zade said. "Cheering up the kids in the cancer ward."

"How the hell did you blend in there?"

"Grabbed some scrubs from a closet and changed fast. Got lucky on the size. I filmed this from behind a food trolley in the corridor."

The kids in the room were hollow-eyed. Some had IV's, some didn't. Most lay on rolling hospital beds. They watched the spectacle as she juggled fruit, did tricks and examined kids with her toy stethoscope. After her show the camera followed her down a corridor. She disappeared into a bathroom. The figure who emerged was shapeless and stooped, wearing the hat and oversized winter coat that Noah had seen on her earlier that day.

"She stopped in here next," Zade said. The camera zoomed in on a storefront.

"Bounce Entertainment?"

"Her current employer, evidently." Zade stared into his phone, syncing up the video stream with Noah's monitor and zooming in for a closeup of the signs taped to the storefront window.

Noah read aloud in a flat voice. "We're the Party People. Unique Themes for All Occasions and All Ages. Ask About Our Balloon Animals Special. That's a big step down from tech consulting."

"Ya think? OK, then she went to the Stray Cat Pub in Greenwood." More footage in the dark. The audio was a confusing babble. Drums started to throb. Wailing instruments cut through the din.

The camera focused in on a dancing figure swathed in purple veils.

"Belly dancing for a bachelor party," Zade said. "That gave us our idea."

Noah stared at the graceful arch of Bishop's slender back. Veils swayed, light flashed and glittered off her jangling belt and delicate chains. Those striking, tilted green eyes were framed with showy make-up. Her tits jiggled as her hips swiveled with insolent grace. And then there was that smile.

An AVP surge started happening, even via digital footage. His ears roared, his heart galloped.

". . . . Noah?" Zade's voice cut through the buzz. "Hey! You tracking?"

"Huh?" Noah dragged his eyes from the monitor.

"I was just saying, the chick's in hiding. Definitely. She wouldn't be clown-slash-belly dancer if she were on Mark's payroll."

"Let's not jump to conclusions," Noah said.

"God forbid we do anything as attention-getting as jumping, even if it's to conclusions," Zade grumbled. "We just stand around like embalmed corpses."

"I bust my ass to keep you from becoming a corpse," Noah said. "Turn that thing off. I've seen enough."

Zade poked his phone with dramatic emphasis. The flickering screen froze.

"You need more proof?" Zade's voice was belligerent. "Call up the entertainment agency. Ask for Shamira."

Noah willed his heart to slow. "What would that accomplish?"

Zade shrugged. "Might shut you up. Our consensus is that she isn't on Mark's team. He wouldn't let her work these two-bit gigs."

"We don't know that for sure," Noah said.

Zade smirked. "You like to run AVP with the lights way down low, right? So order a dance. Schmooze, flirt, suss this girl out. Use your fucking abilities, dude. Besides, she's not the real problem. Mark is. We should have neutralized him years ago."

"I didn't want to. And that was the right decision," Noah said.

Zade's face was grim. "Mark's been hurting people ever since he got out. He's a Midlands monster, just like they wanted us to be. But monsters should stay in cages. We're the ones who turned him loose, so we should shut him down. Because truthfully? No one else on earth can."

"We didn't create him," Noah ground out. "That's not on us."

"Maybe not," Zade replied. "But we owe my brother."

"I know," Noah said. "But we have no proof that Mark's responsible."

"No?" Zade gestured at the monitor. "What do you call this?"

"I call it a mystery to be unraveled," Noah said. "Carefully. Discreetly."

He and Zade glared at each other. Like always, it fell to him to be the hardass.

Zade looked away, shaking his head. "The girl could be useful, if you play her right." Zade tossed a glossy brochure on his desk. "That's from Bounce, in case you give a shit. I'm outta here."

"Zade," Noah said. "Stay away from her."

Zade stopped at the door. "Is that an order?"

"We need to be on the same page for this to work," Noah said.

"Not possible, man, if you're going to be the only one who gets to write on it." Zade reached out as he went through the door and slapped on the lights, all at once.

"*Fuck* you! Jesus, that hurts!"

"Blinded by the light? Deal with it."

Noah turned the lights back off as he heard Zade walk away, whistling.

It drove him nuts, that Zade assumed that he needed to force Noah to save his brother Luke. Nothing could be farther from the truth. Noah was fucking tired of him and the others. Their brains buzzed at uncontrollable frequencies. Outside the box didn't even describe it. More like outside the fucking building.

But they were his best buds, all of them. Until they turned into raging, paranoid maniacs. Who still wanted to be tucked into bed after hearing a reassuring story from Noah.

Fuck them ten times over.

He realized that his sight was returning. No thanks to Zade, who was long gone.

A tentative knock sounded on the door. "Mr. Gallagher?"

"Go away," he said harshly. "Everyone. Stay the hell away. All of you."

It was only Harriet Aronsen, his office manager. He shouldn't use that tone with her, but currently had no fucks to give. Everyone should stay away.

He'd keep his own distance if he could. Just abandon his own rage, lock it up in a reinforced steel box, bury it and forget where he'd left it.

But he couldn't.

The brochure Zade left caught his eye. He picked it up.

Bounce. Your one-stop shopping for party entertainers. Exclamation point. Noah squinted. Make that three exclamation points. He unfolded it. The window signs he'd seen on the monitor didn't remotely cover everything on offer. DJ's, karaoke, clowns, children's parties, fire breathers, sword swallowers, strip-o-grams, Dickens carolers, celebrity lookalikes, giant inflatable rats and snakes, and last but not least, nearly naked representatives of every gender bursting out of cardboard cakes. Plus, hmm, costume design and rental for parties, school, community and professional theater productions. Noah studied a glossy photo of a guy in spangles, exhaling fire *and* jumping through hoops. He could identify.

There were no photos of Caroline Bishop.

Freeze-framed, she gazed seductively over her shoulder from the video monitor, looking at him through long lashes. So maybe she was Mark's spy sent to infiltrate them. Or else Mark's victim, framed for a vicious murder he committed.

The second option was almost as bad as the first, come to think of it. The Midlanders had a crap-ton of issues. They did not need police scrutiny of any kind.

Convincing though their fake identities might be, they were best left unquestioned. And unobserved.

His losses on rebellion day had taught him the price of boldness. All that was left now was a relentless will to keep his freaky tribe alive and thriving. They wouldn't beat Obsidian by acting like victims.

Nope. No grand gestures for him. Slow, steady and secretive would win the race.

But Zade was right, much as he hated to admit it. They needed to know what Bishop knew. How how she fit in to this. Why she was hiding.

He'd never run an AVP scan on a woman who affected him this strongly. It might not even be safe for her.

He might not be.

He wanted a long, private, leisurely, unfiltered look in dim light. AVP running free. No spectators. No distractions. Naked eyes. Raw, unfiltered data. Yeah.

He reached for the smartphone, glancing at the video monitor. The seductive flash of her green eyes.

Hah. He could rationalize his ass off, but he knew why he was making that call.

There was no arguing with a stiff dick. It always had the last word.

SHANNON MCKENNA

Chapter 5

"OPEN THE VAULT, General," Mark Olund said. "You don't want to make me angry."

General Colin Kitteridge's lungs hitched, constricted by the hot air of the high, remote desert and the microscopic dust that drifted endlessly through Obsidian's vast research complex. He struggled against the duct tape that bound him, his eyes bugging out, straining to see his tormenter.

Mark was unable to help with that. He could have turned on lights, but less light gave him more control with AVP. Control meant the difference between victory and disaster.

Kitteridge's rigid ass was taped to a folding stool that Mark had set right in front of the GodsEye Biometric vault door. The man's own brain was the key to open it. Without the general's cooperation, any attempt to open the vault would turn its precious contents into ash and cinders.

The GodsEye brainwave sensor helmet looked ridiculous on Kitteridge's sweaty bald head. But the general couldn't see himself and Mark didn't care. So long as it worked.

"I can't open it," Kitteridge said.

Mark gave the man's sig a quick surface reading and concluded that the general was lying. A strongly fortified lie that almost looked like a truth. But not quite.

The old man was tough. He'd die with honor. Screaming and writhing, of course. But never surrendering. He didn't know that Mark was a genius at finding soft spots and brutally exploiting them.

"Your colleague Lydia Bachmann explained the principles of GodsEye Biometrics to me eight months ago," Mark said. "Right before she died."

The general's sig flashed in startled agitation. "Lydia? You killed her?"

"Never mind Lydia right now. Open the fucking vault."

Kitteridge closed his eyes, but his sig revealed that, far from doing as he was told, he was summoning the energy to fortify his defenses. He was a career soldier and an ex-POW, not a pampered asshole. He knew something about suffering.

Not as much as Mark did, though.

On to the next move. Mark opened the back of the large truck that he'd driven into the complex, and leaped inside. A teenaged boy lay in the cargo space.

"Joseph. You're still breathing." Mark grabbed him by the collar, and hauled out General Kitteridge's grandson. He'd regained consciousness, and his eyes rolled in terror. He was hog-tied with dirty white ropes that showed blood where they'd rubbed his skin raw. Duct tape over his mouth, though. Easier than a gag. Harder to chew, what with the adhesive.

The boy was six feet and weighed a hundred and eighty pounds, but Mark hefted him as if he weighed nothing. Joseph twisted and fought as if dangling from a gallows, groaning as the shirt collar choked him.

"Joey!" Kitteridge's sig turned inside out. Watery green alternated with pulsing yellow. Soul-chilling fear. *Yes.*

"I don't need to describe what I could do to your grandson," Mark said. "Your imagination might be even more creative than mine."

"Don't hurt Joey!" Kitteridge stared at Mark's unflagging one-armed grip. "Who in the hell are you? Are you modified?"

"Me? I'm just a piece of garbage you threw away years ago. It's payback time."

"You're an older gen——? What year? I thought I was familiar with all of the . . . oh. Oh, God. You helped torch Midlands."

"Bingo. You're the second one on my list. You should be honored."

"Second?" Kitteridge's eyes kept darting toward his grandson. "Lydia was the first? Please understand, we had no idea what the researchers were doing. We were horrified when we learned about you kids but there was—it was a breakdown in command—"

"Of course. These things happen." Mark's soothing tone made Joseph groan again.

"We were never able to find you kids after that! We never intended anything like that to—"

Mark gave the man a vicious crack across the mouth. "Shut up, General. The bill's due. You Obsidian pricks are going to pay."

Blood dribbled from Kitteridge's mouth. "I will. Go ahead and hurt me. Not—not—my grandson."

"Shhhh." Mark placed his free hand over Joseph Kitteridge's skull, winding his fingers into the boy's hair. "How about if I collapse his skull and we watch his brain squeeze out? On second thought, that's too quick. I want him conscious when I do this." He reached down and grabbed Joseph's balls.

Joseph screamed behind his duct tape and jackknifed frantically.

"Stop!" Kitteridge begged. "Stop! I'll open the vault! Just put him down!"

"That's the spirit." Mark let go and Joseph thudded heavily down to the concrete floor with an agonized grunt.

Bonus. The kid was crying real tears. Mark almost wished he hadn't let go so soon. He sighed and turned to the general. "Do it."

The older man's eyes darted to his grandson. "I will, but . . . but you can't use it. No one could, not even me."

"Explain, fuckhead. Or your grandson gets something worse."

Kitteridge talked fast, spewing out the words. "The weapons are keyed to the mods of the ultimate generation of enhanced slave soldiers, and they respond only to their specific mental commands."

"Really. Well, I may be just a rough draft," Mark said casually, "but I'm still curious to see the final product. Don't make me wait. Joseph has a low pain threshold. Trust me on that."

"I have to concentrate," Kitteridge pleaded. "It's not easy to use, and it's impossible when I'm agitated! The system recognizes brainwaves generated while visualizing images, and if I can't—"

"I understand the basic principles," Mark interrupted. "I'm a GodsEye client myself, General, and I manage the brain/software interface just fine. Would it speed things up if I cut off a piece of Joseph's body?"

"No! Just let me concentrate, please! Just give me a moment!"

Mark tapped his foot as he watched sweat roll down the General's face. Payback was never as satisfying in real life as in fantasy. He'd cornered his first Obsidian target last year. Lydia Bachmann, CEO of a weapons manufacturing firm. He'd tried to compel Lydia to open a GodsEye safe for him, unaware of the safe's unique biometric design. But the drug he'd used to lower her resistance to interrogation hadn't worked right. She couldn't summon up images strong enough to be read by the sensors.

The safe had stayed closed, to his intense frustration. For months, he'd been hauling the fucking thing around everywhere he went.

Lydia had regretted her sins, but it hadn't been as much fun as he'd hoped. Plus, she'd lost consciousness far too quickly. Silence was not what he wanted out of the encounter. Screaming provided measurable feedback during the infliction of pain. She'd disappointed him.

He was learning how to make agony last, build it into a crescendo as he killed these power-bloated bastards one by one. And then, ahhh. Taking their masterpiece from them, and bludgeoning the living shit out of everyone with it . . . *that* promised to be a fucking blast.

No drugs for Kitteridge. He'd learned his lesson. The general's mind needed to be crystal sharp. The kidnapped grandson was a more efficient stimulant.

Kitteridge squeezed his eyes shut, veins pulsing in his temples. Minutes crawled by. Mark drummed his fingers, monitoring the general's sig for any sign that the man was stalling. All he saw was desperate effort.

Finally, the light panel on the vault door flashed green. The seal popped open.

Kitteridge sagged in his bonds, dangling his head between hunched shoulders.

In between the older man's ragged, sobbing breaths, Mark heard nothing with his augmented hearing. Nothing moved in the desert for miles around other than small animals. He'd taken out the facility's security personnel when he arrived. The place was strewn with their soon-to-be-desiccated bodies. How fortunate that they wouldn't smell, considering that there were ten of them.

Now, it was just him, the two Kitteridges, and the quiet desert evening.

A quickie scan showed that neither Kitteridge was likely to inconvenience him at this point, so he took a leisurely inventory of the vault's contents. Cutting edge weapons designed to be wirelessly synchronized with the newest gen of modified humans, who were basically a slave army awaiting the call to action, if and when it came.

Soon.

Mark was going to take their army and have bloody, noisy fun with it.

It took the better part of an hour to hump all that equipment into his vehicle. With his enhanced musculature, boxes that would take two normal men to lift were feather light for him. But he still hated wasting his time and energy loading fucking crates like a dock worker.

He was better than that. He was one of the original prototypes, goddamnit. Hundreds of millions of dollars worth of research and development had been plowed into producing supersoldiers. There'd been years of rough drafts, failed attempts, trial and error.

Now their worst error, their roughest rough draft, their biggest failure had come back to devour them, suck their living brains and tear at their warm flesh.

He couldn't wait.

He found the flash drive inside the vault that Lydia had described, and plugged it into his laptop. The control freq wands that generated the signal codes were there, too. He entered the general's hacked passwords. Found a folder entitled Control Codes.

But there were only six files in it. There should be files for twelve hundred slave soldiers in there. He already had the names and location of the six prototypes. He'd extracted them from Lydia under extended torture after she failed to open her safe. He knew who and where they were, but hadn't been able to activate them without the freq wand.

Now he owned them. But he wanted the other one thousand nine hundred and ninety-four.

Mark walked out, and nudged the general with his toe. "Where are the activation codes for the rest of the soldiers?" he asked.

The older man's drooping head came up. "Uh—in Lydia's safe," he said dully. "The rest of us only held codes for the six prototypes. Lydia kept the rest. That was our security strategy. We agreed on scattering all the various pieces of the puzzle so that no single one of us could ever—"

"Like I give a fuck." Mark vaulted back up into the cargo bed of his truck, and hoisted the colossal safe he'd taken from Lydia Bachmann. He put it down in front of the general. "Recognize this? Open it for me. Or you get to watch your grandson die real slow."

Kitteridge's horror and despair were clear in his sig. The man was beaten.

"I can't." His voice shook. "I never knew Lydia's image sequence. Kill me if you want, but please let Joey go. He never hurt you."

"If you can't open it, who can?" Mark demanded.

"Lydia's GodsEye coach could," the general said eagerly. "Caroline Bishop. When you can work the interface, you're supposed to re-key with a new sequence of images. But Lydia was so bad with the interface, she tripped security and burned a safe! I doubt she re-keyed the training sequence, just for fear of never getting back in."

"Did you know Caroline Bishop personally, General?"

"Ah . . . ah, no, not personally. Dex Boyd, the GodsEye biometrics designer, sent her to us because she was the best coach—"

"Tell me about her," Mark directed. "What else do you know?"

"Well, ah, only that she's an artist. She gave me an invitation once to a gallery opening. Masks, I think. Dragons, griffins. Not my thing. I didn't go." Kitteridge turned to look at his grandson, who was groaning. "Joey? Are you OK?"

Mark's AVP rage blazed up, hot and maddening. Caroline Bishop, the GodsEye coach who had taught Lydia to use her fucking safe. The only other person on earth who could open it.

He'd been hunting her ever since he'd first heard her name. Now that he thought about it, Caroline Bishop's name had been the last coherent words that Lydia had ever spoken.

So he hired GodsEye himself. Requested Caroline Bishop as his coach. His intention had been to force her to open Lydia's safe and then dispose of her.

Then he saw her with his own eyes, at their first training session.

Her sig made his mouth water. And he, with his visual mods, was the only man on earth who could truly appreciate it. She was meant for him.

He'd changed his original plan. Organized a scenario that would explain away Bishop's disappearance. Framing people was an art form, and he excelled at it.

He'd done all four of the training sessions. He'd asked her out, called her, emailed her, texted her. Dreamed of wallowing in that luxurious haze of shifting colors as he fucked her. Drinking them up.

And after a few drinks and a few coffee dates, the dumb bitch had run away. It must have been seeing that fucking sapphire brooch along with all the other jewel-encrusted crap he'd intended to shove into his new GodsEye safe and forget about. The damn thing had gotten too much press. She'd recognized the piece, and panicked.

She had dared to judge him. She had no fucking idea.

"Joey is innocent. Let him live." Kitteridge was pleading again.

The man's quivering voice spiked Mark's rage. He had to release it or he'd explode.

Over the years, he'd developed tricks that were unique to him, as far as he knew. Siphoning was his favorite. It left no trace. Just a dead body with no outward signs of violence. And it was intensely pleasurable to him. He hadn't had a really good one since Dex Boyd. It had been a long time since then.

The teenager was obviously preferable to his grandfather. Mark kneeled and pressed his mouth to the younger man's throat, pinning him to the ground. Joseph arched, bucking under Mark's weight.

He'd synced to Joseph's vital energy and started to suck the boy's light greedily into his own body. Joseph writhed but there was no escape. Mark didn't break the skin or rupture a single capillary, but on some level the boy knew he was doomed.

Mark faintly heard the general trying to bargain, offering himself, then at the end, hoarsely screaming. He paid no attention. Once Mark started siphoning he never stopped until he was done.

When he lifted his head, Joseph's light was out. Mark had taken it all.

A glance at the general showed him slumped forward, still tied to the stool, no longer breathing. The shock and horror of what he'd witnessed had stopped his heart.

A good night's work. He'd taken out an Obsidian insider, gotten into one of the main vaults for the weapons stash, and replenished his energy. No need to remove the corpses.

Mark hoisted Lydia's safe into the truck and drove into the darkness, dreaming of the rush he'd get when he siphoned Caroline.

SHANNON MCKENNA

Chapter 6

NOAH GALLAGHER FLICKED the lever on the door lock of his conference room. Finally, alone with him. The look in his eyes made her quiver with excitement.

He approached her, stripping off his jacket and tossing it away. Trapping her between his big body and the conference room table.

The cool edge of that hard slab of polished wood pressed her back.

She gasped as he hoisted her up and perched her ass on the table. He gathered up armfuls of her purple and lavender veils, pushing the sheer stuff up to her waist.

Cool air hit her bare thighs. She realized suddenly that she was naked. His eyes flicked up to meet hers. His knowing grin said that he saw all her secret desires. He knew them like he knew his own, and he meant to satisfy every one. He was inside her mind somehow, making her hot, making her mad, making her melt.

He pressed her legs wide, staring down with hungry fascination, and jerked open his belt—

The ringtone buzzing in her coat pocket snapped Caro out of it. The lurch and sway of the nearly empty bus, the blur of traffic lights and neon signs outside the rain-streaked window replaced the intensely vivid fantasy that had filled her mind.

She pulled the phone out, still addled by her fantasy. Her boss at Bounce. At this hour? She tapped the screen. "Hi, Gareth. What's up?"

"Quick question," Gareth said. "I got a call from that guy you danced for this afternoon at Angel Enterprises. Remember him?"

"Of course." Caro's legs went liquid. "What did he want?"

"You! He's fixated on you. And I'll tell you quite honestly, it creeps me out. I hate guys who think anyone they get a yen for is automatically for sale."

Electricity raced, crackling along her nerves. "He said that?"

"Not in so many words. But I just want you to know I made it very, very clear that you're not an escort, and I'm not a pimp."

His indignation was almost funny. "OK."

"But then he kept doubling the fee! He said all he wants is a dance, but in private this time. He got up to twenty-eight hundred before I hung up on him!"

Caro was startled. From what little she knew of the world's oldest profession, that was actually much less than what a high-dollar hooker charged, but to her it was an unspeakable sum of money.

"You hung up on him?" she said blankly.

"Absolutely," Gareth said. "The whole thing was very sleazy."

"Ah . . . wow. Do you think he actually expected me to have sex with him?"

"He'd be an idiot, if so, but there's no shortage of idiots out there. What on earth did you do to this guy?"

"I don't know," she said. "Apparently it was a revenge gig. His sister booked me to punish him for being a humorless prick. His fiancée glowered the whole time."

"Ah. I see. Well, I just wanted to make sure you weren't . . . you know."

She paused, puzzled. "Um, no, Gareth, actually, I don't. That I wasn't what?"

"Oh, sending mixed messages. Getting too flirty with clients. Something like that would be incredibly bad for business."

Outrage prickled up her spine like an electric charge. "I didn't! I can't believe you said that!"

"Don't get offended," Gareth said. "I had to ask. It's my business at stake."

"I behaved with the utmost professionalism! As I always do!"

"Well, good. I'll see you tomorrow morning in the costume shop, then."

Not likely, at this point. Caro ended the call, bristling with indignation.

Gareth knew only a carefully edited version of her life story. Just enough to justify her low profile and why she needed to be paid under the table. As far as Gareth knew, she had a jealous, violent ex-boyfriend on the East Coast, and an ineffective restraining order.

She'd left out the more colorful details, like being framed for grand larceny and first-degree murder and being on the run from a terrifying killer. Gareth had been patient with her limitations. He was a decent guy, and not naïve, but the whole truth would scare the shit out of him. Like he'd just said, bad for business. It would be good-bye and good luck if he found out how serious her problems actually were. She was sick of disappearing. It was exhausting. And expensive.

But given the pony-tailed guy following her, she'd have to do it soon.

It occurred to her, all at once, that twenty-eight hundred dollars would go a long way toward refilling her sadly depleted emergency flight fund.

A fizzy, whole-body thrill startled her. Oh, God. No. A private dance would be so dangerous.

Then again. She'd stabbed a guy in the throat. She'd witnessed a murder and barely escaped herself. She'd lived on the lam for eight months. Noah Gallagher was just a pampered bad boy who wanted to indulge himself. She could take him on with her hands tied. She could eat that guy for breakfast.

After all. Every move she made put her in danger. Just belly dancing at all was dumber than shit, even covered with makeup and draped with concealing veils and all those chains. But she had to eat. Pay rent. Buy bus passes.

So since every move she made could be defined as a mistake, then why not just make more interesting mistakes?

A few passengers had gotten on, staying in the front of the bus where they couldn't hear her. She pulled out the business card that Hannah Gallagher had given her, and stared at it for only a minute before she tapped out the number.

"May I speak to Noah Gallagher?"

"Who may I say is calling?" the receptionist asked.

She hesitated for a second. "Shamira."

The line clicked open after a brief wait. "Noah Gallagher." His voice was deep and resonant.

"Hi." Her voice was too high, but she kept on. "I'm the dancer who came to your office today."

Brief pause. He must have noticed that she wasn't calling from Bounce. The company name would have come up on his caller ID.

"Hello, Shamira. I assume that's a stage name." His tone was affable. "Do you have a legal name?" No edge to that question, either.

"I don't need one, for our purposes. Shamira is fine."

There was another brief pause. "Your agency told me no," he said. "Emphatically."

"I'm not calling through the agency. Which you probably noticed."

"Yes, I did." He paused. "Will you come and dance for me?"

She inhaled, hardening her belly to steel. "Three thousand in cash, for a four minute dance, like the one I did this morning. No touching. None whatsoever."

"Of course not," he said. "I explained that to Gareth. However, I can understand why you might have concerns. If you like, I can arrange for a few admin staffers to stay late. They won't mind the overtime at our going rate."

"Good to know, I guess, but—"

"All women, by the way. And you'll meet them. One is top-ranked in martial arts. She'd personally kick my ass to hell and back if I made one wrong move."

How about that. But Caro hesitated.

"They'll be right outside the office while you perform. It'll be very safe for you. When can you come?"

"When do you want me?"

She could almost hear him smile. "Right now."

The controlled sensuality in that voice made her toes curl inside her rain-sodden sneakers. Her dragging tiredness was magically gone. A feeling she could not name rippled through her, fierce and bright.

Hot, strong. Free. For the first time in so damn long.

She peered out into the darkness, disoriented. Tried to figure out where the bus was on its loop. From what she could tell she was on her way back toward the downtown area. "I'll be there within the hour," she told him rashly.

She sat there restlessly, electrified. And going nuts. Every leisurely stop, each time the door wheezed its rubbery flaps open to let people on or off, every red light made her belly clench with urgency.

After she got closer to downtown, she couldn't stand the pace any more. She had just enough cash in her purse to cab it the rest of the way.

Phone check. The seemingly endless journey had taken fifty-six minutes. The downstairs lobby area was close to deserted. The dark, gleaming expanses of marble looked vaguely sinister. Besides security, there was only an elegant older woman at the marble counter, wearing a lightweight headset that

Caro mistook for an accessory at first. Uh-oh. She would have to clear reception.

She looked up when Caro approached.

"I'm here to see Noah Gallagher," Caro told her.

The woman's discerning gaze flicked over Caro's frumpy coat, hat and glasses, reminding her of the drawbacks of her disguise. It was fine on the street, a bus, a big store. But in a context like this it was memorable because it fit no category in particular. Aside from "all wrong." The receptionist raised an eyebrow as she glanced at Caro's duffel bag.

"I'm from Bounce Entertainment," Caro explained. "He's expecting me."

The woman looked politely dubious. "May I check your bag?"

"Feel free." Caro unzipped it on the counter.

Filmy purple veils exploded out. The woman poked at the contents: wigs, bangles, belt, jeweled headdress. "Let me call up." She punched buttons on a wide console and spoke into the headset. "There's a woman from Bounce Entertainment who says . . . . oh. I see." Her expression became fractionally warmer. "Twenty-fourth floor." Her crisp professionalism never faltered.

The office suite upstairs was quiet, but there were still people there. A white-haired lady in her sixties, glasses hanging around her neck, greeted her at the reception desk and introduced herself as Harriet Aronsen. Probably not the martial arts champ. But you never knew.

"Mr. Gallagher is waiting," she said briskly. "Follow me."

Caro intended to ask if she could change in the same unused office she'd used earlier, but the words froze in her throat. She followed Mrs. Aronsen, who stopped at a door and spoke into a wall-mounted intercom after pressing a button. "Mr. Gallagher? Your appointment has arrived."

She opened the door for Caro, gesturing for her to enter.

Caro walked into the shadowy room, clutching the duffel bag against herself. Mingled fear and anticipation rattled her as she caught sight of him, silhouetted against the glittering cityscape.

"Is there anything else, Mr. Gallagher?" Mrs. Aronsen asked.

"Not right now, Mrs. Aronsen, thank you." It was that deep, controlled voice again, the one that had made her clutch at the phone. "I appreciate you and Karen and Aurelia staying longer. Stanley will drive you home, of course."

"Thanks. I'll be in my office if you need anything." The door clicked shut.

What a set-up. It was supposed to make her feel safe, but it didn't, not quite. It felt too deliberate. Staff expertly nudged into position. Herself, coaxed into coming.

But please. That was bullshit. She'd chosen to come. She made the call herself.

Standing, Noah Gallagher was a shadow against the dusky gray sky, tall and broad. Perfectly proportioned.

"Hello," he said quietly.

Oh, boy. She had never been so aware of a man's sexuality in her entire life. And he wasn't even doing anything. Just standing there on the other side of a very large room. Wearing a dangerously sexy suit and tie.

He flicked a switch on the wall. A row of small lights near the ceiling beam started to glow, warming the gloom to the level of candlelight.

"Excuse the low lighting." He took off his glasses. "I had a head injury a while back, and I can't stand too much light without protective lenses. But by the end of the day, I can adjust if I keep the lights low. I hope you don't mind."

"It's fine." Her voice sounded muffled. *Talk to the man, she lectured herself. Ask for a place to change. Commence Operation Shake It as of now. Go, go, go.*

The words would not come. He was walking toward her. Coherent thought disintegrated. She was close enough now to make out his eyes. They looked different. That luminous, startling flash. Like a wild predator's eyes. A panther, or a wolf.

"Let me take your coat." His voice was so silky. Caressing.

But I don't have my costume on. The words stayed trapped in her mouth as he lifted the garment, weighted by artfully sewn padding. It slid from her shoulders with only a tug of encouragement.

Noah Gallagher took a few seconds to look at the hidden layers, then pushed open a wall panel and hung up her coat.

She felt exposed. "Why did you do that?"

"Just curious. It's an unusual coat."

Well, hell. That sucked. The coat was supposed to be quiet and unremarkable, a wall to hide behind. "It's only a coat," she mumbled.

"It goes with the hat and that wig. And that thing in your mouth."

Her mind had been blank walking in, and now, it was blanker still. Wiped clean by the catlike gold flash of his eyes. Wait. *Gold?*

It hit her with a rush of startled wonder. "Your eyes," she blurted. "They're a different color from this morning."

Not a muscle moved on his face, but she sensed the tension that gripped him.

"Are they?" he asked.

"This morning, they were black," she said. "Now they're golden."

And by saying so, she was admitting to flash-memorizing every minute detail of him this morning. But whatever.

"I wore light-screening contact lenses this morning. Like I said—"

"Yeah, the head injury. I remember. It's just that they're—never mind."

"They're what?" he prompted.

"Amazing," she said. "That gold. How they catch the light. It looks right. It's . . . it's beautiful." She was mortified for blurting that out. So inappropriate.

He looked startled. "Thank you," he said. "Now it's your turn."

"Excuse me?"

"I took off my glasses. You take off yours. And that thing in your mouth and the wig. I want to see you."

There was nothing to be gained by being coy. She fished her zippered bag out of her duffle and did what he asked. Except for the wig.

Maybe that was why he didn't seem satisfied. "Who are you?" he asked. "What's your name?"

"You don't need my name," she replied. "I'm Shamira, the dancer. Do you want your dance? Because that's all I came here to do."

His eyebrow went up. "Let's have it, then."

She was taken aback at his swift change of tone. "I'll need a place to change."

Noah pointed to a door. "There's the bathroom."

She couldn't back out and she couldn't escape. And most likely she couldn't crawl out a small bathroom window and climb down a rope made of her fabulous fake hair from the twenty-fourth floor. But it would have been nice to have the option.

"I have the music file on my phone. Could I just connect it to your—"

"Of course. Cue it up and hand it over. I have a cord."

Nowhere to hide. She handed him the phone and stood there.

"Wait," she said. "Just hold on. This is too weird."

Those piercing eyes transfixed her. "Why? It's a simple economic exchange."

She shook her head. "Really not. It's incredibly complicated."

He passed his hand over his face. "Oh, God. Here we go again."

"What?" she said. "What's wrong?"

"Simple things." His tone was long-suffering. "They become complicated with no warning, and I never get the memo in time."

She swallowed her nervous laughter. "Are you sure you want to drop three thousand for a four-minute dance? I've never studied dancing of any kind seriously, by the way. I just took classes in college because Pilates and aerobics bored me."

"What college was that?"

"Um . . ."

"No one majors in belly dancing."

"Oh—that's a joke." She snapped her fingers. "I don't want to answer questions about myself."

"Understood. And I appreciate your honesty," he replied. "But to answer your question, I enjoyed your performance today. I wanted an encore."

Well and good, but Caro continued. "For that kind of money, you could hire a professional dancer and live musicians playing authentic instruments. Maybe even get a hookah going. Puff puff."

"No thanks."

"OK then. Guess I'll just have to do my best."

"That's exactly what I wanted. Really not complicated at all."

She shook her head. "It's just weird."

"Why?" He crossed his arms over his chest. "You're completely safe here."

True as far as it went but she still almost laughed at him. As if anywhere could ever feel safe again. Not after months of cowering in constant fear, terrified that she'd be chopped into chunks at any minute. She was sick of it.

And why cross-question a guy whose only crime was offering her a wad of cash for a few minutes of her time? *Maybe because you're so goddamn lonesome, you just desperately need to talk to someone. How pathetic was that?*

She had the uncanny feeling that Gallagher had somehow overheard her mental monologue. He looked at her like he had. "You didn't have to do this," he said.

She offered the most obvious thing she could think of. "I needed the money."

"You can go at any time."

"I'm not about to bail," she said. "I just don't get your agenda, I guess."

"I don't have one."

Bullshit.

"Did I make myself clear? There can be nothing else. Not tonight. Not ever."

His stern mouth curved into a sensual smile. "Understood," he said. "And agreed to. There will be nothing else, until the end of time."

His swift agreement left her at a loss for words. "Well. OK, then," she said.

"And by the way, in case you were wondering, I would've preferred not to involve my staff."

"Hadn't thought about that one way or another, actually." Which was a fact.

"It seemed safe to assume that you'd balk at going to a private residence," he said. "So my solution was to have three female pillars of the community, all within earshot."

"I only met one," she observed.

He grinned briefly. "You're not easy."

"That's for sure," she agreed.

"Look, I just want to watch you without anyone watching me do it. Or breaking my balls for enjoying the sight of a beautiful woman dancing like a goddess."

"Oh." The compliment made her face hot, but she still laughed at his rueful tone. "And now I'm the one breaking your balls."

"That you are," he agreed.

Despite his casual tone, she felt engulfed by the incredible energy that emanated from him. It buzzed and shimmered against her body. She'd never felt an emotional vibration so strong from anyone. It was all the stronger for being so fiercely controlled.

"I still don't know why I called you," he went on when she didn't reply. "It was an irrational impulse. I wanted to see what would happen. Every once in a while I do that."

The purposeful glow in his eyes made her breathless. "How often?"

He sighed. "Hell. I lied. This is the first time. Once in a lifetime, right?"

"Why me?"

"Do I have to explain? The feeling is real. You're real. Just let me experience it."

The word kicked open a dark room inside her, letting the light in. Something twisted deep inside her, something hot and soft and vulnerable. Her gaze skittered away, seeking something else to land on, but the big room was a masterpiece of austere, elegant minimalism with Gallagher himself as the only focal point.

Real. Oh, yes. He could have his dance. He could have anything he wanted.

"Ready to begin?" he asked.

Stay dignified. Stay classy. She wondered if he could sense the boundary he'd just destroyed in her mind. "Excuse me. Yes. But I do need to change."

"I'll take care of the music."

"Third cut on the playlist," she said.

"Got it. One more request, though. No jewelry on your face."

She stopped in her tracks. He'd seen her face, so the jewelry was irrelevant. But she'd never danced without it.

"OK. But no photos. And no filming."

"Agreed," he said.

The bathroom was large and luxe, but she was too anxious to notice details. She hurried into her costume and painted her face, stabbing herself with the mascara wand until she started an inky landslide. She put on lipstick, draped the purple veils. The scratchy tickle of synthetic hair brushed her exposed back. Her bare feet flexed against the smooth hardwood flooring. She reached out to open the door and make her entrance.

And hesitated.

It felt like going through some momentous portal, all because of his unexpected reply.

Real. That was all she'd needed to hear.

She opened the door.

Chapter 7

NOAH SAT DOWN in the wingback chair. His AVP was running wild. His heart raced. His face was hot. He'd affected her, too, judging from the fluctuations of rose-tinted light that swirled out from her. She radiated a sensual energy so luminous it was like she wore nothing at all.

The light that had opened up around her like a flower when he answered her question had spread out and out, extending far beyond the confines of the room and his sight, augmented or otherwise. He'd never seen anything like it.

One true fact shone in his mind. He was hopped up to maximum intensity, but he wasn't in freak-out AVP mode. Not at all. No kill plans were coming up.

On the contrary. He felt great. Riding huge waves of scorching lust, yeah, but otherwise, *great*.

He didn't even need to analog dive this time. Fuck glacial caves, mountains, seabirds. This thundering heat felt so much better.

He'd been half hoping the lust effect would fall flat when she walked in. If it did, then all that was left to do was to get the facts straight: Why did she contact Bea? What did she know about Luke? Had Mark sent her?

Noah hadn't told her the whole truth—he did have an agenda. But there was more to it than that. Much more. And it was all about her.

Nothing was ever destined to be simple for him.

The thought that Mark might have been her lover disturbed him. If Noah let himself dwell on that, his combat program would take him someplace very dark, very fast.

He and Mark were both Eyes Guys. Same brain stim, same implants, same mods. Everything Mark knew about himself as a modified human, he knew about Noah. Once the Eyes Guys learned to decode energy sigs, they could literally see people's brain activity projected outside their bodies. Like computer code, but translated into shapes and colors and patterns. Once you learned to extrapolate thoughts and feelings from the data, it got easy.

It often happened that Eyes Guys had surfed the same thoughts together. That was one good thing about AVP. Too bad the stress reaction threatened to drive them all bugfuck.

Unless it was flash-frozen into deep arctic chill. As he had done, mostly successfully, for years. Until today.

No one had a sig like Caroline Bishop. She looked like a walking, breathing passion flower to him. Mark would have liked it as much as Noah did. Mark would have wanted to fuck her. Mark would have known just how impossible it would be for Noah to resist her. He could very well have sent her to infiltrate. Even trained her.

Then again, Caroline Bishop had never approached him. She'd been minding her own business when Hannah hired her to dance.

Their meeting could be defined as random, but it didn't feel random at all. More like inevitable. And fucking incredible.

He clenched his fists and waited for her to emerge.

Real. What a strange word for him. Or her. Her persona was false. She wore a disguise, used a stage name, lived under the radar. Her life was so false, it had swung all the way around to the far side, where it had then become, paradoxically, real again.

He couldn't reason this feeling into submission. Her realness moved him. It gave him a falling-away feeling, a sense of depth and space. He hadn't felt that way since before Midlands. Maybe not since Dad had been killed.

Maybe never in his emotionally stunted life.

She was on the run. He recognized the vibe from his childhood with his mom and dad. He'd buried all those memories very deep, with the other relics of a past he couldn't bear to think about.

His con-artist parents had been an unbeatable team. Noah had been their assistant since he could talk, and probably before as an adorable baby, the ultimate prop. He had a natural talent, they told him. He was a good liar, pokerfaced, fast on his feet, calculating, cool-headed. Asa had been nearly as good, but Noah had the advantage of age and experience, to Asa's eternal dismay.

After Dad was killed and Mom vanished, all his skills had been brutally put to the test. It had been on him to keep pulling rabbits out of hats while Asa zoned out, and Hannah wept. He'd held them all together. Until Asa bailed on them.

And then Midlands. The ultimate fucking forge of hell.

The door to her improvised room creaked slightly. He jerked up in his chair and fumbled with her phone, finding the album cut she'd asked for. Drums started up, in a complex, sensual rhythm. Then the door opened.

Sensations washed over him as a wood flute sighed a low, breathy melody. Sweat trickled down his temples. His fingers gripped the arms of the chair as she shimmied in sideways. The colors of her sig moving around her body were ordered and graceful. Absolutely specific to her.

His heart galloped. Her sig danced in sinuous counterpart to her body, so elegantly that he barely noticed the holes and the uneven spots here and there. Green and blue and violet fountains rayed out from her fingertips and painted the room. Her jade green eyes caught the light.

He wanted to blast his optic nerve with light to max out the AVP and see even more of her, but it was too dangerous. Conversely, he could cut the lights and sit in the dark using infrared. That would give the stress reaction a chance to subside, and bring out the more subtle energetic colors.

But who watched a dance in darkness? She'd run for it.

The lowest light setting was all he needed. Lower than firelight. An intimate oasis of privacy. His dick ached, straining in his pants.

She swayed, delineating a magic circle with the trailing hues of her sig. The shimmering discs on her belt tinkled. Her skin was brushed with velvet shadows, dusted with gold sparkles beneath the shifting colors.

So beautiful. Though too thin. The point of her jaw was sharp. Her wide green eyes fascinated him. And her full, soft mouth made sweat trickle down his spine.

He was tuning to her frequency. He could almost read her completely now. Her sig patterns seemed like a language he once knew but had forgotten. That cornflower blue fading to hot violet above her heart said something beautiful about tenderness and endurance.

A vortex like that could swallow him up. He'd dive right in. Willingly.

He no longer wondered if she were an agent of Mark Olund, despite the data running in the back of his mind. Those frayed, ragged holes in her sig were more important. More worrisome. He'd seen them in his crew in the Midland days and afterwards, when they were in hiding, struggling to find their way. Misfiring energy patterns that resulted from chronic fear, stress, PTSD. Dark, uneven patches consistent with sleep deprivation, malnutrition.

She needed more protection than she would ever admit to. Noah set the thought aside for now. She was safe here with him.

When the music died away, she was arched back on the floor, offering herself in a pool of purple veils. Pulsing petals of pink and violet opened out around her heart like a blossom of light. The music slowly faded away.

The silence extended, filling the room.

The data run finished processing automatically. He felt the slight mind bump as it stopped. The results were in. She was not Mark's employee. She was something far more dangerous.

She was his. All his. Completely open to him. Waiting.

He leaned forward, elbows on his thighs, wondering what the hell he was going to do with this hard-on. He shifted his chair. Afraid to speak.

He'd always made decisions based on what was safest for the people in his charge. Not now. This felt like lunging for survival. He wanted to shout it. *Mine, mine, mine! It's my goddamn turn for once, and I claim this for myself! Fuck you all!*

She rose in one fluid, continuous motion, and bowed to him. The gesture was a graceful ritual, ceremoniously marking the end of one thing, the beginning of another, but he was transfixed by the jiggle of her rounded breasts. The shape of her ass as she bent over. The image filled his mind. Her, on all fours, moaning with delight. Him, naked behind. Cupping those soft tender globes while he slowly penetrated her.

He thought of clapping, but it seemed like not enough. Reverent silence was more like it. But his face felt strange and hot. His throat tightened.

What the *fuck?* Was this what a panic attack felt like? Jesus. He stabbed the remote to turn the dim lights off.

She made an inquisitive sound.

"I'm sorry." His voice felt strangled. "I just . . I can't."

"Are you all right?" Her triumphant glow faded and softened. She looked sweet, now. Colors could be sweet, too. Like flowers in the rain.

"Give me a second," he forced out. "Please. Don't say anything for a minute."

She glowed patiently in the dark, while he silently fell to pieces.

81

"Can I help?" she asked finally.

He shook his head. He felt as if a mask had been ripped off him. Whatever was underneath was not human. "I'm sorry."

"Don't be." Her voice was as light as smoke. "It's OK."

He started to laugh. Big mistake. It intensified the sensation gripping him, which he had not even fully recognized until this moment. Oh God, *no.*

He was fighting not to cry. Noah Gallagher, CEO and owner of Angel Enterprises, ice-cold ex-thief and con man, hyper-trained, tech and bio-enhanced commando warrior, captain of a secret army of fugitive freaks, veteran of bloody battles, on the verge of crying. About *what?*

He hated not knowing. Hated losing control.

He pushed his chair back, rummaged in his desk for the envelope he'd prepared, and stood up, holding it out. "Take it. Go. It's not you. I have no idea what . . ." He cut himself off and tried to swallow. "Just go."

She just stood there in the midst of her cloud of colors. Reached out to take it. His altered vision made the white envelope seem to glow like the moon in her hand.

He realized, abruptly, that he couldn't be with someone like her anyway. His wiring wouldn't sustain that kind of voltage. She'd drive him over the edge.

And it wasn't like he had that far to go.

He went to the closet. Fumbled with the panel and pulled out her coat. "I'll be gone when you come out, so I'll say goodbye now. Thanks for the dance." He held out the coat. "So, ah. Whenever you're ready."

She wasn't ready. She just looked down at the envelope. Puzzlement colored the space around her head. She wanted to know what the fuck his problem was.

He cleared his throat. "Please," he muttered.

She laid the envelope back on the desk. "So, it didn't work?"

He was confused. "What?"

"Your experiment. The good feeling you had this afternoon. You didn't have it this time around? That's too bad. I'm really sorry, considering what you paid."

He almost laughed but stopped just in time. "No, actually. It worked too well."

"Ah. Too real," she murmured. "I know how that is."

He doubted it, but didn't want to discuss it. "You need to go now."

She rose up taller, or rather, her sig rose and expanded, filling the room with its shimmering glow. "Why?" she asked. "What happened?"

"I don't want to talk about it."

Her arms crossed over her chest. She didn't care if he wanted to talk about it or not. Tough shit for him, her body language said. Spill it anyway.

"Look," he said. "I promised not to touch you. I can't keep that promise anymore."

She drifted closer, a cloud of sunset colors. Her scent washed over his senses. His supercharged synesthesia translated her aroma into colors in his head. He wanted to strip her bare. His hands flexed with the impulse to seize her. It almost overcame him.

"Leave." His voice was tight. "I paid you."

"No," she said.

"You finished your dance. You said there could be nothing more. So go."

"Shhh." She stretched up, touching his cheek with soft, cool fingertips. Then, to his astonishment, she pressed a hot, soft kiss to his jaw.

"This is not helping," he growled.

She rose up on her bare feet, her mouth near his. Never quite getting there. No kiss . . . just the caressing heat of her breath. The teasing promise of . . . maybe . . . almost.

He was so close to losing control, he didn't dare inhale.

SHANNON MCKENNA

He stepped back. Not far enough. The sweetness of her perfume taunted him.

She didn't move. Not one inch. She was enjoying this, feeling her power. It made his teeth grind, and his dick ache.

"You're still here," he said.

"I'm not ready to leave." Her voice was a drifting whisper. "I like the way this makes me feel."

"I'm ready," he said. "And it's my goddamn office."

"Yes. After hours. And we're alone. More or less." She closed the slight distance between them with a single step.

So she was seducing him. He got the message—but he still didn't dare breathe.

Then she took his hand, and pressed it against her bare belly.

They both inhaled sharply. She was flower-petal smooth against the hard, callused skin of his palm. A flash of hot lust pumped through him.

A swift, shocked ripple went through her, as if she'd had a small orgasm, and then her hand fastened over his, holding it firmly in place. As if she welcomed the touch but didn't dare allow his hand to wander elsewhere.

"Take the envelope," he said. "Put it in your bag, and we're square."

Her fingers tightened on his hand.

"I asked for a service, you provided it, I paid you," he said stubbornly. All business. Meeting over. Too bad his dick didn't get the memo. He was about to explode.

Without saying a word, she turned and headed to the bathroom, purple veils fluttering behind her.

He didn't have to wait for her to return. But he knew that he would.

She was back minutes later, wearing jeans and a baggy black T-shirt. His exotic dancing maiden was gone but she was as beautiful as ever. Her real hair was a thick, curly dark cloud, caught up in back in a tousled knot of twisted ringlets. Some of them dangled around her face.

84

"Sorry," he said stiffly. "That got out of hand."

"It's OK. Not your fault." She looked down at herself. "I thought it was better to have this conversation in street clothes," she said. "To see if the fantasy melted away for you without the props. Better for both of us to know right now."

He looked her up and down. Blood roared in his ears. "That's not happening."

Her sig pulsed, excited pinks and reds. "So?"

"I promised not to touch you, and I broke that promise. With your help."

She nodded reluctantly.

"If you stay here, I'll break it again. Let me put that right out in the open."

Her eyes were pools of shadow, but with his infrared he saw the pain and longing in them. "I . . . I can't do this," she murmured.

"Why? Are you married? Involved with someone?"

"No." Her answer came without hesitation.

"Then what's the problem?"

She shook her head, after a long pause. "That's nobody's business."

"True," he said. "And yet you're still here."

Her chin went up. "Your sister mentioned that you were celebrating your engagement. Was the woman who sat next to you today your fiancée?"

"Not an issue," he said.

"It is for me." Her voice had an edge.

"OK. We can call it even." He took Simone's ring out of his desk and displayed it. "I was engaged. Now I'm not. I wouldn't have requested a private dance otherwise."

She looked shocked. "Wait. Did you break it off because of my— because we—"

"No. Not at all." He tossed the ring back into the drawer. "I wasn't all that engaged to begin with. I know that now, thanks to you."

"Are you serious?"

"Yes. I'm a free man. Have dinner with me," he found himself saying. "Anywhere. Any kind of food you feel like. Or we can just have a drink. Anything is fine. Your call."

"I can't do that." She sounded miserable.

He crossed his arms over his chest. "Then you're just jerking me around," he said. "Make up your mind. Have dinner with me or walk out the door."

"Well, aren't you the gentleman. Go fuck yourself." Her voice was cool.

"Is that a no?" He didn't miss the brilliant flash of annoyance in her green eyes. *Yes, dancing girl. I can read you. And this is a test of whether you can read me.*

He couldn't tell if she got it. There was a tense pause. He waited her out.

"I have a different suggestion," she said.

"Let's hear it."

Her words came out in a nervous rush. "I don't do bars or restaurants and I don't want to go to any public spaces."

"OK."

"But if you want, I'll go back to your place and, ah, spend the night with you. On the following condition."

He braced himself for who the fuck knew what. "Yeah? Let's have it."

"No questions," she said.

He was taken aback. "Not one? Not even your name?"

"Especially not that. And when I leave, do not try to contact me again."

"Ah. A one-nighter."

"Yes," she said. "I'm sorry, but that's how it has to be."

"No questions at all?" he asked. "Favorite color? Favorite app? Favorite yoga pants?"

"Don't push me," she said. "That's the only way this could work for me."

Amazing. The ultimate horndog fantasy. No-strings sex. No consequences. And he actually felt ambivalent about it. "So what will we talk about?"

"Anything you want," she said. "Except for me."

He gave her an assessing look. "Could I persuade you to change your mind?"

She shook her head. "We could just, you know. Not talk."

His heartrate surged. Hers, too. He was getting a baseline vibe. Hot pink intensifying to an erotic shimmer of scorching red. Undoubtedly what her sig looked like when she was urgently fantasizing about sex. "Let me get this straight," he said. "You don't want me to take you out for dinner. Or let me get to know the real you."

"Nope. Can't do that."

He studied her with narrowed eyes. "You want me to take you home and fuck you up against a wall in the dark with my mouth shut."

She recoiled, but her sig didn't. The colors flared and deepened. "No," she said.

"OK," he said slowly. "We're making progress. I didn't think you were the no-name, one-timer type."

"I'm not," she admitted. "But we do this my way or not at all."

"Can I agree without saying that I understand? Because I don't."

She waved that away. "Forget it. This is a bad idea. I'm sorry I even suggested it. Go home. Heave a sigh of relief and raise a glass of wine to your narrow escape."

"Why? Are you on a Wanted poster? Armed and dangerous?"

"*No* questions," she said.

He snapped his fingers. "Right. Slipped my mind."

She glared at him, and just waited.

"So . . . are we on?" he asked.

"Yep." She held her chin up. Elegant and poised, in spite of her shabby, shapeless clothes, but with his mods, he could see that she shimmered with excitement.

Curiosity was already dogging him. He liked gathering data, knowing all there was to be known, but she wasn't giving anything away

She'd rejected the gallant suitor scenario, so fuck it. She'd have to deal with the lust-crazed predatory animal that was beneath.

A powerful impulse roared up from the depths. He pulled her into a ravenous kiss.

Chapter 8

A CHILDHOOD MEMORY flashed through Caro's mind. Of herself, thirteen years old, diving off a high, smooth granite cliff and into the old quarry. In midair, just before the frightening plunge into the dark, deep water.

The universe had distilled itself to this intersection of space and time, this room, this man. This kiss, charged with worshipful hunger.

Her own hunger roared up to answer it. She clung, melting, craving his heat, his strength. Her nails slid over his shoulders and his suit jacket, frustrated by his starched collar, his thick silk tie. She wanted to rip away all barriers to his hot skin. His lips were soft, seductively insistent. His mouth tasted so good. She drank in the subtle spice of his cologne, his glossy hair, sliding her fingers through it.

She abandoned herself to the sensations. Her body gave her no choice, and it was great not to have a choice. She was exhausted from choice-making. Her body had decided for her that the most important thing on earth was to be kissed as if she were this man's heart's desire.

She'd felt nothing but fear for so long, curled up like a seed in a pod. His touch made everything inside explode outward in a wild riot of color, scent, sensation.

Dangerous. Of course. This man was a luxury that she could not afford, and there would be a reckoning. Yes. Yes, she knew that. Fuck it. The knowing was just a shrill yapping in the back of her head. What was happening was all that mattered.

His arms were steely hard. His erection prodded her belly, made her ache and squirm, thighs squeezing around the hot, surprised glow. Shivering waves of tension convulsed and released, each new almost-orgasm blooming from the one before, each new one deeper. Noah Gallagher was a vast, undiscovered realm, and she wanted to discover him, all of him. To lose herself and stay lost. Seeing him and being seen. Tasting him and being tasted.

Their hands were all over each other. His grip was so warm and strong, gripping and caressing. Hers skittered, frustrated by that damn tailored jacket, trying to dig into the thick muscles of his massive shoulders. He thrust his tongue into her mouth, showing her how wonderful his sensual mastery was going to feel when he entered her.

He lifted his mouth, slowly. The tiny, liquid pop that their mouths made as they disengaged made Caro's eyes flutter open. She was lost instantly, hypnotized by those bright, astonishing eyes that seemed to see all the way into forever.

He spun her around, so that her back was pressed to his front. She felt disoriented until he lifted the weight of her hair and pressed his lips against the side of her neck, and started systematically unraveling her with his slow, dragging kisses, his breath so hot, his teeth gently nipping each and every exquisitely sensitive nerve ending.

His hand slipped inside her belt. Her jeans were very loose, since chronic fear was as much of an appetite killer as her current grocery budget. He caressed her belly, her hip, kissing and nibbling her neck as his hand moved over her mound, his long fingers pressing the springy curls beneath her nylon panties.

He made a low, inquisitive sound, giving her throat velvety, questioning kisses. Wordlessly asking permission to go further, with each touch, everywhere he touched. In no hurry at all. Patiently waiting for a sign. She wanted to give him one, desperately, but her voice was locked in place. Like her muscles, jammed and frozen.

"Can I?" His low voice rumbled in her ear as startled pleasure rippled down her entire body, right down to her fingers and toes.

She nodded, and clung to his thick forearm pressed against her belly, moaning inaudibly as his hand teased beneath the waistband of her panties and then lower, where she was damp and hot. His fingertips slid slowly around the bud of her clitoris until she began to shake with excitement.

He just kept at it, lazy and languorous, as if he would be happy to spend the rest of his life making slow, sweet love to the nape of her neck while petting her into an erotic frenzy. Sweet torment: his melting kiss, the sure touch of his hand. He leaned back against his desk and perched her against his thigh so that he could slide his finger deeper inside her, and found her swollen and slick. She clenched his finger eagerly at each gentle intrusion. Every caress took her higher. Made her want him more.

His erection prodded her ass, his teeth grazed the curve of her neck. She worked herself against him with sobbing gasps, taking his hand into her as deeply as they both wanted it to go.

Explosive waves wrenched her. She wailed and shook, but he held her together with unwavering, implacable strength.

Caro just floated for a little while, unmoored. Forgetting who or where she was. Blushing pink and shy with nameless emotions. Glowing echoes of delight still throbbed through her body.

He turned her, shifting her to face him and settled her on his desk. It all rushed back to her, with a cold thud. Who she was. What was at stake. How crazy this was.

He pressed her gently down, flat onto her back against the cool, gleaming expanse of fine wood. He was backlit by the glittering city lights outside the huge windows again, a dark silhouette looming over her as he pushed her legs wider and pressed the bulge of his groin against the crotch of her jeans. He pushed her shirt up high, stroking up her belly, her breasts. And more.

Even through the layers of cloth that separated them, he got the pressure against her labia just right. Not too hard . . . around and around . . . a well timed, rocking shove . . . and oh. *Oh.*

His hips surged against her as if he were inside her. Still in that suit and tie, for God's sake. Perfectly composed and put together as he slowly, skillfully dry-humped her to molten bliss. She felt so exposed, her back arched and legs spread, the bared skin of her belly and breasts goosebumped in the cool air.

He made a low, feral sound in his throat. "You want to come like this?"

"Yes," she gasped. "Yes, yes. Please. *Please.*"

"Then come," he insisted. "Come now. Give it to me."

Whatever she was going to say lost itself in the rising surge of terrifying pleasure. It crested, broke, and thundered through her once again. Shattering her.

She came back from that one to find him collapsed over her. His breath was ragged and hot against her chest. He cupped her breasts, kissing between them as his fingertips circled over her hyperstimulated flesh. His erection was still pressed against her labia. She could felt his heartbeat in that hot bulge, quick and strong.

She felt so soft now. Like a faint, golden mist.

Caro shifted her hips to wrap her legs around his waist and reached to touch his cheek. She felt it all so keenly. The damp sheen on his hot, supple skin, the fine rasp of beard stubble, the sculpted angles of his cheekbone and jaw. She sensed his unfulfilled need, straining to be released, but he held it in fierce check.

He pressed her fingers to his lips. "God," he murmured. "That was amazing."

She couldn't reply for a minute. The wires weren't connected. When she she found her voice again, she whispered. "You. The amazing part is you."

"This is the thing," he said. "I want you so bad, but I don't have condoms here. I don't carry them around with me and I never assumed that I'd get lucky enough to end up in this situation tonight. With you."

She licked her dry lips. "Um. I don't have one, either."

Noah sagged over her, gave a sharp sigh. "Ah. OK. Let me make you come again, at least. Here, at home, in the car, wherever, however you want. Say the word."

She cradled his head against her chest, feeling his sweat on her fingertips. It was true. He would just keep at it, making her come until she totally melted, and just wait for his own satisfaction indefinitely. Until she demanded that he take it.

"I want to go down on you," he coaxed. "Let me get those jeans off you."

She stroked his hair, soothing the rigid tension in his shoulders. He'd just driven her to a blinding orgasm twice, in minutes. An orgasm that redefined for her what an orgasm was. With her luck, it might never happen again. She intended to make the most of this.

"I think I could relax a little more if we were someplace private," she said shyly. "It's weird, having your admin staff right outside the door."

"Fine." He lifted himself up, and grabbed the phone as she adjusted her clothing. "Harriet? Yes, we're all done here. You, Karen and Aurelia can all go. I appreciate you staying so late. Don't forget to put in for overtime. Stanley's waiting downstairs for you, and . . . . yes, thanks very much. Say hi to Philip for me." He set down the phone. "Our chaperones are leaving."

Caro's face heated as she slid off the desk. "Do you think they heard?"

"No. I had the room soundproofed a while ago. For corporate security," he added when she looked at him sideways. "Not for this."

She burst into laughter. "So what was the point of chaperones in the first place?"

"Hey. Give me credit for going through the motions." He retrieved her coat from the floor, and held it up, feeling the layered hump of foam padding sewn into it. "Looks very natural," he commented. "Professional work."

"No questions," she reminded him swiftly.

"Right." He opened a drawer in his desk and pulled out a small bottle that contained contact lenses. In a few practiced moves, he'd applied them. He shrugged on a coat, slid his dark glasses into the pocket, and picked up her duffel bag. "Shall we?"

Sure enough, the luminous gold glints of his eyes were gone, transformed into inky darkness. She shook herself out of her fascinated trance. "One moment, please."

She twisted up her loosened hair and tugged her wig on over it. Jammed the wide-brimmed hat over the top. Then the jaw-changing thing for her mouth. Pop, suck, and it was in. Then the glasses. Done.

They were both wearing their respective armor now.

He scrutinized her. "Are you trying to beat facial recog bots?" he asked. "I could give you pointers on how to do it better."

"Don't get tricky with me," she warned. "The rules are the rules."

"I'll be good," he said easily.

"You saw through my outfit this afternoon," she said. "How did you do that?"

"Any kind of disguise jumps out at me. You know those online ads with GIFs that jiggle? Disguises look like that to me. But your camouflauge is pretty effective, all in all. Inappropriate for this context, but good in theory."

Great. She'd managed to get herself seduced by the guy with X-ray eyes.

They walked through the deserted offices, and waited for the elevator. She kept her gaze down, partly because of the security cameras, but mostly out of embarrassment.

The silent walk out to the parking garage felt so purposeful, so deliberate. Never in her life had she gone after sex so shamelessly. Just met a guy, and decided to do the deed. That had always happened in the context of a relationship. One that she could fool herself into thinking had a chance to go somewhere.

They never did, of course. Sooner or later, she managed to scare any would-be boyfriend away. She eventually got blindsided by a stress-induced vision, and could never hide her reaction fast enough. It freaked them out. Invariably.

She hoped she could manage not to scare this guy away, at least not tonight. Not until she had gotten herself a nice stiff dose of his sexy magic. Something suggested to her that he was way different from any of the other guys she'd been with.

It was ironic, that this relationship had no place to go at all.

She'd blocked all the exits herself.

* * *

Mark stared down at the GodsEye safe that Lydia had failed to open for him. It was squat and ugly. He'd even say it looked smug, sitting on the floor. Taunting him.

He mentally reviewed every word of the conversation he'd had with. Masks, the general said. Caroline invited him to an art show that featured masks. It made sense. She was a rabbit, a coward. She needed a mask to cringe behind.

95

Masks. To find something hidden, all one needed was the right filter.

Mark adjusted the light on his monitor. It would look like a dead screen to an unmod, but anything brighter than near black and his AVP would zap him into a fugue state.

He'd woken to some gory messes after fugue freak-outs, but he'd gotten expert at cleaning up after himself. Mayhem drained excess toxic energy. It allowed him to masquerade as a normal member of society. When he bothered to.

He took off his glasses and peeled off his shirt, to mitigate the AVP temperature spike. He popped out his shield lenses. Naked eyes were better for digital info dumps. Worth the nervous jitters that followed. It wasn't as if he slept, anyway.

He logged into Caroline's Facebook page, though there wasn't much point in it. She hadn't posted since she disappeared eight months ago, but he still periodically prowled her feeds. Mostly posts from her nothing friends' pathetic lives.

Checking her page was a ritual. Mark liked rituals. They soothed the screaming inside his brain.

Noah had lectured them ad nauseam about stress flashback management. Know-it-all prick. He'd busted them out of that place, so he thought he owned their asses.

Yessir nossir anything you say sir Captain Gallagher, hup hup! Be good soldiers, now, and never use your powers against the unmods because of ethics and morals and blah blah blah di-fucking-blah! Right.

Noah's AVP management techniques had never worked for Mark. He couldn't stand being motionless, concentrating on the inside of his own head. Slow death by boredom. He'd been tortured enough already, at Midlands. Fuck that shit.

Rebellion day had taught him all he needed to know about AVP management. That day had been a mind-opening crash course. Killing those researchers had helped him like nothing else possibly could. Struggle. Blood. Death. *Yes.*

Afterwards, in hiding with Noah's group, he'd begun to slip out alone, hunting for what he needed to calm the constant inner screaming. And he had found it.

He'd been careful. Restrained. He'd picked only lost, wrecked people. Ones that no one would miss. He'd used his AVP to clean up the scenes. The cops never had a clue, but Noah . . . he could read a sig like no one else. Noah had been on to him.

After a few moments of staring at Caroline's boring feed, Mark stopped and scrolled back, nerves tingling.

Caroline was tagged in a photo posted by a dark-haired, toothy woman named Gina Minafra. In the photo, the two women held up masks of dragon's heads. The text read, *A blast from the past! Caroline's magic, from the summer stock production of The Littlest Dragon!*

Masks. Theater. The filter was getting more specific.

Mark set the machine to search for images of masks in recent theatrical productions, and dove back into the data stream. It scrolled on the screen in a blur, over fifty images per second. After a while, he saw it.

Stop. He stopped, worked backwards until he found it again. Not a mask. A costume, of a night moth. Blue-black stretch velvet over a wire frame, ragged edges fluttering. A muscular black girl wore the wings over a black leotard. She was leaping as if she were taking flight. Those wings had Caroline written all over them.

He'd seen enough of her stuff to know her tics, her obsessions. Her so-called "art" was worthless crap made of paper or cloth, wire hangers, pipe-cleaners, chicken-wire. It was full of elements that fluttered and bobbed and swung. Mismatched colors, recycled materials. Her pieces looked like they had been cobbled from repurposed garbage. They bothered him on a visceral level. He wanted to sweep them off his field of vision.

He compared Caroline's eccentricities with the moth costume the way that a criminologist would compare fingerprints, point for point. After fifteen seconds he was convinced that Caroline had designed it.

The website was of a community youth theater group in Seattle, the Mean Streets Players, doing *A Midsummer Night's Dream*. The moth was Titania, Queen of the Fairies. He scrolled around until he could find a clickable playbill with credits. There it was. Costumes by Bounce Entertainment.

Bingo.

In Bounce's online inventory, dozens more pieces bore Caroline's distinctive stamp. Productions of *Beauty and the Beast* and *Thumbelina*. The Blue Feather Playhouse's interpretation of *The Tempest*. *The Bremen Town Musicians*, again by the Mean Streets Players.

Mark studied the owner's smiling headshot. Gareth Wickham. The name sounded kind of fake. He looked fake, too, like a soap opera heartthrob. There was a landline and a cell number. It was after business hours, so he dialed the cell phone.

Wickham picked up promptly. "This is Gareth Wickham." A crisp, professional male voice. Young, artsy, gay.

Mark instantly manufactured his own young, artsy gay persona. "Hi! My name is Rob Vasquez, from the Vermilion Players in New York City? I'm producing a dance piece? And I saw images of masks that your designers at Bounce created for *Beauty and the Beast* and *The Bremen Town Musicians*. It's just beautiful work!"

"Glad you liked it," Gareth said. "What can I do for you, Mr. Vasquez?"

"Please, call me Rob. I was wondering if you could hook me up with that designer. I loved Titania's moth wings. Our director is looking for that ethereal quality. Those wings were built by the same designer who did the *Bremen Town* and the *Beauty and the Beast* masks, right?"

"Ah . . . uh . . ." The guy stammered. "I, um . . . well, we all worked on those."

Mark smiled thinly. What a moron. "But who designed the basic concept? The style is sooo distinctive!"

"Actually, those costumes were a ragbag collection of stuff we had in stock," Gareth's voice gained strength as he figured out his response on the fly. "Mean Streets has a shoestring budget, and they couldn't afford custom designed—"

"Could you put me in touch with the designer? I'd love to talk to him. Or her."

Gareth hesitated a beat too long. "I don't appreciate people poaching my staff."

"Oh, no!" Mark injected mortified distress into his voice. "I'm sorry if I gave that impression! I certainly didn't mean to—"

"Leave your name and number—no, better yet, go to the website form, and do it via email. Tell us what you want and when you need it. We'll send you a quote."

"But—"

The line went dead. That *prick*. No one spoke to Mark Olund like that.

He turned back to the computer screen, and dove deep into the data banks again, until he had gleaned Gareth Wickham's home address. He was going to get a surprise visit sometime tonight, from a fast-assembled team of serious thugs.

Nighty-night, motherfucker.

Chapter 9

NOAH WANTED TO take her arm as they walked, but didn't dare touch her. As wound up as he was, he'd end up bending her over the hood of someone's car.

The contact lenses and shield specs should have blocked enough of the light to zero out his AVP under normal conditions, but proximity to this woman did not constitute normal conditions. His AVP was revved. Data scrolled in a constant stream down both sides of his inner field of vision. He processed it all, crunching numbers, taking measurements, running probabilities. None particularly relevant to the situation.

Some random part of his mind decided to identify all the cars on this garage level and cross reference them. With one swift glance, he identified thirty-eight of his three-hundred-plus employees who had no life and were still at work at nine PM.

Lust was threatening to fry his circuits, but at least it wasn't killing rage.

He just might be able to navigate this erotic encounter without running them into a wall.

Her sig was so damn beautiful. He forced himself to look down so he wouldn't gape at the lights painting the walls. Dreamy pastels were splashed over the rough concrete walls of the garage, transforming them into something magical. If he didn't screw this up for himself, he was going to be inside that with his own body, bathed in colors as he touched and kissed and fucked her.

And when she came . . .

"Would you stop that, please?"

He glanced up. "Stop what?"

"Thinking about me. Just go with it, OK? Don't think too hard or we'll derail."

He laughed. "I'm not supposed to think about you now? Conditions keep getting stricter. You're heavy into control."

"Most men would be happy for a no-strings hook-up," she said. "Why do you want to grill me first?"

Noah shrugged. "Knowledge is power. I like power. The more data you have, the more on top of things you can be."

"Is that your favorite position? On top?"

He glanced at her, curious. "One of them, yeah. You still OK with this?"

"Of course."

The tension in her voice made him slow to a stop to take another look at her sig. Her own unique patterns were not in his lexicon yet, but after less than an hour with her, he already had enough for a quick assessment.

She was turned on, but intimidated. Worried about what she'd gotten herself into, but not worried enough to chicken out.

Having a little sister had forced him to understand the risks a woman took when she chose to go off into the night with a man she barely knew. She was already defenseless and threatened.

He'd make the risk she was taking pay off ten times over.

Maybe he'd come on too strong. But it seemed so right at the time. He'd made sure she was into it every step of the way, and he'd never gotten such an incredible payoff. The lights had blasted the room like a spinning mirror ball when she came.

He pushed that overstimulating thought away before it could mess him up. He was going to need his self-control. Rigorous, constant, always-on-top control.

He'd never let the AVP out of its cage during sex before. Tonight, he wasn't going to have a choice. But for the first time, his AVP might actually be useful for something he totally cared about. Her pleasure. Making her come.

Not that he ever had much trouble with that. But with her, it was different.

He needed it as urgently as he needed his own.

He helped her into his Porsche, got in himself and sat for a moment, keys in hand. She sank into her seat, looking nervous.

"What are you waiting for?" she demanded.

"I'm not sure," he said. "But you don't look OK. What's wrong?"

"Start the car."

He did, letting the engine rev for a moment so she had time to change her mind.

She shot him a nervous glance. "I just hope you're not disappointed, that I'm not, you know, a crazy femme fatale. The sexy costume is just a costume."

Disappointed, his ass. He almost laughed, but she would not appreciate being made fun of in her current mood. "Not at all. I'm flex. And anything but disappointed."

"Good. Go for it, then. Sweep me away. Be masterful. I know you can. You don't have to convince me of anything."

The car sped up. He had to make a conscious effort to ease off the gas.

"I'm glad you think so," he said. "But don't try to snow me. You don't have any intention of letting go. Not for one instant."

She was silent for a long moment. "What's that supposed to mean?" she asked.

"You say, be masterful and sweep me away, but don't ask my name, and no questions or conversation are allowed, and afterwards, never call me again. That's not letting go." He glanced over at her. "I'm just trying to figure you out."

"Don't overthink this." Her voice vibrated with tension. "If the conditions bother you, you can let me out. This corner is just fine."

Right. As if he would let her walk away. "I could use more data."

"Tough shit," she said. "Forget it. Or else stop the car."

He ignored that. They drove on in silence for many minutes while he pondered his next move.

"Tell me just one little thing," he said.

"What part of 'no questions' did you not understand?"

"Your name," he said. "Just that. I'll need it, tonight."

She sighed, wearily. "Courtney."

He couldn't keep from laughing. "Please. Don't insult my intelligence."

She looked at him, startled. "Why? What's wrong with Courtney?"

"Nothing specific. It's just that it's not your name," he said. "People grow into their names, or their names grow onto them. Courtney hangs all wrong on you."

He let the tension build, as the glow in her sig between her throat and heart got hotter. Shades of blue and violet, getting so bright they were almost white.

Truth, rising up at his summons. She couldn't keep it inside. She had to let it spill out, or she'd explode. She had to give it up to him. He held his breath.

104

"Caro," she whispered.

Yes. He was silently delighted. As if he'd made her come with words alone.

"Now we're getting somewhere," he said. "Call me Noah." He reached out and took her hand. Her fingers were slender and cool, vibrating in his grasp. "Caro," he said softly. "I like it."

It was happening again. He waited as they drove along the road that circled the lake. That blue-violet glow brightening as a fresh truth welled up, until it had to emerge.

"It's what my mother called me when I was little," she said.

They were home. He pushed a dashboard remote that opened up a large gate, and drove down the winding driveway. His house finally appeared, the high foundation built into rocks and the land, the terrace on stilts embedded in the lake. He parked, catching her thoughtful look around without commenting on it as they got out. The car chirped in farewell as he touched his key fob. He led her up the walkway.

"When did your mother stop calling you that?" he asked.

Many moments passed before she responded. "I was nine when she died."

"I'm sorry."

She nodded in acknowledgement. He hooked her arm, and drew her onward. "There are security cameras at the front door, and the back patio," he said. "Couple more around each side."

"Thanks. I appreciate you telling me."

He unlocked the door, disarmed the security system that Sisko had programmed for him, and gestured her into the towering foyer.

His fingers flashed over the wall keypad. "Recoding the indoor vidcams," he told her. "OK. They're all off. You can relax."

"Thanks," she whispered.

He put the duffel bag down, and lifted her coat off her shoulders. "Take off your disguise." He waited, as she hesitated. "You're completely safe here."

She still hesitated. Even with the shield lenses, he could see that she'd frozen.

"This is the safest place you've been in a long time," he said with quiet intensity. "I would never do anything to you that you didn't want. I would never hurt you. I would never let anyone else hurt you. I would crush anyone who tried into pulp."

She laughed at him. "Oh, stop. I hate to break it to you, but you're not going to strike terror into the hearts of the legions of darkness in a business suit. Not that it doesn't look awesome on you."

He grinned. If she only knew. "I'm tougher than I look," he said. "Take off your disguise."

Caro did as he asked. The mouth thing went into its hinged container, the glasses went into their case, the yanked-off wig was slung into a satin carrying bag.

He unwound out her coiled hair, loving the way her curls twisted around his fingers. "That's better," he murmured. "Caro."

He clasped her waist and pressed her against the wall, lifting her and setting her astride the bulge in front of his pants. Letting her lean against it. Her eyes looked so wary and dilated, her lush mouth slightly open, her breath quick and uneven. So beautiful. He wanted to admire every detail of her pale face. But there was work to do.

She was too pale. Her lips were bluish. He forced his attention away from his groin and charged up his AVP to scan her.

Borderline hypoglycemic. Dizzy. Low blood pressure. Slightly dehydrated.

He couldn't seduce a woman in that condition. He had to take care of her first.

Food, then. Not a bad idea for him, either. Running AVP burned a lot of glucose. He fueled up with an extra ten thousand calories at one go sometimes. And his AVP had been in high gear all afternoon and evening.

He lifted her and set her down, stepping back. Calling on all of his hard-assed self-control. "Not yet," he said. "Let me get some food into you."

She frowned slightly, as if regular meals were a foreign concept to her. "All right."

He breathed out, to the count of ten. He had to chill. Until her sig looked brighter and steadier.

Ironic, when he thought about it. He had her in his lair, secretly and under cover of darkness. Defenseless. He had every advantage over her that she could imagine, and plenty of others that she probably couldn't. And all it amounted to in the end was that he had to compensate like a son of a bitch for every single one of those advantages.

He had to treat her like blown glass.

Chapter 10

CARO FELT LOST, and awkward. He'd been looking at her if he could see inside her, for miles on end. Then he suddenly withdrew. She felt cut adrift, alone.

She wondered if it was something she'd said.

"I'll order some dinner," he said. "What do you like?"

"Anything is fine."

He frowned. "You'll have to be more specific than that."

Damn. Choosing had never been much of a problem in her previous life, when she could afford what she wanted and didn't worry about money, thanks to solid consulting fees from doing GodsEye Inner Vision coaching. She'd been able to afford New York rent, trendy restaurants and clubs, designer clothes at a discount, and had enough money left over to pursue her art in her spare time.

She might have known she'd have to pay the piper eventually. She just never dreamed that the price would be her life.

Noah was waiting for an answer. "Ah . . . let me think," she said vaguely.

After so long on the run, she'd forgotten what she'd liked. She was grateful if she had milk fresh enough to pour over cereal in the morning. That, and freeze dried soup for dinner were mainstays. Cheap peanut butter was a go-to. A banana was a treat. And to think that she used to get up on her nutritional high horse and scorn simple carbs.

She was coming up blank. She shook her head. "Doesn't matter. You choose."

He pulled out his smartphone and tapped the screen. "This is Noah Gallagher. I have an account with . . . yes, thanks. I'd like a meal for two delivered to my home . . . yes, that's the address. Bring us roasted asparagus, fresh greens, goat cheese and walnut salad, the root vegetable roast, a double serving of oven roasted potatoes with spring onion, fresh thyme and shaved parmesan. Beet and peppercorn salad."

Quite a list. And he wasn't even done.

"Some fruit, berries, melon, whaever you've got," he went on. "A double order of the fresh bread with herb butter. I like it hot out of the oven. Both kinds of cheese. Throw in some extra aged pecorino. Entrée? OK. Grilled Florentine steak for two . . ."

He caught her eye. "Medium rare?" She nodded.

"Medium rare," he repeated. "Apple tart with cream sauce, to finish. Yes, that's fine. Thanks."

He hung up the phone. "Does that sound good?"

She was impressed, and a little overwhelmed by the prospect of eating so much. "More than good. And enough for an army."

"I have a big appetite. And you need a real dinner."

True enough. She was fine with him being in charge for tonight.

He led her into the main room, which was both luxurious and spare. Vaulted ceilings and arches defined the space, its hardwood floors brightened by huge picture windows opening onto a terrace overlooking the dark lake. A set of dark brown leather couches were arranged around a low, smoked glass table. Art hung on the far wall, she noted, as he used a rheostat to switch on and then dim the track lighting.

The whole house was paneled with richly colored wood. Beautiful planks, each with its own subtle pattern of grains and whorls. She felt like she was inside a tree. It smelled good. A resiny tang of summery sweetness.

"Your wood paneling is beautiful," she said. "It feels alive."

He looked pleased. "That's the effect I was going for. Make yourself comfortable and I'll get you a glass of wine. White or red?"

"Red, please." She was drawn by curiosity to wander over to look at the art.

She was mesmerized by what she saw. Millions of dollars worth of original artwork hung on that wall. There was a contemporary painting by surrealist Elisa Keillor, of a strange, deformed male nude crouched on a cliff unfurling clawed wings, paired with centuries-old sketches of demons and monsters by Hieronymus Bosch. A bronze sculpture on a sideboard looked like a tormented swamp thing trying to break free of a tarpit. Painful to look at and, like the other works, faintly bizarre, but beautiful. It struck her as full of hope, straining and yearning. It was by Lara Kirk, a Northwestern sculptor Caro had heard a lot about before her own life exploded.

In the middle of the wall was a Sonia Delaunay. She leaned in closer, studying it. Not one she'd ever seen before. A portrait of an older woman's face, with deep, intense eyes and a stern mouth, but bathed in a blaze of brilliant intersecting colors.

Her mind instantly went into wordless, no-thought mode, forgetting everything but what she was observing. Something about the Delaunay painting was just . . . not . . . quite . . .

"You like art?"

She jerked. She'd been concentrating so hard, she hadn't heard his soft approach. He'd taken off his jacket and tie, and undone his top two buttons.

Just seeing the hollow of his collarbone made her blush, as if he'd stripped off his shirt. "Ah . . ."

"That's a general question," he said. "Here, take this." He handed her a glass of dark red wine.

"I love art." She didn't have to play dumb or lie. "Your Keillor is beautiful. The Bosch sketches are amazing. So is the Kirk. You seem to have a thing about monsters."

"Yes, I do. And the Delaunay? I saw you looking at it. What do you think?"

She looked back at the painting and took a cautious sip of wine, wondering if she should share her reaction.

Better not. She had no business venturing an opinion on that particular painting.

Just tell him it's pretty. You love pretty pictures. La la la.

"It's, ah . . stunning," she faltered.

His mouth twitched. "It's OK. You can relax. I know."

"Excuse me?"

"I know that the Delaunay is a fake. So don't worry."

"It is?" Relief flooded her, then a fresh stab of fear followed. Was he trying to catch her in a lie, or worse, the truth?

"Come on. You picked up on that right away."

"And just how do you know that?"

He shrugged. "Your expression. Couldn't be clearer."

His tone did not invite argument. "Oh. Well, it's a good fake," she said warily. "But I didn't want to be the one to tell you if you didn't know."

"The original is in the vault," he said. "You're the first person who's ever noticed that it's a reproduction."

"It's not like I was sure," she assured him. "I'm no expert."

"Don't lie," he said softly.

Her belly tightened. "Then we'll have a very silent evening."

He gazed up at the Delaunay. "Silence is fine, if lies are the alternative."

"I, ah, took art history classes my freshman year in college," she offered hastily. "I wrote a paper about Delaunay."

"How about that. I'd like to read it."

"And then you'd know where I went to college."

"Hadn't thought about that." His lips twitched in a brief smile, and he gestured toward the glass she held. "Drink. Maybe a little buzz will make you a better liar."

"I'll get drunk instantly," she warned him. "I haven't eaten for a while."

"That's why I put out something to munch on while we're waiting for dinner."

She turned, and saw food on the table. How the hell had he gotten it out there without her noticing? Wheat crackers, sliced cheeses, a dish of meaty Greek olives and another with just cherry tomatoes. A bowl of gold-tinted muscat grapes. "You keep all this fun finger food around to impress the girls?" she asked.

"No, I just burn a lot of energy. I need a lot of high quality fuel. Come on. Eat."

She followed his lead, and it tasted so damn good. The cheeses were nutty, savory, each more delicious than the last. The olives were tart, the tomatoes a salt-sweet explosion, the grapes perfectly ripe. She felt more centered after only a few bites.

"So is your art an investment?" she asked. "Or do you just like having it?"

"Both. I figure, if I like it and I'm convinced that it's genuine, then it's a good bet. Mostly I enjoy looking at them."

He set aside his wineglass and studied his collection for several moments while she covertly studied him, seizing the opportunity to ogle.

When she dragged her gaze away, she noticed another shelf along the opposite wall with a series of striking carvings on it. All appeared to have been done by the same artist. Some were large, some small. All were of wild animals, some still attached to the rough chunks of wood from which they were carved, as if the animal was trying to escape. She went over to take a closer look, struck by the sense of trapped energy.

"Those are beautiful," she said. "Who's the artist?"

He was silent for such a long time, she turned around to repeat the question. Then she realized that he was simply reluctant to answer.

"You?" she guessed. "You did these?"

He shrugged. "I get insomnia." He sounded almost defensive. "It passes the time."

She looked back at the carved animals. They were detailed, dynamic. Original.

"You've never exhibited your work?" she asked.

"I'm not into that," he said. "I just like keeping busy."

"You have a lot of energy," she commented. "I love them. They're great."

He smiled briefly. "Thanks."

"So why do you have a fake Delaunay on the wall, but Bosch originals?"

"Interesting question. I'll answer it if you explain how you learned to tell an original from an excellent professional reproduction."

She shrank back. Put her wineglass on the table. "Some other time. Not now."

"Sorry. I'm just curious. Insanely curious."

Sneaky bastard. She flushed. "So much for not being nosy. That concludes this evening's conversation."

"We'll be all right," he said. "Like you said before. We can just, ah, not talk."

114

Here it was. Her cue to do something sexy and uninhibited. But she felt so freaking self-conscious.

Noah caressed her arm soothingly, as if she'd spoken her thoughts aloud. "Don't be nervous," he said gently. "We both know it'll be great."

If only she could be so confident.

"All we have to do is get to where we were in my office. I suggest we start with a kiss. Unless you have a better idea." He put down his wine glass and reached out.

She shivered as he brushed her cheek with the back of his knuckles. The gesture was tender, respectful, but it went too far somehow. She couldn't handle tenderness, or any real intimacy. She was too raw. She'd set the limits in advance: she wanted nothing but the physical act of sex.

She would content herself with that. They both had to.

Really, it wasn't like she had anything to complain about. She'd maneuvered herself into the luxury lair of a super-hot guy whose plan was to make her come all night long. The only hitch was that he was disappointed because he couldn't take her to a fancy restaurant, where he wanted to wine her and dine her and ask her about herself where anyone could overhear. Awww, tough. Poor her.

He took her hand, enveloping it in his. "You don't have to be afraid."

"Oh, I'm not," she said quickly. "Really I'm not."

"We'll take our time," he assured her. "There's no rush. And I'll be very gentle."

"You don't have to . . ."

Too late. He lifted her hand to his lips and started kissing it. Hot, intense, deliberate kisses.

The experience was new to her. His whole playbook was new. He kissed the inside of her wrist. A swift, hot shimmer flowed right up her arm.

"I . . ." She stopped, swallowed, tried again. "Shall we—"

"Get on with it? Let me have a look at you." He pulled a case out of his pocket, opened it, and removed the dark contact lenses, stowing them. Then he turned his jewel-clear golden eyes squarely upon her.

His gaze triggered an almost unbearable feeling of exposure. She wanted to hide. Sheer stubborn pride kept her chin up.

"You're better," he said thoughtfully. "But not one hundred percent better."

"One hundred percent is not going to happen," she said wryly. "Unless you wait for a very long time."

He nodded, having come to some inscrutable decision. "Come with me, then. If you think you're ready."

She followed him through vaulted spaces full of shadows. Outside, the wind whipped the dark lakewater to rippling whitecaps. He led her into a big bedroom, decorated with the same masculine elegance as the rest of the house. Wood paneled walls, hardwood floor, a vast bed, floor to ceiling windows with vertical blinds made of paler wood.

He let her go in first, then stopped just inside the door. "Lights on or off?"

She shrugged.

"My call, then." He hit a switch. A pair of immense floor lamps began to glow softly.

Caro wished that she'd opted for darkness. She was paralyzed with shyness.

"You wanted me to take the lead," he said. "Now you have to trust me to take you where you need to go."

She wrapped her arms around herself without answering.

"Do you?"

She finally nodded.

He sat down at the foot of his enormous bed, flanked by the lamps. "Take off your clothes for me."

116

She was flustered, and perplexed. "While you sit there and watch?"

"Exactly."

"Why?" she demanded.

His face was too shadowed to read. "To turn you on," he said.

"Oh! So this is all for my benefit?" she flung at him.

"And mine. But I'm not the variable in this equation. You are."

"Not really," she said. "Don't forget that I've already danced for you. Twice. And I wasn't wearing much."

"I remember," he said. "It turned you on then, too. Both times."

His unwavering stare had her pinned to the spot. "What makes you think so?"

"I don't think that it did," he said. "I know that it did."

His self-assurance was infuriating. All the more so because it was true. Caro slashed back with a sarcastic question. "I see. Then does my lord command me, his lowly bed slave, to do his bidding?"

"Hot fantasy. Keep talking."

"When I'm ready," she said.

"I want to please you so badly. Please." His low voice was charged with intensity. "Trust me."

This conflict was winding her so tight, she wanted to scream, break something. But that wasn't going to get her what she came here for. Only Noah could do that.

So often, over the past months, she'd felt trapped in a parallel universe. On another plane, some other free, happy Caro still lived, unaware that her ghost self, this current Caro, was trapped in an alt-world version of her real life. It had crossed her mind, in her darker moments, that maybe she had actually died at Mark's hands on that terrible night and was now imprisoned in an endless nightmare from which she could not awaken. A disembodied soul who floated around, craving human contact.

The kind only Noah Gallagher could give her. Sensual pleasure beyond her wildest dreams.

But ghosts didn't have dreams. She must be real. Noah, too.

And he was right over there. Waiting for her.

* * *

Noah's fingers dug into the bedcover. It was so hard to sit and watch when he wanted so so badly to seize her.

Blown glass. She was much too tense for self-indulgent macho bullshit. He'd have to coax her to where she needed to be, but she needed him to be strong, too. She responded to that. He'd seen it in her sig. It would be so easy to screw this up.

For now, he'd sit, dick throbbing against his pants with every slow heartbeat while she slowly worked it out in her head.

"Take your clothes off first," she said. "Then I won't feel like I'm at such a disadvantage."

"You already are," he said bluntly. "It'd be worse if I were stark naked. You're just going to have to trust me."

Yes. There it was, that hot glow of hopeful pink and violet, blooming outward from her. Trailing off in transparent wisps.

She wanted to trust him. Wanted it desperately.

"You wouldn't be here with me if doing this didn't turn you on."

"This? Could you be more specific?"

He leaned forward, pinning her with his gaze. "Yes. Strip off your clothes. Or else keep them on and think about how it felt when I made you lose it. Move the way you did, but without me touching you. Touch yourself. I want to watch, and imagine how it'll feel when you come for me."

Another pink glow over her chest, this one with the sexy orange sunburst pulsing out of it. Responding to heat with heat.

118

"Why are you looking at me like that? It feels like you're reading my mind."

She'd changed the subject on him. So suddenly. He hadn't seen that coming.

I am reading your mind. He stopped the words, just in time, startled at the overwhelming impulse to tell her the truth about himself. Just blurt out all of it.

Her sig was doing it to him. She wanted him to read her mind. She wanted to be seen, heard, known. She ached for it.

"I'm figuring you out," he told her. "I can't help it. It's just who I am. I observe, gather data, analyze it. I'm designed for that. With no off switch."

"How can you analyze data if I don't give you any?"

"But you do," he said. "It doesn't matter if you talk about yourself or not. You tell me about yourself with every word, every move, every blink."

All at once, she flared so bright, he almost winced. *Yes.* This was the vein of gold he had to follow.

She couldn't resist her own curiosity. "Like what? What am I telling you now?"

"You sure you want to play this game?" he asked. "It might take you someplace you aren't comfortable with."

"I'm never comfortable," she said. "Besides, you're just bluffing."

OK, bombs away. He took a deep breath. Ramped up his AVP to the max, something he almost never did on purpose, but he was already so turned inside out by his reaction to Caro, it hardly mattered. Fuck it.

"You grew up near Boston," he said. "I hear the accent, but I don't hear it very often. You're pretty good at faking Seattle-speak, though. You've made an effort."

She crossed her arms over her chest. "OK. I see where this is going now, and I'm done," she said. "That's enough."

She wasn't done, though. Not by a long shot. Her colors were going crazy.

He pushed on. "You didn't grow up rich. Lower middle class, at best." The look on her face made him quickly add, "Just being objective. I grew up dirt poor myself."

She looked around his bedroom, dubious. "You? Really?"

"Yes," he said. "But we're not talking about me."

"I don't want to talk about—"

"You're alone in the world. No one to turn to." He hesitated, and added, "Until now."

She took a slow step back. "Lucky me."

"You've been running for a while," he went on. "I see it in your eyes. I know that vibe. Constantly on your guard. It wears you down."

"Oh, please," she scoffed.

"Want me to stop?"

"Yes. No."

He went with the last word. "You got involved in something dirty by accident. Someone used you."

She stiffened with shock.

"Tell me his name, Caro," he said softly. "I'll kill him for you."

Her eyes narrowed. "In your dreams."

He ignored that. "What do you do when you're not dancing?" He could guess, and he'd be right. But he was pushing too hard. He needed to back off.

"Noah." There was a quiver of panic in her voice. "Stop it."

He just sat there, concentrating with all his strength. Taking her in. Trying to feel his way to the next step without losing her. "You're scared of me," he said.

"No. Not at all." For the second time in minutes, he was unable to read her. He had to figure out how the fuck she did that. No one ever had.

"OK then," he said. "Take off your clothes."

Chapter 11

THIS WAS HARDER than it should be, for a woman who'd been dancing professionally in scanty clothing to survive. But she had no costume to hide behind here. She was dressed to disappear, not titillate.

And undressing in front of this incredibly charismatic guy would be intimidating even if she'd been wearing silk and lace.

Caro crouched to untie the graying laces of her kicks, wincing as she peeled off socks that had multiple holes in them. Yikes.

She was so excited couldn't breathe. Her heart thudded against her ribs. She longed for filmy layers, something soft or stretchy to peel off and let whisper to the ground. All she had was the black long-sleeved jersey pulled over various other T-shirts, layered for warmth, bulk and blurring.

Once those were off, she had the frayed bra to feel self-conscious about, considering it barely contained her C-cup boobs. It had been bought back in a previous era of her life. Back when she still had reason to display cleavage.

Which she still had, despite living on what she thought of as the fugitive diet. Boobs were great for belly dancing, but aside from that, they were a nuisance for a woman on the run. They had to be contained, concealed. They ached, bounced, and attracted attention. Which she wanted about as much as she wanted a dose of radiation poisoning.

For the first time in a long while, she was glad to have them. She strained to reach the clasp, let the bra fall. Shoulders back. Tits high. In your face, dude.

The energy in the room changed. His face changed, going tense. He swallowed hard. No longer calm.

She was glad. Rattling his cage gave her a rush of power. She posed proudly, just waiting. Savoring the heat. The pressure of his eyes. Like a touch.

"Caro," he whispered. "You're so fucking beautiful."

Aw. Gee. Her face flushed, and her breath got stuck in her chest. She opened her mouth to thank him. Thought better of it.

"Come here," he said.

She inched forward carefully. Gravity got wonky around this guy. When she was within his reach, he began to unbuckle her belt. It was a man's belt, bought to keep her jeans up on her ass so to avoid having to buy smaller clothes.

The buckle gave way. Noah tugged on the ends of the battered strip of leather.

She stumbled forward until she stood between his powerful thighs, his face inches from her naked breasts. Her nipples tightened to rigid points at the heat of his breath. His gaze was so fierce and focused, she felt like it burned her skin.

"Don't," she whispered. Having no clue as to why she said it.

"Don't what? Look at the perfect tits in front of my face?"

"The X-ray eyes thing," she told him. "Not fair. To look at me that way, read my mind, try to tell me all about myself. That wasn't the deal."

"The deal was, no questions. I didn't ask any."

She shook her head. "But somehow you keep pushing me."

Noah put his hands around her waist, his long fingers splayed over the curve of her ass. Her jeans slid down, catching perilously at her hips. One wrong move and they would fall. "I do it because I know you want me to."

"What makes you think that?" she demanded.

"I'm just paying attention."

She felt almost afraid to breathe. "I can't do this," she whispered.

He tugged her closer. "Yes, you can," he said. "You need to. You want it so bad." He pressed his face to her breasts.

Caro moaned as his hot mouth moved over her. He held her in a tight, possessive grip as he suckled and licked. His touch released a torrent of energy, making her vision dim, her head pound. Reality itself warped inexplicably, narrowing down to a single glittering point . . .

And exploded, shooting light all through her body. She blacked out for a moment.

She found herself draped over his shoulder some time after. Clamped in his strong arms, feeling his heartbeat. Her hair hung down over his back.

Her head was too heavy to lift. "What the hell?" she whispered.

"You came," he said softly. "A whole body orgasm. Just from me kissing your breasts for a little while. Amazing. I've never felt anything like that in my life."

It was his fault, she wanted to say. He was the one who did it to her. She could not take responsibility for something so unfathomable.

"Get those pants off." A brisk tug, and they were around her ankles, panties quickly following. He admired her muff, stroking her hips, moving his hands along the tender skin of her inner thighs. Her nails dug into his shoulders as he teased her mound.

"Climb up on me," he urged. "Straddle me, knees on the bed. You are so perfect. I cannot believe you're real."

She swayed there unsteadily, stark naked over his fully clothed body. Her legs splayed wide, on either side of his thighs. Wide open to his gentle exploring touch.

"Take off your clothes," she told him. "I'm going to leave a huge wet spot on your bespoke pants."

"My dry cleaner can worry about that."

"I insist," she said sternly. "I can't handle this. Me bare-assed and you with the white dress shirt, all buttoned up. I know you've got a mysterious plan to drive me mad with desire but those buttons are seriously bugging me."

"It seemed like it was working for you," he pointed out.

"To a point. I'm falling to pieces while you stay cool and composed. Give me the satisfaction of getting you disheveled. Look at you. You could be in a boardroom, closing a billion dollar deal. Not fondling a naked woman in your bedroom."

"Not with this hard-on, I couldn't."

"No one would know, with that poker face," she scoffed. "Someone could be blowing you under the table, and no one would ever know."

His swift grin flashed. "Stimulating scenario. One more orgasm first?"

"The shirt," she said, relentless. "Off with it."

He was silent for a moment. "Whatever." He undid his buttons, tossed the shirt aside.

She was shocked speechless. His torso was covered with crisscrossing scars.

He looked immensely strong, carved and cut, his massive musculature still somehow lean and economical. But scars marked his smooth olive skin, cutting through the hair on his chest and the trail down his belly. Some were in regular, squared patterns. Some were symmetrical and circular, others puckered and random like knife slashes or bullet wounds. Some looked like burns.

He waited patiently, his face somber and watchful.

Her overheated imagination started to generate images of all the possible injuries that could have caused them. She stopped. Nothing made sense. There were too many scars. They practically covered him.

"How did that happen?" she asked.

"Not all at once." He shrugged. "Long story."

"Were you in the military or something?"

"Something like that."

She trailed her finger over a symmetrical cross-hatch on his upper arm. "This isn't a random injury. But it's not a surgical scar, either."

"So you get to ask me personal questions about my past? With a straight face?"

"Sorry," she murmured. "Never mind."

"But there's the other possibility," he said.

"And that is?"

"Show me yours," he said, his voice low and intent. "And I'll show you mine. I will tell you the whole weird, scary story, I swear to God."

They stared at each other. She felt so naked, but he still wasn't satisfied. He wanted every part of her completely bare.

So they had something in common. They both carried the marks of their suffering. His were just more visible than hers. "Never mind," she whispered.

His big shoulders lifted. "All right. So, do you still want to do this?"

She was confused. "Of course," he said. "Why wouldn't I?"

His eyes slid away. "The scars." He sounded uncertain. "They can be a turn-off."

"They're not," she said. "Not at all. We all have scars, of one kind or another."

"It freaks some women out. That was why . . . ." His voice trailed off. "I just wanted to make you come again, before the big reveal. In case it all ended right there."

It squeezed her heart to imagine a guy like him feeling insecure. She kissed the jut of his cheekbone. "I'm not turned off," she said. "Curious, yes. Sorry you suffered all that damage. But not turned off in the least."

"Good." He grabbed her hands, kissed them, and placed them on his shoulders. "Then hold on to me. I want to make you come again."

His erection prodded her thigh through the fabric of his pants. Her hands skittered nervously all over his hot, bare skin, the rough ridges and bumps, afraid to land anywhere, as if he were charged with electricity and every touch was a jittery shock. He stroked her with skill, then got bolder, opening her as he caressed her clitoris with his thumb. A low growl vibrated in his chest as he sank his fingers inside her and found her slippery and drenched.

"All wet," he muttered against her throat. "Later, after you're more relaxed, I want to go down on you and do this with my tongue. For hours."

Her channel clenched eagerly around his hand at his words. He thrust deeper. "Dance over me," he whispered. "Move over my hand."

She swayed slowly, undulating over the fingers he was thrusting tenderly inside her. His hand went deeper, in and out. But what she was doing to him was even more intimate. Touching his skin for the first time, everywhere. The supple muscles under the scars felt wonderful. He smelled wonderful. Wood, smoke, spice, salt sweat, man musk. Her fingers slid through his thick hair, over the taut tendons of his neck.

All that powerful male energy was focused on her. His essential self, reaching for her, merging with her. Touching her soul, and her soul responded, opening, brightening, and then a huge bright torrent of sensation, so strong—

It tore through her, wrenching her with a pleasure even more intense than before.

His low voice had been vibrating for a while against her throat before she put her mind together enough to understand spoken language. ". . . so open," he was saying in a wondering tone. He withdrew his hand from her body and clasped her to him, stroking her back reverently. "Fucking beautiful. How you're so goddamn open."

Caro focused on him, still not quite back from where he'd taken her. "Like hell," she said. "Not me. Not open at all."

"You are with me," he said. "Do you come like that every time?"

She shook her head. "Not ever," she said. "Not once. Nowhere near. It's you."

His head tilted to the side. "Hmm. I like that."

The look in his eyes hit her hard someplace very deep and unexpected. She didn't so much burst into tears as disintegrate into them.

Noah's arms circled her. "What is it? Did I do something wrong?"

She shook her head. His neck was wet from her tears. His hand wound into her hair, massaging her head, slow and soothing. Hugging her tightly.

She finally managed to calm the storm. He held out a handful of tissues.

"I'm sorry," she murmured.

"Don't apologize," he said. "I want you to feel safe. I want you to relax."

"I don't think that's up to my conscious mind," she told him.

"Don't think about it," he urged. "We'll just take this one juicy, earth-shaking, world-rocking, life-altering orgasm at a time."

She wiped her eyes. "That's some big talk, buddy. You have a lot to live up to."

He undid his pants, and let his penis spring out. Large and long, thick and heavy, flushed a hot red. "You have a lot to give in to," he countered.

She stared down at it, taken aback. "Oh, my."

He took her hands, and wrapped her fingers around his thick shaft. Velvety smooth, supple skin, and pulsing vital heat beneath her clutching hands.

He maneuvered her off his body and set her on her feet, and leaned to yank the bedcover down. "Get into bed."

She slid between silvery-toned sheets. They were crisp and fresh and fragrant. The tears on her face felt cold, but her face burned. Noah pulled condoms out of a drawer in his bedside table, and tossed one onto the bed. He shucked his pants and underwear, tossing them on a chair, and just stood there, letting her look.

Yeah. His abs were flat and hard, his flanks lean, his ass tight, his thighs thick and taut, corded with hard muscle. His big phallus jutted proudly from a thatch of dark hair, flushed and thick. The blunt head gleamed with precome.

He ripped open the condom, and smoothed it over himself. Then shoved the covers aside, and climbed into bed. He was so big, so burning hot. He gripped her knees, tugging gently until her legs opened, and rolled on top of her, between her legs, resting on his elbows.

Her face got hotter, legs clasping him, panic slowly rising as she imagined this big, intense, overwhelming man, all over her. Inside her. Watching her with those weirdly attentive eyes while she fell apart. Drawing his own mysterious conclusions.

It was too much.

He sensed the tension gripping her, human antenna that he was. "What's wrong?"

"I can't," she said. "Not with you looking at me like that."

"I have a beautiful, fascinating woman naked in my bed," he said. "You think I'm not going to look at you?"

"I've been trying really hard for a long time to avoid being noticed, Noah. Now there's you. A spotlight, an X-ray machine and a microscope rolled together."

He frowned thoughtfully. "Do you want to be on top?"

She shook her head. "Same problem, different angle."

He caressed her hip, a soothing massage. "Do you want to stop? If I'm, you know. Too weird for you."

She slid out from under the cover and turned away from him. "No," she blurted. "I love being with you. You're the most generous lover I've ever been with. I'm just really tense. A basket case." She crawled toward the edge of the bed.

Noah lunged to catch her, in a gentle grip. "Wait. Let me work this out. You don't want to leave. You want me to have sex with you. And you don't want me to look at you. It's like a riddle. Just please don't suggest that I cover my eyes."

"As if," she said wryly.

Noah scooted until he was kneeling behind her. He swept her hair to the side, pulled her back against himself and began kissing her neck and shoulder.

She started melting, gasping. Tension inside her released with every skilful caress. She was so primed, so wound up, so needy. It was a brutal twist of fate that this panic held her back. His hand lingered over her breasts, sliding over her belly, then venturing lower. He nudged her forward. She caught herself on all fours.

He rose up, holding her hips. Stroking her ass, tenderly. Patiently.

He wanted her from behind.

"Give me your hand." He wrapped her fingers around his penis. "Touch yourself," he said. "And get me nice and wet."

She did as he asked, pressing his stiff, hot rod against her slick divide. Sliding it up, down. His shudders of pleasure echoed her own. She thudded down onto her elbows. Ass in the air, wide open.

Noah positioned himself behind her, nudging her thighs wider. Caro's hair hid her face like a curtain. She moaned, breathless and aching with anticipation as he pressed himself against her, but he just rocked the blunt tip of his shaft at her sensitive opening. Up and down. Teasing and tantalizing.

She pushed against him, trying to take him inside.

"Not yet," he muttered. He caught her clitoris between his fingers as he rocked and stroked. One of his hands clasped over hers, clenched and rigid. Muscles locked with the effort of holding back. Waiting for her.

A secret chamber of her heart opened wide and a deep swell of emotion lifted her in one great toppling wave. She was engulfed.

When her eyes fluttered open, he'd thrust deep inside her and was still waiting. His fingers tightened over hers. "I love when you come around me. Do it again."

He moved inside her slowly. Deep, gliding thrusts. His big penis stroked heavily against a glowing place inside that melted for him. He kept gliding over it and over it and over it, right where she needed him to be, making her whimper and gasp and sob. Feeling so free. So connected. She never wanted to be alone again.

No. Don't go there yet. Don't ruin this for yourself.

She'd thought she could just take what she needed and go when it was time to go. But it wasn't happening like that at all.

She was the one being taken.

* * *

Fuck. Holding her too tightly. Couldn't make his fingers relax. *Grab a hook.*

Couldn't. He was lost in it. Swept away. Noah was aware, through the pounding roar in his ears, that his fingers were sunk too deep into the smooth roundness of her hips. Hard enough to bruise. He'd promised not frighten her, to be gentle. To not be the latest scary dickhead parading through her life.

But he'd never had sex with AVP raging before. It rode him hard, and did not care about the vows he'd made to himself. He couldn't stop now if she were begging him to, if the sky were falling. His body was locked into frantic motion as he sensed where she needed to go, and pursued it. Ferociously.

He was no better than the psycho tool that Midlands tried to turn him into. They hadn't been able to control him with meds or implants. Nothing could, except for massive knock-out drugs. Or chains.

Or euthanasia. Their final solution. He'd been scheduled for disposal, like a rabid dog. A waste of food, a failed investment, like the rest of his Midlands rebels. Almost all of them had been on the discard list. Examples of gene vectoring gone wrong.

He'd somehow convinced himself that he could prove them wrong and regain self-control. But he was losing it now.

The memory intensified the red haze of fury generated by the AVP. Twelve years of struggle every day and night to find his balance, his control. Now, fucked in an instant, with his dick slamming heavily into her, getting harder and longer with every aggressive stroke. Gleaming a hot, angry red. Her rich smell maddened him.

He'd been hijacked by AVP. The wild buzz of combat programming, channeled into sex. Scary combination. Caro was vulnerable, fragile. She'd trusted him, and look how he was treating her. Jesus.

She let out shocked, whimpering gasps at every deep stroke. Having the lights on made it worse. Light was a constant AVP stimulus, amplifying the feedback loop in his mind. He stared hungrily at every pink detail of her slick, flushed folds, clasping him, shiny and luminous. Her hot sea smell. Sweat stung his eyes. He was shoving her forward by the force of each thrust, her face pushed in the pillows, her throaty cries muffled but not by much. Her sig was crazy now, her colors blinding, incandescent.

And he came. Oh God.

The mountains did a vast, slow-motion lift-off into the sky . . . and fell back down on top of him. A thousand tons of broken rock.

He floated back, disoriented. Limp, soaked with sweat. His throat was dry, from panting. The thickness in his throat indicated that he'd been shouting. Who knew what.

He wanted to remember. The effort was beyond impossible.

Caro's lithe body vibrated beneath his. He'd collapsed onto her, still rammed deep inside her. Still stone hard. Pulsing with aftershocks.

He was too big to stay on her, weigh her down. *Let her breathe.*

He lifted himself, felt her inhale. She lay there, flattened on her belly, cheeks flushed poppy red. A flower that had been beaten down to the earth by rain.

But her sig glowed around her, soft and diffuse. It looked happy.

He rolled to his side, fumbling for the cover. Pulled it up over her. Best he could do. It wasn't cold, after sex that hot. But the AVP hadn't totally burned away what gentlemanly gallantry he could lay claim to.

He got up and headed to the bathroom to get rid of the condom. When he returned, Caro rolled over and watched him as he grabbed another one from the bedside drawer. He suited up again, hard as rock. It had been forfuckingever, and no woman had ever wound him up like Caro did. She gazed, nonplussed, at his unflagging hard-on before he dimmed the light to make the AVP ease down.

"Seriously?" she said, with a quick smile. "After that?"

"Yeah. Just won't quit."

Her mouth curved in a quick smile. "I see that."

"You OK?" he asked. "I got a little carried away."

"Absolutely fine," she assured him. "It was intense. But great."

"Did I scare you?" He hoped not.

"Not at all." She propped herself up and brushed dark wavy ringlets off her face.

Data scrolled in his head as he assessed her. She didn't seem traumatized. He pulled down the cover and clambered onto the bed, settling between her legs.

She looked startled. "Uh, Noah—"

"Just let me look," he coaxed. "I was a little too rough with you. I lost control. I'm sorry."

"I'm not. I told you I was OK. Why don't you just believe me?"

"Maybe I just need an excuse to put my face between your legs. Stop wiggling."

"But—"

"Shhh. I'm concentrating." And so he did, holding her graceful thighs wide open, staring at her muff. He needed no light to see every detail. He lost himself in rapt, horndog contemplation. She looked beautiful. Hot and rosy and fuckable.

Temptation overwhelmed him. He spread her lips gently with his fingers, holding them open, and thrust his tongue deep into her.

She cried out in startled pleasure, arching. She was so lithe and strong. Noah stilled her with his hand, resting it on her belly until she lay back with a gasp of fresh pleasure and submitted to his hungry lavish licking.

He lapped upward, trailing his tongue lazily over her slit up to the hood of her clitoris, caressing the taut, pearly bud with his lips and assessing how her sig reacted. A hot pink glow edged with violet pulsed with delight as he tongue-fucked her. Oh, yeah. More of that. Give it to him. He got back to the clit, suckled it. Long, gentle pulls. She convulsed, with a gasp. He could do this for hours. Cheerfully.

She shivered and gasped, whimpering with pleasure at each eager plunge of his tongue into her tight, slick hole.

Didn't take long. In fact, it was over way too soon. After just a couple of minutes she went rigid as a long, violent orgasm throbbed through her.

He drank it in. Waited for the pulsing shimmers to ease down.

"My turn." He settled between her legs. "I want to look at you while I'm inside you."

Her muscles tightened. "Noah . . ."

He froze. "You still can't bear for me to look at you while we have sex?" he asked. "After what just happened?"

"I . . . I don't know why. I can't—"

"I want to see your eyes. I want to watch your tits bounce, I want to play with your clit and watch the colors change on your skin. I want to tongue kiss your mouth while I fuck you. I want it all."

"I don't understand why you're suddenly so angry," she whispered.

"I'm not." He ran his hand through his sweat-dampened hair, frustrated. Tempted to just mount up, push her past the fear barrier, deal with the aftermath later. He was confident he could make her come again.

But even as the thought flicked through his mind, she sensed it. He saw it in her eyes, her sig.

He'd promised that she was safe with him.

He lifted himself off her, fists clenched. "Roll over then," he said harshly.

Her eyes widened at his tone. "I don't respond well to orders."

Shit. Asshole alert. *Grab a hook.*

He closed his eyes, latched on. Counted slowly down from ten. Frigid waves, lapping on the icy shore. Glacial ice caves. Sea birds. Cold. Numbing cold.

"What are you doing?"

"Chilling . . . out." After a brief pause, he added. "Hoping for a second chance."

"Dick move," she said.

"I know."

He sensed her hesitating, then smiled to himself when the mattress dipped as she slowly rolled onto her belly.

134

Yeah. He'd gotten through that without derailing them. Thank God, because he was about to explode. He got into position, nudging her legs wider and nuzzled her graceful back. Pressed hot kisses against her spine. A silent apology.

Apology accepted, if her deep, shuddering intake of breath was any indication.

"Noah?" Her fingers dug into the crumpled sheets, bunching them.

"Don't worry," he muttered. "I've taken the edge off. I'll do it right this time. Arch your back more."

She didn't argue. Just did it, and moaned softly as he nudged his cockhead against her slit, prodding himself into that tight, quivering clasp. Thrusting slowly, deeply inside, with a rasping groan of pure delight.

"Right," she said, breathless.

She rocked back to meet each swiveling shove. He loved the sounds she made. She seemed so surprised by pleasure. Tension released inside her with every stroke of his dick, letting him deeper and deeper inside with each stroke. He ached to get rid of the condom and feel her, skin to skin.

She gave her pleasure to him like a gift. He stared down at his stiff, thick phallus pumping rhythmically into that snug, flowerlike opening. She was so generous, coming for him with crazy abandon. Letting him in so completely. Her depth and openness were insanely beautiful. He felt drunk on it.

He licked the sheen of moisture on her back. "You're so sweet," he murmured. "So hot. I love how deep you take me. Like being licked all over." He reached around to caress the tight bud of her clit. She shuddered, panting sharply in the silence and moving eagerly against his petting fingers, whimpering with each heavy stroke.

Erotic heaven.

Who knew how long it would last. He had no data to compare this to. No clue what it might morph into without warning.

So he gave into it, steering her deeper into a dreamlike state of intense, shivering pleasure. Each sensual moment wonderful in itself, then softly giving way to the next one, just as fine.

She came twice more before he dared to ask. "Turn over now," he urged. "Please. I want to come while I'm looking at you."

Her body tensed. "No," she whispered. "I can't. Don't take it personally. This is incredible. You're the best."

He swallowed his frustration. Dragged his aching dick out of her snug clasp.

"Maybe we should take a break," he said.

She twisted around to look at him, alarmed. "Don't you need to come?"

"I won't die if I don't."

She reached down, gripping him. "But I want you to. I love the way it feels."

"If I follow the rules. Your rules."

She let go of him and edged away warily. "You're angry at me."

He shrugged as he peeled the condom off. "Don't worry, I'll still make you come."

"You think that's all I want?"

He got up and stalked into the bathroom to ditch the condom. Not without effort. His dick was absolutely unconvinced. Incredulous, even.

He headed back out, spurred on by a fresh surge of frustration. "Why do you hide from me?" he asked her. "Whoever you're running from, I'm not him."

She tossed the coverlet aside and got up, going over to the window. She stared out at the dark waters of the lake. "What do you want from me, Noah?"

The question was rhetorical, but the true answer just fell out.

"I want in."

136

That was the truth. He wanted into the heart of her mysteries. To unravel her, master her, keep the keys, know the codes. All for his own greedy, possessive self.

The stab of visceral emotion triggered a sudden stress flashback. All at once, he felt the tight straps that the Midlands researchers had used to restrain him, cutting into his wrists and ankles while they fucked around with his brain.

No. He fought down the hot flare of rage. He could not do this to Caro. She had her own demons to fight.

He rubbed his face, breathed in the chill of the ice cave before he dared to speak again. "Do you want me to fuck you again?" It came out like a snarl.

She'd tell him to get lost. It was what he deserved, for being such a jerk.

She just stood there, straight and dignified, silhouetted against the faint light from the window. With his infrared implants and his AVP, he saw every eyelash in fine detail, as well as the haunted doubt in her eyes, even in the darkness—but she couldn't see his face.

Which was good. He didn't want her to see that look in his eyes. That *oh-please-God-I'll-do-anything-to-touch-you-again* look.

She gazed out at the wind-whipped trees. Her pose was regal. She glowed with bright cobalt blues, edged with a haze of gold. The darker it was, the better he could see an energy sig.

He came up behind her. The warmth of his body made contact with her slender back. He pressed a slow kiss on her shoulder. "Sorry," he whispered.

She turned slowly, laying her hands on his chest, gently trailing over his scars. To his utter surprise, she sank down with a dancer's sinuous grace, and gripped his stiff penis. She kissed and licked his cockhead, sucking him deeply, eagerly into her mouth. Using her hands to grip him, caress, squeeze, stroke as she did so.

He was almost afraid to touch her. The sensation was so intense, he could lose control of the strength of his grip. He hung onto himself, stroking her hair slowly.

So good, that honey-sweet suckling kiss, enveloping his shaft. He couldn't decide which erotic spectacle drove him crazier: taking her from behind, or having her kneel, voluptuously sucking his dick with that soft, full, luscious mouth.

Her excitement spurred his own. Her skill was unbelievable.

He didn't last long, overstimulated as he was. He felt the energy tightening inside him. Tried to ask if he could come in her mouth.

Too late. The storm broke. He was tossed, wrenched by a violent orgasm.

He poured himself into her with a shout, his explosion melding with colors that had no name but Caro.

He somehow stayed on his feet, trying not to sway. Grabbed her upper arms, and lifted her to her feet. Drawing her into a never-let-you-go embrace.

They stayed that way for a while. Lost in bliss.

The intercom buzzed. She pulled away abruptly, startled. The moment was broken. He missed it already.

"Delivery," he reassured her gently. "From the restaurant. No rush. First the gate, then the driveway. But I have to push the buttons."

She hugged herself, shivering.

He pulled his big fleece robe off its hook, and draped it around her. "After we eat—how about a bath for two?"

She nodded. The robe was huge on her. The hem brushed the ground. She looked stunning in it. He threw on sweat pants, a T-shirt, and started the bath before going to pay for the food.

Coming out, he saw Caro looking out at the lake again, drawn once more to the sight of the glittering dark water. He cast a worried glance her way, wondering what she was thinking.

He hoped he hadn't pushed her too hard.

Chapter 12

"BEFORE WE GET too distracted," Caro mumbled around her bite of roasted rosemary potatoes.

"Yes?"

"Do I hear the tub faucets running? I'd hate for your bathroom to flood."

"Not a problem." Noah piled more food on his own plate. "There's an automatic water-level and temperature sensors. Not bathtime yet. Have some more steak."

She swallowed her bits. "Mmm. Am having." She stuck her fork into a juicy pink-centered slice and lifted it to her plate.

The food was incredible. She hadn't tasted such savory flavors in so long. She'd gotten used to a constant gnawing feeling, and the juicy steak and fresh salads and sides overwhelmed her senses. The bread was crusty and golden, hot enough to melt the fresh butter. It made her feel almost faint.

For a few minutes, there was no conversation. She just stole appreciative glances at his big chest in that T-shirt, admiring the faint jut of masculine nipples. She herself was swaddled in yards of fleece. Except for bed-tousled hair and her face, there wasn't much of her to see.

Although she looked forward to getting naked again. Tonight, she wanted to at least play at being whole. Just a normal woman, doing things normal women did. Hooking up with an interesting guy, taking him to bed, seeing where it went.

She'd spin this hot, lovely thing out for as long as she possibly could.

It was going to have to last her.

She had nothing to share but her body. Nothing any sane, healthy man would want, anyhow. If he knew the horrors inside her head, he'd be gone in a panicked flash.

He served her a large slice of an apple puff pastry. Cream sauce trickled down over the cinnamony apples inside. It smelled so good, tears sprang to her eyes. When pastry made you weep, you were in very bad shape. But she fully intended to devour every flaky crumb.

"Can I ask you a question?" she ventured.

His gaze flicked to her face. "For a price."

Her cheeks reddened. "Never mind."

"All right. I'll give you this one for free," he conceded. "But the next one you barter for. And I drive a hard bargain."

"This, from the guy who paid three thousand bucks for a belly dance."

He laid his hand on hers. "Worth it," he said. "Just for a chance to talk to you."

She almost laughed at that ridiculous statement, but stopped herself. Something in his eyes silenced her. He wasn't bullshitting. She knew that vibe. He was for real.

It felt more like he was calling to her, on some level. From someplace very far. She saw the silent longing in his eyes. It pulled at her from the inside.

Oh, please. Get a grip. She was getting mushy and needy. Hormone overload. She tried to bring it back to light banter. "So talk is what you had in mind?"

He grinned. "I won't apologize for what I had in mind. What's your question?"

She had to think for a minute to retrieve it, she'd gotten so distracted. She looked around the muted elegance of his dining room, at the feast on the table. "You said you grew up poor. How come you ended up living in a mansion and driving a Porsche?"

He shoveled some of the pastry onto his plate. "Big question. Long answer."

"You don't have to answer. I know, it's not fair."

"Really not." He ate a bite or two, and pushed his plate away. "But so what."

"Hey, nothing you could say could make me judge you," she said. "We all have to start somewhere."

I'm not sure you'd really want to know how I got started." His voice sounded flat.

Yikes. She'd hit a nerve. Caro set down her fork and dabbed at her mouth with the napkin. "I'm sorry. If you'd rather not talk about—"

"My parents were con artists. Mostly small time. My dad taught my mom everything he knew. They were a team. I got taken along when they needed a prop."

"What for?" She was genuinely shocked. "How old were you?"

"Really little. Who wouldn't trust a nice young couple with a cute kid? Little budding confidence man, that was me. They were training me up to be just like them. Lucky me."

"Oh," she whispered. "I, ah, don't know what to say."

"Don't say anything. I'm not proud of it. It's just the way it was for me."

Caro nodded mutely.

"So this went on for years. They had my brother and little sister. Sometimes we made money, but we still had to get out of town fast. I pretty much grew up on the road. We stayed in one dive motel after another. Cigarette burns on the sheets. Dirty bathrooms. Broken locks."

There was faint bitterness in his voice. He stopped talking and just looked at her.

She didn't reply. He could have been describing the life she'd been living for the last several months.

"Sorry," he said. "You asked."

"I wish I hadn't," she murmured.

"Oh well. You got the short version. No happy ending, though. One day, a guy my dad had swindled caught up with him. Clubbed him practically to death in a supermarket parking lot."

She flinched. "You saw it?"

"Yes," he said. "We had goods that fell off some truck. You do a return for cash—go in just before the place closes, say you lost the receipt. They pay up to get rid of you. Liquor store, here we come. Only we never got there. The guy must have been following us. He waited for us to come out, and jumped my dad with a baseball bat."

She hated to ask, but she had to know. "Did he hurt you?"

Noah's hand drifted up to a patch of thickened scar tissue that showed in the vee of his T-shirt. "He shattered my collarbone when I tried to stop him."

"Oh, Noah." She gripped his arm. His muscles were tightly contracted.

"It took my dad almost a week to die," he said. "He had skull fractures, major brain damage, internal injuries. He never woke up."

"I'm so sorry."

He shook his head. "He was a hard-drinking liar, thief and cheat. No great loss."

"Still. It had to hurt."

"At the time, not that much. Not at all now."

"What about your mom?"

He shrugged. "She took off a few months after that. Just couldn't deal. We woke up one morning, found her gone. I was seventeen. The others were younger."

Caro was silent for a while. It was a lot to take in. "So what happened to you guys after that?"

"We ran wild. Too bad there's no such things as do-overs. I think about what I did back then sometimes. Can't make amends for any of it."

She nodded. Asking anything more seemed wrong.

His gaze met hers. There was a dark fire in the amber depths of his eyes that made her uneasy. "I'm done talking now."

So that was that. "OK. I suppose you have your reasons."

"I do. And you don't get to ask what they are."

She was taken aback. "What's that supposed to mean?

"I spilled my guts," he said. "I just told you some of my deepest, darkest secrets. That's never happened with any woman I've ever been with." His hand went up to the twisted scar, rubbing it as if it ached. "But did I rack up any points with you? Nope."

"I'm not sure what you mean by points," she said warily. "I appreciate your honesty. And your trust."

"Maybe," he said. "But you won't return it."

Caro stared down at her plate. "You really don't want to know my secrets."

He reached across the table and lifted her chin so that she had to look at him. "Actually, I do."

"Noah, please, don't start in on me again."

"Don't tell me no. You're in danger. I see it on your face. Beautiful as you are, you have the look."

"What look?" she demanded, shaken.

"It's hard to describe," he said. "Like a photographer messed with the contrast. It's mostly in the eyes. It sharpens some things up, washes other things out. It happens to people when they're under constant threat of violence. I'm familiar with it."

"How?" Her voice sounded shrill, inside her own head. "Familiar how?"

He shrugged. "I've seen it in the mirror. I've lived on the run. My guess is that you've been doing it for a while now. But I get the feeling you're running for your life, and not just from the law. From something or someone really evil."

She lifted her head defiantly. "Sounds like it's happened to you."

He hesitated for a long moment. "Yeah. It has."

That wasn't possible. He hadn't said those words. Unless she'd hit the jackpot on a bizarro dating website. *Enjoy long walks on the beach?* Check. *Love big dogs and little kittens?* Check. *Shady past? Hidden trauma?* Check. Check.

She wanted to scoff, but a flash of insight told her that he was revealing a painful truth. There were those scars. He'd explained one, but he had hundreds more. Each inflicted by . . . what had he just said? Something or someone really evil.

But whether or not he was comparing his life to hers, she hated being forced to think about what she was up against. It made her angry . . . at the moment, at him.

"Well, you're wrong," she said. "You're wrong about all of it."

"OK," he said gently. "If I am, then you can relax. Your secrets are secure."

"Somehow I doubt it," she snapped.

"OK if I change the subject?" He didn't wait for her to say yes, just pushed up the sleeve of the oversized robe. "You didn't do this to yourself. And before you get mad, that was a statement, not a question." He ran his finger over the jagged scar that extended from her lower arm down to the palm of her hand.

She tried to pull away, without succeeding.

146

"This is healed, but not old, like my scars," he murmured. "Too pink. Someone cut you recently. Last year sometime. You didn't get stitches, but this cut could've used some."

"Stop it, Noah."

But he couldn't help himself. It was his nature. Under any other circumstances, the focused quality of his attention would be a delicious ego-stroking thrill. As it was, it was killing her.

If he looked too hard, he'd see what she saw whenever she closed her eyes.

Slippery hot blood everywhere, the pressure of the box cutter against muscle and tendon, locked into her memory forever. Gouts of blood, spurting. The sight of Dex in Mark Olund's grip, his eyes wide and horrified as Mark pressed his mouth to his head. Beginning to feed . . .

And Tim, who had made the mistake of trying to help her.

She got up. "You won't stop pressuring me. I'm sick of begging you to. Call a car, or else I will."

"No." He tugged her wrist, pulling her right off her feet and onto his lap. "I'll shut the fuck up. I promise. You can't leave. It's the middle of the night."

His arms were so strong. He smelled so good. He'd made her so hungry for him. Damn the guy. Not fair.

He sensed her weakening, and rose up, lifting her easily into his arms.

She struggled, almost panicked. "What the hell are you doing?"

"Being masterful. You said you go for that."

"Put me down this second, goddamnit!"

He went still, then gently set her on her feet and stepped back. "Sorry," he said carefully. "I thought it would turn you on."

She straightened her robe. Tossed her hair back, straightened her shoulders.

She looked him in the eye. His cautious expression made her relent. A little.

"Stay out of my head," she told him. "It was just too much. And I don't like being pushed around."

"It won't happen again." He paused. "So. Still want to take a bath with me?"

She ran her eyes over his tall, ripped, oh-so-fine body. That hot amber flash in his eyes. Those sensual lips. "Oh yeah," she said, unsteadily.

His grin hung on a little longer than usual this time. "Good. Follow me."

Chapter 13

NOAH NUDGED THE bathroom door open with his foot, and went in first. The dim room was humid, and perfumed with lavender bath salts. Wisps of steam rose from a deep tub in the middle of a large, slate-tiled room.

There was a glass shower for two in the corner. Double showerheads, a double marble sink. A tower of fluffy silver gray towels sat on a stand, along with a tray with soaps, shampoos, lotions. Lots of fancy bath stuff for a single guy, she couldn't help but notice. But his love life was none of her business. She only got one stolen night.

"Like everything," she said. "Completely over the top. Awesome bathroom."

"Yes."

Their eyes met. Her head lifted, and her spine straightened with that mysterious rush that only he could give. That smolder in his eyes just did it to her. Magic.

She let the robe open, and then slip off her shoulders. She shook back her hair and stood there proudly. Enjoying the caressing weight of his gaze on her.

The effect upon his body was obvious, and immediate.

Scented steam drifted. The froth of bubbles had cleared. The huge tub awaited.

Noah peeled off his shirt and sweatpants. His naked body was so powerful and sexual, his heavy phallus jutting high, flushed and ready.

Oh, boy. Play it cool. She twisted her hair up into a loose, tousled knot, and Noah took her hand to help her into the high-walled tub.

Her descent into the steaming water felt like a cleansing ceremony. She sank down with a sigh of bliss. Hot baths were another thing she missed.

He followed her in, bringing the water level higher. Her eyes flicked to the old injury on his collarbone, the only scar visible above the water. It hurt her heart, to think of him alone and terrified as he watched his father being murdered.

She had to look away for a second. Close her eyes.

"Don't dwell on it," he said quietly. "It was a long time ago."

God, how did he *do* that? She'd looked at his scar for only a split second.

"Stop reading my mind," she said sharply. "It's rude. I'll feel sad for the boy that you were if I damn well feel like it. Do not tell me what to think or feel."

"I'll try distraction, then."

He surged forward across the tub and seized her.

* * *

They floated and spun, weightless in the water, as Noah plundered her sweet, willing mouth. He slid his hand down to stroke her juicy pussy, coaxing her legs apart. She murmured against his mouth, opening up to let his finger slide in and writhed sensuously around his exploring hand, squeezing it between her thighs. There was too much water between him and that sweet thing. He wanted to taste her again.

150

He lifted her up out of the water, which rushed and trickled down over her graceful curves and hollows. "Your turn," he said. "Sit on the top step. I can't wait for another taste of you."

"Ah . . . that's the thing," she said hesitantly. "It felt wonderful the last time, but it was hard enough for me to relax when it was dark. In a tub, with the lights on . . . I'd freeze up."

He stroked her upper arms. "So I'll stop, if it doesn't work for you. Just try it," he coaxed. "Please. You're a goddess like this. All rosy and wet."

She still hesitated. He waited patiently, sliding his hands down the deep curve of her waist, then downward to grip the luscious swell of her ass. "Strange, that you're self-conscious," he commented. "You're not at all when you dance."

"Performing's different," she said.

"Hmm. But you do it for a living."

"Because I'm broke," she said. "Besides, when I dance, I'm Shamira. All spangles and veils, doing the shimmy-shimmy-shake. When I'm with you, I'm just me."

"Cool," he said. "That's exactly who I want."

"The answer's still no."

He leaned down to press a hot kiss on her shoulder and then the curve of her neck. "Sit down on that step," he coaxed. "Let me worship you with my tongue."

"You slick bastard." She was trying not to smile.

"I can't help it. Everything about you is interesting to me. It's torture that you won't give me more info."

She rolled her eyes. "Suffer."

"I am, I am." He cupped her breasts, tracing faint, stimulating circles with his thumbs. "I'm wondering what kind of artist you are. Not a painter. Maybe a sculptor?" He ran his hand appreciatively over her curves. "At least a sculptor's model."

"Wrong," she said. "I'm not an artist. Or a sculptor. Or a real dancer. I told you."

"I get it. Being a fugitive is a full time job."

She glared at him. "Don't push me."

"So shut me up," he replied. "Keep my mouth too busy to get into trouble."

She pushed off, floating a little farther from him. Too far. "Do you always get what you want?" she asked.

He thought about it. "No. But that was only because I didn't know what I wanted. Now I know, and I'm going after it." He reached out, dragged her back toward him and cupped her ass. Feeling up those beautiful round ass cheeks kept his hands away from her succulent pussy. For the moment at least.

"You're so confident," she commented.

"And you're stalling," he replied. "Give it up to me, or I'll do the X-ray eyes thing. I'll tell you your social security number and your mother's maiden name."

She smiled, but let herself be tugged toward him. He seated her on the top step that led into the tub and knelt before her clamped thighs, trailing his fingertips over her breasts. Her skin was flushed and rosy from the heat. He loved to see her face hot pink instead of pale. Her beautiful soft tits, gleaming and wet. Tight puckered nipples. The fire inside him crackled and surged. Hotter. Fiercer.

He surged forward, kissing her belly as he gently coaxed her legs apart.

It was hard for her to let go. He had to be so careful. Patient and persistent.

She finally opened to him, but he couldn't say she'd surrendered. He still felt her wariness as he kissed slowly up the inside of her thigh and the tender hollow at her groin. Caro vibrated, gasping, and slid her fingers through his hair, but it was too short for her to grab onto. Maybe he should grow the hair an inch or so longer. Just for this.

Concentrate. He scattered a few more kisses to distract her. It was good to have more light, to see a fuller range of those rosy pink shades of her slit. He spread her folds out wide, and let the taut little bud of her clit pop out.

She drew in a sharp breath. Noah stopped, and slowly sank two of his fingers between her labia to stimulate that sweet spot deeper inside. Never forgetting her clit. Circling that with his tongue, around . . . and around . . . ahhh. Big reaction. Yes.

Hang on, girl. More coming.

He loved the taste and feel of her. So sweet and slick and responsive, reacting so intensely to every caress. Opening more and more as she slowly relaxed.

He held her hips in place, licking up her juice. Suckling that taut bud with tender care. He drew back whenever she got too close to finishing, then started again. Over and over, until she lost her patience and just grabbed his head and kept him exactly where she wanted him. Insisting that he finish what he started. Exactly when she said so.

He did, delighted. She gasped with shocked pleasure as her orgasm racked her.

Noah caught her quickly in his arms and held her very tight so that she wouldn't bruise herself on the rim of the tub.

Afterwards, he settled her on his lap, her head cradled against his chest. Her loose knot of hair had unraveled. It trailed out in the water, clinging to him. He loved it. He wanted to make her come again. Take her away from the violence in her past. Make her fears for the future disappear. Just float here together untroubled. So close.

The minute she opened her eyes, he knew he hadn't entirely succeeded.

"Don't panic," he urged. "Everything's the same as before."

"No, not the same. That wasn't normal. Not my normal."

"Give it time," he said. "You'll get used to it."

Mistake. She went instantly tense in his arms.

Time for a fresh distraction. He stood up. "Let's get you warmed up."

He helped her out of the tub and toweled her gorgeous body off slowly and lovingly before drying himself. Then he took her hand, pulling her back to the bedroom.

The room was chilly in contrast to the steamy bathroom. Caro stretched herself out on the bed, displaying himself, arching and stretching with a sensual smile as she scooped up her wet hair and arrayed it behind herself, spread over the pillow. He flipped on the bedside light and rolled on another condom. In case she wanted to watch.

Apparently not.

"Hey," she said. "The light?"

He forced himself to subdue a flash of anger. "Really? You still can't bear to look at me?"

"That's not it."

"No? Then what's the problem?" He slid under the sheets, and slowly rolled on top of her slender body. "Do you need to pretend that I'm someone else to get off?"

She pushed him up with both hands. He went along with it, lifting his upper body and stayed like that, poised over her. "Is this better?"

She gave him a slap that wasn't playful. "No."

He went still. "Do you want me to stop?"

"No," she whispered. "I've never wanted anyone like I want—" She stopped herself. "Never mind."

He'd have to be satisfied with that. "Doing it from behind is great," he said. "Doing in the dark is fine. But I want more. I want you to know who's inside you. Who's making you come. I want you to see me. And know me."

"I don't know you," she said wildly.

154

"Yes you do. You know me better than anyone ever has." The words tumbled out without a second thought.

"Noah," she said nervously. "That's a scary statement. We met today."

"Can't argue with that. " He shrugged. "But so what? We're doing fine. Why stop now?"

She closed her eyes. "All right. Face to face," she conceded. "But lights off."

He twisted around promptly to snap the light off. Good thing she didn't know about his night vision. But this game they were playing was more about her perceptions than his. Besides. The dark brought out the colors of her sig that much more strongly.

He pushed her legs wider, settling between them. Her hands lifted to brace against his chest. Her nails dug in, a little more than he would have thought necessary to keep him at bay. He liked it. A lot.

"You're angry," she said.

Damn. There was no masking anything from her. "I guess I am," he admitted. "Happens. But not often."

"I'm angry too. And I'm not sorry." Her nails sank in more. Then she relented . . . but not really. They dug in again. Scratching him even harder.

He didn't flinch. It excited him. She felt it, and was faintly annoyed by it.

"Guess I had that coming," he said. "Do it again."

Her eyes narrowed. "Would be nice if it actually hurt," she said tartly.

She rested her hands on his shoulders, pulling on him. He took that as an invitation to lower himself. Slowly and carefully. Bad kitty took no prisoners.

"Oh, it did hurt," he assured her. "Hurt just right." He caressed her slick folds with his stiff, aching dick. Slow, voluptuous up-and-down strokes.

She could see nothing besides the outline of his body looming over her, whereas he saw every detail of her. Lithe and luminous, offering herself at last. Caressing his chest.

She cried out as he sank his thick, throbbing shaft into her tight slickness.

"Close your eyes," he muttered. "If you can't stand me looking at you."

She shook her head. "It's like you can see in the dark. I can feel your eyes."

"Keep feeling it," he said roughly, thrusting again. Balls deep in her hot, quivering clasp. "Feel all of me."

"I do." Her hands slid down his sides to his butt. Holding his hips. Digging her nails into the driving muscle, taking him deeper and deeper.

He struggled to master himself. The pleasure was so intense, he wanted to throw himself into it headlong. *No.* He couldn't lose control completely.

He preferred to think about Caro. Experience Caro. She lifted her hips eagerly to meet each stroke. He let his own energy break loose when she was right at the brink.

They both went for it, full force . . . and exploded together.

They stayed like that for a long time afterwards. Twined and motionless, their hearts still thundering. Wet with sweat. He kept his hand on her ass, to keep them joined . . . until she stretched and shrugged him off.

OK. He had to take care of the condom anyway. He got rid of it fast, as if she'd vanish like smoke if he turned his back. But she was there when he returned, sitting up.

"Your smartphone's doing the strangest thing," she said. "It's glittering."

He glanced at it where it sat on the chest of drawers, startled. He'd programmed it to give him a visual signal when Sisko messaged him using their private code. But he'd set it to light frequencies that unmods shouldn't be able to see.

He grabbed the phone and tapped in the password. "This is a work thing. Mind if I deal with it now?"

"No," she murmured.

Sisko's message was brief.

Asa Stone. Specializes in darknet datamining. Auctions illicit information in secret to highest bidders. Big enemies.

The message was followed by several links.

So his brother was active on the darknet in some sort of criminal way. Not that Noah would expect anything else with their background and training. Or from a kid thrown out on the streets at fifteen.

"Are you OK?" Caro asked.

He had a swift, red-tinged data scroll going now. *Damn.* He exited from the message and quickly put the phone down. "Fine. Why?"

"Your vibe. Seems like you got some bad news."

He shook his head. "Just some old stuff." He slid back under the covers, pulling her jealously into his arms again. She felt so good.

"I should go now," she said.

His whole body contracted. His heart thumped hard and the combat program data flickered and scrolled in blurred stripes of light.

"No way," he said. "You said you'd spend the night. We're not even at the half-way point. You're safe here. You can sleep."

She gave him a sidelong glance. "That's not why I came here, Noah."

"I'll fuck you as many more times as you want," he said. "I stand ready to serve. Until then, get some rest." He was working the masterful, steely-alpha vibe again.

Successfully, this time. She was too exhausted to object. Her colors shifted along with her brain waves, colors muting as she sank into a deep, heavy sleep.

He didn't follow her there. Couldn't anymore, not really. He never slept, just rested one brain hemisphere while the other stayed razor sharp. Sentinel sleep, they'd called it. After their escape, he'd never seen any good reason to unlearn it.

Sentinel sleep was perfect for lying around for hours in bed, looking at a beautiful sleeping woman. Soaking it all in. Not missing a single goddamn second.

He could look at her forever. Time was racing by. He listened to the slow thud of her heart, wishing he could slow time down. Make their night last forever. He liked it, that he could always stay sharp and vigilant for her. Her shelter and her shield.

But dawn kept getting closer. The nearer it got, the more intense his feelings became. His AVP started revving in random, intermittent spurts. The damn data scroll was bugging him, making him restless and distracted. He didn't want to share the screen of his vision with the fucking processor display when Caro was on it.

Sometimes kung fu workouts helped chill the AVP. Worth a try. He reluctantly disentangled himself from her slender limbs. She murmured, rolling onto her side, but didn't wake. He pulled on his sweat pants and padded noiselessly to the practice room.

It was a big glassed-in veranda with tatami mats and a floor to ceiling view of the lake. Cold. He stood in the middle of the room. Observed his body. Stilled his mind.

Time to begin.

He usually spent two or three hours a night in here. The night was so fucking long when you didn't sleep. Not tonight. He'd do just enough to take the edge off his AVP buzz and then it was back to bed to wrap himself around that amazing, mysterious woman. Be ready to serve her when she woke up. In any capacity she wanted.

Though a guy could hope for his favorites.

*   *   *

Caro snapped awake out of a nasty dream. A standard nightmare mix of dread, violence, pursuit. For a moment she looked wildly around the room, disoriented.

It rushed back. Noah. That incredible night.

She was alone in the rumpled bed. She slid out from between the sheets and retrieved Noah's fleece robe from where it had been tossed on the bathroom floor.

She padded around the house in search of him, then saw the glass veranda through another window, and the shadowy flash of movement.

When she found the door to the veranda, it was slightly ajar. She pushed it a little further open, and gazed at him, awestruck.

He was naked to the waist, doing a martial art form. His rapid, fluid moves were so beautiful. Sweeping and precise. Full of explosive energy.

He sank down into a deep, wide-legged crouch . . . and sprang upward in a sudden flurry of whip-quick kicks, so fast they seemed like a blur.

He turned to her, put his hands together and bowed slowly.

"I didn't know you saw me," she said. "Didn't mean to interrupt you."

"I was finished," he said. She could barely make out his face in the dimness. He seemed to be smiling.

Caro stepped into the room, which was cold. "That was beautiful," she said. "What is it?"

"A grab bag of disciplines," he said. "Mostly kung fu. It's my favorite."

"Wish I'd studied that, instead of dance," she said, meaning it with all her heart.

He grinned. "I love the way you dance. But it's never too late to start learning. I'll teach you, if you want. Stick around."

Right. As if she could. She shivered as she gazed out the window. "Do you work out at this hour all the time?"

"Whenever I can't sleep, if I don't feel like carving wood or staring at screens. I was just about to come back to bed."

She imagined it so vividly, she could feel the sensations. That long, strong beautiful man sliding into bed with her, making the mattress dip under his weight. The excited delight rippling through her at the contact with his skin as he rolled onto her. His hands, his lips, his smoldering eyes, his big hard cock. Everything.

There was just enough light to admire the lines and curves and cuts of his naked torso. She wanted to run her hands over him, slowly memorizing him by feel. To slide her hand in the front of those low-slung sweat pants and cup him in her hand, stroking until he was stiff and hard and ready.

She could tell by the quality of his energy that he read her thoughts and would be eager to oblige her. But dawn was almost breaking. The deeper she went into this, the harder it was going to be to drag herself away.

She forced herself to turn around and march back to the bedroom.

* * *

Noah followed her, a pace behind, not allowing himself to touch her. She was too tense. Again, after that sensual flare of colors he'd seen back in his practice room. So near, yet so far. Oh, well. Maybe he could cuddle her in bed until she relaxed again.

But once there, she looked at the clock. "I have to go, Noah."

Another flare of irrational rage activated the AVP again and he was right back where he'd started an hour before. He walked a tightrope of self-control to keep his voice even and mild as he responded. "Sun's not up. Have to go where?"

She gave him a stern look. "That's my business." She perched on the edge of the bed. "I can't believe I slept so long."

"You could use more of that," he said. *Weeks of it. Right here. In this bed. With me holding you the whole time.*

"Maybe so." She smiled, but it faded quickly. "But not here."

Another AVP surge, stronger than before. The data feed started to scroll. *Shit.*

"Why?" he demanded, his voice harsh. "Stay with me. I'll drive you where you want to go. Unless you were planning to walk."

"No, but—"

"So I'll drive and I'll wait. Then I'll bring you back here for breakfast."

She frowned. "A cab's fine."

"No. Just no," he told her, exasperated. "Like you could even get one this early in the morning. Listen, Caro—"

"You said last night that you weren't going to pressure me. You promised."

"Yeah. I remember. Now I'm breaking it," he said.

She was outraged. "Don't you fucking dare!"

"Watch me."

Caro looked around wildly. For what? Something to hit him with? Her entire body vibrated with anger.

"No way am I letting you go out into the dark to face all these enemies you refuse to tell me about." He grabbed her hand. "Come on. It's just a ride. Safely buckled up. Going just under the speed limit. Door to door service. And in case you haven't noticed, this is not actually a discussion."

"Bullshit. We established the rules!" She yanked to free herself. "Let go of me!"

He changed his grip so she wouldn't injure her wrist but he didn't let go.

"I can't," he said.

It was true. Letting her just walk out the door was not an option for him. Wasn't going to happen. They stared into each other's eyes. She looked furious and betrayed.

He hated ending on this note, but he wasn't backing down.

"You can't keep me here," she said.

"No," he admitted. "Not indefinitely."

"I mean right now," she snapped back.

"What are you going to do? Call the cops?" He reached for the smartphone on the bedside table and held it out to her. "Go ahead. Be my guest. Tell them your troubles. They'll come and save you."

She crossed her arms. "You son of a bitch," she whispered.

"Right." He set the phone down. "I didn't think you wanted to talk to them."

"You're really crossing a line, Noah."

"Just trying to take care of you."

Caro dismissed that with a contemptuous look. "I can do that myself."

He finally let go of her hand. "Good. My house is your house. Take a shower if you want."

She walked away from him, twisting her hair into a knot that stayed up without pins, a feat of womanly engineering that had always been a mystery to him. "You won't join me?"

He was startled into silence for a second. "Fuck yeah, I want to join you," he said emphatically. "I just thought you'd prefer to be alone."

She shook her head. "Not so much. You just stay right where I can see you."

162

Caro preceded him into the big shower box, shoulders back, chin high. She chose the showerhead nearest to the sliding glass doors, forcing him to slide past her to the one near the wall.

He was erect, of course. Soaped up and standing. They both ignored it, but he couldn't keep from watching the fluffy white foam slide down over her curves and hollows. Looking at her made him hot and stupid.

He slapped off his water and waited in the scented steam until she turned her water off, too. Her sig refracted through the glass, coloring the gray slate tiles like a dark, prismatic jewel.

He took a step toward her. "OK? Do you trust me now?"

"No." She bent over and squeezed the water out of her hair. Her bun had fallen down and gotten soaked. A long, thick rope of wet dark curls. His erection got stiffer.

"I just want you to be safe," he said, staring at the water dripping from her hair.

"I need a towel," she said.

He slid past her, reached out and handed her two. "Why are you bucking me?"

"Stop." She held up her hand. "We're not having this conversation, and you're not driving me home. Now get the hell out of my way."

Chapter 14

HE DIDN'T MOVE. Just stood there blocking the way out. The only sound was the drip of water from the showerhead.

Noah stood there in the steam, his big penis jutting urgently toward her. Drops of water rolled over the striking bones of his face and down to the complicated landscape of muscle and bone and scar tissue. His nipples were tight, dark. Smooth chest hair was plastered to his taut skin.

Her eyes were locked with his. Held and enthralled by that unearthly brightness.

She was furious at him, but her anger was no shield against the ache and pull in her chest. His gaze went right through her, seeing the scared, diminished self she so hated being.

He saw every pitiful detail of it, and somehow still wanted her, with a ferocity that left her breathless. And determined to protect herself.

"Stop it," she told him, adding quickly, "I'm talking about the intense look. It's just another way of pushing me around."

His eyes flashed. "Hey, I'm just standing here, not touching you. Wanting really badly to fuck you again. Can't blame a guy for that."

"Sure I can," she told him.

"But I can't help it," he said. "And I can't stop it."

She reached out, and wrapped her hand around his thick penis. He sucked in air.

She stroked his hot shaft, petting the velvety skin. "It's so strange, being pissed off and turned on at once. It could make me behave . . . badly."

"Really? Awesome. I'm in." He put his hand between her leg, sliding his fingers between the folds, pleased to find her hot and wet and slick.

He withdrew his fingers and hungrily sucked on them. "Caro. Let me." He started to sink to his knees before her.

She stumbled back, panicked. "No, no, no," she said wildly. "No, not that. Not when I'm on edge like this. I just can't."

He rose back up to his feet, his gaze intent. Waiting for a signal.

The bastard. So confident. Making her feel like she'd never forgive herself if she didn't get one last taste of him.

And what felt worse: knowing that he was on to her. He had all the time in the world to wait. He *would* just stand there until she broke down and begged for it.

"I'm prepared." He smiled.

She didn't. "You would be."

"Black cabinet, top shelf, left side."

She shoved past him into the bathroom, and found what she was looking for.

Back into the shower, to sheath his thick shaft. She savored his reaction.

He clasped her waist and she let him lift her and press her back against the cool wet slate tiles, wantonly spreading her legs. He grabbed her thighs, encouraging her to wrap her legs around him, which she immediately did.

He leaned forward, kissed her throat, murmuring in her ear. "Put me inside you."

Caro seized that thick club bobbing at her thigh, and nudged it to where she wanted it. She was drenched and ready. Under his spell. Craving every inch of him.

They gasped together as he drove deep inside her. His thrusts were slow and slick and heavy, each stroke of his big cock the ultimate answer to her body's silent pleas for more, more, more.

She dug her nails into his back, moaning. He was so deep inside. Body, mind, soul. All of her. Her body melted for him, molded around him. A slick rocking give and take of pure erotic bliss. She knew he could hold her effortlessly, pleasuring her with masterful skill for as long as she wanted him to.

Her heart was swelling bigger, too. Hotter, like the sun was inside her chest. Filling her with light. Coming closer, brighter, sharper . . .

Oh. Yes. Sweet oblivion pulsed and throbbed through her.

The wrenching bursts of pleasure eventually eased, leaving her limp in his arms. Just Caro again. Her face was wet. Stupid tears.

Noah's face was pressed against her shoulder. She clutched his hot, slick body, trying to fix this moment and all the others in her memory. His blazing vital energy, the magic space he'd created where she felt safe, desired, beautiful. After months of lonely desperation, this sudden intimacy with him had jolted something dead back to life.

They clung to each other for a long, silent time.

Noah slid out of her, and set her on her feet. He turned the shower on, angling it away until the water was warm, and aimed the stream over her torso and then down between her legs, caressing as he rinsed. There was bold assurance to his touch, as if he had every right to handle her so intimately.

He shut off the water and reached for a fresh towel.

She almost smiled. Couldn't quite manage it. "I can dry myself," she told him.

"Give me that much," he muttered.

So she did. Just stood there unresisting, letting herself be caressed by the long strokes of the towel over her body. Willing herself not to cry again as he slowly and meticulously toweled her hair, with leisurely thoroughness.

He tossed the sodden towel aside. "Stay here with me," he said fiercely.

She felt her body go tense. "Noah. Don't start."

"I never stopped," he said. "I don't know how. The coffee should be ready by now. Come get some when you're dressed. I'll make you breakfast."

"No breakfast, thanks. I'm not hungry." She stared, hypnotized, as he toweled off his own chiseled physique. "Your coffee maker sure is timed to start early."

"I'm not much of a sleeper." He strode out, taking the air and energy with him.

Solitude thudded down. And she'd thought she was depressed before.

How strange it felt to pull on her wrinkled clothes. They smelled unfamiliar somehow, as if they belonged in someone else's life. But this was the only life she had. She was stuck with it.

It hardly mattered if he learned her address. She was leaving Seattle as soon as she made contact with Bea. After that, time to pack and run. Ponytail was probably still looking for her, but she had to risk going home. If she didn't get her stuff, she'd have to buy it all again. Nothing like stark poverty to make a person loathe waste.

Dressed, with her damp hair braided back, she walked through his house, admiring the lofty vaulted spaces and huge windows. The lake glowed, a dissolving mist wafting over the water. There were no lights in the kitchen except for a subtle line of illumination under the edge of a counter.

Noah took a mug from the cupboard. "How do you take your coffee?"

"With cream if you have it."

"I do." Moments later, she was sipping an aromatic French roast lightened with a generous slosh of cream.

"You should eat something," he said, his voice disapproving. "You burned a lot of energy last night. Let me make you some eggs and toast."

Caro set down her unfinished coffee. "No. But thank you. I really do have to go."

He turned his back, as if he didn't trust himself to speak.

She pulled her coat out of the closet in the foyer, and dug into the duffel for the bag with her disguise. Noah saw her.

"Shit," he said, dismayed. "Don't put that stuff on your face. Please."

"I have to," she told him.

"It's not even dawn yet. And it's like spray-painting graffiti on Botticelli's Venus."

She couldn't help smiling. "That's sweet, Noah, but—"

"No one will see you. You'll be wearing a hat. In a car with tinted windows." He waited, and prompted, "Please, Caro. Just say yes."

"I've been doing that since I met you," she said. "It has to stop."

"You mean I have to stop. I will. When your door clicks shut, I really will."

She set the duffel on the table, and packed the street disguise pieces carefully back into it. "Let's hope so," she murmured.

"Thanks for the vote of confidence. Wait. Before you go, there's something I want to show you. Come into the dining room."

She set down her coffee and did as he asked. Moments later, he came in holding what looked like a large painting, swathed in fabric.

He unwrapped it carefully, and placed it upright on the sideboard, angling a gooseneck lamp to illuminate it. "This is the real Delaunay."

Caro moved closer, startled and moved. The spare lines of the portrait and the depths of the layers of color that permeated them opened her inner eye. The unusual painting became a threshold, a connection across time and space that she could actually feel, like a buzzing hum inside her head.

That hum had been lacking when she saw the reproduction, though all of the techniques used to create the painting had been carefully reproduced. The real magic happened on a subconscious level. An original was like a portal into another time and place, another person's vision.

Or, in the case of a fake, it wasn't. A fake just sat there. Competently done, but inert.

"Beautiful," she said.

"I thought you'd like it," he said.

She moved toward it. "May I?"

"Of course," he said.

She picked it up, letting the images resonate inside her. The colors glowed jewel bright even in the darkened room.

Something on the edge of the frame fell into her hand. A locator tag of some sort. Small but definitely high tech. Undoubtedly hidden there to track the Delauney if it got stolen.

She set the painting down, and held the tiny device out. "Your tile came loose."

He pocketed it with a nod of thanks, then walked over to the side of the living room where his art was displayed and stood for a moment looking at the shelf of his carvings. He returned to her with an object in his hand. "This is for you."

She took it, gazing down at a small carving of a wolf. The animal looked watchful and wary, but the carving captured its toughness and wiry resilience. And its inherent nobility.

"I figured you'd prefer something small," he said. "If you need to travel."

She almost refused it. Then she looked up, and something in his eyes made the words stop in her throat.

170

"Thank you," she said, after a moment. "It's beautiful."

Noah didn't reply.

She put the wolf carving in her pocket, and forced herself to step away from him. "I should go now, Noah."

Noah rewrapped the painting, and carried it away without speaking.

Once out the door, he grabbed her hand for the walk to his car. Her hand was happy to be held. His grip was warm and strong, imbued with all the power of his personality. No clamminess, no clutching, no ick factor. Just tingling closeness.

And a sharp longing for what might have been. If her life had been her own.

Their only communication on the drive were the directions she gave him. She sensed his disapproval as they passed the strip clubs, boarded-up houses. She didn't have many options in terms of housing. She was limited to landlords who didn't ask about employment history or credit rating. Or require believable ID.

"Right up the street," she told him. "Park anywhere."

He pulled over. "I may never see my car again."

"Let me off at the curb," she urged. "Believe me, I understand."

"No. It's insured." He got out, and came around to open her door, but she was already out. Noah slung her duffel over his shoulder. "Now where?"

"Long goodbyes are harder. It's a hike. Sixth floor. Spare yourself."

He ignored the advice. "Lead the way."

Noah pushed the battered entrance door of an old tenement building. It opened with no resistance. "Front lock's broken," he commented, expressionless.

"The landlord's been informed," she said. "He says it's unfixable."

He kicked aside some loose tiles from the black and white mosaic pattern that covered the floor. So many were gone, the effect was like missing teeth.

He followed her up on up. The sixth floor had a frayed runner of carpeting, scattered with garbage. A cockroach scuttled beneath a door and disappeared. A sleeping man in a shabby winter coat and knit cap lay slumped against a door.

He opened a reddened eye as they approached.

"Hey, Freddie, what's up?" Caro asked. "Lose your keys?"

"Bitch locked me out," Freddy rasped, and coughed violently.

"That blows," Caro stepped over the man's legs. "Take it easy, Freddie."

Freddie's dull gaze flicked up to Noah and then looked back at Caro beseechingly. "Can I crash with you, beautiful?"

"In your dreams," Caro said lightly.

Freddy took a longer look at Noah. "Ain't he something. Moving up in the world, are we? Nice shoes, buddy."

Noah quelled him with a glance. Freddie seemed cowed. "You never brought home no boyfriend before," he said warily. "What's up with that?"

"He's just walking me to my door," Caro said.

"Uh-huh." He got up awkwardly and stumbled down the hallway, managing the stairs somehow.

Caro stopped in front of a door in which all three of the brass numbers had fallen off, leaving the ghosts of six-zero-eight on it. She put a key in a knob lock.

"Are you kidding me? A fucking knob lock." His low voice was flat. "With neighbors like that."

"I'm not worried about the locks," she said. "Or Freddie. He's harmless. Thanks for accompanying me, Noah. You've been very gallant."

Noah's eyes narrowed. "You only let me see this place because you're leaving."

Something must have flashed over her face, and of course, he caught it. The way he caught absolutely fucking everything.

"Son of a bitch," he murmured. "I nailed it. You'd never let me see this dump if you were staying. But what the hell. It doesn't matter anymore, right?"

"Stop," she said wearily. "It's hard enough for me as it is."

"So make it easier," he urged. "Come home with me. I'll make you a breakfast, and sit you down with a fresh cup of coffee. You can tell me everything. Please, Caro."

"No." Her voice was gaining strength.

"Then give me a few more minutes in your apartment. Just that. And I swear, I'll go."

"You said that before. You're lying. You'll just keep pushing."

"Please, Caro," he pleaded. "Please."

She let out a breath she hadn't been aware she was holding. He was just prolonging the pain. And this was so painful.

Fuck it. He could come in if he was so desperate.

She pushed open the door.

Chapter 15

NOAH STEPPED IN, and stopped on the threshold.

Caro murmured behind him for him to get out of her way. Finally, she shoved him forward, came in behind him and shut the door.

The place was a startling contrast to the squalor outside the door. The floor had been covered with roll-out straw floor mats. One wall was painted a sunny pale yellow, one a robin's egg blue, one pink, one a spring green. Damaged plaster on two walls was decorated with leaves and branches folded from green and brown paper.

Two narrow windows were draped with cloth. The light shone through it on an array of crystal perfume bottles, pink-tinted prisms from a broken chandelier and colored glass wrapped in fine copper wire. What morning light there was refracted through all the glass and crystals, filling the room with shifting colors.

He saw a futon mat on the floor, a folded silver comforter and a pillow on it. A shelf held a hot plate and an electric teakettle, a plate, bowl, glass and cup. One fork, spoon and knife stuck out of a repurposed jar. There was a small sink with a sponge and bottle of dish soap. A shelf with a limited array of food on it. A hanging basket with a few pieces of fruit and a red sweet pepper.

The duffel thudded from his hand onto the floor. "Nice," he said.

"Thanks." She slipped off her shoes, set them by the door. "I fixed it up a little. Good for morale."

"Looks great. Is this a no-shoes type of place?"

She gave him a stern look. "You won't be here that long."

Noah stepped out of his shoes and hung his jacket on a hook by the door.

"Make yourself at home." Caro's voice sounded weary.

"You know something?" He looked around again. "When I came up the stairs, and saw that corridor, I felt sorry for you. I was expecting to feel sorrier when I got inside. I figured it would be a dingy hole."

She waited, arms folded. "I see. And?"

"I don't feel sorry for you anymore," he said simply. "This place says it all."

Her eyebrow tilted. "Ah . . . OK. Is that a compliment?"

"Yeah."

She nodded in acknowledgement. So she didn't like praise, or even being noticed. "It's pretty," he said. "All you. But I hate that goddamn cheap lock. Your neighbors don't thrill me, either."

"Freddy's not my problem," she said.

The edge in her voice clued him in, and he looked at her face more carefully. "Meaning that somebody else is?"

She looked hunted. "I didn't say that."

"But I still heard it," he said. "Who's your problem, Caro?"

She waited a long time to answer. "Just a guy," she said. "Following me. Can't tell you any more than that. It's happened twice. I don't know who he is."

"What did he look like?" Noah demanded.

A troubled look came into her eyes. "You might be about to find out, since you insisted on coming here with me. Check your rearview mirror when you leave. And be careful. Please."

"If I still have a car." He regretted the words the second he said them.

"I wish I had your problems," she muttered.

"At least let me help you with this one thing. Tell me what he looks like."

"Big," she said. "Long dark hair. Ponytail. Hawk nose. Tattoo on his neck."

He relaxed. Just Zade, being careless. "Could be a coincidence."

She looked puzzled. "I doubt it."

"I'll keep my eyes open," he said, trying to calm her. "You're sure you'll be OK?"

"Just shut up, Noah. And go."

"Am I being kicked out?"

"You could leave on your own. That would be easier for me."

He moved toward the door. "Then I guess this is goodbye."

"For the last time."

"Doesn't have to be the last time, Caro."

He knew that it was pointless, but he said it anyway. It had to be said. This was his cue to walk out the door like he'd promised. But he couldn't move. He couldn't stop looking at her, standing there with tears of fury glittering in her eyes.

And something else as well. Her sexual awareness of him. He was so attuned to it now. After one night he knew her well. He loved it when her furious gaze ran hungrily over his body, lingering at the bulge at his crotch.

"Oh, please." Her voice was hard. "Really, Noah?"

He shrugged, unembarrassed, and just waited. Her sig painted the room, but he'd almost stopped noticing it by now. He'd internalized it.

Right now, he was more interested in the sexual hunger pulsing out of her. And the regal angle of her chin. He loved that. So strong and proud and fucking *hot*.

"You son of a bitch," she said. "Jerking me around."

"No. I'm not," he said. "I meant what I said."

She squeezed her eyes shut. "Fuck," she muttered to herself. "You are making this so difficult."

He took a slow step closer to her. "I'm not the one who's doing that," he said. "Tell me what's wrong, Caro."

She shook her head. "I don't want to talk."

"There's a lot we can do without talking."

He had her with that. Once again, she was turned on and pissed off in equal measure.

"Fine," she hissed. "If you're offering."

"Oh, yeah."

She kicked off her sneakers, stepped out of the jeans with sharp, angry gestures. She stumbled, almost falling, as she stripped off her socks, cursing under her breath. The coat fell, the shirts, all pulled off in a tangled wad, plus the bra.

She stood before him naked, cheeks red. Mad as hell. Hot as hell. He could hardly breathe, he was so turned on. So afraid of screwing this up. Sex on a cliff's edge.

She turned to unfold the comforter on the floor. The sight of her naked body bending over like that jacked him up to maximum lust levels.

He drew back just long enough to rip off his own clothes, vibrating with urgency. He kissed her frantically, sliding his fingers between her legs. She was already juicy and soft. She opened to him with a gasp, her nails sinking into his shoulders.

He stopped short. "Are you sore?"

"I'm good. Never better."

"Answer the question I asked. Not a different one."

"Don't give me orders. I want you inside me. Right now."

He rolled on top of her, and then went still. "Condoms?" he asked hopefully.

She shook her head slowly. "Implant."

"Oh." He hesitated, studying her face. "So we're good, then?"

She pulled him closer. "Obviously. Shut up. I keep saying that."

"Yeah. Makes me hot."

His body wasn't giving him a choice, not with her luscious form on full display.

Bracing her slender feet against his chest, he growled as he shoved every inch of his naked shaft slowly inside her.

"Yes," he gasped, shuddering. "Oh yes. So fucking . . . *good.*"

He seized her hands, winding his fingers through hers. Those pale, lush tits bouncing got him even hotter. The deep, rhythmic pump and glide picked up, sooner than he wanted it to. He couldn't help it. Her panting turned into cries of pleasure as her body took him in. So deep.

It overtook them long before he was ready. Both of them were rushing it, on edge, burning up. She gripped his ass, hips bucking with frantic eagerness, and he didn't have a hope in hell of resisting the pull. Straight to the finish.

The energy thundered over them, through them. Huge and obliterating.

He stayed on top of her, eyes squeezed shut for a long time. Unwilling to face it.

He was done. They had come together, but time had run out. This was the mercy fuck before she booted him out of wonderland. He pulled out, turned away and sat on the floor with his back to her, trying to pull on his clothes.

The air was thick with unsaid words.

He finally dared to look at her. Still pale, but her lips and nipples were a hot rosy pink.

"Come home with me," he said, because he just couldn't help it.

She got up and took down a faded green robe. Wrapped it around herself.

"No," she said. "Go. We're done here." Her voice was hard.

He picked up her coat. Hung it up on the hook where he had hung his own, and reached into his pocket for the little thing, small and hard between his fingertips.

The tracking tile that'd been on his Delaunay painting. What to do with it had come to him the second she handed the thing to him back at his house.

So obvious, so necessary. No one could fault him for it.

He adjusted the folds of Caro's coat, and slipped the tile into her pocket. He could not let her disappear into nowhere, knowing that she was in danger.

She stood so straight and unrelenting, her arms crossed over her chest. Not another word from her. She was just waiting for him to get lost.

"Be careful," he said to her. "That's all I'm asking."

"I will," she said. "I always am. Goodbye."

Noah opened the door and propelled his body through it. The door clicked shut.

Freddie grinned up at him from halfway down the stairs between the sixth floor and the fifth. "Lucky boy," he croaked. "Everybody's been wanting what you just got."

Rage he hadn't allowed himself to feel roared up like jet fuel. He ran down the steps and fixed Freddie with his most terrifying stare.

"Just so you know," he said. "Anyone who disrespects her gets his liver torn out. Then I feed it to him, piece by piece. Is that clear?"

Freddie's smirk vanished. So did the leering gleam in his watery brown eyes. "Ah. Yeah. Clear. Got it."

"Spread the word," Noah said. "As a community service."

Freddy nodded, blinking rapidly. Noah moved on down the staircase.

He stumbled out onto the street, and tried, out of force of habit, to do an analog dive. It didn't work. His body still throbbed with the overload of sensations, emotions. He didn't want to put them in the deep freeze. He did not want to chill, after all that heat. He'd changed radically. After one single goddamn night.

He was vaguely surprised to see that his car was still there. Seemed like a week had gone by since he left it.

Zade's ring tone sounded. He fumbled in his pocket for his phone, but then Zade himself walked around the corner. Noah slid the phone back into his pocket.

"Well, well," Zade said. "Imagine my surprise."

Noah had nothing to say. His hard drive was wiped.

"I remember you saying to me yesterday that this was a mystery, to be unraveled carefully and discreetly," Zade went on. "Guess I just didn't hear the part when you said, 'with my dick.'"

Noah's breath hissed through his teeth. "I don't have to explain myself to you."

"Oh yeah? That's Olund's ex! I told you to flirt with the girl, not fuck her!"

"Not his ex," he said. "She wasn't his lover."

"Yeah? Did she tell you that? What makes you so goddamn sure?"

He had no doubts at all. Mark was covered with scars just like his. If Caro had seen such a phenomenon before, it would have been visible in her sig.

But last night was none of Zade's business. "Drop it."

"Fuck no," Zade said belligerently. "I sat around all night in this shitty neighborhood, fending off the creeps who wanted to feel my fine ass for free, or buy drugs from me, or whatever else was squirming around inside their pointy little heads so I could pick up this woman's tail again, and you drive up with her loaded into your Porsche? What, you *forgot?* You've been boning this girl all night, but did you call and say, dude, I'll pick up the tab for your tacos and beer and you wait while I take her home and fuck her—whoa!"

Zade grunted, startled as Noah slammed him against the brick wall, his hand wound into the folded collar of Zade's thick shearling jacket.

"Do not speak about her like that." He barely recognized his own voice.

Zade made no move to defend himself, though he was supremely capable of doing so. He just stared at Noah, his dark gaze alive with suspicion. "Holy shit," he said. "What the hell? Are you in love with this woman?"

"No!" He couldn't seem to breathe. All the strength ran out of the arm that clamped the other man against the wall.

He let go, and just stood there swaying, fists clenched.

Zade looked almost scared. "I've never seen you like this. What the fuck is wrong with you? Are you OK? Do I need to call—"

"No." Noah waved his hand in negation. "I'm just . . ." He broke off, rubbed his mouth. "It's the AVP. And stress hormones. The combat program is kicking my ass."

"Oh." Zade studied him intently. "So. What about the Ice Maiden?"

Noah frowned at him blankly. "Who?"

Zade rolled his eyes, disgusted. "Your fiancée? Simone? She doesn't deserve this kind of shit, you two-timing pig."

"We broke up," Noah said.

Zade's eyebrows shot up. "Say what? Did she cry?"

"No," Noah said, uncomfortably. "She dumped me. Gave me back the ring. Told me I was a prick, not in those exact words. That was it."

"Wow. And your rebound is Mark's fugitive ex? You're keeping it interesting, I'll say that much for you."

"Don't call her that," Noah snapped. "She's not Mark's ex."

Zade's own unique design of augmented sensory processing, with different brain stim and implants, made him as good at reading people as Noah, in his own way. It felt strange, being observed so intently. Not that he had any goddamn right to complain.

"So what now?" Zade said finally.

"You'd better up your game, for one," Noah said. "She saw you twice and remembered every detail. She thinks you're a hit man for Mark, with good reason. She's skipping town because of you. Mark's trying to destroy her, but she wouldn't tell me a goddamn thing."

Zade grunted. "She saw me, huh? Sharp eyes, for an unmod."

"And you dress to impress."

"Now is not the time for cracks about my personal style," Zade said. "You practically broke my ribs on that wall, dude."

"Boo hoo, poor you. Go check yourself into the hospital."

Zade snorted. "So, what's the deal? Why bring her back to this dump at all? You could have sent one of us to get her things."

"I'm not taking her anywhere right now," Noah said. "She threw me out of her place."

"Ah." Zade looked puzzled. "That sucks. I'm, ah, almost afraid to ask—"

"So don't."

Zade didn't, for about three seconds. Then he cleared his throat, and did. "For twelve years you've been kicking our asses, pushing us around. You can wrangle a bunch of crazy mutant freaks, but you can't lay down the law with a pussycat artist? Just be the man! Tell her how it is!"

Zade had a point, but still. Pushing Caro around might keep her alive, but it would kill something else, something he treasured. But he didn't know how to say that in a way that Zade could understand.

"I put a locator tag in her coat," he admitted.

Zade shook his head, bewildered. "Hope she doesn't take it to the cleaners. Did you get her story?"

"No," he said bleakly. "None. Best I could do was guess at some of it."

"You rock, secret agent. So did you take out the lenses and do the scary glowing eyes thing?"

"Yeah," he admitted. "All night long."

"And she still didn't talk? That gonzo yellow cat stare would make me confess to anything."

He was too miserable to tell Zade to get stuffed. "Didn't have much of an effect on her," he said. "She wouldn't spill a goddamn thing."

Zade whistled. "She's tougher than she looks. What signal did you plant?"

"The tile Sisko put on my Delaunay painting. I'll tail her myself, today."

"Did Mark hurt her? Can we kill him now?" Zade's eyes gleamed.

"She wouldn't tell me. But she has knife scars, and probably PTSD or something like it. Whatever happened, she barely got away with her life. I'm giving her some breathing room for now."

A grin split Zade's lean face. "You know, I've never seen you like this."

Noah was irritated. "Like what?"

"All turned on. Fired up, but not AVP freak-out mode. Not deep-freeze robot-king either. This one's new. Hey, I think maybe you annoy me a little less this way."

Noah tapped data into his phone to monitor her locator tag. "You're making me all soft and warm inside. Stop it, before I get confused about who I am."

"Awww," Zade crooned. "Am I emasculating you, Noah? I'm so sorry."

"Get lost," Noah said. "Go have some tacos and beer."

"Too late, asshole. But thanks." Zade strode away without looking back.

*　*　*

Mark peered through the chilly mist of the autumn morning. His phone burbled in his pocket. He checked the display. It was the leader of his Seattle team.

"Carrerra," he said. "Give me good news."

"You got it, boss. We're following her. She's on a bus. We're behind it."

"Good," he said, circling the mud puddles. "Gareth Wickham gave you her address?"

"He knew her street address, but not the apartment number. Pain in the ass."

"Did you push him hard, like I told you to?"

"We scared the living shit out of him. He would have handed over his own grandma and given us all blowjobs by the end. But he was still fucked if he knew, and the building has sixty goddamn units. But we just got lucky. She came out the front door of the building, alone, just as we were getting out of the car. So we just got back into the car and followed her to the bus stop. She's heading downtown now. How do you want us to wrap this up?"

"Isn't it obvious?" Being forced to micromanage was annoying, and he could see his target already, barely visible through the trees.

"I don't wanna screw up. Tell me what your comfort level is when it comes to making noise," Carrerra said. "It's business hours downtown, so we'll have to—"

"Be discreet," he snapped. "Be creative. Don't get caught, don't be seen, and stay away from surveillance cameras. Most of all, do not make me wait one second longer than I have already. When I get to Seattle, I want her waiting for me. I don't want problems. That's why I pay so well. Do we understand each other?"

"OK, boss. Got it."

Mark cut the connection, enjoying the hot buzz of pleased anticipation as his target approached. His first prototype slave soldier, and he could finally activate him now that he'd retrieved the freq wand from Kitteridge's vault. R-Gen, serial number 57-878, who went by the name Brenner Jameson to the outside world. Once entirely human and now . . . not. Six foot four, two hundred forty pounds of enhanced muscle and super-dense bone, sprinting through the morning drizzle with the speed of a pro athlete.

When Brenner was done with his workout, which he was programmed never to miss, he showered, ate a huge high-protein meal, and went to his job in a local big box appliance store, humping stoves and refrigerators. Working super hard. Lacking the slightest idea of the specialized knowledge and training hidden inside his highly compartmentalized brain.

In his research, Mark had noticed that Brenner had bucked his programming in the past two years, to the extent of getting romantically involved with a woman in the town where he lived. He'd even had a child with her. The woman had since died, but the liaison should never have happened. Probably a programming design issue.

He was ten yards away when Mark stepped out of the trees. "Brenner Jameson?"

The young man turned to look at him as he ran. "Yes?"

Mark pushed the button on the small freq wand he had taken from Kitteridge's safe, activating the silent shriek, a coded pulsation of an ultrasound frequency, designed to tear down firewalls inside Brenner's barricaded brain.

The younger man stopped, staggering. His momentum drove him to his knees in the mud with a grunt. His energy sig exploded in a chaotic burst of wheeling color as energy was released, suppressed memories liberated. What an incredible sensation it must be for him. And painful, perhaps. Always entertaining to watch.

"Your real work just began," Mark told him. "I'm your controller now, Brenner. You have to do anything I tell you."

Brenner stared up at him, his hand at his throat. Struggling to speak.

"I heard you got involved with a local girl," Mark said. "Started a family."

Brenner staggered to his feet, swaying. "Callie," he said thickly.

Callie. That had been the name of the child. He wondered if he should eliminate her, just to simplify things. Might attract too much attention, though.

"That's all finished for you now," Mark said. "You'll never see Callie again. Forget her and everyone else. Starting right now. Never think about her again."

Brenner's eyes narrowed. "Callie," he blurted out, more fiercely this time.

"Forget her," Mark snarled. "You're mine, now."

Brenner just stared at him. His breath was sharp and panting, his face shiny with sweat. His hands kept clenching into fists. He looked like he wanted to kill Mark.

Mark was pissed. The guy didn't even look happy to be activated. He should be thrilled, to finally be able to use the power inside him. It was a gift that Mark had given him. He should be fucking *grateful*.

Brenner's brow furrowed. He was trying to resist the programming.

Eight more iterations of brain stim research after Mark's time at Midlands, and subjects were still rebellious? Was that the best the researchers could do?

It took ruthlessness to get results. He had no problems being ruthless. He adjusted the wand, pointed it at Brenner's head and activated a suitable punishment.

The effect was instant. Brenner screamed, arching back and writhing in the mud. Mark watched the spectacle for a few minutes with enjoyment.

"Get up," he ordered Brenner. "Come back to the truck with me."

Brenner obeyed, haltingly. He was a sorry sight, all soaked in mud.

At the truck, Mark dug his keys out of his jacket pocket, and flung them at Brenner, who caught them one-handed. "You drive," he directed.

Brenner climbed into the driver's seat without a word.

Mark used his time to access all the road maps of the state stored in his database. Seeking the perfect out-of-the-way place. Brenner's punishment had restored his good mood.

He was jonesing to play with his new toy.

Chapter 16

THE DOOR CLICKED shut. Caro leaned her forehead against it and sobbed.

The only way to get him out the door was to be an icy-hearted bitch. She'd had her fun and now she was done. Goodbye and fuck you, too.

It killed her to play that role. She was starving for more of him. Pushing him away made her so fucking angry, she wanted to scream and break things.

Such a goddamn stupid waste.

Don't be needy. You don't have the luxury. Grow . . . the fuck . . . up.

She forced herself to think about what happened to Tim. He'd been a tough guy by anyone's standards: martial arts, military training, concealed weapons permit. He'd tried so hard to help her.

Mark and his thugs had tortured him to death.

She got into the tiny shower. The trickle of tepid water soon turned ice cold, but she barely noticed. She dressed mechanically. Packed fast, to be ready to blast out of there the second she got back. Ditched anything that would not fit in her roller bag.

Travel light. Leave no trace. Those were the rules of her current life. She'd broken one of them bigtime. Now she had to pay for it in blood.

A city bus got her downtown and to the coffee shop half hour earlier than the appointment. Not too smart, wandering around in the open, but she was too exhausted and pissed off to care. She didn't even bother with the disguise. Just shoved stuff into her coat pocket. Walked around with rain misting her bare face, her real hair. Fuck it all.

Nine o'clock came and went. No Bea. The crowd in the café changed. Someone switched the music from the cheerful Vivaldi to a melancholy adagio for strings. Violins sobbed in agonizing pathos. She hated it.

Minutes ticked on. Nine twelve. Nine-nineteen. Nine twenty-eight.

At nine forty-one, she saw the slight figure huddled in the entrance wearing a drab raincoat. She was shrouded by her big hood, but Caro caught a glimpse of a pale, anxious face and lank black hair. Caro waved and the woman approached warily.

"Were you followed?" Bea demanded.

"Not as far as I could see," Caro replied. "Thanks for coming."

"I was across the street for a while," Bea said. "Wasn't sure if it was a trap."

"It isn't. Want some coffee? Something to eat? The cinnamon rolls look good."

"No. I can't seem to eat much," Bea said. "Not since . . . you know. Luke."

"I know," Caro said. "Me, neither. There's a brick wall in my stomach."

"Yeah, exactly." Bea slid into the chair, perching on the edge. Her nervous gaze darted around the room. "Todd keeps asking me about you," she muttered. "I think he's afraid I'm into drugs or that I embezzled money. I wish it was that simple."

"Tell me," Caro urged. "Tell me about the footage. Please."

Bea pressed her lips together for a second. "I haven't talked about it to anyone."

190

"You mentioned video footage yesterday evening, before Todd interrupted us," Caro said. "Tell me more about that."

Bea rubbed her mouth and took a moment to gather her thoughts. She looked like she was struggling to concentrate. "Luke was doing security in Chicago," she said in a low voice. "His boss had a meeting that got changed to a new hotel at the last minute. I remember Luke bitching about that over breakfast, saying it wasn't safe. He brought a wireless camera to record the meeting, like he always did. He'd given me a fresh password that would give me access to his remote server if anything happened to him."

She let out a bitter laugh. Caro tried to stay calm.

"I remember thinking how silly and paranoid that was," Bea went on. "He changed the password every day, and I was supposed to give the latest one to his brother if anything happened to him. Then he disappeared, and they found his boss's body with a bullet in his head. So I retrieved the video."

"Did you watch it?"

"Yes." Bea pulled a tissue from her pocket and dabbed at her nose, her gaze still darting around. She was clearly reluctant to go on. "I never believed in supernatural bullshit in my life," she said under her breath. "Thought it was total crap. But I saw that guy say a few words and freeze Luke. As if it were a spell. He couldn't move."

Caro pondered that. "Could he have been drugged?"

Bea shook her head. "I know what I saw. This guy shot Luke's boss right in front of his face. Taunted him. Some guys came in, put Luke in a box and carried him off. Luke knew every kind of martial art there is, and he couldn't even move."

"You never gave that last password to his brother?"

"No. I didn't have the nerve. His brother might have given it to the cops." Bea's tone was defensive. "That would be like begging for that guy to catch me and kill me. He has to be watching Luke's family."

"But this video proves that Luke is innocent and Mark is guilty, right? Why the hell not take it to the police? Let them stop him."

Bea shook her head. "I'm telling you. It would be suicide. My apartment was robbed a few days after, and my electronics were taken, so I know he's looking for that video. I just happened to have the flash drive in my purse that day because I was afraid to leave it." She stared around the room again. "I've been hiding ever since. But if you can find me, he can, too. Maybe you led him right to me."

Caro ignored that. No need to feed the woman's paranoia. "Can I copy what's on it?"

"I don't carry it around with me," Bea snapped. "I sent it to the lake."

"The lake? What lake?" Frustration put an edge in Caro's voice.

Bea shook her head. "I can't help you. I'm having a hard enough time as it is."

"We could work together," Caro urged. "He killed my friends. I want justice for them. I need help. So do you. Let's help each other."

Bea rubbed her mouth. "You don't understand. There's something, I don't know, almost supernatural about that guy. Prison can't hold him. We would never be safe."

"Maybe not." Caro hesitated for a long moment. "So let's kill him."

Bea's fidgeting suddenly stilled. She was dead silent for a long moment.

"Seriously?" she whispered. "Do you have a death wish?"

"Nope," Caro said. "Just tired of being afraid. I want him gone. If this is the only way . . ." She shrugged. "Do we really have that much to lose?"

The other woman edged back in her chair. "Are you crazy?"

"Maybe," Caro said. "I don't much care, at this point. Are you in?"

Bea's shadowed eyes were full of fear and reluctant longing. "I think you're fucking nuts, and you're going to get me killed."

"We've both survived this long," Caro said. "Give yourself credit."

"Do you have a plan?" Bea demanded.

"Not yet," she admitted.

"Oh. Well, that's inspiring," Bea snapped. She craned her neck to scan the coffee shop and the street outside again. "Oh fuck. We're being watched."

Carol looked around. A young mother was feeding chunks of poppyseed muffin to a toddler in a stroller. A chubby guy in a goatee was tapping into a laptop. Two lovers were forehead to forehead over their lattes, giggling. An old man read a paper.

"I don't think so," she said. "Tell me more about this lake."

"Not here. We can't stay here." Bea leaped up. "Meet me outside. I'll head east."

Caro cursed under her breath and hurried out after her, catching up with Bea halfway down the block. "What lake, Bea?" she panted. "Just tell me."

Bea spun around. "Do not say that name," she hissed. "I am *Marika*."

"OK, fine. Marika. Just tell me what you mean by lake."

"Shut up." Bea looked over Caro's shoulder. "Those guys are following us."

Caro started to turn, but Bea swatted her arm. "Don't look now, you stupid cow! You were followed! Oh fuck, oh fuck . . ."

Bea took off like a gazelle. Caro glanced back over her shoulder, looking for Ponytail. He was nowhere around, but she saw two guys about twenty yards away. They wore earpieces, and both moved toward her, a stony, purposeful look in their eyes.

She took off running as fast as she could. Bea was already some distance ahead, veering into a busy intersection—

Brakes and tires squealed. There was a horrible *thud*.

Bea's body rose high above an SUV, turning in a somersault, suspended in air for several moments.

Caro skidded to a stop when she heard the windshield shatter. Bea's tumbling body hit the ground a second before another car braked. Not fast enough. The SUV got slammed forward. More broken glass. Shouts, screams. Horns blared.

A crowd began to gather. Caro ran faster, shoving, weaving around stalled cars, until she could see Bea, sprawled on the street, arms wide, staring at nothing. The hair on the side of her head was a dark mass of blood.

Caro fought to get closer, a scream of denial shredding her throat—

An arm caught her around the waist. She flailed, scratching and twisting—

"It's me. Calm down." Noah's voice. Noah's arm, Noah's big, powerful body.

She went limp, utterly confused. "What? You? Why? What are you doing—"

"Not now. Not with those two after us." He set her on her feet. "Run!"

"But what about Bea?"

"She's dead, Caro." He scanned the crowd as they wove through it, dragging her alongside him. As soon as they were clear, he gave her a hard push. "Go!"

His command worked like the crack of a starting gun. Caro dashed in a frenzied sprint on a zig-zag course through streets, alleys, parking lots. He herded her behind one of the bigger buildings under renovation. Scaffolding was still up. It was a mess. Dumpsters heaped with trash, piles of bricks and rebar.

Noah stopped short, and shoved her back into a narrow space between two parked trucks until her back hit rough brick. He cupped her face in his hands and gave her a swift, hard kiss. "Stay here. Right here."

She gasped for breath. "But what are you going to—"

"Shhhh. Not a word. Don't move." He pressed her back against the bricks, and darted back the way they had come.

194

She was locked into place for a confused moment. Then she heard the slap of running feet getting closer. She scrambled behind the trucks and eased her way forward along the wall so she could see what was happening.

She heard a heavy thud, a startled yell. Gasps, grunts. Cursing, punctuated by slapping sounds. A harsh, chopped-off shout. The guy had attacked Noah.

She crouched down and saw a second guy's feet flash by. Still more pounding footsteps were getting closer.

Three to one? Fuck that. She had to help him. *Now.*

Various lengths of rusty rebar were scattered on the ground. Some lay across the path between the trucks and the dumpsters. She grabbed the end of the longest piece of rebar she could see with one hand, and a brick with the other. Just as the running footsteps and panting breaths got louder, she jerked the rebar up—

Yes. The guy tripped. Went flying with a shout and hit the ground hard.

Caro pounced on him, screaming as she swung the brick she held downward.

Her opponent twisted, blocked her blow so that the brick glanced off the side of his head, but he still roared in pain. Caro whipped back to avoid his punch—

A rush of air moving, a blur of rapid motion. She was lifted. Tossed to the side.

Noah kicked the guy's face. The whipping sound, air moving, flashes of color. His moves were too fast for her eyes to register. He yanked the guy's arm, wrenched his knee sideways, slammed a fist down on his chest.

The guy lay still, his face a mask of blood below the nose. Arm and leg bent at impossible angles. Out cold.

Caro stared up. Noah didn't even look rumpled. A glance behind her revealed that the other two attackers lay on the ground, in the same condition.

Noah grabbed her wrist and lifted her up to her feet. "You were supposed to stay put," he said with disapproval.

"I haven't survived these past few months by doing what I was told," she said.

She barely caught his appreciative grin just before he grabbed her hand and pulled her into a stumbling run. "Let's move."

"Yeah," she coughed out.

They spotted a back door that opened onto a loading bay and ran inside. An exit sign pointed them toward a stairwell, which led down into a basement corridor with a low ceiling hidden by insulated pipes.

Caro barely kept pace with his long, purposeful strides, held up by the arm around her waist. It was like being swept along by a powerful storm wind. One which knew exactly where it was going.

They came to the battered doors of a freight elevator. Noah jabbed the button and dragged her into his arms while they waited, hugging her fiercely. His heart thundered against her ear. He threw off so much heat. It was life-giving.

She tried not to see it, but now that they weren't in frantic motion, the loop in her head started to play. Bea, catapulted into the air. Bea crumpled, bleeding and silent. She pressed her face to his chest.

His arms tightened. "You OK?" he asked.

"Fine," she said fiercely against his jacket.

He grunted, unconvinced, but the doors were sliding open. Into the elevator. Up another level. She followed where he led and tried not to stumble. At some point, they were outside again, running through an icy drizzle that gave her goosebumps.

He came to an abrupt halt, and she heard the *thunk* of the car locks opening. He opened the Porsche's door and helped her in. "Seat belt," he directed.

She fumbled with it clumsily as he got into the drivers' side.

He clicked his own seatbelt into place as he he started the motor. She noticed the dark wet splatter on his jacket sleeve as the car surged into the street. "Noah, you're bleeding!"

"Not my blood," he assured her.

She sagged back, relieved. "How the hell did you *do* that?"

His elusive smile showed. "No big deal. There were only three of them."

"Only three . . . ?" Her voice cracked, failed her. Only three, her ass.

After a moment, she tried again. "So, were you some kind of commando once? Is that where you got the scars?"

"You don't get to ask questions right now. I'm taking you home. And you're coming clean with me."

"I don't think so." Caro's voice gained strength. "Slow down. I'm getting out of the car now."

"Not at this speed. I want to know who's messing with you, and why."

She sat there, too exhausted to protest. Astonished, too. She'd been mooning helplessly at this guy nonstop since the moment he'd entered her field of vision, but she'd realized in a sudden, spine-tingling rush, that she'd never really seen him at all.

Not until now.

* * *

"Escaped?" Mark snarled into the phone. "How in the fuck did she do that?"

Carrerra hemmed and hawed. "I sent in my three best operatives. But the guy with her had serious combat skills. He took them by surprise."

"But you didn't go."

"No."

"Three trained, armed professionals, and she got away. Again." Mark's AVP was starting its nasty buzzing drum roll inside him. "Where are you now?"

"The hospital," Carrerra admitted. "Two of my team have broken knees. Ripped ligaments. All three have broken jaws. They're being checked for brain bleed—"

"As if I gave a shit. As if they had any brains. Why aren't you out looking for her right now?"

"I'm about to—"

"To leave the fucking hospital? Good move." Mark bit the words out with lethal softness. "Do it. This minute. Find Caroline Bishop."

"I'm on it."

"Don't fuck up a second time." Mark slid the phone into his pocket.

It took a few minutes of concentrating just to drag his raging AVP under control and remember what he was doing. Product testing.

He'd found the perfect place for it. The abandoned gravel pit off the highway was protected on three sides like an amphitheater. No people for miles around. He'd checked for thermals, listened with his augmented hearing for approaching cars. He was eager to get to Seattle and collect Caroline, but he had to be realistic. When he activated the rest of the slave soldiers, they would outnumber him twelve hundred to one.

He had to develop his control technique very quickly.

Marc wrenched open the nailed crate and lifted out the multi-mode slave soldier control unit. Lydia Bachmann had babbled on about the amazing new special weapons back when she was still hoping that she might survive the encounter.

Hadn't taken long for her to realize that she was so fucking finished.

The equipment wasn't elegant in its design. Just a large, clunky helmet. The freq wad was inserted into a larger amplifying console. Commands synched wirelessly with implants inside the slave soldier's brains and could be sent to multiple subjects at once.

Plus, there were many modes. Verbal commands relied on the slave soldiers' programming and brain stim, but wireless commands from the console went straight to their cerebral implants. There was also an FMC mod, fine motor control, that gave the controller complete command over the slave soldier's nervous system, but that required more equipment and was more complicated to learn. Later for that. There would be time.

He wanted to play with the quick and dirty toys right now.

He looked out the back of the parked truck. Brenner was out in the gravel pit, setting up two extremely realistic dummies that Mark had found in Kitteridge's vault. They even had fake blood pumping through surgical tubes and artfully simulated soft tissue and organs. A young woman dummy, and a child dummy, a girl about the size of a five-year-old. The little girl dummy held a doll, a detail which he found perversely kinky. Those Obsidian pricks thought they were so fucking cute.

Brenner had finished getting them in place. Now he just stood, staring at them. There was a sickly gray green pulsing in his sig around the level of his liver. Dread.

Mark's anger flared. Sloppy design. Brenner should have no emotions aside from an eager desire to serve his controller. Mark had to burn those feelings out of him.

There would be plenty of opportunities for that coming up real soon.

Mark approached him, savoring the moment. He could have used the pain setting on the freq wand from a distance, but it was more fun up close.

A long, hard zap broke the pattern of colors in the slave soldier's sig into a muddle of disoriented agony. Better. Softening him up.

Mark gave Brenner a moment to recover as he looked over the settings on the amplifier. The one he was most intrigued with was the last option. TOT. DES.

Total destruction. At his fingertips. He liked it. Felt right.

Mark pointed at the female dummy. "First target," he said. "Go."

He pointed the console at Brenner, and pushed the TOT. DES. button.

The effect was immediate and violent. Brenner threw back his head and roared like a wounded bear. He leaped at the female dummy, knocked it to the ground, and proceeded to rip its limbs off. Then its head. Realistic high-pressure blood spurted out of the breached fake arteries, drenching him.

After he'd torn off all the limbs, he began to claw and bite the tissue away from the skeleton.

Mark was so enthralled by the spectacle, he let it go on for a while. Lydia had warned that leaving the soldiers on total destruction mode for too long would compromise their function, but Brenner needed a good hard whack to get him into line.

Brenner clawed and gnawed at the bleeding shreds of the dummy like a maddened dog. He would just keep at it indefinitely until Mark told him to stop, or until the target was pulped.

He pushed the stop button. Brenner rolled over onto his back, gasping for breath.

When the slave soldier's sig once again looked more or less human and he'd struggled back up onto his feet, Mark pointed at the child dummy.

"That's your next target," he said. "Go."

He pushed TOT. DES. and Brenner roared again. Then he staggered, and stopped. He stood there, swaying. His arms swung around, fingers clutching and fisting, seeking a target to strike and rend but remaining motionless. Three seconds. Five. Ten.

Mark cursed under his breath. Bullshit implant and stim design. Worthless turd was resisting his programming. If Mark pushed too far, he'd trip the autodestruct and Brenner would be toast. A huge investment of energy down the drain.

He stopped the amplifier, pulled out the freq wand and set it to maximum pain.

He let Brenner scream and writhe for a good ten minutes. He'd almost ceased to care if he damaged the guy. He had to learn his lesson, or else he'd be useless anyway. So why the fuck not? Better to just have at. Get it out of his system.

He let Brenner catch his breath after his punishment, sweating and shaking, and then gave the man a rousing kick to the ribs. He pointed to the child dummy.

"On your feet," he barked. "Again. That's your target. Go."

He pushed the button and Brenner leaped on the little girl dummy with a hoarse roar. He began to tear it to pieces, yelling the entire time, but his hoarse bellows no longer sounded triumphant. They sounded desperate.

Mark observed carefully. After a while, he concluded that as long as he functioned, Brenner could suffer as much as he liked. His inner conflict was irrelevant as long as the programming held. And it seemed to be holding. So it was all good.

He watched with enjoyment as the process ran its course. The bloodsoaked, howling Brenner reduced the child dummy to something unrecognizable as human. Skull crushed, bones shattered, tissue torn apart. Almost liquefied. It was enough.

Mark lifted the console and stopped him. A strange silence descended. Even the bird and animal sounds were gone.

"Go down to the creek," Mark told the slave soldier, pointing to the nearby gulley. "Get cleaned up. There are fresh clothes for you in the back of the truck."

Brenner got to his feet. "Callie." His voice was scratchy and ruined.

"She's not here," Mark said. "If she were, I would tell you to kill her. And you would do it. So shut the fuck up. Go clean up."

Brenner was looking at the ground. Mark realized that the slave soldier was staring at the doll that the researchers had shoved into the girl dummy's hand.

It was a baby doll, drenched with blood. Now missing an arm and an eye.

Brenner lifted his head, and fixed his eyes on Mark. His blue eyes shone weirdly bright, their color only heightened by the slimy fake blood that covered his face.

Brenner's gaze was pure concentrated hatred.

It didn't bother Mark. Hate was good. Hate was fuel.

He should know.

Chapter 17

COLD, BRACING AIR rushed in when the car door opened. They were at Noah's house again. She'd come full circle. She got out, squinting in the white light from the overcast sky. Glimmering gray lakewater and evergreens. It smelled good.

Her legs wobbled for a moment when she tried to stand. Adrenaline aftermath.

Noah offered his hand to walk to the house. She took it, entwining her fingers with his, comforted by the warmth of his touch. The lethal war machine she'd just seen in action had been locked away somewhere deep in his psyche.

The guy was a walking contradiction.

They reached the door and went in, making their way into the big kitchen. Noah switched gears, going into alpha-male domestic mode. She was fine with that.

Strong coffee and a ham and cheese sandwich grounded her a little. She was starting in on her second cup when Noah sat down opposite her, silently waiting.

She struggled inwardly for a few minutes as she sipped her coffee. Her first instinct was to stay silent, which seemed like the only way to protect him and herself. Although she'd never in her life met a person less in need of protecting than Noah Gallagher.

What a weird and excellent rush that was.

The urge to resist his curiosity was still there, but it was mostly habit. The desire to tell him the truth was getting stronger by the second.

"I'm not sure where to begin," she said at last. "But I do want to talk."

"Good."

"OK." She stared down into her coffee as she chose her words. "Last night, you made some guesses about me. You pretty much nailed every one. I do come from near Boston and yes, I'm an artist. I also make theater costumes and masks—that's how I got started at Bounce."

"That fits."

What did he think it fit? His calm expression gave away nothing.

"Anyway, I used to have a much more lucrative job with a company called GodsEye Biometrics. My boss, Dex Boyd, bought a small firm that did everyday biometric security—you know, retinal scans, iris scans, voice recognition, even fingerprints. Old school stuff."

"If you say so."

"Dex developed a brain-based system and hired me to train new clients in its interface. So that's how I started. I loved the work. But all that's gone. GodsEye can't exist without my boss, Dex Boyd. He was murdered eight months ago."

His eyebrows went up. "So then. Security. Biometrics. Don't tell me, let me guess. Somebody wants you to open a vault for them. Right?"

She gave him a startled look. "Ah . . . how did you figure that out?"

"It's not much of a leap," he said. "What's in the vault?"

"Don't know," she said. "Not my business to know. It belonged to this woman named Lydia Bachmann. The CEO of a weapons manufacturing firm. I was her coach."

He frowned in perplexity. "Coach? For what?"

"I didn't explain the system yet," she said. "Dex Boyd developed biometrics for vaults and safes using brain waves patterns generated while visualizing a sequence of images. Clients who weren't good at visualization struggled with it. Dex was always looking for staff to demonstrate the interface and work on it too, make it more user friendly."

"How did he find you? Is he an art school alum?"

"No," she said. "We connected through a mutual friend." She looked at him warily. "I was in a mental institution at the time."

He didn't answer for a several seconds. His voice was gentle when he finally spoke. "Huh. That came out of nowhere."

"Yeah." She looked down at her clasped fingers. "All my life, I've had this thing. I used to call it a problem, but I've trained myself not to. If I imagine something, I actually see it. As if it were real and solid. Right in front of me."

She looked up at him. He said nothing, but his eyes urged her on.

"It was odd, but nobody really noticed it until after my mom died," she continued. "I saw her everywhere. I freaked everyone out. It took me a while to sort out what was real and what wasn't."

"Can't have been easy."

"No. But I—well, anyway, my Aunt Linda took me after Mom died. Nice lady, but not very imaginative or open minded. I got older, and when it kept happening, I scared her a couple times. Ended up in the psych ward more than once. Antipsychotic drugs stopped my visions, along with everything else. They have a lot of side effects."

She tried to read him. His expression was neutral, but she sensed how intently he was listening. That focused amber glow in his eyes made her catch her breath.

She wouldn't react like that if he were judging her. She hoped.

"How did this GodsEye guy find you?" Noah asked.

"A friend that I'd met in the psych ward had heard about Dex," she said. "She thought it could be an opportunity for me. 'Put your crazy to work for you,' she said, or something like that. Made sense to me, so I contacted him. Dex invited me to come in. He'd designed a new test to measure the capacity of the visual center of the brain, and I placed in the top one percent. He offered me a job on the spot. I worked for him ever since. Software development, research, coaching."

Noah nodded thoughtfully. Her slight smile in return faded as a wave of grief clutched at her throat. It took her by surprise. She wasn't used to feeling much of anything besides fear lately.

Noah slid his hand beneath hers on the table, fingers open, as if he hardly dared to squeeze. Just warm, gentle contact. No words.

She didn't dare speak. Starting to cry would mess her up.

"You miss him," he said finally.

She gave him a tight nod. "We trusted each other," she said. "I was lucky to have him in my life. We were very close."

Noah didn't ask the question, but she could feel it hanging in the air.

"Not like that," she clarified. "He was thirty years older than me, and in a wheelchair with degenerative arthritis. Plus, I think he was gay, though it never really came up."

"Ah." She sensed him relax. "More like an uncle, then."

"Exactly," she murmured. "A benevolent uncle."

There was an awkward silence.

"Anyhow, it was a dream job. I made pretty good money, and Dex gave me flexible hours so I could go to art and design school and rent a cool little studio. I did freelance art design too. It was awesome. I loved my life," she finished, a little wistfully.

His fingers curled around hers and gave them a brief, encouraging squeeze. "I can see why."

"OK. So how did I end up here? I know you want to know."

"Yeah, I do."

"Months ago we got a new client, Mark Olund. He requested me as a coach but it turned out he didn't need coaching. He got the interface on the first try. I offered to refund the fee, but he refused. Then he started coming on to me during our sessions."

"Happens."

"Well, I didn't want it to happen. I mean, it was flattering, but I just wasn't feeling it. He was smart, good looking, and he had to be rich to afford a GodsEye vault, but he made me tense. It just didn't seem . . ." She shook her head.

"What?" he demanded.

She shrugged. "Real," she said. "It was all shiny and pretty and . . . nothing."

"Good," he said, with rough emphasis.

"So one morning, I'm reading online about a murder and theft in Chicago. A security expert murdered his client and stole a lot of money and some art pieces. One of them was a brooch worn by French royalty in the seventeenth century. Priceless sapphire the size of a golf ball. There was a picture in the article. Very beautiful."

He nodded. "OK."

"So that evening, I did my last coaching with Mark. He'd requested that we do it in his own apartment rather than our open workspace in the West Village. It was odd, but he made the request through the main office and paid the premium fee for a home coaching. That was an extra that we offered for problem clients like Lydia, which wasn't Olund's case, but I figured he had the right to use the services we advertised. And he'd always been polite to me. Flirtatious, yes, but nothing scary. I thought I was a good judge of character. So I went."

Noah's thumb was stroking her palm. Slow, soothing circular movements. She realized that her hand was shaking.

She tried to make it stop, but the agitation came from deep inside.

She braced herself and went on. "So anyhow. We do the session, and afterwards, he insists on offering me a glass of wine. While he was out of the room choosing a bottle, I wandered around. There was a door open to a room with a table heaped with stuff. All kinds of things. Antiques. Extremely valuable. Made of gold, encrusted with jewels, just piled up and tangled together as if it were junk. But it was genuine. I have an eye for that kind of thing."

"I know."

"That sapphire brooch was there," she said. "I'd just seen the photo. I remembered every detail. That's just what my brain does."

He nodded. "What did you do?"

"I panicked," she said. "I ran away. I'm still alive right now just because he took so long to pick out that bottle of wine."

"Did you go to the police?"

"No," she admitted reluctantly. "Like an idiot, I second guessed myself. Started wondering if maybe the brooch was a reproduction. Or if maybe he'd bought it from the thief in good faith. That maybe he was the normal one and I was crazy. I went back to GodsEye headquarters to talk about it to Dex. He always worked late. But Mark followed me there."

Noah squeezed her hand, but she no longer felt it. She saw the memory as if she was there.

They'd grabbed her right after she walked in. The big leering guy with body odor and huge groping hands held her down on Dex's work table while Mark told her how she was going to go with them to open Lydia Bachmann's safe. About the trail of evidence he'd planted to show she was stealing trade secrets from Dex and selling them to other biometric startups. So that when they found Dex's body, the police would suspect that she was the killer and the DA would charge her with first degree homicide. No priors. But no bail either.

Go straight to the slammer and say hello to your public defender, because Mark had cleaned out her bank account just in case.

But if she was very good, Mark might keep her alive. As his pet.

The images were horribly bright, fragmented. Pinching, groping hands. Foul breath choking her. Rough hands curling her fingers around a gun butt and then the trigger. Planting her fingerprints. They were going to shoot him.

Dex was gagged, and watching from his wheelchair from across the room. His horrified eyes begged her for help.

Then Mark grabbed Dex. Fastened his mouth to the top of Dex's head as if he were sucking it. The look in Dex's eyes gave her a burst of strength.

She jerked a hand free from the man holding her, kicking and scrabbling on Dex's cluttered worktable. Her hand landed on an open boxcutter.

She whipped it up. A lucky jab.

Blood spurting. Arms flailing. He sliced her arm in that moment right before he realized what she'd done to him. Blood all over the desk, all over her. Hot, spattering drops.

The guy trying to hold his blood inside his throat with his hand. Failing.

He collapsed to the ground. She scrambled for the emergency exit door. Everything felt horrifically slow. Mired in tar. Dex's eyes had gone empty and blank.

No sounds, just her heart pounding. So loud.

Mark had been intensely focused on Dex, but his gaze snapped up and fastened onto her as she dashed out the emergency exit. He bellowed with rage as she yanked the heavy door closed—and locked it from the other side, with the GodsEye lock.

That bought her time to run out into the night, sticky with blood—

"Caro? Talk to me."

Noah was bending over her, his hand on her shoulder. His kitchen swam into focus. His worried face.

Caro licked her dry, numb lips. "I'm fine," she whispered.

Noah circled the table and reluctantly sat back down. He waited for a few minutes while she gathered her thoughts.

"Mark was there to kidnap me," she said. "He was going to make me open Lydia Bachmann's vault for him, and then kill me in cold blood. He had it all planned out, including framing me for Dex's murder. He didn't expect me to fight back. I killed the guy who was holding me down. I barely got away alive. But Dex . . . Dex didn't."

She suddenly realized that she held his fingers in a white knuckled death grip. She let go abruptly and whipped her hand back.

Noah's hand stayed outstretched on the table, as if hoping to reestablish the contact. "You knew Lydia Bachmann's combination?"

"If it's still the fucking training sequence, then I do," Caro said bitterly. "It's not likely she ever followed our recommendations to reset a definitive combination. Lydia sucked at the Inner Vision interface. She even tripped the auto-destruct once. Almost killed us both. We had to tweak her software so that she wouldn't blow herself up."

"And where is she now?"

"She's a missing person," Caro said. "Since before Mark Olund showed up at GodsEye. I don't know what happened to her. I'm sure it's nothing good."

Just a nod, and a thoughtful frown between his eyebrows. No other reaction.

"You seem so calm," she said. "I can't seem to shock you."

"I don't shock easily," Noah said. "And I suspend opinions or feelings when I'm taking in data. That lets me calculate strategy more quickly."

She crossed her arms over her chest. "I don't remember asking you to do that for me, Noah."

He looked taken aback. "You think you don't need any help with this? Really?"

"Of course I need help," she said. "Teach me how to fight."

Noah's face went absolutely blank for a moment.

Caro hurried on. "Look, I killed that guy by accident. I won't get that lucky again. And I'd prefer to use a gun, not a blade. I don't want to get that close to Mark Olund. I assume you're as skilled with guns as you are in hand to hand combat, right?"

Noah's eyes were incredulous. "Sure, but . . . you're actually planning to stalk and kill this guy by yourself?"

"If I could find solid proof that he's a killer and I'm not, then I'd go to the cops," she said. "But I'm in no position to do that. So yeah, Noah. That's exactly what I propose."

"That's crazy," he said.

She shrugged. "I get that a lot," she said. "At least I'm consistent.""

"I can't let you—"

"Not your call," she said. "Don't make me regret telling you everything."

He studied her carefully, saying nothing.

"Teach me to use a gun," she repeated. "I'll be so focused. You'll be amazed."

"I already am," he said.

"It's not like I want to ask you this," she said. "Did I mention that I got a friend to help me a few months ago?"

"No."

"His name was Tim. Big, tough guy. Military training. Big believer in open carry."

Noah looked like he was bracing himself. "And how did that turn out?"

"They got him," she said flatly. "Tortured him to death. Cut him to pieces. Gouged out his eyes. I'm not risking that again. So you can either help me do this entirely by myself, in my own way, or—"

"Or what?" Noah asked, drumming his fingers on the table.

"Or nothing. I'm a jinx, if you haven't figured it out. I have to go it alone from here on in. Although I have to thank you for saving my life so far. I really do appreciate that. But it's on me from here. Really. It's best for both of us."

Holding his gaze when he was angry was a challenge. She could feel the force of his frustration and disapproval pushing against her.

Caro clenched her hands into fists and held her ground. *Be tough, Bishop. Fake it til you make it.*

Right. She tried, but she felt very fake right now, with all her tough talk. Who the hell was she trying to kid?

Herself, for sure. She didn't have a choice about any of this. But it was very hard to maintain the necessary fuck-you attitude under these conditions.

"I can't say I agree." Noah rose to his feet and walked out of the kitchen.

It looked like she had her answer. She stared after him with tears in her eyes.

Chapter 18

BLASTING THROUGH. FELT good. Noah rode a huge, energizing surge of AVP energy on the way to his office to get his laptop. But it wasn't making him feel crazed and frantic. Just fiercely focused on the job ahead.

Caro needed help on her own terms or he wasn't allowed to help at all. OK. Seemed easier to agree. She'd been too upset to notice that Noah was already formulating a plan. On *his* own terms.

He grabbed his laptop, stopping when he caught a glimpse of himself in the hall window. His reflection floated on the tinted glass, his weird yellow cat eyes glowing brighter against transparent gray. At the moment, he was too. Even people who knew and trusted him got creeped out by them. Almost no one had ever looked into his eyes unshielded.

He usually didn't allow himself to notice or care, but right now, he was suddenly, intensely aware that being so different annoyed the living shit out of him.

He went into his study and pulled down all the blinds. Which didn't help him find his laptop in the clutter. Fuck fuck fuckity fuck . . . there it was. He picked it up, thinking about how Caro looked at him unshielded. She could gaze deep into his naked eyes even while he was inside her, his AVP blazing hot, staring at her and the whole universe sliced up, cross-sectioned, analyzed in every way. She was fine with it.

Noah loved that.

He tried to figure out what she saw in his eyes. Obviously, something very different from whatever repelled all the others—something that she wanted. Exactly what that might be, who the hell knew. He gave up thinking about it after a couple of seconds. He could go back to the kitchen and look at Caro herself instead. That was way more interesting and compelling.

A feeling was nagging at him. Not a good one. Guilt. Fear of what was going to happen when she realized that he knew Olund and Luke Ryan personally. But he couldn't tell her now and risk her disappearing on him.

And he couldn't neglect to follow any clue that might lead toward Luke.

He got back to the kitchen and opened up his laptop, typing rapidly. She'd clammed up. Just as well.

He could focus better, get started on the kind of data dive he'd do if was just a gifted hacker who had never heard of Luke Ryan. Knowing exactly where Luke's lake house was situated and exactly which shell companies owned it made it easier. He wasn't literally lying to her. Just setting a scene that suggested a different truth. While never directly stating it.

Yeah. He could just keep telling himself that. For all the good it would do him. "What on earth are you doing?" she asked.

"Researching Luke Ryan," he said. "Look at this."

Caro circled the table and leaned over his shoulder to peer into the screen. A heavy lock of her ringlets draped over his shoulder and tickled his neck. He was careful not to move for fear that she would brush it away. He liked the way it smelled.

She studied the impenetrable block of data. "What am I supposed to see here?"

"Look there, and there." He pointed to bits of data as he scrolled. "This piece of property was bought on behalf of Luke Ryan by Wilkes and Meryton, LLC, six years ago. Stoddard Lake. A little more than three hours north of here."

Her sig showed a flare of cautious excitement. "You think that could be the lake that Bea mentioned?"

"Could be," he hedged. "Even if it is, don't get your hopes up. Let's go see."

"Not you. I don't want you involved. You've done too much already."

"Please," he said. "We can drive up together, right now. You wouldn't have to rent a car. There's no risk. We'll talk about your weapons training on the way."

She hesitated, and he stroked her hand. Willing her to give in.

"OK," she conceded finally. "Just a ride, though. No more."

* * *

It rained most of the way, sluicing the windshield with a wavering blur of water that the wipers couldn't keep up with. Instead of discussing weapons training, Caro fell fast asleep as they drove deeper and deeper into the mountains. He wasn't surprised to see her crash after the adrenaline dump from this morning.

The rain finally eased off, though mist clung to the dark green sides of the mountains. The road was a shining ribbon of gray, winding up the tree-covered slopes.

Stoddard Lake was a vacation town right off the highway. The lake itself was long and narrow, surrounded by skeletal white trees. The GPS led them far out on a road that ringed the lake. Cabins and vacation houses dotted it at intervals.

Noah slowed to a halt in front of a thicket of firs. A faint path led through them. A chain that had once been strung from two posts now lay across the road. He gunned the car. They lurched through and over small trees, bending but not breaking them.

The house by the water was luxurious, though not large. Lots of plate glass overlooking the water, a wraparound deck. Luke made good money doing specialized security work, and he'd denied himself nothing. It was plain that no one had been there for a long time. Drifts of pine needles were blown high against the doors and walls.

Noah's AVP surged as he got out of the car, though his heart was steady. He wasn't walking a tightrope of killing rage, either. Just a jangling rattle of overstimulated nerves. Scents registered. Earth and water, trees and moss, animals and fish—all translated into an array of crystalline colors, knife sharp in their clarity.

Caro gazed over the choppy lake under the heavy gray sky as he scanned the place, using every diagnostic ability that he possessed. Caro's was the only heat sig within a hundred and fifty yards of the place, aside from a few small animals. The house was silent and dark. No heat, no electrical activity. The houses nearby seemed equally quiet. Not a ping on his array of supercharged sensors.

Caro herself was cloaked in a halo of blues, indigos and violets. She gazed up at the sky, out at the stormy lake, her hair flying like a banner. Her exposed throat looked so vulnerable. It made something twist in his chest. She was too exposed. Unprotected.

And that was about to change. He slid his arm around her, pulling her against him so fiercely, she stumbled.

"Noah? I—"

He cut her off with a hungry kiss. She felt so good. Her lips were so sweet, tender and yielding. The impulse that roared up was huge. *Go for it. Right now.*

216

But the wind was raw and damp, the pebbles on the shore slick from the recent rainstorm. Caro's eyes were wary as his outsized sexual energy beat against her secret inner senses like waves of heat.

Too much. Pull back. "Come on. I want to see what's inside," he said.

The place had no alarm. Luke didn't want this place on any security grid. But the front lock was gouged and scarred. Someone had forced it.

The door opened without resistance.

"Shit," Noah muttered. "Totally trashed."

Couches and chairs had been slashed and overturned. Through the door into the bedroom, he saw that the mattress had been pulled off, sliced open. Every drawer in the bedroom and kitchen was yanked out and overturned, every cupboard and cabinet emptied onto the floor. The electronics were on the floor, in a haphazard tangle of black cables and wires.

"Someone got here before us," Caro said bleakly.

At the same moment, they saw the pile of envelopes below the mail slot.

"It could have been delivered after this break-in happened," Caro said. "Bea told me she retrieved the video from a remote server after the murder." She crouched down and started sifting through dusty envelopes.

Noah joined her, rapidly tossing aside junk mail, brochures, credit card offers, past due notices, debt collection threats. On the floor beneath all of it was a small white padded mailer. The address was scrawled on it in bold black pen. No return address.

Caro hefted it. "Chicago postmark," she said. "Dated about two weeks after Luke Ryan disappeared."

Noah hid his impatience, waiting as she ripped the padded envelope open and shook a flash drive into her hand.

She looked up at him, her eyes bright with tears. "Do you think . . ."

"Let's go," he said harshly. "Right now. We'll look at it when we're home."

Caro gave him a puzzled look, reminding him that he wasn't supposed to be personally invested in this. He had no stake in this but hers, as far as she knew. But he was intensely affected, and she saw it.

She saw everything far too clearly for an unmod.

But now was not the time to tell Caro about Mark, or Luke, or Midlands, any of the rest of it. She'd just witnessed Bea's violent death. She'd barely started to trust him.

He had to go slow. He turned away. "I have to make a couple calls."

"To who?" she called after him.

"People who need to see this footage," he said, quickly adding, "People who can help you." But it felt like an afterthought, even to himself. *Fuck.*

"Are you sure that's a good idea?" Her voice had an edge. "Wait, Noah!"

He punched in a number he knew by heart, and Zade picked up fast.

"Yo, Romeo," he drawled. "Chilling with your fugitive lady fair? Having fun?"

"I'm at Luke's cabin on the lake," he said. "Bea got killed this morning. And we found a flash drive. Something Bea sent to the lake. Could show Luke's meeting with Mark. We haven't looked at it yet."

Zade was dead silent for a few beats. "Holy fucking shit," he breathed.

"Meet me at my place in three hours. Tell Sisko." He killed the call, and turned to find Caro's shocked eyes blazing at him.

* * *

"Wake up, you piece of shit. Malcolm! I'm talking to you."

The building superintendant woke with a gasp, knocking over the warm beer that sat next to his bare foot. Beer foamed over his toes as he tried to bat away the huge fist which seized his shirt front and heaved him upward.

218

"Huh?" he asked, looking around wildly. "Who?"

Two men looked down at him. A big one held him suspended over his sprung out couch, watched by a smaller, beady-eyed bald one. A porn film played on the TV behind them, a cluster of bodies, lips and holes and hands, pumping and sucking.

"You're the super of this dump, right?" the smaller man asked.

Malcolm struggled to breathe against the pressure of the huge fist at his throat. "I—yes—but—"

"Shut up," the smaller one said. "We're looking for a woman. She lives in this building. Hold on. Where is that photo?" He patted his pockets. "Tell us which unit and we'll leave you to jerk off in peace."

Malcolm realized that his pants had been left open and were now starting to fall. "I have no idea who—"

Whack. The blow rocked his jaw. Hurt like a motherfucker. The big man let him fall back down onto the lumpy couch cushion and wandered off.

"This is her," the smaller guy said. "Take a good look."

Malcolm's eyes watered as he peered at it. The girl in the photo was hot as hell. Big eyes, lush lips, long dark hair. Out of his league and his budget.

He shook his head. "Never seen her."

"She could look different," the guy said. "You know, like wearing a wig, or glasses. Think about all of your tenants. Rule out the ones that couldn't possibly be her. Tell us what's left. We'll do the rest. Of all the young white female tenants in your building, which one of them could be her?"

"I don't know," Malcolm said desperately.

"Check this out." The big guy held out another photo for his colleague to look at.

Malcolm blinked to to focus on it. His six-year-old niece and eight-year-old nephew at a birthday party. He'd taped the picture on the fridge.

"Love to Unky Malcolm from Emil and Isla," the guy read from the back of the picture. "How sweet. So, Unky Malcolm. If you give us the unit number, we'll walk out the door, and we won't hunt down Emil and Isla and do things to them that oughta make their bodies impossible for their mother to identify."

"There's a young white woman in six-oh-eight," Malcom blurted. He kept on babbling. "It could be her, but maybe not. She came about four months ago. Thought she gave me a fake ID, but I didn't argue, not with four months rent in advance and—"

"Thanks, Malcolm. We don't need the details. Of course, you never saw us." The bald man smiled, showing off silver eye-teeth. He tucked the photo of Malcolm's niece and nephew into his coat pocket. "I'll keep this. Do we have an understanding?"

Malcolm nodded frantically.

"This woman will be gone soon," the man went on. "Clean out the room. Rent it again. She never existed. Any records you had of her have to disappear. Understand?"

"What did she do?" he blurted out.

"She's bad to the bone," the bald guy said. "Your building will be safer without her. Good man. You did the right thing." The man's glinting teeth flashed again. "Thanks for your help, Malcolm."

Malcolm sat there after the door closed behind them, his feet resting in a puddle of beer. After a while, he realized that the couch beneath him was soggy with warm piss, and he was still nodding.

He just couldn't seem to stop.

Chapter 19

MARK LOOKED AROUND the restaurant table at the faces of the five prototype slave soldiers he'd awakened. He was struggling with rage. His AVP bubbled hot and crazy.

It had been easy to pick them up. They had been situated relatively near to each other. After taking Brenner in Cheyenne, he'd picked up Rich Hobbs from a gym in Rock Springs, and then driven to collect Ty Matthews at a stereo store at a strip mall in Logan, Utah. Then came Raquel Mendoza who cashiered at a pharmacy in Baylor Flats, Utah, and Mike Breyer, who worked on a road crew outside Salt Lake City.

Gathering them was no big deal, but now that he had them, they were bugging the shit out of him. They were perfectly capable of speaking, but none of them would speak a word to him unless directly commanded to do so.

They defied him constantly in the only way they could. With passive silence. Although the place was otherwise empty, so no one but him was noticing.

Brenner's huge hands kept flexing and clenching as he stared at Mark. His fingernails were still stained with the dummy's fake blood. The man's unrelenting rage had been unsettling at first, but Mark had quickly gotten used to it. Sort of like riding a half-broke horse.

But now the phenomenon was multiplied by five. They glared at him en masse. He recognized the look of trapped, seething rage. He'd felt it on his own face.

Too fucking bad. Everybody had their time to squirm. He'd done his time and now they could do theirs. In his service.

They'd pay for their attitude. At his earliest convenience, at the highest pain setting and for the longest time he could risk without causing neurological damage.

But in the meantime, they needed fuel. Which dovetailed with his last pickup.

This was the last of the prototypes. A female, R-Gen 57-1221, also known as Sierra Horst, aged twenty-four. She was a waitress at a strip mall steak house outside Salt Lake City. She'd just served them all big glasses of ice water.

She gave them a big smile as she brought the man across the room his bread basket and soup. Like the others, she was a stunning specimen. Tall and stacked, with blue eyes and a bouncing blond ponytail, she did the waitress uniform more justice than it deserved. Maybe her shoulders were a little too heavily muscled and her calves too stringy and defined for his tastes, but even so. She'd had a much more advanced iteration of Braxton's muscle-and-bone cocktail vectored into her genes than Mark, and would have been brainwashed into compulsive exercising just like her other fellow slave soldiers, so it was hardly her fault. They'd been sculpted by psychopaths.

Mark's eyes slid over Raquel's smooth golden skin and perky tits, and then eyed Sierra's eye-catching ass. He was rethinking his plan to skip stopping for rest as they drove toward Seattle. An hour in a roadside motel exploring the possibilities of using a control freq wand as a sex toy would be better than sleep.

She approached them with a bouncy step and gave them another brilliant smile as she poured their coffee. "Have you folks decided what you're having?"

Mark looked around the table. The five slave soldiers glared at him fixedly. For fuck's sake. "Bring us all steak, baked potato and string beans," Mark said.

Sierra scribbled on her pad. "Right away!" she chirped.

Mark assessed the restaurant as they waited. It was late for the lunch rush, early for dinner, and their section was empty. He decided to activate Sierra now. Risky, but he was trading one risk for another.

When she came back with the tray of plates, he waited until she had set them all set on the table before pulling out the freq wand and giving her a long, hard zap.

She stumbled forward with a grunt, hitting the table. A water glass fell over, scattering ice cubes and water across the table and onto the lap of R-Gen 57-629, also known as Ty Matthews. Ty did not react to the ice water. He just kept staring.

Mark put his hand on her shoulder, speaking low and clear, keeping the freq want pointed at her. "You real job just started, Sierra," he said. "I own you now, and you'll do everything I say. Do you understand?"

Sierra swayed drunkenly as the spilled water soaked into the front of her apron. Her sig showed the same violent color upheavals as all the others had done. Her lips were forming words, but she couldn't force them out. Or wouldn't.

He dialed up the pain setting, careful not to overdo it. He didn't want her to make a scene or fall to the ground. Just a sharp jab. To show her how things were going to be from now on.

The sudden shocking pain made her bite her lip. Blood welled up on the full, sexy curve of her plump lower lip. It made his cock stiffen and throb. He smiled at her.

"Come closer, Sierra," he ordered. "Lean down . . . and kiss me."

She took her time, so he took his. He just let the freq wand buzz. The combo of intense, racking pain and her obedience programming finally won out.

She slowly bent over him. Her formerly rosy face had gone sickly pale, shiny with a sheen of sweat. The blood on her lip was a striking contrast to her pallor.

And she still hesitated, inches from his lips. Fighting it. Dumb, stubborn cow.

He seized her chin, his fingernails digging brutally hard into her smooth skin as her lips touched his. His cock thickened at the contact, a hot pulse of lust, sharpened by the revulsion showing in her sig. He licked the salty drop of blood off her lower lip. Thrust his tongue into her mouth. Intensive retraining was in order for this one.

He could hardly wait to administer it.

Fresh blood had welled into the bite wound on her lip. He spread it with his fingertip like lip gloss, covering the bluish pallor of her lip. He took his hand from her chin. His nails had dug half moons into her skin. They too had filled with blood.

"Nice to see a bitch who knows her place," he whispered. He pinched her nipple through the white polo shirt with his bloodstained fingers. His fingers left a rusty smear.

Her face contracted, mouth trembling. But she couldn't say a word.

"Listen carefully, Sierra," he said. "We're going to eat our meal. You will continue as if nothing had happened. Bring us refills on coffee. Bring us our check. After we leave the restaurant, follow us to the parking lot in back of the fabric warehouse at the end of the mall. I want you out there in ten minutes. No longer."

Her eyelids fluttered. She made a short, choked sound.

"Go," he snarled. "Go do as I told you."

She lurched across the room, knocking over a chair in the process.

The distilled loathing in the eyes of the other slave soldiers had intensified, if that was even possible. The puddle of ice water kept dripping steadily onto Ty's lap. He didn't seem to notice.

"Eat your fucking food," he snarled.

They picked up their forks. He wondered if he'd have to tell them when to piss.

Sierra came back to refill their coffee. She was sweaty, hands trembling, but still functioning. She offered no more chitchat.

Mark paid the check that Sierra had left. The other slave soldiers clumped along behind him, not even pretending to behave normally. Still defying him.

They walked in absolute silence to the remote, empty parking lot at the end of the strip mall where he'd left the truck. When they arrived, he got out the freq wand and turned the pain setting to the highest level.

"This is what happens when you show me attitude," he said.

He punished them all, one after the other. Their shrieking and writhing felt good. He prolonged the session for the last one, Raquel. He particularly enjoyed the way all that violent arching and twisting made her tits bounce.

"Mommy? What's that guy doing to that lady?"

Mark spun around, startled. He'd been so involved in Raquel's punishment, he hadn't even heard them approach. A young, pimply woman with messy pink hair and an old army coat was gaping at them. She held the hand of a little boy in a gray down jacket. Her hand was covered with tattoos. The kid was maybe four years old.

More footsteps, but a glance behind him showed that it was only Sierra, following his orders. She hadn't changed her clothes or put on her winter coat. She was still in her waitress uniform, displaying an attractive nipple hard-on in the frigid wind.

Which meant he would have to dress her himself. Fucking great. Details. Multiply them by twelve hundred, and his head was going to explode.

"Mommy? Is that a mean guy?" the kid quavered.

The pink-haired girl edged away. "Let's just go, baby." Her voice was high and thin.

The girl took off running, dragging the kid behind her. In a moment, she picked him up and continued onward through the empty parking lot in a heavy, awkward lope.

Mark turned to Sierra. He couldn't have devised a more perfect maiden voyage for her if he'd planned it to the last detail. "Kill them," he ordered.

Sierra's eyes were bleak as she looked at the pink-haired girl with the kid on her hip, who lurched onward, casting panicked looks back over her shoulder. She was calling for help, screeching like a bird, but there was no one in earshot to hear her.

Mark pointed the freq wand at her. "I said to kill them, you dumb bitch."

Sierra gasped at the pain. She let out a sharp, desperate sound and took off.

The pink-haired girl had gotten a good lead by now, but Sierra ran faster than any professional sprinter. She soon overtook the girl's clumsy trot.

But just before she made contact, she veered off to the left. She ran incredibly fast, her feet in the white waitressing kicks a blur of movement. Right past the pink-haired girl . . . and onward . . . and then she curved back around the way she came.

She couldn't run away. She was resisting her programming to the absolute limit, but it was dragging her back to him in a big parabolic loop.

But she'd let the pink-haired girl and her kid go free. They were now scrambling into a battered pickup which peeled away, tires shrieking. Off to tell her crazy story to whatever meth-head pal of hers would listen, the trashy slut. His secrets were safe. But still.

He'd been disobeyed.

Sierra was almost back, but her pace was faltering. She staggered, stumbled.

About thirty feet away, she fell to her knees. She tried to get up. Fell again.

She began to crawl toward him.

Mark walked out to meet her. She was bleeding from her nose and ears. The auto-destruct was punishing her. Cheating him of the pleasure. She gasped for each gurgling breath. Blood flecked her lips. Her lungs were probably full of blood by now.

He turned to Raquel. "Bring one of those big sheets of plastic from the truck," he ordered her. "And duct tape. She's leaking. I don't want a mess out here."

Raquel did as he asked, and stood there, looking down at Sierra. Tears streamed down Raquel's face.

The tears irritated him. Raquel had no business feeling emotions. She was just a tool, a doll, a fucktoy. "Wrap her up in plastic," he snarled.

Raquel knelt, spread out the plastic and did as he'd directed, but the manner in which she did it annoyed him. So careful. Wrapping Sierra like she was swaddling a goddamn baby. Just another subordinate cunt getting in his face. Enough of this shit.

He shoved her roughly to the side and finished wrapping Sierra himself, jerking the flap down over her face. Duct taping her until she looked like some sort of strange, oversized larva. The less bodily fluids that stained the asphalt, the better.

When she was fully contained and sealed into the plastic, he started kicking her.

Sierra was tough. It took a long time, which suited him fine. He kept at it, viciously, until every last sign of her sig was snuffed out. Then for some time beyond that, just for good measure.

When he stopped, the plastic-wrapped form looked like a bag of blood.

The other slave soldiers had ranged themselves around him. Fists clenched. Eerily silent. Raquel's face was still wet. She sniffled loudly with each breath.

He slapped her so hard, she hit the ground rolling.

"Load that garbage into the truck," he told them. "We have to find a place to dump it. Defective piece of *shit*." He wrenched open the back of the truck. There was just enough space among the crates of weapons for the five of them to huddle. "Get in!"

They all hesitated. He lifted the wand, and gave Brenner a long, rattling buzz of agony. That shocked them all into obedience.

They hoisted in Sierra's limp body and clambered over it, huddling down into the truckbed among the towering stacks of boxes.

Five pairs of burning eyes stared back at him over the plastic-swathed corpse.

Mark slammed the door on them, closing them into pitch darkness.

Chapter 20

THE DRIVE BACK was excruciating. Noah had no one to blame but himself.

What the fuck was he thinking, calling Zade right in front of her? As if she were one of his group. As if she knew their secret history.

Noah was used to having people angry at him. He was a leader and it came with the territory. But with Caro, it made him feel like shit. And now she was going to watch them all watch the footage. Which was a brand new clusterfuck in the making.

He concentrated on the road, trying to ignore the furious silence and the angry colors that filled the dark car. She was pissed off, confused, scared. With good reason.

She spoke up as they got off the highway and sped through a strip mall business district. "You can let me out right now," she said. "Anywhere around here is fine."

He did an instant dive to counteract the surge of the combat program that flickered furiously to life on his inner screen. "We're almost home," he said.

"Noah." Caro's voice vibrated with fury. "I don't know those men you called. Whatever's on that flash drive is my business, not theirs. You're being an asshole."

He focused hard on the blue glow of the ice cave in his inner vision, keeping his breathing deep and slow, while trying to think of a way to explain himself that wouldn't freak her out still more. There wasn't one.

"You said you trusted me," he said, finally.

"I did, before you started pushing me around."

"Those men are brothers to me," he said. "I trust them with my life."

"Your life," she said. "Not mine."

"Too late, anyway," he said. "They're waiting for us there. It's a done deal."

Her angry colors surged and pulsed. "So this is Noah Gallagher, being on top," she said. "Calling all the shots. Making all the hard decisions."

The car sped up on the wet road. "I will take care of you, Caro."

"I didn't ask you to. And even if I had, you're jerking me around. It's not the same thing."

There was no short answer to that, so he pretended not to hear as he braked in front of his gate and buzzed it open. "Time to meet my people," he said he drove the car through. "Brace yourself."

Two cars were parked at haphazard angles in front of his house. Noah cursed under his breath, and parked in the driveway. "Can't believe I taught those lazy bastards to drive," he grumbled.

He wanted to take her hand when she got out of the car, but she kept a haughty distance, staying a few steps ahead of him as they entered the house.

Sisko was the first person they saw, his long body sprawled all over one of his couches. "Caro, this is Sisko," he said.

"I remember you," Caro said to Sisko. "I saw you at Angel Enterprises."

"Yeah, I was there." Sisko stood up to greet her. His face was calm and his body appeared outwardly relaxed, but Noah was bare-eyed and could see the jagged spikes of emotion in Sisko's sig. A complicated blend of excitement and dread.

"Where's Zade?" Noah asked.

"Coffeeing up," came a deep voice from behind them.

Caro turned, and gasped when she saw him.

"He's one of mine," Noah said swiftly. "It's OK. This is Zade."

"But . . . but I saw . . ." she faltered. "He was—"

"Sorry if I scared you," Zade said. "Believe me, I'm harmless. To you, at least."

"Why were you following me?" she demanded. "You were tailing me even before I even got the call from Noah's sister! What the hell is going on?"

Zade's eyes flicked to Noah in silent question. Noah shook his head slightly.

"I'll explain," Zade said. "Let's see that footage, first."

"Hell, no." Caro looked wildly from one man to the other. "Not until I understand what's going on."

"Later," Noah said.

"I need an explanation right now. Why the *fuck* was that guy following me?"

"We'll get to that." Noah kept his voice carefully even. "Calm down, Caro."

"Noah, do you have to be such a colossal dickhead all the time? Seriously, don't let him get away with it." An amused feminine voice sounded from behind them.

Noah looked around, dismayed to see Hannah in jeans and a sweatshirt, her curly red hair twisted in a thick braid. She held a big white pastry box.

"Shit," he muttered. "Who told you about this?"

"Sisko was at my place when he got Zade's call." She set the pastry box down. "Have a cruller," she said to Noah. "Emergency fuel. And there's a sandwich platter on the coffee table if you want protein."

Noah ran his eyes over the pile of sandwiches and the pastry box. He'd been running AVP off and on the whole day, and the combat program beast was screaming to be fueled. But he just couldn't do it. Not while contemplating what could be on that flash drive. "Thanks," he muttered. "Maybe later. You weren't invited, Hannah."

"I so totally do not give a fuck," Hannah said. "You need to start including me. Especially if it's something I'm interested in. Or working on. Or would just like to know about, goddamnit."

"Excuse me. Why would my personal business be of any interest to you?" Caro demanded.

Hannah smiled at her. "What I mean is, no way would I miss a chance to check out my brother's new girlfriend," she said, gesturing toward the pastry box. "Care for a sugar hit?"

Caro shook her head. "No thanks."

"Take off your coat, at least." Hannah lifted Caro's coat off and draped it over the back of a chair before sliding her arm through Caro's and towing her gently across the room. "Come sit by me," she urged. "All this testosterone creates static interference. Makes it hard to think."

Sisko wandered over, grabbed a cinnamon pecan roll out of the box and ate it in a few purposeful bites, watching Hannah guide Caro to a couch and sit down next to her. His sister's cheerful friendliness got a wan smile or two from Caro, but the smiles faded quickly.

While Caro was occupied with talking, Zade sidled over towards Noah.

"Dude," he hissed under his breath. "What the fuck is she doing here? We can't watch this thing with her. It'll scare the living shit out of her. At best."

Noah shrugged. "We have to," he said simply. "She was the one who found it."

"What are you planning to tell her about us?" Sisko said.

"Don't know yet," Noah said. "Hadn't really thought about it."

Sisko and Zade exchanged a startled glance.

Zade gulped the last of his coffee and wiped his mouth. "So play the goddamned thing already," he said roughly. "I can't stand waiting any more."

Noah plugged the flash drive into a laptop connected to the flatscreen TV. A download box appeared on the blue screen. Noah selected it, and hesitated, looking at Caro.

Hannah had pressed a coffee cup into her hands, but when Caro met his eyes, she set the cup down on the lamp table and clasped her hands.

"Don't look at me for permission," she said. "You'll do whatever the fuck you want anyway."

He picked up a remote and hit Play.

* * *

Caro regretted the sweet, strong coffee that she'd sipped at Hannah's insistence. It was making her stomach churn.

This scene felt wrong. Everyone in the room exuded a buzz of controlled excitement that made no sense. There was no reason for them to be here, or to care about this. If they were here only as a favor to Noah, their vibe would be more flat.

The video had begun. She'd worry about Noah's people, as he called them, and their hidden agenda afterwards.

The video began. The concealed camera that took it had a fisheye lens which distorted the features of the man who peered into it. But it was clear that he was handsome. Buzzed dark hair, a strong nose and jaw, and keen eyes that looked intently into the lens as he adjusted the angle. She recognized him from the pictures that Tim had dug up of Luke Ryan. Behind him, another man, fortyish, talked loudly on a cell phone. He was heavyset and bearded.

A knock sounded. Luke's hand reached back to touch a gun in a holster inside his coat. The bearded guy yelled, "Who is it?"

A muffled voice answered. Caro couldn't make out the words.

"I'll get the door," Luke said. "Stay back."

He opened the door to someone wearing a sweatshirt with a hood that shadowed his face. "Calliope banner ibex," the man at the door said.

Some sort of code? Except that Luke didn't react to it. The man at the door pushed back his hood.

It was Mark Olund

Grinning, he chucked Luke under the chin, then shoved him as if to test if he'd hold still. Luke Ryan remained motionless.

The bearded guy ended his call, belatedly alarmed. "What's going on? Who the hell are you?"

Mark grabbed Luke, heaved him into the room and shut the door. At this angle, Caro could see Ryan's tense face. He was struggling to breathe.

"Hey, Lukie," Mark said. "Remember me?"

Caro didn't understand what she saw but it was awful and sure to get worse.

The bearded guy's voice was edged with panic. "What the hell's wrong with you, Luke? Are you having a goddamn seizure? Who's this guy? Do you know him?"

Luke's eyes blazed with helpless fury. He seemed frozen. He dragged in tight breaths, fighting for air, but he was still on his feet.

Mark pushed him against a wall. He stayed there.

Then Mark lifted a gun from Luke's holster with a latex gloved hand, and deftly screwed on a silencer.

The bearded guy's eyes went wide with terror. He lunged for the door—

234

Two muffled gunshots to the head. The bearded man thudded to the ground.

Mark put down the gun, seized Luke's chin in a cruel pincer grip and kissed him aggressively. "Alone at last," he said. "Great to see you again. The brave warrior who saved us all! What a man. You always had the biggest balls. Mind if I squeeze?" Mark reached down, grabbed the other man's crotch and just about wrenched them off.

Luke's face contracted with agony, but he didn't make a sound.

Mark slapped him brutally hard. Caro half expected Luke to spit out teeth or crumple to the floor, but his tormenter steadied him before he could topple.

"Poor bastard," Mark crooned. "What a fucking mess. They invested so much money in you kill code boys before they scrapped the program. Everyone with clearance knows your fucking codes, plus anyone those people feel like telling . . . and anyone who's good at data theft, like me. I have your brother's codes too. I think you two are the last of the tribe." He patted Luke's face. "I'm almost sorry for you. But not really."

Luke was motionless, his gaze fixed on Mark.

"Want to know a secret?" Mark chortled. "Obsidian improved the product. No verbal codes this time, though. No more of that calliope-banner-ibex crap. Too sloppy. Full of bugs. Not anymore. Now it's coded ultrasound. One pulse to activate. And now there are hundreds of them. Trained like us, only better. Stronger, faster, more mods, more implants, more power genes."

Luke's chest hitched as Mark leaned closer. "Aww. Don't be jealous. I'm going to take their army . . . and I'm going to fuck them with it. I'm going to fuck them really hard. And you, my old friend, are going to help me do it."

Luke made a strangled sound.

"Yeah, I know, it's crazy," Mark agreed. "But you're the decryption man. You and Zade and Sisko decrypted all the Midlands info before rebellion day. I know exactly how good you are. I have the files on the slave soldiers in a biometric safe, which I can't get into. But you can." Mark's manic grin showed all his teeth as he leaned in and licked Luke's neck. "I could have had so much fun with you. Too bad I'm not into boys."

Luke gurgled painfully, dragging in a little air.

"Shut up. Don't even try to move. You can't until I give you the release code. I have six prototype slave soldiers all in the Wyoming-Utah area, and as soon as I get access to the frequency wands, I can pick them up and start practicing."

Luke looked pale. Gray in the face, blue in the lips. Fighting Mark's mind control was quickly draining his strength.

"By the way, as far as the police are concerned, you shot that rich asshole, took his eighty million and his fucking fancy jewelry collection and left the country. I could tell them where to find you. Want to know?" He leaned closer, to Luke's ear. "You'll be six levels underground, at my secret place. Being my bitch."

Luke jerked, helplessly.

Mark Olund pulled a small device out of the pocket of his sweatshirt. It looked like a wide, heavyweight elastic band that he put around Luke's head, clamping a series of sleekly designed electronic devices against it. Mark adjusted the band carefully and peered down into his phone, syncing the device. He gazed at his own phone for a few moments, tapping and scrolling.

Apparently satisfied, Olund went to the door and opened it. Four huge men came in, carrying a case that looked like it was made for a big piece of sound equipment.

They upended Luke Ryan's stiff, unyielding body into it like a corpse into a coffin, locked it and carried it out of the room.

Mark followed them. The door clicked shut. Minutes passed, in utter silence.

The video stopped. No one moved.

Caro had no reason to be surprised by any of this. She knew only too well how violent and disturbed Mark was. But she still couldn't move or speak. It was so horrible.

Then she saw Hannah, sobbing into her hands. Sisko paced behind the couch. Zade sat, white-faced, fists clenched so hard his knuckles were white.

Noah just looked at the blue screen, his face a blank mask.

Her neck prickled, as Mark's words in the video floated through her mind. *You and Zade and Sisko decrypted all the Midlands info before rebellion day.*

Oh, God. Zade and Sisko? "What the hell is going on?" she demanded.

No one answered. The tension in the room intensified as she stood up.

"You guys are not being straight with me. Especially you." She pointed at Noah. "I don't know what the fuck happened in that video, or what connection Mark has to that poor guy, or why you even care. But none of it matters to me."

Hannah's wet eyes widened with outrage. "How can you say that?"

"Framing people for murder is what Mark does," Caro said. "That's all that's relevant to me. This video will prove my innocence, or at least help me prove it. I have to take this to the police right away."

Noah stood up, and removed the flash drive from the laptop. The TV went dark.

"No," he said.

Caro braced herself. "Care to explain?" She knew he wouldn't.

"I'm taking him down," Zade said. "Nobody can stop me."

"Zade." Noah's voice was flat. "Think. If what he says is true, and we have no reason not to believe him, then he has your codes. You can't get near him. He'd take you just like he took Luke."

"But Luke's in the dungeon," Zade insisted. "Mark's hurting him *now.*"

Caro looked around at Zade. "So that's why I saw you before Hannah called for me," she said to Zade. "You guys know Luke Ryan personally. Mark Olund, too?"

Noah broke the silence. "Yes," he admitted. "We have history with Mark."

"So you've been stalking me?"

"Not exactly," Noah said. "We've been stalking Mark. We only stalked you by reflex. You popped up on our radar when you made contact with Bea."

Caro tried to wrap her mind around that, and drew a blank. As blank as Bea's empty blue eyes. No mental flexibility was possible today. She felt fragile, brittle.

"Guess we all want to bring down Mark Olund," she said. "Right? So why not go to the police? Why not help your friend?" She gazed around their shuttered faces, feeling the weight of their tense silence. Her heart sank.

Caro straightened her shoulders, and held out her hand for the flash drive. "Give me that," she said. "It's mine. I found it. I paid for it. And the price was very high."

"I'm sorry," Noah said. "I can't let you take that file to the police."

Caro drew her hand back. Her stomach roiled. So. There it was.

She'd had an awful, sinking sense that something like this might happen. Ever since Noah insisted on calling his own crew to view the footage they had found.

She'd been betrayed, fucked over, deceived and used. Again.

This time, it was incredibly personal. Noah had made an absolute fool of her. She'd opened herself to him completely. He'd made her fall into something like love with him and then betrayed her trust. She was almost too shocked to be angry. But not quite.

"You lying, treacherous prick," she said.

Noah let out a controlled sigh. "Caro—"

"You had your own agenda from the beginning. The whole time you were just manipulating me. Jerking me around. All those things you said."

"They were all true," Noah broke in.

"Oh, shut up. How could you play me like that?" To her dismay, she was dissolving. This asshole didn't deserve her tears. She barely remembered the other people in the room. She was alone with Noah. The others were wallpaper.

"I meant everything I said to you," Noah said. "And the two of us are on the same side. But my people and I have secrets that have to be kept at all costs."

"Secrets?" She laughed wildly. "Oh, great! All costs, huh? I'm the cost, Noah. Who the *hell* are you guys? What is your deal?"

The others exchanged uneasy glances and looked to Noah for their cue.

"It's complicated," Noah said.

"I just bet that it is." She glared at him through a haze of furious tears. "Let's keep it simple. Just give me the flash drive."

"If I do that, everyone I care about will die," he said. "Or worse."

Something in his voice undercut her anger. An intuition of some shadowy threat that loomed over all of them. Noah was not lying.

And that helped her not one bit. She had her own monsters. She had no compassion to spare for anyone else. Maybe if he had not sucked her in so completely, she might have been more open-minded, but as it was, no.

"Guess what, Noah?" she said. "That is not my problem. *You* are my problem. You stalked me, seduced me, lied to me and fucked me left, right and sideways. I will not smile and make nice. Give me that flash drive, you son of a bitch." She dove for his hand.

"Flush this." Noah tossed it into the air toward Zade, who caught it one handed. Then Noah seized her in his arms.

Panic exploded in her chest. "No!" She fought like a wildcat to free herself. Nothing doing. He was insanely strong.

"You sure about this?" Zade said to Noah.

"Get it over with." Noah's voice was implacable.

"Don't!" Caro yelled. "Don't do it! Please!"

Zade flashed Caro a pained look, and did as Noah commanded. They saw the bathroom light switch on. Heard the swoosh and gurgle as the flash drive was swept out of reach.

Zade came back, avoiding Caro's eyes. "Done." His voice was subdued.

The strength that outrage had given her drained away. If not for Noah's hold on her, she would have crumpled. All that effort. Months of plotting, searching.

"I'll fix this for you," Noah said forcefully. "I'll find another solution. I'll protect you from Mark for as long as you need protection. I promise, Caro. Just please, be patient."

She started to laugh, but it degenerated into tears. She choked them back.

Noah deposited her in a big easy chair and stood looming over her as if afraid to turn his back on her. "Relax," he said.

"How?" she asked, with a bitter laugh. "Maybe you should just fuck my brains out. It worked so well for you the last time. Too bad it's just a temporary solution."

Zade and Sisko edged warily toward the door. "Hannah," Zade said in a warning tone. "Let's get the hell out of here. These two have things to discuss."

"No. We don't." Caro's voice rang like out a bell. "I'm not likely to live long enough to be a problem for Noah."

"Caro, shut up and listen to me!" Noah's voice was harsh with frustration.

240

Sisko snagged a big black wool overcoat from the closet near the door. "You won't go all AVP apeshit on her, are you?" he asked.

"Get lost," Noah said curtly. "All of you. Fast."

They filed out fast, eager to be gone, but Hannah stopped at the door and turned to look at Caro.

"I am so sorry," she said. "I never wanted to hurt you. It's not who we are."

"Really," Caro said icily. "I'm touched."

"Don't hate us," Hannah persisted. "Please."

"I don't hate *you*," Caro said. "Good enough? Now get out of here, unless you want to watch me rip off your brother's arms."

Hannah's eyebrows shot up. "Good luck with that," she murmured.

She scurried out. The door slammed. The two of them looked at each other.

"Caro," he said. "I swear I won't let anyone hurt you. Is that understood?"

Caro crossed her arms over her chest. Her neck felt sore, looking up at him. "You mean, except for yourself?"

"I couldn't tell you secrets that weren't my own to share," Noah said.

"You lied through your teeth to me!"

He waited for a moment. "Last night you asked me what happened to us after my mother disappeared," he said finally. "Do you still want to hear that story?"

"Sure. Why not. Like I have a choice."

Noah made a frustrated sound. "Are you going to bust my balls indefinitely?"

"That is the least of what I am going to do to you, Noah Gallagher."

He shook his head wearily. "OK, here it is," he began. "For what it's worth. I told you about our mother disappearing. After that, Child Protective Services sent us to foster homes. Asa and Hannah and I ran away. We shoplifted to get by, when we weren't eating out of supermarket dumpsters. Hung out on the streets when we weren't stealing. Slept wherever we could. Then one day, I get approached by this guy, out of nowhere. He told me about this amazing experimental program for young people. An awesome opportunity for us all."

Oh, shit. Dread tightened her belly, but she kept her face sternly blank, and nodded for him to continue.

"He didn't talk like a pimp, for what it was worth," Noah said. "And we prided ourselves on knowing how to dodge them and the chickenhawks looking for underage kids. There was something different about him. Even so I figured there had to be a catch. But Hannah was sick. I needed medicine for her. If we'd gone to a clinic, we would've ended up in juvenile detention. I couldn't risk that."

"Got it," she said. "And?"

"I figured, I'd go along, check it out. Walk out whenever I wanted to. Lying and cheating and stealing, picking locks, deactivating alarms—I was an ace at all that."

Caro couldn't afford to sympathize with Noah's desperate younger self. He'd tried to parent his brother and sister as best he could, yes. But she had to stay in the center of her own goddamn story. "Go on."

"So I said yes. Asa thought the whole thing stank. He wanted nothing to do with it. So he disappeared, and Hannah and I went to Midlands." He paused for a moment, his eyes bleak. "I'll have to live with that decision for the rest of my life."

"How old were you?" she asked, in spite of herself.

"Seventeen," he said.

Shit. Already, she was falling into his trap of feeling sorry for him. He was playing her again. "Finish your story," she said. "Be quick. I'm not enjoying this."

"It seemed OK, the first couple of weeks," he went on. "The food was great. Hannah started getting better right away. As soon as her lips stopped looking so gray, I began to plan how we'd get out. Which was when I realized that the place was a prison."

She was leaning forward, she realized. Hanging on his every word. Damn him.

"There was no way out," he said. "I was in over my head. Things proceeded. They got our group organized, told us we'd be a beacon of hope for humanity. They didn't tell us how much it would hurt. How many of us would die in the process."

The haunted shadow in his eyes could not be faked. It chilled her.

"What did they . . . how . . ." Caro's voice trailed off. She wasn't sure she even wanted to hear the rest.

"Our odds of survival weren't good to begin with," he went on. "And if the experiments didn't go the way they wanted, their plan was to plow us under and start over with fresh meat."

Caro hugged herself against the inner cold. She wanted to say something, but couldn't.

"We were ideal subjects. Intelligent, relatively healthy children who weren't addicts, and about whom no one on earth gave a flying fuck. My crew all has the same sad story."

"How many of you are there?"

"Not as many as there should be. I led a rebellion at the research facility when I found out that a bunch of us, including me, were scheduled for disposal. I had to move fast. Before they took out the trash."

Caro bit her lip and waited for the rest. She couldn't bring herself to ask any more questions.

"There were twenty-seven of us fighting on rebellion day," Noah said. "It was bloody. High casualties on both sides. I can think of twelve more who died before that, during the trials. We lost seven in the battle. Twenty of us escaped. Four more died over the next few years. PTSD, depression, suicide. The rest of us are still hanging in there. New names, new lives. Lethal secrets."

"And Mark?"

"Mark was one of the twenty," Noah said. "He was in my group. One of the Eyes Guys. Didn't stay with us long. He wasn't a team player."

"I bet he didn't like taking orders from you," she commented.

"No, he didn't. I made rules, about not using our abilities to take advantage of people. Mark found that insulting. After what was done to him, he felt entitled to grab whatever he wanted as payback. But nothing could repay what they took from him. It was driving him out of his mind, even then. He'll never be satisfied."

"I see," Caro said, though she didn't. She felt numb, and stupid.

"We've followed his career," Noah said. "He changed his name, of course, but so did we all. And he was never hard to find. We just follow the death and destruction."

"You never turned him in?"

"How could we? He would retaliate, and I'm still responsible for fourteen other people. If Obsidian tracks us down, they'll wipe us all out. We're a threat. We could go public, expose them, I guess, but it's not like the quality of our lives would be improved. Our existence would scare the living shit out of everyone."

"So Mark is stealing Obsidian's secrets," she said. "To punish them."

"Mark wants to punish the whole world," Noah said. "And he will never stop."

"Well," Caro replied, after several seconds. "In spite of all this, you have a wonderful life. I don't know how you pull it off. I'm huddled under a rock, eating ramen, and you're making gazillions helping humanity with visionary biotech. You live in a lakefront mansion with art by Delaunay and Bosch on your wall, you drive a Porsche, you eat filet mignon for dinner and hand-peeled grapes for dessert. I am in awe."

"I've been at it longer," Noah said. "You learn some tricks."

She raised a skeptical eyebrow. "Is that so. Tell me more about these modifications. Are you, like, Superman?"

An ironic smile flashed across his face. "Hardly," he said. "We have implants. We had to undergo brain stimulation and intense biofeedback, plus experimental gene splicing. Muscle fiber mods, intensive combat training, ultra-heightened reflexes. They wanted supersoldiers. Each of us has a specialty, according to our dominant abilities."

"What's yours?"

"Eyes," he said simply.

She sighed. "Of course. Can you see in the dark?"

"Yes. I have hardware in my eyes, for far vision and night vision, and AVP uploaded into my brain. Augmented visual processing. I see a wider spectrum of frequencies, and I process visual information extremely fast. And react the same way."

"Kill first, think second?" The question just came out.

"It's happened," he said, unfazed by the question. "Not lately. Took me years to learn to calm down the stress response."

Caro got up from her chair and grabbed her coat from the back of the couch where Hannah had draped it. She shrugged it on. "That is just an amazing story, Noah, but I don't want to hear any more. It's time for me to go now."

"No." Noah moved between her and the door, blocking her. His huge body was a wall between her and and escape.

Her throat constricted. "You can't force me to stay."

"I don't want to force you to do anything. But I can't let an angry person with a grudge who knows my family's secrets just go walking out my door."

"Oh," she said. "So, you're a super-assassin, right? You don't even need to outsource a hit. Shall I say my prayers? Is this my big moment?"

"I already told you." His voice was stiff. "I would never hurt you."

"You already did," she said. "You've hurt me more in the past half hour than I ever have been hurt by anyone. Including Mark. Open the goddamn door, Noah. There's no danger in letting me walk away. I won't say anything about you. No one in their right mind would believe me if I did. You're perfectly safe from me."

He shook his head. "I'm sorry, Caro," he said. "Not happening."

The look on his face made her want to scream. He felt completely justified in what he was doing, no matter how supposedly sorry he was to do it. It made her feel so alone.

A thought crept into the back of her mind, which was right where she had to keep it. It had to stay small, huddled up. If it got any larger, he would sense it. The way he sensed fucking everything. Always.

Sexual energy buzzed between them. She couldn't stop it if she wanted to. Her body responded to him without her consent. That heat in his eyes did something to her that was light-years outside her conscious control. It made her frantic. Furious that he had so much power over her. Besides all the other powers, all his crushing advantages as an adversary, he had this, too.

Sex was the only weapon she had to turn back upon him, as alert as he was. If she could keep her thoughts small, and cold, and secret.

Sex might distract him for a crucial moment. If she could manage not to get totally swept away by it herself. A very big if.

She took a step closer. Shrugged the coat open. Shoulders back. Tits out.

"So what's the plan for me, then?" She made her voice go low and husky. "A golden cage? A collar and leash? Is this going to be my life now? Will you keep me naked in your bedroom, ready to fulfil your every sexual whim?"

His eyes narrowed. "That's a fast change of subject."

She shrugged. "I suppose. You make me so angry. And even so, we always find ourselves . . . right here." Another step brought her close enough to reach out and stroke the thickened bulge at the front of his jeans with her fingertip. "Every damn time."

He shuddered but stood tall, a hot flush on his cheekbones. "Oh fuck."

"Screwing me over really turns you on," she said. "Look at that."

"You too," he shot back.

"You think?" Caro grabbed the hems of her layered T-shirts and pulled them up, baring her breasts and tight nipples. "Well, would you look at that. You're so right."

His eyes had that hot amber glow that made her crazy, but she controlled herself, sliding her hand into her deep coat pocket as she sidled closer. "If you're not going to let me go, what do you propose to do with me? I'd love to hear the details."

Noah's body heat made sent a shivering ripple of excitement through her body, making her nipples tingle wildly.

"No," he said unsteadily. "We're not doing that now. You're too angry at me."

"That's not going to change," she told him. "But I'm in a crazy mood."

"Caro." His voice was strangled. "Anytime you want it, just take it."

Caro kept her purpose cold and clear as her trembling fingers closed around the smooth cylinder in her pocket. "Not this time," she said. "*You* take it."

She whipped out the pepper spray and blasted it into his startled eyes. Then she grabbed one of the brass candlesticks from the table.

The sound he made was awful. A bellow of betrayal partly drowned out by her own screaming. She screamed with horror, and guilt, and anger, at having been driven to do something so fucking horrible to someone she loved.

Loved. Yes. She did love him, goddamn him. She realized that fully the same instant that the brass candlestick connected with the side of his head.

She felt it through her own nerves as if she'd taken the blow herself.

Noah grunted at the impact, dropping to one knee, hands clamped over his eyes. He let out another roar that rattled her bones. Caro scrambled away from him.

Everything was overbright, disjointed. The world through a shattered mirror.

The keys to the Porsche. She snatched them, stumbling and weaving through a smear of colors out the door. Something broke behind her. He was still bellowing.

She was crying so hard she could barely breathe. She dropped the key fob, had to fish for it in the wet grass. Once she was in the car, her legs couldn't reach the pedals, and she lost precious seconds groping for the button that slid the seat forward, terrified that Noah would descend upon her in an avenging fury.

She hesitated before putting the car into drive, and groped in her pocket for the phone she'd kept for calls from Gareth. She turned it on. She couldn't leave Noah like that, after hitting him on the head.

She got the information across to a methodical 911 operator, then turned the phone off and shoved it back into her secret pocket, the one she'd sewed way down in the seam. She'd toss it the next chance she got.

The paramedics would come to his rescue—while she sped away in the luxury car that she'd stolen from him. It was so fucked up. Tragic and twisted. But it wasn't like she could go back and minister to him. He might actually feel justified in killing her after what she'd done to him.

At least the Porsche wasn't a stick shift. She'd be doomed.

Still crying, she blundered through unfamiliar streets, constantly expecting sirens, strobe lights. When she finally made it home she left the car in a tow zone. Noah must have a GPS tag on it. She'd leave the keys in her apartment for him to find, along with a note of apology.

When she put the Porsche keys into her pocket, she felt the carved wooden wolf between her fingers. All she needed right now. A reminder of the one moment when he'd seemed real. She fished around in her big overstuffed pockets for the key to her apartment and found it as she ran up the stairs, taking them two at a time.

She unlocked her door, and went in, reaching for the light—

A hand clamped her throat, stopping her breath. A damp cloth reeking of chemicals pressed down hard over her nose and mouth. Someone else caught her wrists, crushing them.

She fought, frantically. The huge hand holding her wrists tightened, until the small bones and tendons ground together, crushed tight, and oh God, that *hurt* . . .

Two shadows, in the gloom. One spoke, in a mocking tone, but she could hardly hear him over the roaring in her ears, her thumping heart.

". . . Olund wants her, he can have her."

Her lungs demanded air, forcing her to inhale the nasty stuff on the smothering cloth.

It plunged her right down into the dark.

SHANNON MCKENNA

Chapter 21

NOAH COULDN'T STOP bellowing. He crashed against the wall, lurched away and thudded to his knees again. He blinked away streaming tears, his body's desperate effort to wash the chemicals out of the blistered whites of his eyes.

No longer human. Not even close. Not in this red haze, combat program raging, so far from his right mind he didn't even know where he'd left it. He could feel it back there, struggling, but it couldn't reach the control panel.

Arrogant shithead, thinking he was so on top of himself.

He put his fist through the top of the glass coffee table.

He hunched beside it, head dangling, panting. Hannah's sandwiches were scattered on the glass shards below the metal frame. Fat red drops of blood plopped down from his fingertips. He stared around the room, dripping, panting. Seeking with his burning, swimming eyes. Finding nothing else to break.

Blood trickled down his shins from his lacerated knees. The smell maddened him with ugly associations. His friends at Midlands, the ones that didn't make it. Sprawling in an ocean of blood. So many of them.

He staggered in the direction of the kitchen. The sink. *Yes.* That was what a normal human would do. Wash the wound, stanch the blood. Logical. Sequential.

But as soon as he made it into the kitchen, some random association made AVP rage sweep over him again. He forgot the sink, the blood, the logical sequential plan, and swept his arm over the kitchen counter. A big glass blender sailed high into the air in a slow, lazy arc ...

It hit the brick wall. Chunks of glass rained down over the kitchen. He was peppered with small, stinging darts.

He hardly noticed. His eyes stung, burned. Fucking *hurt* ...

He flung containers, flour, pasta, sugar, garlic, contents scattering across the floor, the counter. He was possessed by a demon, programmed to someone else's specs, and he had to play their game or pay an unspeakable price.

I found it. I paid for it. And the price was very high. Her words echoed in his mind.

He shoved his guilt aside. Sneaky bitch, flashing her tits at him, and he'd panted and wagged like a hopeful hound. Fury at his own stupidity made his arm sweep out at the knife block. The contact would have broken a normal man's arm. Not his reinforced bones, not his super-toughened muscle fibers. The block hit the ceramic floor tiles, shattering a few into a spiderweb of cracks and fragments.

Knives slid out, skittering over the tiles, through glittering shards of glass and ceramic. Another sweep caught the big fruit bowl, piled high.

It crashed to the floor. Apples, oranges, grapefruits bounced and rolled.

His eyes streamed, his chest hitched. He hated this. *Hated* it. He groped again for a shred of rationality, stabbing out into the hot red darkness, searching for it.

His eyes, his eyes, his fucking eyes. Take care of the eyes. He should flush them with water. A soothing eye wash. Bathroom. Medicine cabinet. Yeah.

His head throbbed. Anger flared, hot and murderous, as he touched the lump on his scalp where she'd clocked him with one of his own fancy-ass candlesticks. Fucking brilliant. He had an extremely high pain threshold, and quick recovery to trauma was vectored into his genome, but the injury triggered memories that flooded out, full force.

They raged through him now as if it was all happening right now.

Twelve boys in the room. The first lucky punks to get Braxton's Mr. Muscle and Bones of Steel gene cocktail. Flailing in their restraints as they burned with fever, choking on snot and vomit, leaking from every hole. Just a few of the side effects of the hollowed-out flu virus that carried improved genes right into the cell nucleus and into the genome itself. The first change that would make them a beacon of hope for goddamn humanity.

Five boys died that day alone. One right next to him. He still saw blood streaming out of the kid's nose as he croaked. His cells overwhelmed with waste toxins.

He barely made it to the downstairs bathroom before he lost what was in his stomach. He watched it swirl down the toilet, disgusted. With all his optimized cerebral function, he still hadn't come up with a better solution than this stupid shitstorm.

He held his streaming eyes open for a long squirt of eye wash, hissing as the stuff made contact with the blistered whites. His eyes looked like stoplights, but already his rapid healing was at work. The huge sickening *whanga-whanga* caused by the candlestick to the extra-hard bone tissue in his skull had subsided to a throbbing ache that synchronized with each heartbeat.

He put the eye wash back in the medicine cabinet, and saw the flash drive in there. Zade had left it for him, and flushed a plastic contact lens case instead.

He'd signaled for Zade to stage the scene, never thinking things would get so out of hand. No way in hell would any of them have destroyed that flash drive. They needed to study and analyze that footage.

But Caro hadn't know that. He grabbed the flash drive. Shoved it in his pocket.

He was in control again, but the anger raged on, running on a separate track from his rational brain. It lit his mind with a hot red haze.

One thing was simple. Retrieve Caro. Stick to her like glue. Keep her safe, and keep his people safe from revenge on her part. Be smarter than he'd been so far.

The trick would consist of not morphing into a one-man barbarian invasion and scaring Caro out of her mind. Anger and sex were wound too closely in that knot in his head. Those hack neuroscientists had crossed his wires backwards and upside down, just to see what would happen. They'd already written him off, so why not just fuck around, get more useful data to crunch before they pulled the plug?

He'd learned to walk that tightrope using the analog dives, meditation. He'd fooled himself into thinking he was normal enough to get married, have kids, and live like a normal man. He'd been able to have great sex without being emotionally engaged in what he was doing, and he'd considered that to be a step in the right direction, a sign that he had a hope of being civilized. Sex was just a physiological need that he fulfilled, for pleasure, entertainment, and optimal health and function.

Guilty as charged. Brand him with a big red M for Man.

But he couldn't cut himself off from Caro. And the red-tinged images writhing in his unhinged imagination were all of frenzied, conquering-warrior-style fucking.

Caro would not welcome that vibe from him in her present mood.

He touched the lump again. His fingers came away gummy with drying blood. His hair stuck up, blood-stiffened. He looked like shit, and he wasn't going to be able to tolerate the shield lenses on his inflamed eyes for a while. He'd have to rely on shield specs alone, which was too much light exposure. The light that came in the sides would keep the AVP combat program revved to screaming, wild-sex-or- pitched battle levels. Just to keep things interesting.

The other option was to call his people, have them bring Caro in for him. Safer for everyone. Except that he would be likely to burst a blood vessel, if he were waiting at home like an asshole.

Caro would just have to deal with the problematic thing that he actually was. He staggered around, looking in vain for the Porsche keys until he remembered with a fresh surge of fury that Caro had taken them.

He dug out the keys for his Mercedes SUV. Stopped for a moment to plug the flash drive into his laptop to copy the video file for future study. It went back into his pocket, and he sped out the door.

Caro had awakened the beast. He'd bent over backwards to be a perfect gentleman for her, and it hadn't worked out. He couldn't keep the mask up any longer. He had nothing left to hide behind. And this naked, jacked up, deformed thing that he was, both more and less than human . . . here it was. In your face, girl. Good luck with it.

At this hour of the night, the road was his, which was a good thing at this speed. He had the reflexes of a race car driver, and the high speed mellowed him out a little.

Until he spotted his Porsche parked outside her building. In a fucking tow zone, no less.

The front door of her shitty tenement building was still unlocked. Weirdos skulked in the foyer, but they scuttled into the shadows when they saw him. He must look like something straight out of the crypt right now.

He leaped up the six flights, four steps at a time. Most of the wall lamps in the corridor were burned out, and the remaining one flickered fitfully, choked by a drift of dead bugs.

Freddie was stretched in front of his door again, snoring. Noah loped past him, alarm bells buzzing in his mind. The shadows on her door were the wrong depth. The door was tilted at a different angle with respect to the other doors in the corridor.

There was no way that a young woman alone in a run-down tenement would leave her door hanging open at night. For any reason on earth.

Panic threatened to drop-kick him off the AVP deep end. *Stay cool. Breathe. You need your whole brain functioning for this.* Wrongness thrummed as he approached the door, like the throb of an infrasound weapon. He wished he'd brought a gun, but he'd been too busy wallowing in agony to think of it.

Her door squeaked against the warped floor as he opened it. No one there.

Without light to activate it, the visual magic of the room was gone, and he saw it as it truly was. Cramped and shabby, without Caro's transforming influence.

The duffel was there, and a battered hard-case wheelie, pawed through, contents flung upon the floor. A hot plate, a toothbrush, a snarl of cotton underwear, bags of instant oatmeal. A spoon. The keys to his Porsche lay on the floor. A single sneaker. The one she had been wearing.

He grabbed his Porsche keys, staring at that grayish, shabby kick, once white, very worn. From what he'd seen, in this place that had no drawers or closets, it was the only pair of shoes she had, and it had no mate. So Caro had gone out on a cold, rainy night, leaving everything she owned, with her door hanging open. Wearing one shoe.

The carved wolf he'd given her lay on the floor in two pieces. The tail and one of the hind legs had snapped off. He picked the pieces up and shoved them into his pocket.

For the sake of certainty, he peeled up the floor mat, and checked where she'd stowed the envelope he had given her. Still there. The entire wad of cash, intact.

256

He pulled up the program on his phone to monitor her tile, hoping desperately that she still had her coat on. A map appeared. An icon moved north on the Interstate, going too fast to be a bus, and she hadn't had time to catch one. She'd still be moving through Seattle toward the station, if a bus were her plan. Not heading north into wintry mountains with no bags. And only one shoe.

He exploded out the door, then on impulse, skidded to a halt next to Freddie. He nudged the guy, none too gently. "Freddie! Wake up!"

"Huh?" Startled, Freddie peered up. He shrank back, eyes wide with alarm when he saw Noah. "What? I didn't do nothing, man!"

Noah grabbed the guy's sweatshirt under his chin and hauled him a foot or so off the ground. He leaned into the man's rank body odor. "Who took Caro, Freddie?"

Freddie's eyes rolled frantically. "Caro? Who's Caro?"

"The chick in six-oh-eight. You slime her every time she walks by. Someone came and took her away. Did you see them?"

Freddie blinked, disoriented. "What? Are you talking about, like, her dealers?"

"Dealers? What dealers?" He shook the guy the way a terrier shook a rat.

"Uh . . . some guys," Freddie sounded bewildered. "I saw her leave with them."

"Left how? What condition was she in? Was she injured?"

Freddie plucked at Noah's knuckles. "Dude, that hurts! Let go! She, uh, looked stoned out of her fuckin' mind. They were dragging her. Musta been some really good shit. I asked if I could score a hit when they came by." He rubbed his ribs. "Scumbag kicked me."

"What did they look like?" Noah demanded.

"I don't know!" Freddy whined. "Just a couple of guys. And one of 'em kicked me! Prolly cracked my ribs. I never saw either of them before."

"White, black, Asian, Latino? Wearing what? Age? Weight? Anything!"

Freddie looked panicked. "One guy was bald," he offered. "The shorter one. He had a goatee. The other one was big. And white. Yeah. Both of 'em were white."

"What made you think they were her dealers? Their clothes?"

"Don't remember their clothes," Freddy said. "I thought that because of you."

"Me?" Noah was bewildered. "What does that have to do with me?"

"Come on. Bitch needs to cop a buzz. She turns a trick, and calls her dealer. It's so easy for bitches, especially ones like her. All they have to do is spread their legs."

Noah smacked the guy before he could stop himself. Freddie burst out crying, cringing away from him.

He dropped Freddie on the floor, and ran.

* * *

Buried alive, under tons of earth. Head splitting. Can't breathe. Mouth full of dirt. Her chest bucked and heaved. Couldn't . . . get . . . any . . . air . . .

The line between her stifling dream and waking reality was blurry for a long time. She wavered, reaching toward consciousness, then collapsing back into nightmares again. Then the movement stilled. That buzzing hum had stopped.

She was in a car. It had stopped moving. Full consciousness forced itself upon her, and along with it came horrible images of whatever might be in store for her.

Someone dragged a smothering blanket off her head, and hit her face. She tried to cough, but couldn't, with the gag in her mouth. The man's face was slack and grotesque at that angle, his chubby cheeks and the bags under his eyes flushed and dangling. Metal glinted in his dental work. He had a black goatee. "Wake the fuck up!"

She was in the trunk of a car, arms fastened behind her. The upside-down man's hands hooked her armpits. He dragged her out, flung her against the side of the car.

She would have slid to the ground, but he pinned her there, and swatted the back of her head. "On your feet, you lazy cunt." He cut the ties on her arms. She cried out with pain when the numbness wore off and stumbled to her knees.

The bigger man kicked her in the buttock, the toe of his boot shooting a bolt of pain up her spine. "Get up, bitch," he growled. "I ain't carrying you this time."

She tried, but her balance was shot. Whenever she was kicked or shoved forward, the dirt roadway tilted up and whacked her hard in the face.

They were on a deeply rutted, unpaved road carved through a thick evergreen forest. The tangled bottom branches were packed so tightly that the boughs seemed black and lifeless in the dim light of dawn.

The huge guy grabbed her arm. "Move it. Stupid whore."

She was shoved and kicked all the way down the overgrown driveway until a building hidden in the woods slowly came into view. It was a shabby prefab box set on cinder blocks. No porch, just temporary aluminum steps in front of the door.

The bald man rapped on the door. "It's us," he said. "Open up."

The door opened. Caro was heaved inside, cracking her shins against the bottom of the door frame before scrambling onto her hands and knees. Four pairs of jackboots were ranged around her on the dirty linoleum. She fought to control her terror.

One of the four men grabbed her under the armpits, heaved her to her feet, and shoved her before him through a dim corridor that stank of mold.

In the back was a room with a window showing a dark wall of trees. There was a wrought iron bed. The mattress was covered with a sheet of heavy plastic. She closed her eyes and hung onto her guts.

She was flung onto the bed. She'd lost her coat, at some point. The plastic covering the mattress felt damp and cold against the small of her back.

"Get out of here. Leave us alone," the bald goateed man said to the man who had dragged her.

He waited for the big, thick-featured guy to leave, and then smiled wide, flashing metal in his eyeteeth. He pulled up a chair to the foot of the bed and straddled it backwards, facing her. "Good morning, Caroline."

It took her several tries to get the words out. "You work for Mark Olund?"

The man's close-set black eyes narrowed slightly. He didn't reply.

Caro massaged her own wrists, and tried to flex her numb fingers. "I don't have what he wants," she said.

"Not my problem. I was paid to pick you up and keep you here until he comes for you, which will be soon," he said.

"But—"

"Nothing you say will change that. Keep your trap shut and don't annoy me. When he gets here, you'll give him whatever he wants. You'll give him everything you have. Count on it, bitch."

She stared at the flat emptiness of his eyes. Her ears roared. That nightmare was coming due. She'd tried so hard to outrun it, but it was here.

She had no idea if she could open Lydia's safe at all. Caro had urged the woman to change her training image sequence to something new and private. It was sloppy and dangerous to leave an interface coach with potential access to goods and secrets that others would kill to have. Changing the sequence protected everyone.

But Lydia had been reluctant. What a freaking idiot.

"They say you killed a colleague of mine," the guy said. "With a boxcutter. Hard to believe that a dumb cow like you could pull that off. Did you wait until he was fucking you? That makes some men stupid, but not me."

He bent down and kissed her, clamping his hand over her nose and thrusting his tongue into her mouth. It was muscular and slimy and huge. He slid it to the opening of her throat. No air.

She'd almost blacked out when he lifted his face.

"You know what? I can think when I fuck," he confided. "When Olund's done with you, I'll show you." His grin showed his eyeteeth before he attacked with another vile, smothering kiss. This time, he grabbed her crotch, groping and squeezing. Her muffled shriek was lost against his mouth as his long tongue thrust into her mouth.

She bit down on his tongue with frantic force and clawed wildly at his face.

He yelled and tried to pull away. She bit down harder. Hot, coppery blood flooded her mouth. He whacked the side of her head and freed himself, but she kept on moving. She slid off the slippery plastic and onto the floor. Sprang to her feet.

He dove after her with a shout. She bolted through the communicating rooms, bare feet pounding. Two men in the front room turned startled faces toward her as she ran at them, screaming. One of them stumbled back. The other tackled her.

She staggered at the contact. Hit the floor hard, the guy landing on top of her. Gasping for breath, screaming and clawing and squirming. The other guy piled on, too.

Too many of them. Too much rank, stinking dead weight. She was immobilized, but she was possessed. She could not stop shrieking and twisting.

Another blow to her head stunned her. Her vision swam back into focus to see the big, thick-faced guy who had kicked her down the driveway rubbing his jaw. Angry.

"What the fuck was that about?" he demanded. "Why'd you hit me? Asshole!"

"I told you, dipshit. She's not supposed to be harmed. Olund's orders." The man with the goatee again. "That kick would have knocked out all her fucking teeth!"

"Don't think she'll need teeth where she's going," the third man observed.

"That's not our call. Shut up, you asswipe moron. Olund wants her intact for whatever he has planned, and if she looks like hamburger when he gets here, he'll kill us. Here, help me. Get her legs. And hang on tight. This bitch can kick."

She started screaming and flailing again as the three of them hauled her back into the bedroom and flung her onto the bed. This time, they jerked her arms up and immediately fastened them to the iron bedframe with a zip tie, yanked brutally tight.

The three men stood there, panting. The goateed man had flecks of blood on his lips, his cheeks, his chin. Her fingernails had left angry stripes down his cheeks, and his eyelid was bloody and reddened. As their eyes met, his lips stretched in a horrifying smile, showing bloodied teeth. He moved forward, holding up his knife.

She couldn't shrink back, just cringed away as he slid it into the fabric of her layered T-shirts and sliced through necklines with a twist and flick of the blade.

He then tore the shirts open all the way down, wrenching them wide.

All three men stared at her bared breasts. That fixed, hot, mindless stare.

The knife tip was cold, tracing and then piercing her skin at the collarbone. Then again, and again. She clenched her body, and made no sound as the knifetip dug in. A trickle of hot blood made its way slowly down her chest. Then another.

262

"You scratched me," the guy said softly. "Now you have to bleed. Whore."

The big one licked his heavy lips until they gleamed wetly. "Nice tits," he said. "Can we, uh . . ."

"No," the goateed man said. "Olund said no damage."

"It wouldn't damage her." The big guy's voice was sulky. "Not much, anyhow. Besides, you're cutting her. Fucking hypocrite."

"Maybe after, when Olund's done. If there's anything left." He dipped his finger in the blood pooling in her navel. "I've seen that guy work people over," he told Caro. "He knows all about pain. And he's got something special planned just for you." He wiped the blood off his mouth with his sleeve. "I just hope he lets me watch."

Chapter 22

NOAH PEERED THROUGH the trees, teeth gritted. He had an arsenal of guns and he practiced regularly. Even with extensive mods, marksmanship was a perishable skill. Not one he could let slide, considering Obsidian's looming shadow over their lives.

All his effort and paranoia did him no goddamn good at all right now. He'd been too out of his head when he left his house to think to to bring a weapon.

He wanted to kick his own ass, he was so disgusted.

Ransacking the SUV for anything useful turned up only a tire iron and a coil of climbing rope. Sisko and Zade had raced to equip themselves after his frantic call, but they still hadn't showed.

One single unarmed man. That was Caro's whole cavalry. *Fuck.*

The sig of the guy circling the house showed him to be the human equivalent of an attack dog. An inflamed red-orange glow in the area of the belly and groin pulsed like a lava lamp, and a dull yellow haze hung around his head. His chest area was blank. No energy at all, just a cold dark sinkhole.

He'd seen sigs like that before on some of the Obsidian researchers. Their colors were even worse. Like pus or gangrene. For some reason, that project had attracted brain-eating sociopaths.

Mark's sig had gotten just as ugly by the time they'd parted company. Midlands had changed Mark. It had killed his humanity.

Men with sigs like that could do unspeakable things to Caro before Sisko and Zade caught up with him. The urgency that assailed him wouldn't let him wait for back-up.

He slid the tire iron into the sleeve of his leather jacket and edged closer. He'd have to thin them out. Get his hands on a gun. There were two men in the front room. He read their thermals through the wall. Caro's would be instantly recognizable if he saw it. He itched to identify how many of them there were, what room she was in.

But not yet. Better to get rid of some guys in the front. Improve his chances before he got anywhere near Caro.

He studied the man pacing not thirty feet from him. Tall, massive. His face was thick, his eyes dull. Not a take-charge type. He might hesitate before shooting Noah in the throat, for fear of fucking up.

He'd hold back, if only for an instant. All Noah needed.

Cut plastic cuffs lay on the ground behind one of their vehicles. They had pulled her out of the trunk of the car and cut off her bonds.

Seething rage got the better of him for a moment. He fought it down. He could not let rage run the show. His enhancements gave him an edge, but he was alone, unarmed, outnumbered. No margin for error.

Go. He stumbled drunkenly out into the roadway, flapping a roadmap as he strode toward the guard, slurring his words.

"Ah, exshcuse me! Hey, sir? I, uh, crashed my car a few miles back, and walked here, can you believe it? No offense, but this place is the ass end of nowhere. I can't get any bars on my cell and I was wondering if you—"

"Fuck off, dickwad," the guy snarled.

Noah staggered closer. "Dude! Don't get uptight! I'm not gonna rob you, I'm just—whoa! You don't need . . . Holy shit, dude, put that fucking thing down!"

The guard pulled his gun. Noah shrank back, angling his body so that the other man wouldn't see the tire iron slide out.

With a blow too fast to see, he whipped it down and shattered the man's arm.

The gun dropped. The guy stared at his arm, startled. It dangled, floppy and useless. His eyes rolled to the whites as he sucked in air—

Noah whacked the tire iron across his throat, crushing his windpipe.

The man dropped, gasping. He made a choked, wet sound, lips turning blue.

Not his lucky day. Shouldn't run with a pack that laid hands on Noah's woman. Bad call. Die alone and gasping, shitbag.

He grabbed the guy by the ankles, dragged his twitching bulk behind the Jeep. Jerked up the man's pant leg, took the knife in his boot sheath. Scooped up the guy's Glock. Two more in that front room to deal with. One stationary, one moving.

He ran back, snatched up the coil of rope, checked the tree limbs over their parked Jeep. He clambered swiftly on top of it, the rope around his shoulder.

His leap from the Jeep's roof had all the power of Braxton's enhanced muscle gene cocktail behind it. He caught a branch several feet above the Jeep and nearer to the building. He swung there, fingers scraped by the rough bark, his body dangling over the overgrown path. The smell of pine pitch stung his nose. The branch bent dangerously under his weight as he crawled higher into the sticky boughs, seeking a clear drop onto the path. He uncoiled the rope.

The knot didn't need any enhancement to remember. Just a hangman's noose.

He held himself still until the branches stop swishing. Patience was a bitch, with Caro inside, suffering and afraid. He shut that thought down when it threatened to unseat his mind. After several agonizingly slow minutes, the screen door squeaked as it rasped wide. A tall, skinny guy in black leather with buzz-cut black hair peered out.

"Matt!" he bawled. "Where the fuck are you? You're supposed to check in!"

Matt made no sound, being too busy dying behind the Jeep. The man in the doorway cursed. Someone behind him spoke in a sharp questioning voice.

"How the fuck do I know? He's not answering," Buzz-cut complained, gesturing with a gun as he emerged from the house and peered through the early morning gloom from the top of the. "Matt! Where the fuck are you?"

He got no answer. Noah, peering down through the pine needles, holding the end of the rope he'd draped over a strong branch, saw the man's sig shift colors. It shrank, went from greenish to snot gray. The guy was unnerved.

He clattered down the steps and onto the path, no longer calling out, the gun kept close to his body in case he had to shoot fast. Preoccupied and antsy, he didn't look up—until the noose thudded down onto his shoulders, around his neck.

Noah dropped himself down as a counterweight, yanking the guy up off his feet.

The man dangled and danced as Noah's weight pulled him higher. They swung together. Holding the rope with one hand, Noah stared into the guy's purpling face as he swayed there helplessly, clawing at his throat.

"I hate this shit, man," Noah said to him softly. "But your number's up."

The guy twisted, groping desperately for a hidden knife. Noah saw it flash, seized the man's wrist and torqued it until bones splintered.

The knife thudded to the ground.

It would take too long for the guy to suffocate on his own. Noah didn't have the time to wait. He hoisted himself up, let the guy drop a couple of feet further down, wrapped his legs around Buzzcut's neck, and finished him off with a lethal squeeze.

The man's neck snapped with a sickening crunch. Noah let him hang for a moment just to be sure. The wind sighed. The rope that Buzz-cut dangled upon creaked.

Noah secured the end with a strong knot and dropped to the ground. He snatched up the knife. Sharp. Notched. Good.

The thermal splotch of the last guy in the front room was approaching the closed door. Noah dove for the open space under the building and scrambled behind the temporary stairs.

The door rasped open again.

Noah peered out through the space below the top step. Black leather boots appeared in Noah's field of vision. They stopped a few steps down. Noah could see the back of the man's thighs.

Creak . . . *creak* . . . the hanged man swayed in the morning breeze.

Noah felt the moment that horrified realization exploded in the guy's mind as he dragged in breath to yell for help.

Just before Noah stabbed through the open space under the stair and sank the notched blade deep into the guy's hamstring. The man lurched forward with a gurgling cry.

Noah slithered out and jumped him, knocking him to the ground. The leg wound had crippled him, spurting blood and sapping his strength. Noah snapped his bull neck after less than a minute of pitched wrestling.

He left the guy where he lay, dropped the knife into the thigh pocket on his cargo pants, and slid noiselessly into the house, gun in hand.

Light filtered from a corridor that led from the open door off the front room. A male voice droned from it. He crept closer, bracing himself for whatever hit his eyes.

Caro lay on a plastic-wrapped bed, her shirt sliced open, arms stretched up, ziptied. The man he'd heard talking was leaning over her.

Caro saw him. Her sudden eye movement betrayed him.

Noah jerked back as the guy dropped down behind the bed into a crouch and opened fire, right over Caro's naked torso. Noah dropped to the floor and aimed beneath the bed, for his feet.

Two shots. A hoarse yell. He'd scored a hit. Caro screamed.

"Get out with your hands up, or she dies," the guy said. "On three. One . . . two . . ."

"Don't hurt her," Noah broke in. "Olund needs her alive to open that safe. He'll kill you if you hurt her. Count on it." He held his breath, waiting.

The silence was broken only by sobbing gasps from Caro.

"Get out with your hands up, motherfucker," her captor said. "I don't give a shit what Olund wants right now. I swear, I will kill her, if you fuck with me."

"Don't do it," Noah said. "Don't shoot me, either."

He crawled forward. There was rustling and grunting from the direction of the bed, which made his heart thud. But Caro was alive. So far. That much he knew.

The guy was cursing, hissing through his teeth. Caro made a sharp sound. A cut-off cry of pain.

"I bet you hate that prick Olund, because everybody who knows him does," Noah said. "But how about his money? You want some of that?"

"What the fuck are you talking about?" The rustling stopped. Raw, choppy breaths from the man.

"Want to be rich?" Rolling the dice, betting on greed and curiosity. Distracting him.

"Fuck you, man," the wounded man gasped out. "This ain't no game show."

"Just hear me out. Before anyone else gets hurt." Noah rose slowly, letting the gun dangle from his spread fingers as he stepped into the doorframe, hands up.

A bald man with a black and silver goatee crouched against the wall. Blood coursed down his face. More leaked from his boot. He'd slashed Caro's restraints, and pulled her down on top of himself as a shield. He held the gun to her temple and held Caro clamped against his chest. Blood trickled down in long rivulets between her breasts. A knife lay next to them on the floor. The blade was bloodied. He'd been using it to cut her.

The bastard was pretty fucking quick, for an unmod. But there were claw marks on his face. Caro had done that. Good for her.

She looked up at Noah. Her lips tight, but her eyes were clear. Her sig was ablaze.

"Take the ammo out of the gun," the thug commanded.

"Don't hurt her," Noah said.

"I swear to God, I will cut her throat right now if you don't empty that gun and kick it over to me." The blade dug in deeper. Blood pooled in her navel.

Noah pulled out the magazine, dropped it to the floor, kicked it.

"Take out the chambered round," the man said. "Toss the bullet over here. And slide me the gun. *Now*, fuckface."

He did as he was told. The bullet bounced and rolled right into the puddle of blood at the man's feet. The gun rattled across the plywood floor.

"Don't hurt her," Noah said again. "She's the only one who can open Olund's safe. She doesn't know what's inside it. But I do. Major money. You in?"

"Shut up, asshole, or she'll feel it." The guy whacked Caro in the side of the head with the gun butt. Noah buzzed on the raging edge of a supernova.

271

Not now. Not yet. Not with a gun to Caro's head. *Not. Yet.*

"You must be the son of a bitch who fucked up my team yesterday," the man snarled. "I'm not doing any goddamn deals with you."

"Hear me out," Noah said. "I hate that psycho prick, and I want him dead, preferably slowly, and screaming. But I have nothing against you . . . yet. There's no reason you and I couldn't cut a deal."

"You are so full of shit." The man shoved the gun barrel against Caro's face. She winced as it dug into her cheek. "What the fuck would I need you for?"

"Getting the job done right," Noah said calmly. "You'd have to take down Mark on your own otherwise. It'll be a whole hell of a lot easier to do with me."

"Oh, God," Caro said shakily. "No! No, you can't—"

"Shut up and do as you're told," Noah said curtly.

"Talk fast," the bleeding man said. "I'm getting bored."

More like about to pass out from shock. The wound was serious. But the guy was tough. "Mark never told you what was in that safe?"

He watched the guy's sig carefully, filtering out Caro's overlay.

"It's not my fucking business what's inside," the guy growled.

Noah read defensiveness, conflict and anger. The man holding Caro really didn't know what was in the safe, and he was curious, even if he was afraid of Mark. He was smart, and his survival instincts were good.

"So you're that kind of guy," Noah said softly. "You toe the line. Take what you're given."

The other man gripped Caro tighter, making her catch her breath. "Right now, asshole, I have the gun, and you have jack shit. Tell me what's in the fucking safe."

"Bearer bonds," Noah said. "Eighty million bucks worth. Half are yours."

"I don't believe you," the man hissed.

Noah smiled thinly. "That's a forty million dollar payday. Why else would I be here?"

"You tell me."

"To get rich. So how much did Mark pay you to pick up this chick? Fifteen thousand? Twenty thousand?"

"More than that."

"Chump change," Noah said. "You call that money?"

"Yeah. With benefits. Like this." He squeezed Caro's breast. She gasped sharply.

Noah's hands clenched. "I need her alive and functional. She set the biometric parameters on the vault. Only her brainwaves can open it. The safe is programmed to destroy anything you try to extract by force. Kill her, and you kill the money."

"Hmmm." The thug ran a meaty, bloodcaked hand over Caro's tangled hair, and cupped her head. "Brain waves, huh? You could just shave off all this pretty hair, stick on some electrodes. Record the brainwaves. Crack the safe with a playback. Beats hauling this whiny bitch around." He yanked hard at her hair. "Then you'd look like me," he crooned, licking her throat. "Only scared."

The rage almost ran him over. Noah forced it down. He'd make that piece of shit pay in blood for every humiliation. Later. When Caro was safe.

"Won't work," he said. "The sensors pick up body heat, blood flow and electrical fields, all keyed to her. Not my preference. I like to eliminate all witnesses. But shit happened, and I had to improvise."

"Big fail, fuckface. Right now, everything belongs to me. The girl, the safe, the bonds. You."

"Only until Mark Olund gets here," Noah said. "I'm telling you I can help you flatten him like the piece of shit that he is. Then you and I get to split some serious money."

The doubt on the guy's face was reflected in the frantic fluctuations of color around his head.

"One thing at a time," the guy said. "To start with, I want you restrained. You make me tense." He extended a hand without taking his eyes off Noah, feeling around for a canvas bag next to the bed. He pulled out thick zip ties and put them in Caro's hand. "First, take off your jacket and throw it toward me," he said to Noah. "Then turn around. Kneel. Put your hands behind your back. She puts the cuffs on you. I hold the gun to her head while she does it. Then she cuffs your ankles. One wrong move and she dies. Bye bye brainwaves. You follow me?"

"Yes," Caro said, when he prodded her with the gun barrel. "I hear you."

Noah shrugged off his jacket and tossed it. It landed halfway between them. His smartphone slid out of the pocket and onto the floor.

"Turn around!" the man barked. "Get down! Cross your wrists and keep them crossed!"

Noah sank to his knees. Echolocation formed an exact picture of where Caro and her captor were in space, as if he had eyes in the back of his head. Caro was moving. A masculine grunt and a sharp hiss of pain showed that her captor was on his feet as well.

Muted sounds. Zip ties scattered on the floor. A thud of a gun butt connecting with Caro's head again. A stifled grunt of pain.

He hung on to himself. Patience. Wait for it, goddamnit. *Wait.*

"Pick them up, you dumb cow, and don't drop them again," the guy snarled.

"You won't have to split the take with anyone but me, once Mark is dead," Noah said. "There's no one else to pay off. No witnesses but me. And her," he added, like an afterthought.

The other man hesitated. "What about my men?"

Noah shrugged.

"Shit!" He sounded irritated. "All of them?"

"You need a better crew," Noah remarked.

"So do you. And why did you stash her in that flophouse dump if she's the key to all that money?"

Noah stared straight ahead. "I was keeping an eye on her there. Neither one of us has a crew, but together we could take Mark. Are you in?"

There was a long silence as the man thought it over. "Ninety percent for me, ten for you," he said slowly. "Since I'm the one holding the gun."

"Get real," Noah said. "Fifty-fifty. You can't take down Olund without me."

"Maybe. Maybe not. That guy is one hard son of a bitch."

"So am I. Just keep in mind that it's him I want to kill and not you." Noah eased around to look at him. "Just look outside, if you want proof. I'm good at killing."

The thug was holding the gun to the back of Caro's neck and clutching a bedpost with the other hand. He studied Noah through slitted eyes. "Who the fuck are you, man?"

"Does it matter?"

"That's not an answer. Tie him up." He shoved Caro forward. "Move!"

She stumbled forward. He felt her cold fingers fumbling at his wrists, her hair swinging, brushing his forearms.

"Tighter," the man barked. "I want it to hurt. Now the feet."

Caro kneeled and struggled at his ankles with the zip tie until the guy was satisfied.

The guy pulled her roughly back against himself, his arm pressing down on her throat, the gun pressed to her temple. Noah turned his head.

"So?" Noah asked. "How about that forty million? Do we have a deal?"

"I didn't say that you could look at me, dickhead. I should just give you to Mark as a bonus. Bet he'd be happy to have you to play with."

"Put the gun down," Noah coaxed. "I'm restrained, and she's harmless."

"Don't tell me what to do," the man replied.

"We need her alive and functioning," Noah insisted.

"You keep saying that."

"Look at her," Noah said. "She's a basket case. The gun is overkill."

"Yeah," the other guy said, with a harsh laugh. "Right. Funny."

"She'll do whatever you say. Right?" Noah looked at Caro.

She drew in a hitching breath. "Yes," she whispered, through bluish lips.

"See?" Noah said. "She'll cooperate. I'm restrained. She and I both want to live. And all of us want that money."

Caro nodded.

Slowly, the guy lifted the gun barrel from her head.

Noah snapped the zip tie effortlessly and sprang up, twisting in the air. "Dive!" he yelled.

Caro hit the ground. Mark's thug opened fire. Bullets whizzed past Noah's cheek, but he evaded them, with his combat reflexes and his AVP. One barely clipped his ear. Others pocked the walls.

 He landed, slamming the man to the ground. The guy's gun skittered under the bed. He rammed his knee up toward Noah's groin.

Noah twisted to protect himself as the guy snatched up the bloodied knife he'd dropped on the floor earlier. He whipped it up.

Noah blocked the stabbing blow to his face, but his opponent's blade sliced through his sleeve and carved a gash in his arm. Noah yanked the knife from his pants pocket. With a yell, drove the notched blade down through his opponent's hand, pinning it to the floor.

The knife bit deep into the damp plywood.

The guy screamed, convulsing. Blood spread beneath his hand. He stabbed at Noah with his knife, but his wild, slashing strokes didn't reach, not with his other hand pinned to the ground.

Noah snagged the man's knife hand, torqued it . . . and crushed it. The knife fell.

Noah straddled the guy. That fuckhead had hit Caro. Cut her. Now he paid.

He started in on the guy's face. Then his ribs. Instinct and training took over, and he let it roar on through him like a flash flood—

. . . *Noah . . . Noah! Stop! It's enough! Stop it, goddamnit!*

The words came from faraway. Caro's voice. He fought his way back.

Those strange, rhythmic rasps were his own panting breaths. His throat was raw. He had a vague memory of screaming.

He stared down at the broken, unrecognizable man beneath him. Mark's bald, goateed thug was a gory mess. Blood gushed from his nose, his jaw was askew, his eye socket was crushed, trapping his eyelid so that it could not blink. His other eye watered, rolling frantically.

His own knuckles looked like raw meat.

"Noah?" Caro's voice was barely a whisper. "Are you OK?"

He nodded, struggling off the guy. Feeling weak. Just when he needed to be strong for her.

She grabbed him. His forehead pressed the cool skin of her belly, but just for a second. He had work to do. He heaved himself off the guy. Reached to touch his carotid artery.

There was a pulse, barely. He was shutting down. He saw it in the man's sig, too. No tears when this one went down the drain. "Dying," he said.

"Good." Her voice hardened. "Wish I'd done it myself."

"I killed the ones outside," he said. "Three more out there."

Caro got to her feet and swayed for a moment, clutching the bedpost for balance. Her eyes looked glassy, but he could see her fighting the drop in blood pressure by sheer force of will. "What now?" she asked. "I assume you don't want to involve the police."

"That's right," he said. "My DNA would confuse the living shit out of a crime lab. But Mark won't call the cops either when he shows up. This is his mess. Let him deal with it. We just need to get you away before he shows up."

Noah looked around and spotted a crumpled wrapper from a breakfast sandwich on the floor. He retrieved it, fished a pen from a pocket of his own jacket and smoothed the grease-stained paper out onto the window sill. "You write this," he said.

"Write what? Why me?"

"Mark might recognize my handwriting, even if I try to disguise it. I don't want to identify myself to him yet." He pushed the pen into her hand.

"OK." She poised it over the crumpled wrapper. "So?"

"Write, 'Oblio.chat. You're the Keyseeker. I'm the Keyholder. When I find you, we'll talk terms.' Just that. Nothing else."

She looked up, eyes wide and wary. "Terms? With Mark? Are you nuts?"

"We have to establish a point of contact. I'd finish this right now, if I could, but I'm not prepared. And I don't want you anywhere near him." They stared at each other. Finally, he made an impatient gesture. "Write it. Now. So we can get out of here."

She wrote it, asking him what was capped and what was not along the way. Noah crumpled it, bent down, and shoved the ball of paper into the dying man's mouth.

Caro turned her gaze away, shuddering.

His own jacket lay stuck to a thick smear of blood. Too bad. He would have liked to use it for Caro. He scooped it up anyway, along with his phone.

Her coat caught his eye in the corridor, crumpled and forgotten in a corner. He picked it up and draped the ugly thing over her shoulders. Her bare, bloodied feet looked so vulnerable, poking out from the frayed hems of her blood-spattered jeans. He hated that she had no shoes on. "Come on," he said shortly, tugging on her hand.

She followed him out the door, stopping short when she saw the bodies. The one by the door lay in the dirt, face turned to the side, mouth gaping. Buzzcut swayed from his tree, his rope creaking in the rising wind. She gazed at them without flinching, her face pale and stiff.

"There's another one behind their Jeep," he told her.

Noah dug car keys out of his jacket pocket, vaguely surprised they were still there. He pulled out his phone, and immediately called Sisko.

"Hey," Sisko's usually mellow voice had an edge to it. "So?"

"You can turn around," he said. "Go on home. It's handled."

He could hear Sisko sigh. "Ah. OK. How many did you have to take down?"

"There were only four. Mark wasn't there yet. He's on his way. I left him a note. Pointed him to a chatroom. We'll talk with him soon."

"Only four, huh?" Sisko grunted. "You're getting soft. You need challenge."

Noah glanced at Caro. "I have enough."

"By the way," Sisko said. "Don't go home. It's compromised. Use the Kirkland house. Someone found you. I swung by to pick up your guns, and the place was trashed."

"Oh. Yeah," Noah said. "About that. That wasn't, uh, Mark."

Sisko was silent for a moment, bewildered "Holy shit. *You* did that? To your own property? What the fuck? What happened? Did you have a combat program freakout? But you were the one who taught us to beat those! You wrote the book!"

Noah was too exhausted to tell him to shut the fuck up. "It ran me over."

"Do we need to do any clean-up?" Sisko asked. "Body bagging? Floor bleaching? Anything?"

"No, don't get near it. I don't know when Mark is coming."

"OK," Sisko said. "We'll meet you in Kirkland. Later."

Sisko hung up before Noah had a chance to tell the guy that he didn't need a welcoming committee. He looked into Caro's set face and bluish lips, and lifted her up into his arms. "I know you have a thing about this," he said. "But you need make an exception to your rule today."

She wrapped an arm around his shoulder. "I can walk," she told him. "I'm fine."

"You're barefoot," he said. "It'll take us five times as long to get to the car through those woods if you walk. We need to move fast."

"But aren't you tired?"

"It's what I'm made for," he said. "It's easy to carry you."

She sighed, and shifted in his arms, arranging herself more comfortably. "Whatever. Put me down if you get tired. Please."

Not likely. It took a while to bushwhack through the gullies and the thicker undergrowth, but he ate up the clear ground in a swift, easy lope on his way back to the clearing where he'd hidden the Mercedes. He opened the back seat, nudging her inside, and got in after her.

He sagged against the car seat. Smelling blood, the trees, his own sweat. Hearing only wind, and the rustling trees, and the loud galloping thuds of their heartbeats.

Caro put her hand on his, looking down when she felt the rough, torn skin and dried blood on his knuckles. "Noah." She sounded exhausted.

"Yeah," he said, taking her hand in his. "It was bad. But now it's over."

They sat for a moment, staring mutely down at the blood caked on their clasped hands. But she wasn't done. She looked up, wide green eyes meeting his.

"Why did you come for me?" she asked. "After what I did."

He was at a loss for a long moment. The part of him that could process a question like that was not working right now. AVP and his combat program and all his many mods could not help him with complicated shit like this.

"I don't know," he said. "I just did it. Without thinking. I had to."

"You didn't have to," she said. "You had the footage already. You had all that you needed from me."

He shook his head. "No," he said. "Not all."

Her gaze dropped, but she looked up at him again after a minute. "I still can't believe you did that for me."

There was an awkward pause. He shrugged. "The AVP is fucking my impulse control," he said. "I no longer give a shit if what I want is bad for me."

"But I'm not . . ." Her words trailed off, and her eyes flicked away, abashed.

He squeezed her hand. He'd been so angry at her before, but the fighting and killing burned all that away. He felt empty and hollow now.

"Well, you were crazy, to do that," she said, her voice muted. "But I'm glad."

He nodded, hoping she was done. No such luck.

"Mark's going to be all over your ass now," she said. "You know that, right?"

"Good," he said. "Bring him on. I cannot fucking *wait* to deal with him."

She looked startled. "Seriously?"

"Fuck, yeah. He has Luke. He hurt you. It's war, and he is going down."

He stared her down, his eyes full of challenge. His AVP sputtered along, the processor mostly burned out and needing rest and fuel to rev up again, but he could still see her sig a little bit.

That soft golden glow, filling up the car.

Like sunrise come early.

Chapter 23

IT COULDN'T BE real. Being alive at all was improbable. Let alone having been rescued by a gorgeous, valiant, more or less superhuman guy.

But here she was. Bloody, exhausted, and amazingly, alive.

Caro smelled the salt tang of his battle sweat, stared at his scabbed, battered fingers on the steering wheel. He'd come to her rescue. Saved her from her worst nightmares. And the sun had come up.

Noah gave her a quick, assessing glance. His face was pale, cheek scraped and bruised, shadowy eyes still reddened from the pepper spray. A red stain soaked his gray, torn-open sweatshirt sleeve.

"Noah! What happened to your arm?"

He glanced at it. "I got stabbed."

A modified man was still just a man, she thought. Pretending he wasn't hurt to look tough. "What if you need stitches?"

Noah shook his head. "It won't. It's clotting. Rapid cell repair is built in. And I'm pretty much immune to most pathogens and toxins. Even radiation is no biggie."

"Oh." She shook her head. "I don't want to watch you put that to the test."

"I fucking hope not." He started the car and maneuvered out over the bumpy terrain until he got onto the narrow road, handling the wheel stiffly and wincing as he shifted lightly in his seat. "Guns and knives are about all I can handle right now."

She looked closely at the dark, wet stain, making sure it wasn't spreading. "How did you find me?"

He stared straight out at the dirt road that wound through the trees. "Later for that."

She reached across the console and laid her hand on his thigh. The denim was damp with sweat and stiff with blood, but her fingers gripped the steely bulge of his thigh muscles. "Noah," she said. "We have to talk to each other. No more secrets."

His mouth tightened. "You'll be angry."

She sighed. "Please. At this moment, you can do no wrong. Just tell me."

"OK. If you insist. I geotagged you," he admitted. "With the tile that fell off the painting you liked. I stuck it in your coat pocket in your apartment. After we made love."

She stared at him, astonished.

"Look in your pockets."

She did. Both of them. Finding a bus ticket, a laundromat token, a button that had been missing in action, a couple receipts, a pack of spearmint gum . . . and something small, square and hard. She held it up.

"So?" His voice was defensive. "Yes, I'm controlling. And obsessive. I can't help it, so what the fuck? I knew you were in danger. I know what Mark is. What he could do to you. If you want to have a fight about this, go ahead."

He looked like he was bracing himself.

Caro reached out, and stroked the side of his face with her fingertips. "No," she said. "I don't. I can't believe what you just did for me. After I attacked you. And hurt your eyes. And stole your fucking car."

"Oh, yeah. The car," Noah muttered.

"It might still be there. I parked it in a tow zone on purpose."

"Don't make me laugh. I'm on the edge as it is."

She traced the shape of his cheekbone, feeling the velvety heat of his skin and his harsh beard scruff. His mouth was set in a tense line.

"Noah," she said. "I have something to say to you—"

He exhaled sharply. "Here we go. Here it comes."

"No, don't get nervous," she soothed. "This is a compliment. You are a world class bullshit artist. If lying were an Olympic event you would win the gold."

A wary grin flashed across his face. "Comes from growing up on the streets," he said. "Thank you. I feel proud. Even though I should be ashamed."

"Lying to that guy got us out alive. That's what I'm talking about."

He shrugged. "I was just blowing smoke."

"Yes. At gunpoint. Tied up, no less."

Noah looked at her sideways. "OK, so I'm really good at it. But what's your point? Are you worried that I'll lie to you?"

"You already have. I'm just thinking out loud."

Noah groaned under his breath. "Go ahead. Beat me up."

"No. Just saying that you're a different person when you lie. You project a different frequency."

He frowned. "Sounds like I'm ready for the psych ward."

"Not at all. And trust me, I'd know."

"You would, huh?"

"Yes," she said. "I wouldn't recognize the man talking to me."

Noah braked suddenly, turning onto a narrow, half-hidden road overgrown by stubby evergreens that scraped against the sides of the car. Noah killed the engine.

They sat in silence. Noah looked away from her. It looked as if he were struggling to breathe.

Was that why he stopped? Caro undid her seatbelt and leaned towards him, trying gently to turn his face back toward her. He resisted, so she just kissed his cheekbone, his hair. Tasted salt, grit. Blood.

"Don't do that," he said harshly.

"It won't kill you, Noah."

"I'm not so sure about that." He turned toward her, spread open her coat and pressed his face against her naked breasts. His breath was a hot caress against her bare skin. "Maybe not yet."

She wrapped her arms around his neck and buried her nose in his sweat-stiffened hair.

"I want you," he said.

They kissed, madly, passionately. No more talk. Just gasps, sighs.

He tasted like life itself. Heat and salt, fire and blood. She was starving for him. His hand cupped her tangled hair, and she clung to him, trying to get closer. Frantic need yawned, a fiery chasm that could swallow them. She caressed the hard contours of his body until she found the unyielding bulge of his cock, trapped in his jeans.

He growled low in his throat, and pushed her suddenly away. On her knees, half naked, nipples tight in the chilly dawn. They panted, wildly aroused by the strange energy flaring between them.

"We need to cool it." His voice was uneven.

"Please," she whispered.

"No. Mark is on his way, and he wants to eat your brain. I shouldn't have pulled off the road."

She nodded, resigned, and put the seatbelt on.

Caro watched the landscape slide by, amazed at how calm she felt. All the horrible things she'd just seen were burned into her visual memory but for some reason they stayed under control, not taking over her visual field in hallucinations as they so often did when she was violently stressed.

Noah Gallagher, in all his glory, charging in to rescue her . . . that was an image more compelling than terror, blood and death.

The thought steadied her. She hung on to it.

*   *   *

Caro awoke from a restless half-sleep as the car slowed down and stopped.

They were parked outside a modern mansion on a wooded hillside. Simple but luxurious, with walls of glass on all sides, big decks and patios, and a long, winding driveway. One other car was parked there. A black van. "Where are we?" she asked.

"One of our safe houses," Noah said.

It resembled his own place. Which made sense, she supposed.

Sisko and Zade sauntered out the front door just as she got out of the car. Looking worried, they both gave her and Noah a thorough onceover.

OK. She'd had better days, been better dressed. She pulled the shabby coat tighter, and held her head up as high as she could. Screw them both.

"Jesus, man. You look like shit," Zade said to Noah. "Especially your eyes. What happened out there?"

"Long story," Noah said wearily. "Not now."

He took her hand and led her inside. "Make yourself at home," he said.

The inside of this house was beautiful. Understated, oversized furniture that looked custom-made was highlighted by austere lamps that cast a rich glow over equally rich fabrics in soothing earth tones. Decorator coordinated, to be sure. Exactly what she would expect to see in a Noah Gallagher crash pad.

She heard Sisko and Zade come in as she wandered around the place, enjoying the silky smooth texture of the wide plank flooring under her bare dirty feet, the tastefully arranged furniture, the big, airy kitchen with top of the line appliances. Huge plate glass windows offered beautiful views of the surrounding greenery on all sides.

"I'm taking her up to the master bedroom to settle in," Noah said to his men, who stood there looking awkward. "Zade, get that shit-eating grin off your face and call Hannah. Tell her Caro needs stuff. Clothes, whatever else she doesn't have right now. And tell her to arrange for some food. Something really good, and a whole lot of it. We're going to lie low for a while."

"Excuse me?" Caro said. "You're ordering *what*?"

"Clothes," Noah repeated, as if the answer was obvious, gesturing toward her bloodstained jeans and coat.

"Hannah's going to enjoy that," Zade observed. "Unlimited shopping, with your credit card? A dream come true. Watch out."

"For once in her life, her shopping mania will be good for something." He looked at Sisko and Zade. "Sorry you guys didn't get to see any action today, but things should get interesting soon. When Mark gets to town."

"Ah, yeah. About that," Zade said pointedly. "Can we talk?"

"Later," Noah said. "Soon. Let me get her settled. Then we'll talk." He glanced at Sisko. "Keep monitoring the surveillance video feeds while I'm upstairs."

"Love to." Sisko rolled his eyes. "Thanks, boss."

"About time you took a turn," Zade observed. "I'm always on call."

Caro left them to their bickering and headed up the stairs. Noah ran up behind her and swept her into his arms again, carrying her into the big master bedroom.

"Let's get you cleaned up." He shrugged off his jacket, and disappeared into the bathroom. Soon she heard the roar of water jets filling a capacious tub. Scented steam floated out the door. Lavender, honeysuckle, a hint of manly mint? Nice, whatever it was.

She smiled at him when he emerged from the bathroom. "Mmmm. Smells good. OK, you can take care of me."

He unbuttoned her coat, tossing it away and smoothing his hands slowly down over her bare shoulders as he looked her body over, before pulling her gently into the bathroom. He pulled swabs, gauze and ointment out of the medicine cabinet.

"Let's see those cuts," he said. "Lift your chin."

He examined the nicks at the base of her throat, washing and disinfecting them, treating every little wound with his usual focused intensity. He smoothed adhesive bandages over them, and pressed a slow, searching kiss against the nape of her neck.

Her nipples tightened. But she had to return the favor. "Now you."

He sighed. "If you must."

"Sweatshirt off, Mr. Gallagher."

He tried. "Can't roll up the sleeve. It's stuck to my arm. You do it."

Slowly and carefully, she peeled the ripped, bloodstained sleeve up and away from his forearm. The gash underneath looked messy and painful, but Noah was stoic, pulling the sweatshirt all the way off as soon as she was done. No longer bleeding at all. Just as he'd said.

Avoiding the still raw but rapidly healing tissue, she rinsed the dried blood off with careful pats of a wrung-out washcloth, and saw to his scabbed knuckles as well. She smoothed antibiotic ointment over both wounds and bandaged them.

"This is terrible," she fussed. "I'd bet anything you need stitches. And a tetanus booster, and serious antibiotics."

"No need," he said calmly. "It won't get infected, and it'll heal very fast."

"But it'll leave a scar!"

He let out a short laugh and glanced down at his heavily scarred torso. "Oh, no. Anything but that."

"You should see a doctor," she snapped.

"Look who's talking."

Before she could reply, he pulled her closer, cupping the back of her head. His masterful kiss changed almost instantly into something lingering, pleading. His tenderness melted her.

When their lips parted, she looked away, and sniffed back tears. "Don't kiss me just to shut me up," she said, her voice wobbling. "That's unfair."

He shrugged and bent down to turn off the thundering jets. There were still surging bubbles below the surface of the water. She wanted to sink into it almost as much as she wanted him to kiss her again.

"Your bath is ready. But before you get in, I have something for you," he said.

Apprehension gripped her. "What's that?"

He pulled the flash drive from Luke Ryan's lake house out of his pocket and held it out to her. "We didn't really flush it," he said. "I'm sorry I jerked you around."

She just stared at him, open-mouthed.

"I copied it, of course, so that we can analyze every second of it," he said. "This one's yours. But as a favor to me, don't take it to the police yet. Let me see if I can resolve this somehow, without exposing us all. Please."

She couldn't even trust herself to speak. She didn't know what to think.

Noah went on, his voice gruff and uncertain. "But, ah. It's your call. Like you said, you found it, and you paid for it. And if you need to use it . . . well. Whatever."

She curled his fingers back down over the flash drive and pushed his hand away.

"Thanks, Noah," she said. "Keep it safe for me."

"OK. Thanks." He put it back into his pocket, and kissed her forehead.

It felt like the seal on a truce.

He started in on the buttons of her jeans. When they lay in a crumpled pile with her underwear and the remnants of her slashed open T-shirts, he helped her into the tub. In a startling rush, she became aware of her body again. Her nakedness. The hot amber flash of his eyes made her heart speed and brought a burning flush to her face, a tingle to her nipples and between her legs. His eyes dragged over her, lingering.

Instant energy pulsed through her. A deep inner heat. It made her head rise and her back straighten and her shoulders go back. Boobs proudly out. On display. *Take that.* Nipples tightening eagerly, as if his ravenous gaze were a skillful, caressing touch.

There was an impressive bulge in his pants. She wondered if it had been there all along, or if she'd just woken up to it now.

"Coming in?" she asked.

He didn't answer, but images flashed through her mind, just as she knew they were flashing through his. The caressing lap of warm water over flushed, gleaming skin, and sloshing against the tub as she wrapped herself around him, straddling him, kissing him. All the while penetrated and tenderly rocked by the slick, rhythmic thrusts of his cock inside her. This tub wasn't as big as the one at the lake house, but more than big enough for anything they could dream up.

His mouth tightened. "Not a good idea."

She could have screamed in frustration. "Please?" she urged. "Isn't Sisko downstairs, keeping watch?"

"Yes. But I'm too jacked up to relax. I want to patrol the perimeter with an AK-47 right now."

She sank down into the water very slowly, eyes locked with his. The heat of the water embraced her skin, inch by slow, taunting inch. Her hair touched the water and spread out on the surface like a lily pad before sinking down. She dipped down to her neck, and then rose up again, letting her gleaming breasts bob right at the surface. "I want to be with you," she said. "I want to feel you. Inside me. Right now."

He let out a low, rasping groan. "Oh, fuck, Caro. Not fair."

"Nope," she said. "Suffer if you want to. Or . . . not. You decide."

Noah let out a shuddering sigh and kneeled behind her. He leaned over the tub, smoothing the wet hair off her shoulders, and sudsed up his hands with scented cleansing gel, slowly massaging it over her shoulders and chest. Drifts of scented foam floated out onto the bathwater. "Lean back," he said. "Let me wash your hair."

That was such a delicious sensation, she could almost reconcile herself to the forced waiting. She floated in the hot water with his strong fingers massaging her scalp. Gazing up at his gorgeous face, fiercely intent upon the task of washing her hair.

She made sure her breasts were bobbing right at the surface. Pink-tipped, gleaming-wet islands in the foam. For his viewing pleasure. Sweet torture.

He took the torture stoically, kept his focus, refusing to yield. When it was time to get out, she rose slowly. Dripping. Succulent. Alluring. He remained in full control of himself, though he did seem to have silently decided that playing the part of the mouthwatering sex god bath attendant was a reasonable compromise. He was naked to the waist, which could only have been improved by him being stark naked.

But naked to the waist was already a hyperstimulation to all her senses. He was so big and powerful, with that wild predator glow in his eyes, looming over her protectively with the towel. Squeezing water out of her hair, turning her, swabbing off the drops of water beading her skin with long, slow, caressing strokes and pats. Making sure there was no spot left untouched.

Then he positioned her naked in front of the bathroom mirror and just stood there behind her for a moment, their eyes locked in the foggy reflection. She wasn't sure if it was him, moving forward, or herself leaning back, but soon they were touching. His hand clasping her, stroking her belly. Creeping up . . . and then stopping.

He grabbed the towel. Wrapped it around her. So damn close. Stubborn hard ass.

"Let me comb your hair," he said gruffly.

Fine. She watched Noah's blurry reflection as he slowly and patiently worked a comb through her hair, never once making her flinch.

He took his own sweet time. When he was done, her hair was almost dry, and so was the mirror. It reflected them with crystalline clarity, but all she could look at was his hungry eyes. She craved that bright, luminous amber glow. It meant joy, pleasure, power. It connected her with all the strength she had left.

Noah put down the comb, and ran his hands gently over her shoulders. The towel had come loose, so he tossed it away.

"Should I get dressed?" she asked. "Do you have a robe?"

He sank his fingers into her hair and separated the strands, draping them. "Yeah, but I don't want you to wear it. You're more beautiful like this. You're a goddess."

On impulse, she trapped his hands, and pressed them against her breasts.

Noah went rigid. As if he was afraid to breathe.

She couldn't breathe, either. But he hadn't pulled his hands away. They were so big and warm. Her skin tingled madly at the contact. Heat bloomed in her chest, sweeping up until her face was poppy red. His fingers curled, stroked in tender circles.

His face was a taut mask, but the hot glow of his eyes betrayed him. "Caro," he murmured. "Don't push me."

"I want you," she said. "I want to look into your eyes, while we make love. It feels incredible."

He looked wary. "What do my eyes have to do with anything?"

"That thing your eyes do, when your AVP is working," she said. "The way light gets caught in them, and flashes out. I just love that."

"Oh." He opened his fingers slightly and trapped her nipples, tugging.

"It makes me all hot and bothered," she whispered.

He seemed puzzled. "That's the first time anyone ever . . . oh, never mind."

"Tell me," she urged.

"Just the idea that someone could actually want to look into my eyes . . . it's strange."

"Not strange," she told him. "Beautiful." She covered her hands with her own, arching her back to heighten the sensual pressure and rubbing her ass against the thick, hot bulge in his pants.

Noah dragged in a harsh breath, his fingers flexing, stroking her. "Just tell me what you want." His voice was rough.

"You," she said. "Now."

"Jesus, Caro," he muttered. "You know just how to yank my chain."

Oh, yes. She exulted silently, took one of his hands, kissed it, and moved it down to her belly. Then lower.

His fingers tangled eagerly in the puff of damp ringlets, teasing and petting and parting her. He groaned when he found her already slick and hot. Ready.

"Those eyes," she murmured. "Told you."

She arched her back with a soft moan as he pressed his lips to her shoulder, her neck, kissing, licking. His hand slid, stroking and delving into her slick channel.

She squeezed his hand between her thighs, like she wanted to trap him there, as he slowly, expertly teased her closer to an erotic edge . . .

294

And then took her all the way over it. *Yes. Oh, yes. Ohhhhh* . . .

A blinding flash of oblivion. Intense pleasure throbbed voluptuously through her.

Her eyes fluttered open to see him still holding her tightly against himself.

Caro shifted, putting both hands on the edge of the bathroom sink, and bent over. Standing on tiptoe, legs apart, in silent invitation.

Noah stared down at her posed body, his color high. He stroked his hands slowly down over her hips. "You have bruises." His rough voice was concerned. Still.

"Make me forget about them," she said. "You're the only one who can."

He opened his belt, then his pants, shoving them down, and finally, she felt the blunt pressure of his cockhead, prodding at her sensitive folds. He swirled it around in that hot well—and drove inside her all at once.

They both cried out at that moment of exquisite intimacy. She felt like a flower blooming wide open, a blaze of colors, and with each caressing stroke inside her, he became another color blending into her where their bodies joined. Molten, marvelous.

Each stroke was a lash of erotic pleasure. Each thrust propelled her deeper into her own wildness. She braced herself for all that he was giving her while still craving more. Biting her lip to keep from screaming at how shockingly good it felt.

Pleasure swelled . . . and then erupted, overwhelming her.

Afterwards, they couldn't look at each other for a long while. He bent over her, spent, his cock still throbbing. She steadied herself against his body, loving the feel of his weight, and the ebbing sensation of his explosive release.

Finally, he withdrew and fastened his pants. She swayed, clutching the sink for balance. He caught her tightly against himself, hungrily kissing the curve of her neck.

"Wild thing," he murmured.

She almost choked on a burst of startled laughter. Her, wild?

But the more she thought about it, the more she liked it. Wild was good. Wild was hot, wild was strong. She needed wildness to survive.

"Fuck being tame," she said.

His answering grin was so beautiful. Lingering on his face. Always before his smile had fled so quickly, as if afraid to be caught in the act. Not this time.

"I'm going to run downstairs for a while," he said. "I promised to debrief Sisko and Zade on what happened out there. I'll come back up soon. You get some rest."

She stood there for a moment after the bathroom door shut after him, staring at her own feverishly bright eyes and flushed cheeks. She stared down at her battered, scratched hands, clutching the shining white porcelain sink. Rocked by feelings, too strong to suppress, too sweet to deny. Crazy wild feelings she was afraid to examine.

Ever since Tim's death, she'd been so careful to organize her life so that she didn't have to feel afraid for anyone but herself. She'd just plod along on her lonely quest, and if the powers of darkness won out, hell. Everybody had to bite the dust sometime. And at least the damage would be limited to her alone.

That had been her strategy so far. Such as it was.

But Noah had dragged Mark's attention onto himself by brute force, just to keep her company. She could hardly believe he was for real. He wanted to protect her, bind her wounds, buy her clothes, wash her hair, fuck her senseless.

And make her care. When it was just too goddamn dangerous for her to risk it.

Falling in love was all she needed to make her destruction complete.

Chapter 24

"HEY." HANNAH SHOVED her way through the door with difficulty, what with all the shopping bags. The expensive kind made of fancy thick paper with silken cord handles. Silver, cream, pastels, embossed with velvety patterns. Matching tissue paper poked out of their tops.

"What are you doing here?" Noah demanded. "I said to have stuff delivered!"

"It is being delivered. By me." Hannah looked around. "Where is she?"

"Resting upstairs. She needs peace and quiet." He looked at the size of her haul with disapproval. "Holy shit, Hannah. Seriously?"

"Just following orders," she said. " Everything a girl needs, Zade said. She just went through hell on earth. The least I could do was get her some nice lingerie. A little high end denim. Some cashmere and silk. It soothes the soul."

He glanced at the bags, feeling vaguely that this was going to get him into trouble with Caro, causing more problems than it solved. His own damn fault for involving Hannah, who always had to put her own stamp on everything.

"Besides, you never give me anything to do. If I don't get to kick some bad guy ass, I'll kick the living shit out of your credit card instead. And I didn't just buy clothes. There's toiletries, perfume, hair stuff and makeup. Hope you have nice big shelves in that bathroom, buddy."

Noah sighed. "Did you have to take this as a personal challenge?"

She gave him a cold look. "You didn't call me to help."

"Of course not. I had no idea what we'd be getting into—"

"Neither did Zade or Sisko," she said. "But they came because you called. Exactly like I would have." Her whiskey brown eyes were full of hurt.

"Hannah, don't," he said, frustrated.

"You think I'm still nine years old," she said. "And you still feel guilty about taking me to Midlands. But you know what, Noah? I survived. I'm as tough as the rest of you."

She fell silent, waiting, but Noah was spared the necessity of a reply by Caro's voice, floating down from above them. "Hey, you two."

Caro stood on the landing above, bundled up into the thick terrycloth robe she'd found in the bathroom and leaning over the railing, her hair dangling down. "What's all that stuff?"

Hannah held up her bags. "Your interim wardrobe," she explained. "And there's more on the way. Hope you don't mind."

Caro watched Sisko stagger in, barely visible beneath bales of plastic-swathed goods. "Hannah, a pair of jeans and a sweatshirt from Target would have been fine!"

"No way," Noah surprised himself by saying. "You need nice things."

Hannah turned a startled look on her brother, and laughed. "Finally, something we agree on," she said. "Caro, look at it this way. If you're going to do battle with the powers of darkness, you should look as hot as possible while you're doing it."

Caro rolled her eyes. "That's just silly. And extravagant."

"No, it isn't," Hannah said firmly. "So pick out whatever fits and looks best on you, which I bet will be everything, because I know what I'm doing."

Caro tried to catch Noah's eye without success. Hannah noticed.

"He's totally on board with this," she assured her. "Right, Noah?"

He gave his sister a pained look. She ignored it, turning to Sisko. "Did you get everything out of the car?"

Sisko lay down the bundles. "Yup. Want me to take it upstairs?"

"I'll do it." Noah loaded himself up with Hannah's purchases, tossing a big, puffy bagged thing perched precariously on top. "What the hell is that? It's really light."

"An excellent down parka," Hannah said. "And mukluks."

He whipped his head around. "What the fuck are mukluks?"

"Snow boots." Hannah followed him upstairs with a stack of shoeboxes. She stopped at the landing and rested her hand on Caro's shoulder. "Don't say no. I shopped my ass off for you."

"I appreciate it. I really do."

Hannah smiled. "And Caro, in case you haven't noticed, my brother is rich. He makes huge money, and then his money makes more money, while he's not even looking. He's insanely good at generating money. In fact, he's insanely good at a whole lot of things."

"Yeah, I noticed that today," Caro said. "Is that because of Midlands, too? I mean . . . the incredible combat skills?"

Hannah stared at her, and dropped two shoeboxes. "He told you about Midlands?"

"Of course I told her." Noah pushed past her, kicking aside the spilled shoes and packaging. "She saw the video with Mark and Luke. What was she supposed to think? That he used a voodoo spell?"

"But I . . but you . . ." Her voice trailed off for a bewildered moment. "But you just met her!"

"That's true. But she's one of us by now," he heard himself say.

His sister's wide brown eyes darted from him to Caro, shimmering with tears.

He heard a car outside, which was as good an excuse as any for a quick retreat.

"Sounds like someone's here," he said. "I'll be downstairs."

The door flew open as he got to the bottom of the stairs. Zade shoved through it, loaded up with takeout bags that smelled amazing.

"What the hell is this?" he complained. "Why did you come back?"

"You need fuel," Zade said. "I found a good taqueria. Eat with us or starve alone, you ungrateful son of a bitch."

"I want the place quiet for Caro. She's still in shock."

"Hannah's taking care of her. And we'll be as quiet and gentle as fluffy little lambs," Sisko said, emerging from the kitchen. He grabbed the taqueria bags. "Go back to the car and get the beer," he told Zade. "I'll just get this food set up in the dining room."

Noah stood there for a while, at a loss. Activity bustled around him. Soft female laughter came from the bedroom upstairs. The popping sound of beers being opened eventually came from the kitchen. Zade and Sisko clinked bottles.

Bizarrely, the place had taken on a party mood.

Zade appeared, and shoved a beer into his hand. "Drink up. You did good today. We were just toasting the fact that your life has finally begun. And about fucking time."

"Huh?" He stared blankly at his friend. "What is that supposed to mean?"

The other two men exchanged telling glances.

Sisko finally took pity on him. "It means we're tired of watching you knock yourself out trying to protect us. Especially since Luke got taken. Here you are, finally doing something for yourself. We've never seen you do that. Since we've known you."

"That's bullshit," he mumbled.

"True thing," Zade said firmly.

"And we like this new development," Sisko announced.

"Which one?" He was baffled. "You mean, me almost getting myself killed? Putting us all in danger?"

Sisko waved away that inconsequential detail. "I mean, you going nuts, kicking ass, giving a shit. It's great. A messy, stupid, all-around bad idea, but we like it. A lot." Sisko took a long swallow of his beer, wiped his grinning mouth, and added, "We are entertained."

"Drink," said Zade. "Here's to fucking up your life like you mean it."

Noah was too tired to think of anything to say in reply. He lifted the beer. Drank.

It tasted great.

Chapter 25

"WHAT WAS THAT all about?" Caro asked. She didn't want to go through all the bags and boxes dumped on the bed where Hannah was sitting.

Hannah sniffed, and dabbed at her eyes. "It's just that Noah's always been so intense about keeping the Midlands story a secret," she said. "He's so paranoid."

"Knowing him, there has to be a good reason," Caro said.

"Yeah, there is. He's afraid that Obsidian will come after us. He's never told a single soul about what happened, or allowed any of us to tell, either. And he spilled the whole thing to you, after what? Two days?"

"Today makes three, I think," Caro said, distractedly.

Hannah shook her head. "It's strange, that's all. That he trusts you. Noah never trusted anyone. Not even when he was a kid. That was how we survived."

"You mean at Midlands?"

"And before," Hannah said. "He kept me and Asa alive for months, before we ended up there. They scrounged money or stole stuff to sell. Then he amped it up. Wouldn't tell me how. He's crazy smart. This was before Obsidian jacked his brain up to the stratosphere. And they were going to euthanize him." Her expression was stony. "Almost all the boys in our group were on that kill list."

"But why? Why kill him? Or any of you?" Caro asked.

"They went too far," Hannah said. "They got scared. Noah was light years smarter than those assholes to begin with, and they just kept maximizing him. When they realized what they'd done, they panicked. But Noah made his move just in time. Saved our asses." She shook her head. Her eyes were haunted. "That was a bad day."

Caro's neck prickled with horror as she imagined it, all too vividly.

"Noah's a natural leader," Hannah went on. "And he's a good guy. He saw kids exploited and hurt, and he fought back. Kinda got to be a habit with him, I guess."

"I don't doubt that for one second," Caro said wryly.

"Yeah, well, he still tries to do most of the fighting, even though we're all grown up, more or less. And then you came along. Looks like he feels responsible for you, too." She wiped her eyes and gave Caro a tremulous smile. "You're lucky. We were lucky. Believe me, I know."

So, Caro thought. Noah was used to being a hero. Nothing more personal, or specific, to it. Like love. Clearly not a Noah concept.

"What about you?" she asked Hannah. "What did they do to you in that place?"

Hannah let out a short, harsh laugh. "Oh, plenty. Noah didn't say anything to you about our mods?"

"Just about his eyes," Caro said. "And some ominous hinting."

"Yeah, it would take a lot of telling. His mods are extreme. My main thing is frequency processing. I have brain implants that let me send, receive and jam various frequencies with my mind. I don't need any hardware."

"You mean inside your skull? Right in your brain?"

"Yeah, they drilled a lot of holes in my head. Not fun. But I wasn't on their kill list yet when Noah busted us out. Me and some of the others were younger, so the researchers held back a little. We got a shitload of implants. Intensive brain stims."

"It's a miracle you're alive," Caro said.

Hannah shrugged. "I try not to think about it. So when did he tell you about Midlands?"

"After you left last night," Caro said. "I saw his scars the night before."

"Yeah, we all have them," Hannah said ruefully. "Some are from rebellion day. Some are from the do-it-yourself surgery right afterwards."

"I'm not sure I want to know." Caro looked at her apprehensively.

"You might need to know someday," Hannah said.

It sounded like a warning. Caro nodded. "Go on."

"Noah and Sisko and Luke had hacked into Obsidian's computer system, and memorized all our geotagged implants. After we escaped, I jammed our internal frequencies until Noah could get bandages and disinfectant, and sterilize his pocket knife. Then he cut them out." She shuddered. "There were a lot."

"My God," Caro whispered.

"Yeah. But Noah got it done, and he kept us all in one piece afterwards. I don't know how. Figured out how to damp down our augmented sensory processing so that we wouldn't go batshit. We survived, more or less sane. Most of us. We lost a few." A shadow flitted across her face.

"Did you still have . . . any . . ." Caro's voice trailed off. "Sorry. Shouldn't ask."

"Yeah. Some. There was nothing Noah could do about the implants inside my skull, but I could jam those myself at will, so they were no big deal. I had four implants on each shoulder, six on each of my upper arms, a few on my thighs. Nothing compared to the boys."

Part of her didn't want to ask more questions, but the rest of her won out. She sat down on the bed next to Hannah. "Tell me," she said.

Hannah exhaled slowly, shaking her head. "They went absolutely nuts on the boys," she said. "Plugged them full of anything and everything. No long-term strategy. We weren't scientific experiments so much as toys that they didn't care about breaking. Nobody was looking. The psychos did whatever they wanted."

Caro could think of nothing to say that wasn't hopelessly inadequate, but Hannah didn't seem afraid of silence. In fact, she almost seemed to have forgotten that Caro was there. She was deep in the grip of some haunting memory.

Caro sat next to her and waited quietly.

After a few moments, Hannah shook herself out of her reverie. "Sorry," she said. "Didn't mean to stress you out with that old shit. I'll go downstairs and see if the boys are on top of dinner prep. Come down when you're ready."

"OK."

Caro sat for a while after the bedroom door shut, trying to make space in her mind for this new info. Noah had told her the story the night before, but she'd been too angry to let it in before. To feel any of it. Now she felt everything.

She got up, jittery and restless, and rummaged through the shopping bags, pulling out stuff at random. Underwear. Some jeans. Socks. A bra, just the right size. A warm sweater.

The clothes felt good when she pulled them on. Good fit, top quality. Hannah had even nailed her shoe size. She dabbed on some minimal makeup, brushed her hair, and looked into the mirror, trying to connect what she saw to how she felt. Her face was thinner, and she had assorted cuts and bruises, but she looked very like her old self.

But from the inside, she barely recognized herself. Everything was different. Everything she had been before was gone. She'd felt so empty.

But not now. After that intense encounter with Noah, she was feeling a sense of . . . well, she could almost call it hope for the future. If she dared to.

But she didn't, really. That would be tempting the gods. She'd rather not be noticed by them right now. She was getting enough attention already.

She went down the stairs and headed toward the lights, smells and murmur of conversation coming out of the dining room. Noah, Hannah, Zade and Sisko were seated at a table covered with foil takeaway platters heaped with fragrant Mexican food.

It was always a fresh zing to her senses, seeing Noah after having looked away for any length of time, even a minute. Every sensual, starkly chiseled, larger-than-life detail of him. He seemed bigger, denser, brighter than everything around him.

He reached out and clasped her hand, tugging until she moved around the table to sit next to him.

"Thank God you're here." Zade said. "Noah wouldn't let us start without you. We've been sitting here, snorting flavored steam."

"Should have gone right ahead," she said.

"She's here, so stop whining," Noah squeezed her hand under the table. His hand was so big and strong and warm. Her own tingled deliciously in it.

The food was very good, but she couldn't eat very much of it, or follow the conversation. Considerable good-natured teasing was directed at Noah, but he ignored it, eating his tacos deftly with one hand while clasping her thigh under the table with the other. The contact made every luscious detail of their recent lovemaking run through her mind again, over and over, making her breathless and muddled.

Eventually, the conversation turned to her pepper spray, which sat displayed on the kitchen bar along with the other items that had been in her coat pockets. Plus her wig, her mouth thing, the tile from the Delaunay. Not her phone, though. That had been in the hidden pocket way down in the seam.

"Where's my coat?" she asked.

Everyone abruptly stopped talking. Noah answered. "Down in the garage, sealed in a garbage bag. You don't need it anymore. You have new stuff."

"I'll decide for myself about my own things." She tugged her hand out of his grip and left the kitchen, heading down the staircase to the garage.

She untied the plastic bag that sat next to the trash bag and fished the filthy thing out. It was bloody and trashed, but she'd made it herself, and she was still attached to it.

She turned it inside out and slid her fingers into the small hidden pocket she'd sewn into the lining, and pulled out her phone. There was a smidgen of battery power left, so she checked the log. Six unanswered calls and a voice message, all from Gareth.

She accessed the voice mail as she went back up the stairs. Gareth's recorded voice was so high and thin, she barely recognized it.

"Caro, I don't know what you're mixed up in, but a gang of thugs just assaulted me in my home! They wanted your address, and I'm so sorry, but I gave it to them. So look, if you're there, run, and if you're not there, don't ever go back. And Caro, I hate to say this because I really like you, but just stay away from me, OK? Like, forever. Your problems are too big for me to deal with. Have a nice life. If you can."

The message ended. Her coat thumped to the floor at her feet.

Noah joined her, in a few swift strides. "I didn't see the phone," he said.

"Hidden pocket," she said.

"Turn it off," Noah said. "Your sig just went nuts. What happened?"

"Gareth. My boss at Bounce." She struggled to catch her breath. "Mark's guys found him. Roughed him up. Gareth gave them my address. That was how they found me. He called to warn me. Left a voicemail."

He held out his hand for the phone. "Let me hear it."

His eyes were fiercely thoughtful as he listened to the message. Beard stubble shadowed his jaw, his chin.

"It's happening again," Caro said. "Tim, then Bea, now Gareth. You and your family are next. I thought Gareth would be safe. I walked into his agency right off the street and asked him for a job. He had no past connection to me. He never knew my real name. No one but you knows my name! How the *hell* did they connect him to me?"

Noah pried open her phone, pulled out the battery and tossed it onto the table. "Did you do artwork for Gareth? At Bounce?"

"Of course," she said. "But not as a designer. Nothing that I took credit for. Not even using a fake name. Let alone my legal name."

"But you did do design work for him," he said. "Credited or not."

"Well, yeah. It was a costume shop. I built costumes, made masks."

"Were those featured online?"

"Of course. Theater or dance productions are all over social media."

He shrugged. "So he saw your stuff online."

"But I never got credited. I made sure of that. I'm not stupid!"

"Mark would recognize your style if he'd seen your work even once," Noah said. "So would I."

She bit her lip. "Gareth took a chance on me. Now he's paying for it."

"He'll be OK," Noah said. "They have no reason to hurt him now. According to the message, he gave them what they wanted. Now those men are dead, and Mark has me to think about. He won't bother Gareth." He stroked Caro's hair. "But I didn't want for us to discuss this now. You need rest."

"Rest," she repeated. "Right, Noah. A soul-sucking psycho maniac is searching high and low for everyone my life has ever touched so that he can punish the whole world with an army of lethal mutant freaks, and I'm supposed to *rest.*"

Noah shrugged. "Well, for what it's worth, we're lethal mutant freaks, too. The good kind." His arm went around her shoulders, squeezing gently. "We'll work on this after you've had twelve hours of sleep." He turned back toward the dining room. "Everyone else, clear out of here," he called.

"Except for me, to stand guard and man the monitors," Sisko called back. "Right. Lucky me."

Caro headed up the stairs. Noah followed her. Inside the bedroom, he flicked on a light just like those in his house. Dim lighting, as soft as firelight.

He pulled a lens case out of his pocket, removed his lenses, and turned that gorgeous, unearthly flash of amber in his eyes directly upon her.

The probing sensation was unbearable. "Quit it, Noah."

"I'm just looking at your sig," he said. "You're so fucking beautiful without those damn lenses. It's wild."

Wild. That word anchored her. After a moment, she could breathe deeply again and gaze right back at that uncanny luminosity. Wildness. It spoke of full moons, huge spaces, sweeping winds. A timber wolf running through snow.

And power. Strength, from deep within.

He made her feel it. It grounded her, straightened her back up, sent a rush of energy through her whole body.

Noah sensed the shift in her, and heat crackled and leaped between them instantly. His raw sexual sorcery was so potent. She couldn't get enough.

She kicked off the shoes, the socks. Peeled the tight sweater off her head, and tossed her hair back. Shimmied out of the jeans and stood there in only bra and panties.

"Come here," she said.

He came closer. "I'm yours for the taking," he said. "Anytime, anywhere."

"Good," she whispered as he approached. "Right now, then. Right here."

"Nice lingerie," he said. "Take it off."

"You do it."

Her words were cut off by his hungry kiss.

They only stopped long enough for him to rip off his sweatshirt. He pressed her against him, unclasping the bra, tossing it away, clearly enjoying the way the tips of her breasts rubbed against his broad, scarred chest. He hooked his thumbs into her panties, nudging her back until she ran into the bed and sat down on it, bouncing.

He crouched by the bed to peel the panties off her ankles, then knelt between her knees and pressed hot, demanding kisses against her inner thigh, caressing her knees with his warm hands. The contact left a shimmering glow that spread out, everywhere.

"I want to go down on you." He stroked the seam of her labia, just a slow, tender swipe with his thumb, up and down. That teasing contact and the aching hum of tension between them made silky wetness pool inside her. Her body's instinctive demand.

Noah's fingers slipped inside her and emerged gleaming, slick and hot. He made a low growling sound of pure satisfaction and sucked on them hungrily.

"So sweet," he muttered. "You taste amazing."

He put his mouth to her, his lips and tongue lavishly caressing every tender fold, lapping them, loving them.

And all she could do was give into it, lost and incoherent with the exquisite erotic sensations. Every part of her opening wider with every pulsing surge.

SHANNON MCKENNA

Chapter 26

NOAH WAS DEEP into his analog dive. It was one of his favorites; a moonlit rock climb high in the Cascades, an old standby that chilled him fast. He could do it driving, during martial arts, while conducting business. Even when working on engineering designs.

It kept the restless, twitchy, damaged part of his brain too occupied to mess him up while he had an actual, real-world job to do. He'd even used this dive during sex on a few occasions, to keep from coming too fast. But that was pre-Caro.

Everything was different with Caro. Like night and day.

Every detail of the actual climb was burned into his memory. Every instant of the muscle popping, finger-bleeding effort as he crawled up under the last steep overhang. The physical, real-world climb was dangerous even for him, and he only undertook the real thing when no one could see him free-climbing it. Doing things that should be physically impossible attracted unwanted attention. His feet dangled over the empty abyss, wavering and jerking with each lurch upward.

Suddenly, freezing rain was pelting down on him. Out of nowhere.

What the *fuck?* This was his own goddamn analog. Like always, he'd gone with cool, sharp moonlight. A clear, empty sky. He had not visualized sleet into it.

Imbed.

Fuck. Imbeds were floating triggers for stress flashbacks. They sometimes drifted up from his subconscious mind and appeared in an analog dive without warning. He didn't know what provoked them. Not only stress. Fallout from long-ago brain damage was his best guess as to their origin. Always scary. Always painful.

Cerebral implants and brain stim, the gifts that kept on giving.

It had been stupid to analog dive within twenty-four hours of pitched combat. Stupid, too, doing it while touching her. Contact with Caro flooded him with hormones, and affected his judgment. His heart and mind raced and his dick throbbed, still more than half hard even after a long bout of desperate sex. He was in a state of constant wonder and astonishment.

That was why he dove in the first place. To force himself out of this oversexed mindset. He needed to focus with laser-beam intensity to find a way to keep her safe from Mark forever.

He gently disentangled himself from her embrace, retaining his mental connection to the compromised analog. It hurt him to break physical contact with her. Every nanosecond that he wasn't touching her was a nanosecond wasted.

He lay down naked on the floor. The contact cooled his hot skin as he dragged himself back into the mental rock climb, grimly resolute. He was going to beat this, damn it.

An icy imaginary wind blasted around him again. Night vision and infrared revealed every crack in the rock, each dangling root, scrap of lichen and creeping insect. He remembered it all. The images were in his long-term memory. Catalogued, indexed and available for instant recall whenever he needed them.

His brain had been forged into a motherfucking monster of a learning machine. He'd spent a lot of time pondering whether it was a curse or a tool. In the end, he'd given up trying to decide. It just was. Shut up and deal with it.

The analog was out of control. Ice pounded his face, made the stones slippery and his fingers stiff. His naked body convulsed on the floor, shuddering in reaction.

The analog was hijacked. He couldn't alter it. He could only stop the dive and admit defeat—but if he did that, the analog was burned for good. Which sucked.

He tried to wrestle the imagery back to his chosen template. A few more feet, and he'd scramble to the summit and see the white-topped mountain range. The satisfaction he'd feel was the point of the exercise. The endorphin rush, that bright zing of positive reinforcement, was the reward for his concentration. Every muscle quivered with effort as he stretched . . . almost reached it . . . *yes!*

Crack. A jutting rock broke off. Then the overhang. He fell, with a shower of shale and dirt, sliding, and barely caught himself on a lip of stone. He hung there, shock reverberating through fingers and arms, shoulders stretched past the point of pain. Wind shrieked. The handholds were gone. The face of the rock had changed.

No way up. No way down. Bolts of lighting stabbed the mountain. Missing him. Not by much.

A climbing rope thudded against his shoulder. He peered up, squinting through the darkness and the rain to see who held it. A tall man. Narrowed eyes stared quizzically down at him. A flat mouth. Dark beard scruff.

Asa?

He jolted back to the bedroom, with a jolt of adrenaline that goosed his AVP to combat level. Asa, imbedded in his deepest, oldest analog? What the *fuck?*

SHANNON MCKENNA

He got to his feet, knees rubbery. The combat program data scrolled madly inside of his eyes as he pulled on jeans and a shirt. He left Caro sleeping, padding silently out of the bedroom on his bare feet.

Sisko looked up as he came down the stairs. He'd arranged the security monitors in a half-circle on the big coffee table, and was sprawled on the couch, feet on the table, tapping away at a laptop poised on his knees.

"Hey," Sisko said. "What, you don't trust me to stand guard anymore?"

"Can't rest," Noah muttered. "Tried to dive. Got ass-kicked by an imbed."

"Should have known better than to dive right after combat, dude," Sisko said absently. "You taught me that yourself. Did you fry your analog?"

Noah waved that away. "Never mind. What are you up to?"

"Researching your brother, among other things," Sisko said. "Interesting guy. Got a lot going on."

"Yeah? Illegal?"

"Some of it must be. He specializes in deepnet data mining, like I told you the other day. Auctions off targeted data. Makes flaming crap-tons of money. And plenty of enemies."

Noah went still. "What kind of money?"

Sisko kept staring into the screen. "Half a billion, at least. I've been poking around in his stuff . He's got some sweet algorithms. I was checking out a few just now, when you came down. If I didn't know better, I would have thought he was a modified."

"Huh," Noah muttered. "Weird, for a kid who would never do his math homework or pick up his dirty socks. What kind of enemies?"

"The kind you wouldn't want to have," Sisko said. "There's a price on his head. He stays on the move. It's hard to pin down his location."

Noah padded into the kitchen to get a beer, and then went to stretch out on a couch. He was a couple yards away from Sisko, but he could still read all the data on the screen without appearing to look.

"Data auctions, huh?" he said. "With that kind of money socked away, he must do it just to keep score."

Sisko shot him a thoughtful glance. "You've got that much money," he observed. "More, even. Are you just keeping score?"

Noah opened his beer and took a swallow. Light from the unshielded computer screen was making his eyes water, which made the combat program sputter and scroll in his inner vision, in jarring fits and starts. He rubbed his eyes, squinting. Didn't want to put on the lenses, or the shield specs. He was so sick of them.

"That's different," he muttered. "I'm creating stuff that improves the quality of people's lives. He's just exploiting greed and vice for profit."

Sisko's narrow gaze met his. "Wow. Pissed at him much?"

Noah took a swallow of beer. "Why would I be? Haven't seen him in years."

"You're not usually so quick to judge. Cut him some slack."

"Doesn't matter if I do or don't," Noah said. "He doesn't give a shit."

"Ah." Sisko's tone was thoughtful. "So it's like that. After all this time."

"What of it? Don't preach. It's been a long day, and I'm not in the mood."

"I don't make adjustments for your moods," Sisko informed him. "I just spent hours replaying that footage of Mark's attack on Luke. About a thousand times."

"Insights?"

"That thing he stuck onto Luke's head," Sisko said. "It reminded us of something. Zade noticed it first. We were going to mention it to you. Then things got crazy."

Sisko's hesitance was bugging him. "So? Let's have it."

"It looks like a miniature brain scan and brain monitor design," Sisko said. "There's something similar in the line of Batello products that are currently in development."

That startled him. "Simone," he said.

"Yeah," Sisko agreed. "It looks like one of Simone's designs."

The implications of that were sweeping and ugly. Noah pondered them briefly, and then shoved them into a box in his mind. For later.

"One thing at a time," he said finally. "This has to wait."

Sisko nodded slowly. The laptop on his thighs was the only source of light in the room, which made it easier to scan his sig. It was usually a mellow, uniform pulsing alternation of purples and blues. Today it was bigger, darker, with more extreme contrasts, and it was shot through with agitated spikes like solar flares.

"What's up with you?" Noah asked. "You OK?"

"No," Sisko said. "I'm just trying to distract myself from the thought of what's going to happen to Luke once Mark realizes that we have his shiny toy."

"Caro isn't his toy," Noah said. "I have to take him down before he finds out."

"See? That's what I'm talking about. We, Noah. *We* have to take him down."

Noah clenched his fists. "Are you going to get up in my face?"

"Someone has to," Sisko said. "You're being a goddamn dictator."

Anger flared, ramping up his combat program. A kill plan for Sisko suddenly flickered on his inner screen. He ignored it.

Sisko heaved a weary sigh. "But hey. You saved our asses on rebellion day, and afterwards. We all know it. We'll never forget it. Still and all, you can't carry us anymore."

"We saved each other at Midlands," Noah said. "We all did our part. I couldn't have done it without every single one of you guys."

Sisko rolled his eyes. "Maybe in the battle itself. But after? We were wrecked. They would have scooped us all back up and tossed us right back into the shredder if not for you."

Noah scowled. "So what's your point?"

"You can't do everything yourself," Sisko said.

"What about Zade?" Noah demanded. "You really think that he should be involved in this? Mark has his fucking codes. He can kill Zade in one second. From across the room."

"Yes, that is a problem," Sisko conceded. "Let Zade work it out. He's not a kid. And Hannah--"

"No way. She can't get near this."

"Why? Because she's your baby sister? She'll tear you to shreds if you cut her out of the action."

"Let's argue about this when I'm not chewing nails."

"You could spit out the nails," Sisko suggested. "Just a thought."

Then Noah saw the colors, slowly revolving on the walls and ceiling. Caro had sneaked out the bedroom door. She leaned over the railing, trying to listen in, her sig like a huge peony blooming in the darkness. He glanced up, and she pulled back with a guilty look.

"Why aren't you sleeping?" he asked.

"Same reason you're not, probably."

"Don't think so," he said. "I do soldier sentinel sleep. It's a Midlands thing. We toggle brain hemispheres, resting one while we function at a hundred percent with the other. You, on the other hand, need regular sleep. I can see it from here. Go get some more of it."

Her sig got bigger, unfurling like the fan of some huge fantasy peacock, like it always did whenever her pride was involved. The image filled the room, silently defying him.

It drove him nuts. OK, he could be a controlling bastard. But for a damn good reason. Controlling people was sometimes the only way to protect them. Worked sometimes. Or it crashed and burned. He hadn't been able to control Asa. He hadn't been able to protect Hannah. But God, he had tried. So fucking hard.

If he couldn't control Caro, then he couldn't protect her.

Caro ignored his command and descended the stairs, dignified as an empress. She seemed to drift an inch or so above the ground, in her swirling cloud of colors.

"How did you know I was there?" she asked. "That door doesn't squeak."

Sisko snorted under his breath. Noah shot him a quelling look. She didn't need to know how acute their hearing actually was. At least not right now. Best to let details like that sink in gradually over time.

"Your sig. It's really bright," he said. "I could see you from space."

"And I try so hard to be unobtrusive," she murmured. The lights were ebbing now, Noah noticed. He wondered if she could control it.

"So what are you guys doing?" she asked.

He shrugged.

"Fill me in, Noah." Her voice was adamant.

"You don't need to know about things that don't concern you."

"How could you conclude that this doesn't concern me?" she demanded. "I wrote that note to Mark myself, remember? You're the Keyholder. Mark's the Keyseeker. I'm the goddamn key. Me, Noah. So yes, I'm pretty fucking concerned."

"You're not getting anywhere near it," he said.

"I appreciate your protective instincts, but Mark won't walk into your trap so easily. Plus, I assume you mean to take him alive, so you can question him about Luke. Then there's the safe, which is a huge threat to everyone as long as he has it."

"Anything else?" She was on it, he had to admit.

"So, with all that, you still think you have to go after Mark alone because only superduper you can handle him? Get over yourself."

Sisko crowed under his breath. "Amen, sister. Nailed it."

Noah exhaled slowly. "But it makes sense," he said tightly. "It was my decision to let him run around loose for so long, so it should be me who makes it right. Plus, we're evenly matched. Same advantages, no surprises. It'll be like fighting myself."

"Yes, except that he's a psycho."

"I don't intend to fight fair," Noah said. "When my AVP is running hot, I could give fucking Satan a run for his money. I can send Mark a video of you when we make contact with him."

"Send him what you want, but he still won't show for a meet-up unless he knows for sure that I'm there," Caro said. "And he'd be an idiot to come alone. So you can't either. It would be a suicide mission. I'm vetoing it."

"Is that right." His hands clenched into fists as the data scroll speeded and flickered. "Since when did you get veto power?"

"Since I took it for myself."

They stared at each other as her sig billowed out. If he were outside the house, he'd see it filling the whole dark forest. Rising up into the night sky.

"Throwdown time." Sisko's voice was hushed.

"Shut up," Noah snapped. He turned back to Caro. "Got some brilliant alternative?"

"No," she said. "So far, my biggest ambition was just to prove that Mark killed Dex, and see him go to prison. Everything's different now that you guys are involved."

"Yeah, well, somebody has to die," Sisko said. "And it's not going to be any of us. If he lives, he'll punish us by hurting Luke. Unless we take him alive."

"Don't know if we can," Noah said. "He was the best back in the day, and he's had twelve years to hone his killing skills. And even if we did take him alive, that doesn't mean we'll get Luke's location out of him."

"That's true," Sisko conceded.

The man was on his side again, at least for now. Noah continued. "We all had strong resistance to interrogation vectored into our genes. Midlander researchers probably built in some tricks to pry us open, but I don't know what they are."

"If we make contact, he'll follow the breadcrumbs right back through our security and Luke will be fucked," Sisko said. "We need someone else to be our front man. Someone with no connection to us and genuine ties to the criminal underworld. Only a real-life, drug dealing, human-trafficking crime boss would be credible to Mark."

Noah's heart thudded heavily. As if it was his body that had this crazy idea, but his brain lagged behind, unwilling to allow it fully into his consciousness.

Even though it was kicking and banging. Breaking down the door. *Asa.*

Sisko went on with his musing. "But dealing with those guys is such a fucking mess. Like handling a bag of rattlesnakes."

"A con." Noah blurted. He stopped, and swallowed to keep his voice from vibrating. "You're talking about running a con. On Mark."

"I am?" Sisko said. He and Caro glanced at each other, uncomprehending.

"What do you mean?" Caro asked. "What kind of con?"

"You lost me," Sisko said.

"Shhhh. Let me think." He buried his face in his hands.

This explained that crazy imbed. His subconscious mind had already known exactly what he had to do. This was the only way through this mess.

But it was going to cost him big.

He pulled out his phone and retrieved the message he'd received the other day after Caro's dance. Waiting wouldn't make this idea any less insane. He hit 'call.'

The line connected. He didn't look at Caro or Sisko, who both watched him, bewildered. Five rings. Six. Seven . . .

Click. He waited in the taut silence of the open line for a few seconds.

"Danny." An expressionless baritone voice. Deeper than he remembered.

"I don't answer to that name anymore," he said. "I'm Noah now."

Asa grunted. "OK. So what? Did you know it's two AM? Don't you sleep?"

"Hang up, if you feel inconvenienced. I won't bother you again."

Asa just waited. "So?" he said, finally. "What do you want?"

Noah controlled himself somehow. Too much backed up feeling, unsaid words. *Keep it simple.* "I need your help," he said.

"Tell me more," Asa said.

"Not on the phone. Are you in the Seattle area?"

"I'm around. Should I come to the lake house? You never even brought that fiancée there. Or ex-fiancée, I should say. You have me to thank for dodging that bullet."

"I'm not thanking you for that or anything. And no, not the lake house. Come to this address." He gave Asa the address of a nearby roadhouse bar. "How long?"

"I could be there in forty minutes," Asa said.

"OK. See you there." He hung up.

Sisko's eyes were wide. "Holy shit," he breathed. "Is that who I think it was?"

Noah let out a careful breath before he could trust his voice. "Only one person I know has the cred to pull off a con like that."

Sisko cleared his throat. "Uh . . . I wasn't serious when I proposed it," he said. "You said you didn't even know the guy anymore. You sure it's a good idea?"

"No," Noah snapped. "It's what happens when you're driven into a corner. You do dumb things, because you have no alternative."

"Can someone fucking fill me in?" Caro snapped. "What dumb thing are you about to do?"

"Get your shoes on," he said. "You're about to meet my long lost brother."

Chapter 27

CARO WARMED HER chilly hands with a cup of reheated coffee. Not worth drinking, but it served its purpose. The roadhouse restaurant was dim, and a live band played in the next room. The twangy music not improved by a muddy, blatting sound system.

She tried at intervals to speak to Noah, but he had retreated behind a wall of ice.

Sisko kept at him, though, too stubborn to quit. "You should have talked to me before you called," he said heatedly. "You don't know if you can trust him."

"I know that I can't trust him at all," Noah said, his voice remote and cold. "But we need specialized help. From a crook." He hesitated. "He's a crook I can control."

"What makes you think so?" Sisko snapped. "You haven't so far."

"He reached out to me," Noah said. "He wants something from me. Whatever it is, I'll bargain with that."

Sisko made a disgusted sound. "And what could that be? Your kidneys? Your firstborn? Jesus, Noah. What are you going to tell Hannah?"

"Nothing." Noah gave them both a hard look. "She has no reason to know."

"She's going to find out. You can't protect her forever."

"All the more reason to protect her for as long as I can," Noah said.

Silence descended between the three of them, but the clatter and hum of the bar got louder. Out-of-tune rockabilly music floated through the greasy smoke that hung in the air. They'd been waiting a half hour when Noah's gaze flicked to the door.

Sisko and Caro craned their necks to look at who had walked in.

Asa Carr was big and tall, muscular and built, which was no surprise. He wasn't similar to his brother in any obvious way, aside from his height and size. Asa's long body was somewhat narrower than Noah's, and his long-lashed eyes were a clear silver gray beneath a thick slash of dark brows. He had the same strong chin and stern mouth, and his dark hair was buzzed off short. The battered brown leather coat, jeans and heavy boots amped up the intense, brooding vibe. In fact, the subtle vibration of danger was the biggest similarity he shared with Noah.

That, and the way every woman's head turned as he walked by.

Unsmiling, he walked toward them, his eyes locked on his brother's. Caro sensed violent emotion beneath their blank expressions. The disconnect was eerie and unsettling.

Noah slid out of the booth and stood up. "Hey, Asa."

Asa nodded. "Noah. Been a while."

"Yes," Noah agreed. "Thanks for coming."

Asa nodded, and his gaze flicked to Caro and Sisko. "Thought you'd be alone."

"This concerns them too," Noah said.

Asa made no comment, just studied Sisko. "I've seen you on surveillance photos. Edward Sisko?"

Sisko inclined his head in cautious assent.

Asa turned his eyes on Caro. "Not you, though. You're not, ah . . ." He slanted a questioning glance at Noah.

"She's not a Midlander," Noah said, answering both the spoken and the unspoken question. "But she knows everything."

"I see," Asa said. "That's a first."

"How do you know about Midlands?" Sisko demanded.

"Don't want to get into that right now." Asa looked at Noah. "So. You got a new girlfriend so soon?"

The question had a strange edge, which Noah ignored. But he answered it.

"This is Caro Bishop," he said. "Caro, Asa Stone. My brother."

"I'm glad to meet you." Caro held out her hand.

Asa took it, and pulled her subtly closer to his towering body, as if he meant to somehow let her know who was boss. Caro pulled her hand away, taken aback.

Noah took a menacing step forward. "Never touch her again," he said.

"Sorry," Asa said.

The single word conveyed bored contempt. Noah locked eyes with him.

"Guess you're serious about this one," Asa commented, after a moment.

"What's it to you, Asa?"

His brother looked at him hard. "Women get in the way. You know that. Or you did. Now look at you. Pillar of the community. Philanthropist. Job creator. Tight-assed tycoon with custom-built closets full of tasteful shit. You were on track to become a major criminal. What happened to you, my brother?"

"You already know everything about me. I don't want to bore you with the recap." He gestured toward the space in the booth next to Sisko. "Sit."

Asa slid into the booth, staring. "Weird, how much you look like Dad now."

"I don't want to talk about the past," Noah said. "It's dead and gone."

Asa pondered that for a moment. "If you want to talk about that tip I gave you the other day, I can't discuss my sources." His eyes flicked to Caro. "Not in front of unvetted strangers, anyway."

"Forget it. I don't give a shit about that right now."

Only stillness betrayed Asa's surprise. "I see," he said. "You don't want to talk about the past. You don't care about the mess I just saved you from, including that stupid engagement. So why am I here?"

"What do you know about my engagement?" Noah snapped.

"That the buttoned up blond chick was all wrong for you. What were you thinking?" His eyes flicked to Caro. "Was this the one who convinced you?"

Caro calmly returned his scrutiny, refusing to drop her gaze. It took some effort.

Asa's gaze slid over Caro's cuts and bruises, then turned his gaze to Noah's scabbed knuckles, the long scrape on his cheekbone. "Rough night?"

"That's why we're here," Noah said.

Asa's large, square fingernails tapped on the tabletop. "So? Tell me."

Noah looked at Caro. "Go ahead."

"It's a long story," Caro said.

"I get it." Asa said. "Not your story. It's *her* story. You didn't call me to help my family. You want me to do a favor for your new girlfriend. For fuck's sake."

"You can leave," Noah said. "Feel free."

"Hell no. I'm curious. What could be so scary that a pack of bad-ass mutant freaks have to beg a low-life thug like me for help?"

Noah didn't answer.

"Spill it," Asa said. "If you want anything from me, I require full disclosure. Real name. Verifiable details. And be warned. I can smell bullshit a mile away."

"My full name is Caroline Anne Bishop," Caro said. "Eighteen months ago, that was the name on my driver's license and passport. Before Mark Olund stole my life."

"Mark Olund," Asa mused. "I believe that was a post-Midlands alias. Right? But not one of your core group."

"He broke off from our group a few months after the rebellion," Noah said. "He went on alone."

"And became a--?"

"Criminal. He's good at it. Rich. Not as rich as you."

"Huh. He wasn't around when I started my surveillance on you guys."

"How in the hell did you do that without us noticing?" Sisko sounded personally insulted.

"Some other time, Sisko. You can buy me a beer," Asa said. "Focus. Tell the damn story."

Caro did. Asa's eyes took on a look similar to Noah's when he was on AVP; both far away and laser-focused. Caro faltered when she came to the part about the belly dance at Angel Industries, but Asa's eyes gleamed with enjoyment.

"You came in to shake your stuff during the meeting with Batello and the blonde? Wish I could have seen their faces." He turned his gaze on Noah. "But let's stay on topic. Why am I here?"

"We're not done." Noah went on to recount the events of the last few days. "When we make contact, Mark will follow us right back through our security," he concluded. "There's no keeping him out. The minute he figures out who he's dealing with, he'll try to control us by hurting Luke. Assuming Luke is still alive. That's what we have to prevent."

"OK." Asa thought for a few seconds. "You need a proxy with a solid backstory that stands up to stellar hacking. Nice to know I'm so believable as a ruthless villain. I'm a data pirate, not a kidnapper."

Noah shrugged. "Don't take it personally. I just don't know anyone better. Or worse, as the case may be. And an opportunist is an opportunist."

Asa snorted. "Fuck you, Noah."

"Didn't know you were so sensitive," Noah murmured.

"Neither did I," Asa admitted. "Did you tell Hannah about my text message?"

"Yes," Noah replied. "She wants to see you."

"Ah." Asa stared down at the table for a moment. "So what makes you think that I could pull this off?"

"Everything about you," Sisko said. "I checked you out. You're the perfect bad boy. We liked the data mining, the secret data auctions, the luxury properties. And you gotta tell me how you keep such a low personal profile. It was hard as hell to find a recent picture of you."

Asa shrugged.

"And the real estate," Sisko went on. "Buildings in Manhattan, penthouse apartments, mansions in Malibu, San Francisco, Santa Fe, Chicago, Boulder, Boca Raton. Bank accounts, stock portfolios, brokerage accounts, offshore accounts, foreign properties. And I liked your algorithms. There's some good work there. "

Asa's jaw sagged. "Holy shit," he said. "I don't know whether to kill you or offer you a job."

"Neither," Sisko said. "I won't let you kill me and I'm not looking for work right now. But if you need a consultant later, when things calm down, I'd tweak that latest algo to increase precision and speed. I'm expensive, though. Be warned."

"I'll think about it." Asa turned back to Noah. "There's the matter of payment."

"Money is no object," Noah said.

"It isn't an issue for me, either," Asa said. "That's not the point. Although I will expect a huge advance. Upfront expenses, that kind of thing."

"Anything else?"

Asa's mouth curved in a thin smile. "Yes. If you want to take advantage of my cred and my resources, you have to give me something that I give a shit about. Aside from money. I have plenty of that."

Noah waited. "What do you want?"

Asa's eyes glittered. "Depends on what you've got."

The three of them stared at him, blank.

Asa made an impatient sound. "Don't insult my intelligence. There's a crucial detail that you all left out. What's in the safe? And what's my cut?"

The pause was glaringly awkward. "Nothing of monetary value," Noah said.

"I didn't ask what it's worth," Asa said. "I asked what it is. What it's worth is based on a constantly shifting set of relationships between who wants it, why they want it, how badly they want it, and the extent of their resources. Calculating that value is my thing. I'm very good at it." He tapped impatiently on the table. "So what's in it?"

No one answered him. Asa leaned forward. "Understand this," he said softly. "I owe you nothing, and I will not be your tool. Do not fuck with me."

A muscle pulsed in Noah's jaw. He hesitated so long, Caro had almost concluded that he had decided not to speak at all.

"Obsidian has made a new generation of genetically and technologically enhanced supersoldiers," Noah said finally. "More powerful than in our day, according to Mark. Their memories were suppressed. They've been folded back into normal civilian life until they're called for. That safe holds their control frequencies and activation codes. All twelve hundred of them." He gestured toward Caro. "And she set the code."

Asa's eyes widened. "She's the only one who can open it?"

Noah nodded.

Asa whistled. "Control of twelve hundred cyborg supersoldiers? I could monetize the living fuck out of that."

"No," Caro snapped. "Absolutely not. Nobody will do that."

They looked at her, startled at her vehemence. "Why not?" Asa asked.

"They're slaves. If you even have to ask, then you're so far gone you wouldn't understand my answer anyway," she retorted. "Those twelve hundred people are human beings."

Asa made a noncommittal sound. "Worth saving?" he murmured. "I'll do what I can. But they'd be a hell of a lot better off monetized by me than by Obsidian."

"The slave soldiers aren't part of the bargain," Caro said. "Now or ever."

"Who even asked you, sweetheart?" Asa sounded only mildly curious.

"I'm not your sweetheart," Caro said coldly. "And I have the brainwaves that open the safe. That makes it my call."

Asa's eyebrow tilted up, genuinely startled. "You talk tough for someone who needs a life or death favor."

"You could help us to help them," she said. "You've got the resources."

Asa held up his hand. "Count me out. That would wreck my image of selfish villainy, and isn't that what you needed from me in the first place? I'm sure you guys can figure out how to redeem the twelve hundred without me."

"Let's hope so," Noah said. "Selling them is not an option. But we still need your help."

Asa rolled his eyes. "Fine. Wouldn't want to compromise your principles. If you're not going to split that ocean of profits, what else can you offer to tempt me?"

Noah hesitated for a long moment. "I can't interest you in a simple, straightforward contract? Monetary payment for services rendered?"

"Nah," Asa said. "Boring. Come on, big brother. It's been thirteen years. Thrill me. You guys have special abilities, right? Genetically enhanced this, tech-augmented that? I might find it handy to call in favors from people like that from time to time. Things come up all the time."

Noah shook his head. "I can't speak for the rest of the—"

"I can," Sisko said. "I'll speak for all of us. For Luke's sake. Just don't ask us to kill or hurt anyone innocent. Barring that, we'll do favors for you."

"Watch it," Noah said swiftly. "Shut up, Sisko. That's way too general."

"Take a few hours," Asa soothed. "Talk to your people. Work out the details." He slid out of the booth and rose to his full height. "I'll see you tomorrow at midnight in the Kirkland house, and we can nail down the deal. Then we work out how to make contact with this scumbag and get this thing rolling."

"What the *hell?*" Sisko said. "How do you know where we're staying?"

"You mutant types underestimate the obsessive-compulsive paranoia of the one percent," Asa said. "Will Hannah be there tomorrow?"

"No," Noah said. "She won't be involved in this."

The brothers' eyes met. Tension throbbed in the air like a huge bass note. A complex mix of intense emotions. Anger, fear, pride, guilt. And under it all, the magnetic pull of each man's own gravitational force fighting for ascendance.

"You were right," Noah said. "About Midlands. If that's any satisfaction to you."

Asa's eyes slitted as he gazed down at his older brother. "Satisfied," he repeated. "That's how you think I'd feel. To see you and Hannah get hurt."

"That's not what I meant," Noah said. "I just know that you like to be right."

"It's not that I like it," Asa said slowly. "It's just that I *am.*"

Caro stared at the two men in wary fascination as they locked horns. It was plain that neither one of them had ever succeeded in dominating the other, but they were compelled by their essential nature to keep on trying, no matter what.

Noah finally let out a short bark of laughter. "So you're infallible?"

"I never said that," Asa said. "If I were, I would have found a way to stop you from going to Midlands. Or at least taken Hannah and run like hell."

"I would never have let you do that," Noah said.

"I know." Asa's voice was bleak. "So you see? Not infallible."

Noah scowled. "The Midlands fuck-up was on me. I take full responsibility."

"It's a family trait," Asa said. "When we fuck up, we go all out."

He turned and walked out without looking back.

Chapter 28

ONE OF TWO things was certain, Mark had determined. One: that incompetent shithead Carrerra was already dead. Two: he was about to die, for not answering Mark's calls. It had been over twenty-four hours since Carrerra's triumphant phone call announcing that he'd picked up Bishop and was heading to the meet-up.

Nothing since then. Carrerra knew better than to be incommunicado.

It was not quite dawn, but for him and the five prototypes, equipped with visual implants and new, improved AVP, light levels were no issue. Mark drove through the canyon of dark pines, noting the glaring lack of guards.

Sloppy. Or ominous. He was betting on the latter. His tension mounted.

New kill plans generated on his inner eye screen every time he happened to look at one of the prototypes. He was accustomed to the constantly changing display. Multiple kill plans were useful when he needed to kill large numbers of people in a short amount of time, but at the moment, they only served to remind him how much he would enjoy annihilating the slave soldiers.

Who continued to annoy the living shit out of him.

Besides the palpable hostility they displayed, there were serious glitches. Brenner kept blurting out the name of his kid at random intervals, and Raquel was a river of tears, which swelled her eyes and dripped from her her nose. In addition to making him want to smack her puffy, reddened face, the snot and the gurgling and the constant sniffling obliterated her sexual appeal.

He'd been keeping Brenner and Raquel in the freight container, just to prevent himself from acting on the temptation to hurt them. Life had been simpler when he was alone. The other three in the cab up front had the sense to keep their mouths shut.

When he saw the building, he knew instantly that Carrerra's entire team was dead. There were no live thermals within a hundred meters of the place, aside from some small forest animals. An unmistakable stench wafted through the window. Not terribly strong yet, but his sense of smell was acute, and he had extensive experience with that particular odor.

He stopped the truck, ordered the protos out, and let the other two out of the freight container before starting the damage assessment. The smell indicated that he was going to need the whole crew for the cleanup.

One corpse lay in the gravel driveway, throat crushed. Dead of asphyxiation, judging by the bulging, sightless eyes.

Wind whipped the treetops. A rhythmic creaking led him to the hanged man, swaying over the narrow path that led to the house. The third corpse lay facedown in front of the aluminum steps, his livid face turned at an improbable angle on his neck. He'd soiled himself in death. The reek of terror-shit blended with the developing taint of human decomp made Mark circle the corpse as widely as possible.

He mounted the stairs that led into the small building. The door hung open, banging against the aluminum siding in the wind, letting out a stench of of blood and death that was stronger still.

Brenner tried to follow him through the front door, but Mark spun around. "Stay out, until I call for you!" he snarled.

336

Brenner faded quietly back outside.

Mark found Carrerra pinned to the floor by the knife stuck through his hand. His face was unrecognizable, swollen and dark, crusted with blood. His eyes were hidden in pockets of swollen, purplish flesh.

Mark catalogued every detail. The bloodsmears, the bullet holes, the broken plastic restraints. Whoever did this had been looking specifically for Caroline Bishop, but she had no friends or allies capable of rescuing her. She'd been all alone, living off crumbs, huddling in dark corners. The closest she'd come to a bodyguard had been that dickwad Tim Wheaton. Easy enough to crack.

Whoever had pulled this off was in another class altogether. Considerably smarter than Wheaton. Someone who knew the potential of the info she held in her head. Probably the same man who took down Carrerra's last team. Acting alone, by Mark's guess. Stealthy, highly skilled, and possessing formidable strength.

An extremely gifted professional . . . or else he was modified.

Carrerra looked like he'd fought hard. Mark had hired him for that, and he'd proved to be ferocious. He'd met his match this time.

He walked around Carrerra's body, peering at it from the other side, and saw the yellow paper poking out of the stiff, purplish lips and fragments of broken teeth. He pried the dead man's mouth open, and extracted the crumpled, bloody paper, smoothing it out.

Even with AVP, it was a challenge to read. When he did, his combat program surged and seethed. Terms? Arrogant shithead.

He forced himself to study the note more closely. Looked like a woman's handwriting. Caroline. Had to be. So she was alive, conscious, functional, and under the other man's control.

She's mine, the note said. The bastard was probably fucking her in the ass right now.

He pocketed the note and left the building, looking down at his crew of hollow-eyed, staring supersoldiers. Still glaring at him, in spite of their frequent punishments. They looked like zombies who hadn't gotten around to rotting yet. Soon, though.

"Take the bodies into the woods," he told them. "Bury them deep. You get to burn the house before we go. Special treat. Say thank you."

They stood there, mute and glaring, until he raised the freq wand and gave them all a pain zap. That shocked them into action. Except for Brenner, who didn't move.

"Callie," Brenner blurted hoarsely.

Moaning about his goddamn kid again. It was too much. He punched Brenner, sending the big man flying right off his feet. When Brenner crashed heavily to the ground, Mark extended the wand and gave the stupid fuck an excruciating buzz of neural punishment.

Brenner writhed and screamed for long, satisfying minutes.

Mark pocketed the wand, walked over and kicked the whimpering man in the crotch, hard. The cerebral inhibitor blocked Brenner from defending himself against his controller. He just curled up, panting heavily with rasping, sobbing breaths.

"Say that name one more time, and I'll take you back to where she lives and make you kill her with an axe," Mark told him. "And when you're done, you can set yourself on fire. Got me? Do we understand each other?"

Brenner choked out the name one last time.

Mark sighed in frustration, switched the wand's setting to knock-out, and zapped him unconscious. Best to power him down. Let them both chill. It was impractical to flush a thirty million dollar investment down the toilet for nothing. There were cheaper necks to squeeze if he felt the urge.

Talk terms, his ass. He'd teach the Keyholder all about terms before he was done. That arrogant shithead was going to get a special, intensive private lesson.

While Mark gouged his eyes out with his thumbs.

*   *   *

The ride back to the Kirkland house was weirdly silent. Sisko slid behind the wheel and took over the driving, as if by prior arrangement. Noah sat in the back with her, but would not respond to anything she said. After a few frustrating minutes, he put out his hand and pressed his finger gently against her lips, without meeting her eyes.

"Not now," he said. "Sorry. I can't."

"Caro. Let him be," Sisko said.

"Do I have a choice?" she asked bitterly.

"He's doing an ASP management thing," Sisko explained, keeping his eyes on the road. "Self-imposed sensory deprivation. You isolate yourself and blank out all sensory input. It's problematic, because you have to lower your guard, but when analog diving isn't working, it's an emergency time-out, so you don't blow something up. Or hurt somebody."

"I see," she whispered, even though she didn't.

"He'll be back soon," Sisko assured her. "Just be patient."

Patient, hell. She wanted to blow something up herself. It was not freaking fair.

Sisko parked outside the Kirkland house, and held up his hand when she opened her mouth to speak. They sat in utter silence for a couple of minutes, just waiting.

Finally, Noah opened his eyes and looked at Caro. "Sorry," he said.

The raw pain in his eyes made something clutch in her throat. She knew how that felt. Painful memories were hard to control. Seeing his brother Asa after so long must have triggered a torrent of them.

Once inside the house, Sisko looked Noah over keenly. "You OK?"

"I'm good." Noah's voice was flat.

"Call if you need me. I'll be down in the basement tech room." Sisko nodded at Caro, and headed for staircase.

Caro took Noah's hand and tugged it. "Let's go up and rest."

"No," he said. "I'm going out for a while."

She was bewildered, and alarmed. "Out where?"

"Just outside. I need space."

Ouch. Her whole body contracted. "Well. That's a classic."

"Caro, please," he said wearily. "Don't get your feelings hurt. It's not you."

"Oh, just shut up," she snapped. "If you need to blow off steam, I know just how that might be accomplished. Without isolating yourself."

The room charged instantly with sex. His eyes flashed, right through the lenses. She could feel the hot magical light on some level other than just sight, and her body answered, softening and melting. Preparing for him.

He swallowed, hard. Hands flexing, clenching. "Not now," he said thickly. "My AVP is bugfuck. Happens, after half a lifetime of getting fucked over and pissed off. You do not want me naked on top of you while I'm metabolizing it."

"Stop carrying on," she said. "I trust you completely. AVP or no AVP. You just need to trust yourself."

He shook his head, and walked out the door.

She forced herself to breathe down the hurt. *Suck it up.* This issue was bigger than her tender feelings, and nobody could criticize the man for not trying hard enough on her behalf. She had to grow up. Go upstairs. Wait patiently for him to work through his crap. He was entitled to his weird strategies. Whatever worked for him was fine.

Her mind raced too frantically for sleep, so she sat down in the living room for a while, and leafed through a stack of files Sisko had left there.

One caught her attention. A list Sisko had compiled of the people who had been reported missing the past week in Utah and Wyoming, the states Mark had mentioned in the video they had found in Luke Ryan's lake house.

It wasn't hard to winnow the list. The supersoldiers had to be young, physically powerful, and without family connections to fit the supersoldier profile. In the past few days, ten had met the criteria. Seven men. Three women.

Caro studied them for a while, staring at the photographs. She opened one of Noah's laptops, which lay on the coffee table, and did internet searches on each one. Not much to be found. No missing-person alerts either, statewide or national.

She lingered over Sierra Horst, a waitress who'd disappeared from a restaurant during her shift. Blood found in the parking lot. Active investigation.

While searching one of the names, she found a video clip from a local news channel covering the disappearance of Brenner Jameson from Cheyenne, Wyoming. The attractive blonde reporter gazed earnestly into the camera, her lips not quite in sync with the audio. Caro listened closely.

"Brenner Jameson left his two-year-old daughter Callie with his mother-in-law at seven AM, just like he always did, for his daily ten mile run. Every other day, he'd come back, have breakfast with his daughter, and take her to day care on his way to work. But the day he disappeared was not like every other day . . ."

The blonde babbled on, speaking over a shifting display of photos. Brenner, muscle-bound and proud of it. Callie, a laughing toddler with dark hair. Callie's mother, a pretty, slender woman who, the reporter said, had died of leukemia only a few months earlier.

Caro stared into the big, liquid eyes of the motherless toddler gazing back at her from the screen. Big, brown, owl-like eyes. So innocent. They hurt her heart.

It was a pain in the ass to have all these inconvenient goddamn feelings waking up again. Blindsiding her.

She'd bet good money that Callie's dad Brenner was one of the unlucky ones.

She'd be so fucking happy to lose that bet.

Chapter 29

CARO STARTED UP out of an ugly dream. It took a moment to orient herself.

Oh. Yeah. She was in Mansion Two. She'd dozed off on the couch, laptop still on her lap. But where was Noah? There wasn't a sound from any direction.

Looked like she'd be sleeping alone. She closed down the laptop, gathered the files together and set them in a neat pile on the coffee table. She went upstairs and stripped off her clothes, sliding naked between the cool sheets.

A half hour of ceiling-staring later, she felt the air currents shift as the bedroom door opened. And there he was. She wasn't surprised. She was so acutely aware of him now. She wondered if hanging out with enhanced people sharpened her own senses somehow.

She reached for the bedside lamp. Stopped herself just in time. He'd had enough drama today. Getting jabbed with light would not help his mood. Or her own agenda.

She gazed at his tall, broad form, a deeper darkness silhouetted against the dark framed by the bedroom door. A breath of the outdoors came in with him, a whiff of the forest: dampness and leaves, needles and resin. Sweet wild earthy smells.

He'd taken off his lenses, and his eyes had that uncanny reflective gleam even in the dark, catching all the available light and flashing it back at her. It was a glimpse straight into the heart of the unfathomable energy of nature. The flash in a wolf's eyes, the deadly grace in a mountain lion's spring, the infinity of the night sky. Pure, distilled masculine power, armoring the secret tenderness inside him.

He was so beautiful, he stopped her breath. She held the sheet to her chest, warmed by delicious, toe-curling, very female desire as he tossed his jacket on the chair and stripped off his sweatshirt. What light there was gleamed on the wide, powerful contours of his shoulders as he bent to kick off his shoes.

She felt intimidated, shy, exultant. She needed so badly to be close to him, and sex was the most direct way. Besides, just looking at him made her ache to wrap herself around his big, hard, sinewy body.

Her lower body clenched in anticipation as he padded barefoot to the bed. He jerked the coverlet down, baring her.

"Didn't Hannah bring you something to sleep in?" he asked.

Her hair shifted silkily against her bare shoulders. "Of course. Cami jammies, she called them. Very nice top and bottom. But I was hoping to get lucky. And here you are. Feeling better?"

He shook his head. "I tried to analog dive. Got slammed by another imbed."

"What's that?"

He waved the question away. "Never mind. Didn't mean to talk shop. Sometimes I forget you're not up on all our mutant mods terminology."

"I'd love to learn," she offered.

"No. Not right now."

She noted his sharp tone and waited for a moment. "Then just tell me what an imbed is. That's not too much to ask, is it?"

Noah blew out a breath, staring out the window into what looked like impenetrable darkness to her but wasn't to him. "OK, if you really want to know," he said. "An imbed is a hidden trigger for a stress flashback. This one was bad. I burned another analog. I can't dive again tonight. I can't use any of my usual tricks to chill myself out. And they're all I've got. Except for you."

"Hmm."

Talking about all his enhanced whatevers wasn't getting them anywhere. It sure as hell wasn't enough for her right now. By no means.

She rose up on her knees, and grabbed his belt buckle. "Come here, Noah."

He covered her hands with his own big, warm hands. "I'm wound too tight," he warned her. "I don't know if I can be gentle once we really start. You know how it gets with us."

"I don't care. Go wild." She jerked his belt open and undid the steel buttons on his jeans. "I need you. Right now."

"You talked me into it." He pulled his jeans down, and his big, heavy penis sprang free.

He stopped talking as she seized his thick shaft, her hands squeezing and swirling around his velvety skin. She bent to lick up precome from the swollen tip, pleased to feel him jerk and shudder. She took him into her mouth, cupping his balls, swirling her tongue. Pulling him deeper. Inviting him with every touch of her tongue to take his own pleasure.

He did, thrusting slowly. She responded with sensual, rhythmic pulls.

Each stroke deepened her excitement. A hot glow of light raced through every nerve ending, centering within seconds in her lower body, her swift arousal matching his. Her nails dug into his steely muscled ass. Her excitement ratcheted higher, fueled by his ragged gasps of pleasure. She was

345

exultantly sure she had him already thundering full speed ahead when he groaned suddenly and dragged himself out of her mouth.

Oh, no, no, no. Not now, when she was burning to feel that hot, liquid explosion of male energy in her mouth. "Let me," she begged.

"No. Not yet."

"But I need you," she said wildly. "I need this."

"You've got me. You can have me. As much of me as you can handle." He gasped sharply as she squeezed his shaft again. "But don't make me come yet."

"Why not?"

"Because I want to be inside you when I do. If there's anything that could make me feel better right now, it's that."

Caro sighed, and hooked his jeans, shoving them further down his thighs. "Then take what you want. Just don't make me wait!"

She tried to yank him down on top of her and onto the bed, but Noah stood strong. He stripped off his clothes and then kneeled on the bed before her, pulling her closer.

"Be patient." His tone was implacable as he slid his hand up between her legs, cupping her mound. He thrust his fingers tenderly inside her, pulsing and stroking. "You'll wait if I say that you will."

"Goddamnit, Noah—"

"Shhhh," he murmured. "Don't rush me. I'm getting you ready."

She gasped as his fingers circled inside her, and clenched around him, wriggling with pleasure. "You are such a control freak."

"Yeah. Fun sometimes."

Anger and excitement and pleasure fought for dominance as one sensation melted into the next. He touched her with incredible skill, unlocking new desires she never knew she had. She'd never imagined being so open to a man.

346

Noah was exactly what she craved. Whatever she'd been bitching about before the clothes came off and they got down to it, she couldn't remember. Not for the world, while being caressed by his long fingers. His tongue would be next. And then . . .

"More," she said shakily. "There. Yes."

"I don't need you to tell me that," he muttered against her throat, between hot, dragging kisses. "Your sig never lies."

"Damn it, Noah. Not fair."

"You're so right. But I don't care. Too bad for you."

But it wasn't, not at all. It was good for her, so good, and he knew it. It was obvious, how much he loved making her whimper and writhe. He knew just where to stroke, where to press and circle inside her in ways that sent pulsing throbs of erotic energy through her entire body.

"Put your hands on my shoulders," he commanded.

She did so, trying to dig her fingers in. His muscles were so hard, so dense.

"I imagined this, the first time I saw you dance," he whispered against her ear. "Just us. Alone. You naked, dancing for me. But with my hand shoved up deep inside you, so sweet and tight. Sliding in and out of you. Your juice making my fingers all slippery and hot. Rolling your hips, getting closer and closer to coming right around my fingers. Made me hard as a rock."

"Oh . . . God," she whispered.

"I wanted it so bad," he said. "I love how your lips get so red. Your eyes go almost black, and I can see inside, all the way into your secret, hidden places. Let me in, Caro. All the way in. Sweet fucking surrender."

"Noah . . ." Her voice was low and pleading.

"Dance for me now," he said. "Dance around my fingers. Come around my hand. I want to feel it. Make me hot, Caro. Do it. Move!"

The snap of command in his voice startled her into motion.

She did just as he asked, clutching his shoulders, face damp and hot, breath rapid and ragged. She thrust her hips down and around, her arms draped over his shoulders as she rode his expert hand, maxing out on strange new sensations.

He was doing it all to her. Noah. Her man, if that's what he was. And if he was more than a man, she craved it all. Everything he was. *Hers.*

Noah withdrew his fingers and opened her legs all the way. Then leaned her back, his hands cradling her.

"Yeah," he murmured. "That's how I want you. Wide open to my hands, my tongue, my dick. My mind. You make me so hot."

Caro moaned with pleasure at his weight, his heat, as he settled himself between her legs and teased her labia with his penis. Painting her with long, slow, licking, strokes, dipping deeper now and again, to bathe himself in her slick opening. His glans shone with it.

Ooh yes. *Yes yes yes.* His fingers encircled his dick, touching the tip to her quivering bud. Letting her enjoy the tiny thrill every time he did it. Keeping the action unpredictable. Delicious, maddening, marvelous. He continued, relishing her building frustration, until she rocked forward, squirming with eagerness. She clutched at him, trying to pull him deeper.

"Please, Noah," she whispered. "Give it to me now."

"You're ready?"

"You know I am," she said. "Don't play games with me."

"No games." He thrust inside her with controlled, deliberate slowness.

She gasped at the heavy slide of his thick member moving into her inner flesh. He surged in, filling her completely, eased out. She could feel his strong pulse throbbing inside her.

"Look into my eyes," he demanded softly. "Don't look away."

He clasped her hands, twining his fingers with hers. She lost herself in that amber glow, in the sensuously deep connection, every point of contact as intimate as a kiss, as steady as a heartbeat, shimmering with intense emotion.

348

Light blazed through her. She wondered if it was like the light he saw with his altered eyes. Wild joy lifted her, launched her into the heart of that brightness.

Her fingers held his with desperate strength as pleasure crashed over her.

She came back from far, far away when he nuzzled her neck. Caro shifted her body, and realized that he had not come. Still super hard. Still inside her. He just rocked against her. Waiting. She had no idea for what.

"I thought you wanted to come together," she ventured.

"I do. And I will. I'm just not done yet." He rocked his hips against hers, nudging deeper. "Caro. Listen. I want you like I want to breathe. In my bed. In my life. I want it it all."

"What?"

"You know. The whole thing." He waited, his body taut with expectation.

Caro shook her head, momentarily lost.

As if he'd read her mind, he rocked back and surged forward, swiveling his thick rod inside her, stimulating all those hot glowing sweet spots. Which was great, but it didn't do much for her ability to think. She wanted to understand him. "What are you talking about?"

"Marry me," he said.

She stared at him, mouth open.

He waited. "Say something."

"You're proposing to me?" she squeaked. "Now? You're inside me!"

"Yeah," he said, with evident satisfaction. "Feels fantastic. The last time I proposed to someone, it was so much more calculated. Champagne, candlelight, fancy ring, memorized speech. This is realer. I like it."

She didn't. "And I get a flying tackle from out of left field? Come on. That was the absolute best hot sweaty sex I ever had but if you think that I— Noah, this is crazy timing."

349

He looked perplexed. "Do I have to give you the option of saying no? I don't have a plan B."

"I don't even have a plan A," she said hotly. "I don't have squat right now. And when people get close to me, it does not end well. Don't do this to me."

"I'll keep you safe," he said intently. "We'll get through this. I promise."

She reached up, tracing the sculpted shape of his cheek. "Please. Let right now be enough for us. It's enough for me. I'm grateful."

He responded by nuzzling her neck, like he didn't want her to see his face.

He finally lifted his head, stroking her hair away from her face. "I'd do anything to keep you with me. Sex as a strategic device? Yeah. Multiple screaming orgasms to wear down your resistance? Sign me up."

"It won't work," she said. "And don't joke around. Things are too dangerous. I can't make promises and neither can you."

"Why can't you?" His amorous mouth whispered the question against her ear before he nipped her earlobe.

"Come on." Her lips trembled. "I've got a big, dark cloud hanging over my life."

"It's my cloud now. I own it. So? What do you say? Where do you stand?"

She smacked at the solid wall of his chest, poised over her. "Who's standing? I'm flat on my back! With you about three miles up inside me!"

"We could get engaged."

"You must be kidding."

They stared at each other for a long moment. He shifted, as if about to roll away, and she tightened her legs around him, trapping him inside her with a spasm of what felt almost like panic. "Don't you dare move," she whispered.

His smile flashed. He kissed her lips, her chin, her jaw. "Never. That's the whole point."

She gripped his big shoulders, fingers digging in. "It's sweet of you to ask," she said. "Very romantic. But it's way too soon. Let it go. Please."

"Don't say yes or no," he urged. "Just think about it."

"I'm not going to say anything," she said fervently.

He nibbled her ear. "I'm going to finish now. You good with that?"

"Yeah," she said. "I love that. I love all of it, with you."

He wound his arms around her shoulders. They clung to each other desperately as his hips drove against hers until he climaxed with a shout, and pulled her along with him, freefalling into sweet oblivion.

Some time later, he rolled onto his side, keeping her clasped tightly against him.

"It's dawn," he said.

Caro yawned. "I noticed," she said. "Sort of."

He'd stayed on his side, keeping her clasped tightly against him. He ran a hand over her from shoulder to hip. "You OK?"

"Why wouldn't I be?"

"Good. I'll make you breakfast."

She heard a faint ringtone. Waited for him to ignore it. He did, but after a few moments he stretched out his arm and grabbed the thing, tapping the screen.

"Hell," he muttered. "Gotta call my crew. Sorry."

"Why?"

"Looks like we have to figure out exactly how to sell our souls to my problematic brother." He slid from between the sheets, sat up and reached to snag his jeans. His mind moving forward with the task at hand.

All business again.

Chapter 30

"IF YOU WANT him to bring the safe, you have to show him the girl." Asa sounded irritated. "He's not stupid."

"Not an option," Noah said again, implacably.

Asa squinted up at the ceiling. "You keep telling me how hard it's going to be to outwit this genius psycho. And now you tell me that we're supposed to trap him without bait. What the fuck do you want, Noah? Miracles?"

"We'll send him a video of her," Noah insisted. "If anything fails, he'd cut her to pieces. She cannot be there."

"I hear you, and you have a point, but still."

As he spoke, Asa's curious gaze kept flicking to the glow in Noah's unshielded eyes. Noah had taken his lenses off, figuring what the hell, he had nothing to hide from his brother at this point. Besides, he wanted to take a good, long look at Asa's sig.

He'd been surprised to find it as atypical as Caro's, though for opposite reasons. Asa's sig was unreadable. Shielded, as if he were generating some sort of interference. When Noah tried to read his brother's energy pattern, all he saw was an eye-watering shimmer. Like heat rising from hot asphalt on a desert highway.

Which was very interesting and thought-provoking, but not worth a good goddamn when it came to making guesses as to his brother's mysterious agenda.

"He won't go for it," Asa said.

"Noah," Caro said. "I should be the one to decide if I—"

"No." His harsh voice smashed down on the suggestion.

He locked eyes with Caro. Her color was high. Pissed at him, but he was pushing all that aside for the moment. Focusing on the task at hand.

Asa blew out a frustrated breath. "You're not being rational."

"That's how it has to be," Noah said. "You'll have your favors to call in. You know we're good for them."

"Yeah?" Asa challenged him. "How do I know? The last thing we did together before we bashed each other's brains out was that fill-a-basket con, remember? We scored bread, lunchmeat, milk, some M&M's and Tylenol for Hannah's fever. And you were an awesome liar that day. You're one of the best liars I've ever known."

"He's not lying now," Caro said. "He couldn't lie to you."

Asa looked amused. "Sorry, beautiful," he drawled. "You're not impartial, so your opinion is worthless."

"Let's cut the bullshit," Noah said. "Mark's sniffing around out there. Sooner or later, he'll catch our scent. We need to make contact soon. Give him something concrete to focus on. Something of our choosing. On our schedule."

"The financial outlay for this enterprise will skyrocket if you insist on being unreasonable," Asa said. "And no matter how many guys I hire or what gear they get, our probability of success is about to fall off a cliff. You're being an asshole, Noah. Not that this surprises me."

"Are we going to get to work, or not?" Noah asked.

Asa opened up a slim silver laptop. "So you want him to trace these messages back to me, correct?"

"That's right."

Asa nodded, staring at the screen with an abstracted frown. "So I have to make it hard for him. Really hard . . . but not too hard."

"Right," Noah said impatiently.

Asa pressed a small tab of gummed paper over the vidcam on the laptop and tapped a few keys, humming to himself. "Oblio.chat," he murmured. "Creating an account . . . username, Keyholder. What a super-nerd gonzo gamer username. Couldn't you think of anything better?"

"Not at the time. I was rescuing Caro," Noah said. "Give me a fucking break."

"Logging on," Asa murmured. "Let's see if this guy is . . . shit." He looked up, eyes sharp. "He's waiting for us."

Dread fluttered through the color patterns of Caro's sig, quickly calmed and stilled. Caro joined Sisko and Noah to peer over Asa's shoulder. Mark's opening was terse.

took you long enough

Asa typed back.

been busy with the girl. She's so happy to be saved! and grateful = on her knees to me ☺ kickass aphrodisiac.

"What the fuck do you think you're doing?" Noah snarled.

"My job," Asa said calmly. "I'm destabilizing him. Pissing him off. Wounding his pride. Manipulating him into making snap decisions that are not in his best interests."

Noah sat down next to him, staring at his screen. "Is that a good idea?"

"We'll find out soon enough. What's important is that I'm being me, and not you. Which is why I put a sticker on the camera."

"I noticed."

"He'd feel something was off if you just used me as a mouthpiece. Shut up and let me do my thing. He'll find me when he does his research. I'm a smart-ass by nature, and people know it. You're not."

"Yeah, I remember that," Noah muttered.

"I just bet you do," Asa said. As they spoke, Mark had typed back.

not interested in games. name your terms.

Asa looked up at them. "How much do I know?"

"Everything you could have learned from her if she'd never met us," Noah said. "And you being you, you don't want a flat fee. You want in. That's what turns you on."

Asa's white teeth flashed. "You got my number." He began to type.

I have contacts/network to maximize value. 50% of what's in the safe

Mark did not reply for several tense moments. Slowly, letter by letter, his response appeared on the screen.

U don't know what the product is so how can u talk value or buyers?

Asa flexed his hands, wiggled his fingers, and banged out a response.

U want it bad. Lydia Bachmann died for it. That's enough 4 me. I want
in.

Mark responded.

There is no place 4 u. Sell her 2 me.

Aw where's the fun in that? Besides I want 2 keep her. She can open the
safe 4 u, but I want my new favorite toy back in 1 piece

There was a long pause from Mark's end, and then the response:

that won't work.

Asa typed again:

u bring the safe. i bring the girl. she opens the safe. we split the contents. she
gets back down onto her knees. the end.

Caro's mouth was flattened and colorless. Noah could almost feel
Mark's rage, pulsing through the computer screen and into their faces, like a
hot wind.

Sisko shot a glance at Asa. "Pushing it a little?"

"Fuck, no," Asa said. "This is me holding back."

Noah's jaw ached. "Stop sliming my girlfriend. Or say goodbye to your
teeth."

Asa laughed under his breath. "Don't cramp my style. I'm doing this
for you, OK? And her, incidentally. Trust my instincts. Leave me the fuck
alone and let me do my thing."

Sisko grunted. "We have to kill Mark now, or you're a dead man," he told Asa.

talk terms not bullshit

Mark, waiting.

Asa typed:

i told u. bring the safe. i keep the girl. i keep half.

There was another tense pause, and then:

5 million for the girl

Asa grinned.

Lmfao

Fast reply.

6.5 million last offer

Asa's response:

dont waste my time

Asa logged off. "Let him stew for a while," he said. "When we get back to him, he'll be frothing with rage and getting nervous."

"He's going to try to kill you and take Caro," Noah said.

"Of course he will," Asa said. "The only unknown is the size of his team."

"Mark by himself equals ten topnotch professionals," Noah said. "If not more."

"But I'm not supposed to know about his mods," Asa said. "So I can't prepare for the encounter as if I knew. My team has to be as small as possible. And concealed, along with you guys."

"It'll be hard to hide from him," Noah said. "He sees thermal heat signatures and energy sigs, right through most walls. He senses electrical activity too, and his hearing is acute. Also his sense of smell."

"Great," Asa said lightly. "Bring him on. I need a challenge. What can block all that? Maybe we can throw something together. Thermal cloaks. Made of dental aprons and black garbage bags."

Noah shrugged. "I have some stuff."

Asa waited for him to say more.

"OK, by stuff I mean rough draft concepts for thermal cloaks. We made a few. Not super hero level. Sisko and Zade and I started developing them a few years ago. I designed them to be invisible even to me. No thermal signature, and almost no energy sig. Not a hundred percent effective, but they're a hell of a lot better than nothing. And they don't restrict movement or the wearer's visibility. Not much, anyway."

Asa's eyes gleamed. "And I thought you were all about save-the-world medical biotech. You do secret gear and weaponry, too? Hidden depths, man. Hidden depths."

Asa's knowing smile irritated the shit out of him. "If Obsidian comes after us, I need to be ready."

"Sure. You ever want to leverage your defense tech, just let me know."

"I'm not an arms dealer," Noah snapped.

"You're missing out on big money," Asa said absently. "Everybody needs to survive. Don't forget that us mere mortals have to hustle."

"Noah," Caro broke in. "There's a vehicle at the gate."

Noah quickly turned to scan the security screens that monitored every approach to the property. "What? Who?"

"That's Zade's van," Sisko said. "On it. Buzzing him in."

"What the hell he doing here?" Noah leaped to his feet, dismayed.

"Hannah's with him," Sisko informed him.

Noah happened to be facing Asa, or he wouldn't have caught the instant his brother's sig shield wavered. A pulse of intense colors flashed, and quickly subsided.

His AVP kicked up in furious battle readiness. Fighting the kill plans that were loading made his muscles contract. He rounded on Sisko. "You told them, didn't you?"

Coolly unrepentant, Sisko stared him down. "They deserved to know."

Through the window, peering out into the darkness, he saw the flash of red hair as Hannah got out of Zade's van. "God *damn* it, Sisko!" He slammed his hand on the sideboard table. It collapsed, broken in half.

"Noah," Caro's voice was that soothing, velvety violet shade. "It'll be OK."

He turned to her. "The hell it will."

The soft gold cloud spreading out from her chest shut him right up. He stared into her eyes while the colors embraced him. Images of all had happened between them the night before played vividly in his head. The frantic scrolling slowed.

One by one, the kill plans began to wink off his inner screen.

Strange. With all his mods and implants, he felt like he'd only really started seeing since he met her, as if there were new eyes deep inside him now, and they were wide open. Seeing more than all his other techno shit combined. So much data.

But unlike the AVP, he didn't want it to stop. Bring it on.

Hannah came through the door first. Zade followed. Hannah's gaze fastened onto Asa, who looked uncomfortable. For the first time, his brother seemed at a loss.

Hannah made an almost imperceptible movement toward Asa, but stopped short. She opened her mouth to speak, and closed it again. Her throat bobbed.

After an agonizing minute, Asa broke the silence. "What's with the red hair?"

Hannah's chin went up. "Really? After thirteen years, *that's* your opener?"

"Gotta start somewhere," Asa said. "You're blond or you were. I'm thinking you should've gone lighter, or darker brown. Even platinum would be more convincing than that shade of red."

"Who asked you? My hair is my business," Hannah said haughtily.

"Argue later," Noah told her. "You two weren't invited."

Hannah shot him a mulish look. "I don't care. I never care. Get that through your head."

"Mark took my brother," Zade said. "I'm here to plan payback and I don't have to ask your permission to fuck him up."

Noah held still, trying to calm down the combat program with just the breathing exercises, but it wasn't working. His muscles tensed to the point of pain.

"Stay away from him," he said, biting out the words. "He has your stun and kill codes."

"At least I know he has them," Zade said. "That's more warning than Luke had. Maybe I can break Mark's jaw or tear out his tongue before he can spit the codes out."

"Good luck with that," Noah growled.

"I'm all over this, like it or not," Zade told him. "And you need us. Even with this guy in the mix." He gave Asa an unfriendly onceover, which Noah's brother ignored.

Caro watched the scene from where she stood behind the couch. Her sharp, level green eyes caught everything.

"You'll definitely need a freq weaver," Hannah said.

"What's a freak weaver?" Asa asked.

"Freq as in frequency," Hannah explained. "A freq weaver is fitted with intracranial implants and nanotech that receive or block various frequencies." She pointed to her head. "All kinds of crazy stuff in here underneath that red hair you hate. Life's been interesting since you took off."

"I'm sorry," Asa said, stiffly.

"For what?"

Asa shrugged. "That I didn't come back sooner. That you got modded. For everything that happened."

"Well. Whatever." She looked away for a moment, and turned to Noah, a belligerent set to her jaw. "I'm not going to rock on a goddamn porch swing and listen to crickets while you fight Mark," she said. "You need a freq weaver. So eat it."

"You guys aren't tracking," Noah said. "If Mark recognizes any of us, we're screwed. And the more of us there are, the more likely we get noticed by the police, the media, and Obsidian."

"I won't let him see me," Hannah said. "Not that he'd know me if he did. Last time he saw me, I was half dead and totally bald."

Asa frowned. "Why?"

"Brain surgeries. Holes in my skull. My cool neon hair means it's really unlikely that Mark would make the connection.

"He'll recognize your sig," Noah pointed out, staring at his sister.

"So? He'll know yours too, if it comes to that." She met his gaze, her eyes full of defiance. The air hummed with tension. Caro was watching from

362

behind the couch. Catching his eye. Silently telling him to chill with her eyes, with the colors around her body. But he couldn't.

"I can't let you do this." He was slammed by the flat certainty that he couldn't control her or protect her any longer, even as he said it. So fucking futile.

"You'd keep me in a padded room if you could," Hannah said. "I love you for wanting to protect me, even though it drives me nuts. But no more. I'm done with that."

"Listen for once," he said. "It has to be me. Only me. You guys need to disappear, to locations that aren't in my head, so they can't be drugged or tortured out of me."

"Sounds like the doomsday plan." Hannah crossed her arms over her chest. "Updated?"

"Yes," Noah said.

"You have got to be kidding me," Zade muttered.

Caro looked around. "Doomsday plan? What the hell? Somebody explain."

"Noah's way of keeping us safe," Hannah said. "Scatter us across the world to randomly selected destinations, with new identities, and no connection to each other. No past, no future, not a chance of getting back together, ever. What fun."

"Got a better idea?" Noah demanded, eyes narrowed. "Let's hear it."

"Uh, no, but we're only dealing with Mark alone," Sisko argued. "Not all of Obsidian."

"None of you seem to get how dangerous he is," Noah pointed out. "And don't forget. We agreed years ago that I would be the one to make this call."

Zade and Sisko exchanged telling glances. "Here we go again," Zade said. "You self-important prick."

"Too bad," Noah said. "The party's over. Everybody out of the pool."

Appalled silence followed his pronouncement. After a few moments of it,

Caro shook her head.

"No," she said. "You can't do that, Noah."

He was taken aback. She was supposed to be on his side—at least he'd assumed as much. The Midlanders bitched and moaned and pushed back, but they always deferred to him in the end. Caro just defied him. In his face. No compromise.

His vision was overlaid by a haze of hot red. The scrolling, the flickering. *Fuck.*

Hannah gave Caro a startled look. "Right," she seconded quickly. "Amen."

"I'm not gonna toe your line either." Zade said, his voice steely. "That shit's over."

Sisko's clear gaze was just as unyielding. "You're outmaneuvered, buddy," he said. "We'll all come up with a plan together. It's cool."

Noah closed his eyes, flexed his hands, breath shuddering.

Giving in could be fatal for them all. But what the fuck else could he do when he was outnumbered? He looked one by one at the familiar faces of his crew. All of them waiting in silence for him to cave.

"Everybody has to be ready to bolt," he said. "Plane tickets, documents. We salvage what we can, if it all goes to hell. Sisko, warn the out-of-towners."

Sisko nodded.

"Don't forget me," Asa said, his voice wry. "If your people all run off to the four corners of the earth, I'm screwed."

"Tough," Noah said. "If that happened, you'd be long past caring."

Asa looked faintly impressed. "Fuck you, too. Expenses just doubled, brother."

Noah met his gaze. "Give me an itemized bill when we're done."

Caro spoke again. "I'm going to bait the trap," she announced.

"The *fuck* you are," he said savagely.

"Like Asa said," Caro went on. "Mark's too smart to walk into an empty trap. I have to be there. I'm the only one who has what he wants."

"But not what you need to survive," Noah said. "You're not combat trained yet, or modified for speed and resistance."

"I'm the only one who can lure him in," she said stubbornly. "And he can't kill me until he gets what he wants from me."

"But he will get it," he said harshly. "Could take him hours. Or days. He'll break you. Brutally. He's good at it. He lives for it, in fact. He won't kill you until you're begging to die. Which will be long after he's forced you into opening the safe."

Caro sighed. "Noah, please shut up. I can share the risk with all of you."

"No." His voice was a whip crack, making her flinch back. "Get out of this room. You've done enough damage."

"What?" Her eyes widened.

"Just go."

She didn't move an inch. Sudden fire with a white-hot blazing center bloomed out of her sig. It hurt his eyes.

When she spoke, her voice was cold and clipped. "I didn't go through fucking hell on earth to be sent to my room like a bad little kid."

No one else dared to speak.

Asa finally broke the silence, chuckling under his breath. "Yeah, you tell him," he murmured. "Someone has to. Way overdue."

"I did not ask for your input," Noah ground out.

"Like I care." Asa went back to staring into the laptop, his rugged features lit by its faint blue glow.

Noah closed his eyes and walked a tightrope inside himself, trying to block sensory input until he could breathe again. Asa's voice dragged him back.

". . . prefer to rip my arms off and beat me to death with them?" Asa's tone was casual. "Or look at Mark's counterproposal, instead?"

Noah positioned himself at a safe distance with a clear line of sight to Asa's laptop screen. Caro ignored him, perching with a dancer's grace on the edge of the sofa.

A little too close to Asa. Who didn't seem to mind.

Noah got the unspoken message. He wasn't in charge unless he wanted to fight for it.

Good thing fighting was what he was made for.

Chapter 31

SITTING CROSSLEGGED ON the bed, Caro smoothed the final fold of the origami Pegasus. Various other paper creations were scattered over the bed. Making mythical animals out of squares of colored paper was her latest tactic to distract herself from the solitude and suspense of the last few days.

It wasn't working.

The bedroom door opened. Noah came in, carrying two large suitcases. He didn't meet her eyes. Just set the suitcases down with a thud. "Time to pack."

Tension seized her whole body. "You're making a mistake," she began.

"It's not up for discussion." His voice was expressionless. "A team from SafeGuard will pick you up tomorrow morning." He held out a bulky manila envelope.

She took it, and shook the contents out. There was a flawlessly faked driver's license for a Melissa Brodhurst. He'd taken the picture on it two nights ago, using her wig, her glasses and the face-distorting mouth insert.

There was a cell phone, a set of keys for a car and another for a house or apartment, by the looks of them. The pen drive from Luke Ryan's house. A sheaf of documents.

Lots of documents. Bank accounts for Melissa, with breathtakingly high balances. A car title. The deed to a condo. A birth certificate. High school transcripts. A college diploma. A graphic design resume featuring multiple jobs.

"Enjoy your new condo in Mendocino. Good security. And an ocean view, when the fog lets up," he said. "Car's in the garage."

"OK." Her throat was so tight, she could hardly say the word. It was a lie, in any case.

He continued in the same matter-of-fact tone. "I ordered you a passport. It'll arrive in the mail, at your condo. Then you could leave the country. If you want."

Caro squelched the urge to crumple the papers. Furious at him, for making high-handed decisions for her. Grateful that he cared so much. The conflicting impulses made her want to scream. As if her life would be worth a damn if she ended up needing another faked identity. Like she could hide or run for it, knowing that Noah was either dead or else imprisoned and tortured by a madman.

"Don't look like that." Noah sounded defensive. "We all have emergency escape plans, if things go to shit. This is yours. Best I could come up with on short notice."

"You controlling bastard," she said.

"That's me. Pack your stuff. I'll see you in the morning."

Hurt stabbed deep, cold and sharp. "You're not staying?"

"I have more work to do. Gotta focus. Everything else can wait."

"Guess that applies to me, too," she said.

A muscle pulsed in his jaw, but his blank expression did not change. "I need to stay in control." His voice was rigidly even, almost robotic. "I'm having a bad time with imbeds. My old analogs are compromised, so I have to construct new ones every time. Takes time and privacy. It would be stupid of you to take it personally. Good night."

He walked out, and shut the door. Like he'd been doing ever since their clash after they first got in touch with Mark in the Oblio chatroom.

His withdrawal had been subtle. Impossible to protest. Of course he was busy and preoccupied, largely on her behalf, so she had no right to complain. But ever since the flurry of preparations had begun, he'd been lost to her. Light years away.

Truth was, he'd spoiled her. When he was switched on, he radiated a wild, hot, reverent passion that was healing. It made her feel beautiful and powerful. After her long stint of barely surviving, she'd glommed onto that like a starving creature. Passion, closeness. She'd lapped it all up.

Then, all at once, he'd yanked it away again, leaving her lost and bewildered.

Well. Almost. Not the sexual intimacy. Every night he had come to her deep in the night, after his secret planning sessions to which she was not invited. He'd stripped off his clothes, slid into bed and made fierce, focused love to her. No talk. No cuddling.

He peeled off her panties and hungrily licked her into a whimpering frenzy, keeping at it until she was aroused beyond belief. Then he rolled on top of her, kissed her senseless, and took her for a hard, pounding ride, driving her to wave upon crashing wave of erotic surrender. And as soon as she drifted back to reality, he promptly positioned her for the next round. And on, and on.

Sexually he was as eager and generous as he'd ever been, but emotionally, he was gone behind a thick wall of glass.

But still. He'd taken the weight of the world on his shoulders to help her. And she was feeling miserable because he wasn't focused on her tender feelings? Please.

It made her hate herself. Which was really all she needed right now.

She folded over, pressing her hand to her belly. That falling-away feeling was like those last weeks before Mom died. Something so bad was bearing down on her like a train, and she was tied to the tracks. Helpless to stop it.

Then the train hit. The worst happened. It happened all the time, with monotonous regularity. Grief, loss, violence, disaster, brutality. Catastrophe. She knew. Falling in love was a trap. She'd tried so hard to dodge it.

Fail. Major fail. It embarrassed her.

Then again. Any woman's ability to reason clearly would break down in the presence of a man like Noah Gallagher.

One thing was for sure. She could not leave for California tomorrow. She couldn't blame Noah for trying so hard not to involve her in this encounter with Mark, but his fear and stubbornness was going to drive them off a cliff. He was tightening his control over everything and everyone, including himself. She'd seen it in his face, heard it in his voice. He was wound to the breaking point.

Fuck this. She was not going to let him push her away tonight.

Opposing his strength and will would take all of her energy and nerve, but she couldn't be intimidated by the man she loved. She desperately wanted to believe they had something good going on. That they might still actually have a future.

She scattered origami animals in every direction when she got up, with no clear plan of action, just a restless hunger to be close to him and force her way through the wall he'd put up. They had no time for that shit.

She wished she still had her belly dancing outfit. That would have been good for a tension-relieving laugh. Still, thinking of her costume made her want to dress up for this. Maybe make him smile. Probably too much to hope, but hell. She could try.

She pawed through the dresser drawer where Hannah had dumped all the finery she'd gotten for Caro at the lingerie store. There was lots of silky, lacy, wispy little nothings in there to choose from. Pretty, understated, pastel.

Too tasteful. Nothing that could be characterized as an in-your-face sexual weapon.

She wanted something fun, playful, loud. A bustier, a garter belt. Fishnet hose.

Then her hand brushed a little velvet bag. The mysterious object Hannah had left. She pried open the drawstring and upended a sparkling tangle of chains into her hand. At first she thought it was a necklace, but the clasps were positioned wrong.

Body jewelry. Oh, yes.

She peeled off her clothes, untangled the thing with some difficulty, and put it on. The top part was a collar, from which a long sparkling chain connected, plunging straight down between her breasts and hooking to a belt that draped low on her hips. Glittering chains draped from the belt over her hips, as well, and the belt let a richly embossed pendant dangle on her lower belly, just over her mound.

She studied at the ensemble in the mirror as she unwound her hair and shook it loose over her shoulders. The look would definitely have been improved by a Brazilian wax, but her life hadn't permitted that kind of fancy grooming in a long time. Not that Noah had ever complained about her small puff of ringlets.

The ensemble had sort of a kinky, porno bed-slave sort of vibe. Perfect.

She shrugged on the peach silk dressing gown that Hannah had deemed essential for her emergency wardrobe, and padded down the corridor to the room where Noah had been retreating to do his analog dives.

She paused before entering, about to knock. But he never bothered to knock when he came to her at night. Why should she?

The room was dark, but enough moonlight filtered in to show Noah's long, powerful frame, stretched out on the bed. He was stripped down to a pair of loose sweat pants which rode low on his hips. The room was chilly, but even naked to the waist, he radiated heat.

She moved closer, drinking him in, her gaze moving over the sensual contours of his massive chest and shoulders. He was lost in silent meditation, so deeply he didn't seem to hear the sigh of the door or her barefoot tiptoeing. His body heat intensified with every step she took. She felt like banks of blazing stadium spotlights were switching on and lighting her up, one after the other, in the deepest levels of her being.

Everything about him pulled her.

* * *

The new analog dive was in place, every element chosen to do exactly what Noah needed it to do to stay chilled, sharp, in perfect control. The summit was just over that outcropping. Jagged fingers of of black rock poked through the powdery snow that crunched under his boots. At the summit, the soaring peaks of the mountainscape would calm both body and mind. One last step—

Fuck. He reeled back from an unexpected cliff. A volcanic crater lay below him, exhaling steam, gray with ash. At its heart, a gaping cave glowed a hot, wounded red.

Another imbed. So his new analogs were compromised, too.

Flinching away from the imbeds never worked. He had to stare that bad bastard down, and see what happened. Even if it hurt.

He descended into the crater. His boots kicked up clouds of ash as he got closer to the cave, coughing from the acrid fumes.

To the side was a larger opening. Light blazed out. Not the sullen red glow. This light was paler, yellowish. Like sunlight.

He moved closer, steeling himself, and peered through the opening. Cracked asphalt, baking in desert sunshine. His mind fought it, but this place was too much a part of him not to recognize it. The grocery store parking lot. A waffle house down the block, a used car dealership, a dollar store. Cheap, prefab structures of fake adobe, aging fast in the pitiless sun.

The wet, hollow thwack of a baseball bat, connecting with a skull.

He turned, braced to see the grizzled man, his face splattered with Dad's blood.

It wasn't him. It was Mark clutching the bloodied baseball bat, grinning wildly. And it was Caro who lay crumpled and bloody and still at his feet. Her head caved in.

Noah? Noah, do you hear me?

He exploded upright, startled back into the physical world, his fist stopping just before it connected. She jerked back, and thudded to the floor on her ass.

"Never touch me when I'm having a flashback, Caro! I could have killed you!"

She recoiled. "I . . . I'm sorry!" Her sig tightened to a clot of anxious greens and grays. "I didn't know it was a flashback. You called out my name, so I thought—"

"You scared the living shit out of me!" He flung his arm out, sweeping the a ceramic lamp off the night table, sending it crashing to the floor.

"Yo!" Sisko's voice floated up from downstairs. "What's up?"

Noah couldn't get an answer out. He hunched over, fists clenched. Caro tried several times before she could speak. "We—we're—we're fine," she called out.

"Noah?" There was a harder tone in Sisko's voice.

"We're good," Noah called out. "Lamp fell. No problem."

He was horrified at what he'd almost done. For years he'd thought he'd licked this. He was wrong. One bad imbed, and he was nailed right back to the wall. Falling to pieces before her eyes.

Caro was huddled on the floor. Afraid of him.

Desperately, he slid off the bed onto his knees and seized her. He nuzzled her silky hair, inhaling its silken, perfumed warmth. The sensory data of her perfume formed incredible visuals in his mind. Even with eyes shut, she dazzled him. His whole body was a wide-open eye, worshipping her.

He held her tighter. *God.*

"Sorry I yelled," he muttered. "It scared me, that I almost hit you."

Her hands slid into his hair, petting and soothing him. "I'm sorry, too. That I startled you. Was it . . . what do you call it again? An imbed?"

"Yeah. My analogs are all compromised. Even new ones. Don't know why."

"Tell me about it," she suggested. "Maybe it would help."

"No."

Her fingers stopped for a moment, and then resumed their slow, soothing caresses. "OK," she murmured. "Whatever."

He should have sent her away days ago. He'd kept her for his own comfort. And not just for the sex. She kept him balanced. His pre-Caro equilibrium was trashed. If he couldn't keep the combat program under control with his analogs, then proximity to Caro was his only alternative. She reinforced the underlying structures inside him so that the ASP and AVP could rage full force without driving him nuts. He retained his capacity for rational thought, impulse control. Decision making.

With Caro, AVP was a powerful resource, not a caged monster.

But she had to go. He'd have to stay on top of the AVP without her. Unchilled. Unsoothed. No diving. He had no idea how he'd pull it off. He was terrified to fuck things up. Let them all down. Get them all killed.

He was ashamed to have Caro see him in this condition. His own fault, for keeping her here.

They ought to get up off the goddamn floor at the very least. The bed was a whole lot softer.

He got up and onto the bed, fully intending to sit her right next to him.

She sat down on his lap, before he could stop her. His body's reaction was instantaneous.

She kissed his forehead, shifting and wiggling her ass over his stiff, aching cock. Her lips were so soft. Light bloomed on his skin like bioluminescence wherever she touched him. She kissed his lips, her tender tongue flicking against his.

He pulled away, and slid her off his lap and onto the bed beside him. "Bad idea," he said roughly.

"Bullshit!"

He was startled by her sharp tone. "What? What the hell is your problem?"

"Don't play dumb," she snapped. "I want you. I need to be close to you. We both need it. I'm sorry you got zapped by your imbed, but you appear to be fine, so get over it." She reached out and gripped his stiff, aching cock. Her skillful stroke and twist made him gasp sharply, a shudder of pleasure racking him.

He trapped her hand, held it still. Sweat broke out on his forehead. He was trying so hard not to drown in this thing, and she just would not get it.

"I'm not playing hard to get," he said. "Of course I want to fuck you. That's a given. But I'm messed up right now. Thirteen years I've been busting my ass to manage my stress reaction and maintain impulse control. I thought I'd beat it. I was wrong."

Her fingers tightened, stroking. The sensual caress made him clench his teeth.

"What's wrong with this impulse?" she asked. "I love this impulse."

He dragged her hand away from his shaft and held it tight to make it fucking behave. "You're not listening," he said roughly. "I always lose control with you."

"Have you heard me complain?"

"That's not the point," he snarled.

She huffed out an impatient breath. "So what the fuck is the point? I'm lost."

He grabbed her other hand, and squeezed. "Be patient," he begged. "Please. I have to come up with an analog that's not mined with imbeds. Not easy, OK?"

"I think a blow job would work better for you."

His heart revved, and his dick twitched and throbbed. His combat program was scrolling madly, but he barely noticed it, staring at the hot challenge in her eyes.

"Uh . . ." He stopped and swallowed carefully. "Not a good idea."

"Let go of my hands," she said. "I'll show you exactly what I mean."

He maintained his tight grip, but his mouth felt dry. "Don't push me."

"I'd grip you, right at the root. And lick you up and down," she said. "Until you're shiny and wet. Hot and thick. Filling my mouth. I love that. I'll pull you in deep, and suck you, and lick you . . . and make you scream with pleasure." Her voice was throaty and caressing. Her fingers curled around his, squeezing. "Until you're helpless and gasping. Out of control. Exploding in my mouth. Mmm. Love that. Yum."

"Goddamnit, Caro," he growled.

She lifted his hands and kissed his knuckles. Hot, silky kisses that he could feel against his cock. Where he automatically felt all her seductive suggestions.

She looked up, meeting his eyes. "Can you tell how turned on I am, just by looking at my sig?"

He scanned her shifting halo of colors. He was so used to being bare-eyed with her by now, it seemed as normal as any other sensory detail he might notice, like the way her nipples poked through the fine silk robe. "Yeah." His voice felt raw.

"Not fair," she said. "My feelings are written in neon for you to read whenever you feel like it. But I can't read you. Not when you shut me out."

"I'm trying to keep you safe," he said.

"I am safe," she said sharply. "You're trying so hard to control everything. Yourself, me, everyone else. It's not working. It's not necessary, either. Let go."

His jaw ached with tension. "The last time I let go, I almost put my fist through your throat."

She shook her head. "I'm not worried about that."

"You goddamn well should be," he told her.

"I know you, Noah. Way down deep. And I want to make you come. Let me."

The hypnotic cadence of her voice were like magic, softening his rigid grip. She felt the moment her spell worked on him and her smile flashed, wide and delighted.

"I don't know how to let go," he warned. "Don't get your hopes up."

"Don't worry. I got you covered." She slid off the bed and leaned forward, fumbling with the drawstring of his sweatpants. Letting his hugely erect dick spring out.

She took him in hand, squeezing and stroking, then leaned in to swirl her hot tongue around the head of his rod, licking up precome. He sucked in air, muscles clenched, fingers digging into the edge of the mattress. AVP surging and red hot.

He should stop her, but he couldn't. Too damn good. Every wet, pulling, suckling stroke destroyed him. She was taking him to pieces . . .

No. Panic surged, along with the explosion. No retreat. No escape.

A huge blast. Deep throbbing pulses of pleasure. Blinding light.

His eyes opened. He was flat on his back on the bed. Limp and gasping.

Caro was still there. She was OK. He hadn't done anything terrible. Not yet.

He focused on the vision before him. Her hair was draped over his thighs like the folds of a silk scarf. She smiled at him as she discreetly wiped her mouth.

Delirious pleasure still pulsed through every nerve. "God, Caro. That was . . ."

"Yes indeed. Absolutely. It was." She sounded pleased with herself. "I don't know about you, but I call that progress. Oh, I have a surprise for you. Want to see?"

The last thing his nerves needed was a surprise. He jerked up onto his elbows.

She read his expression. "Just for fun," she reassured him. "To make you smile."

She stood up, and let the silk robe fall to the floor.

He sat bolt upright with a gasp, his hard-on refreshed in a hot instant. "Where the hell did that come from?"

"Do you like it?" She lifted up her hair over her head and spun around, displaying herself proudly.

"You didn't answer my question. But fuck, yeah, I like it. A lot." He stared at her, dazzled. "My dick is going to explode. Again."

She looked mystified. "It has that effect on you, even in the dark?"

"What dark? This room is flooded with light. Some of it is blazing out of you."

She smiled demurely. "I could wear this pretty thing under my clothes, and you'd see the collar as you look at me across the dinner table, and know I'm wearing it under my clothes. And thinking about you. Inside me."

"I don't need the slightest encouragement to think about being inside you."

"Good." She spun, swaying her hips. "I thought that a romp with the naughty nympho playmate from the porno planet might lighten you up. It's your turn to be the bed toy."

"Bed toy?" That startled him out of his horndog reverie. "What the fuck is that about?"

"You've been freezing me out," she told him. "And then coming in to ravish me in the night. My demon lover."

He studied her, slit-eyed. "Seemed like you were into it," he said cautiously.

"Of course I was into it," she said tartly. "The sex is not the problem. But I didn't come here to scold you tonight. I had other plans." She swirled her fingertip tenderly in the slick drop of precome pooling on the head of his cock, and licked it.

Still, he hesitated. "Is this a trap?" he asked warily.

She gaped at him. "What?"

"You're pissed at me. I see it in your sig."

She laughed out loud at him. "What if I am? I still want you. And I'm tired of tiptoeing around you. Get used to having me all up in your face. This is a very straightforward seduction. No traps or tricky stuff. Don't be a humorless jerk. Lighten up."

"Oh, babe." A burst of laughter shook him. "I would do anything for you. But lightening up is too much to ask of me."

"OK, fine." She swung her leg over him. "Be dead serious, then." She smiled down through the shadowy fall of her hair. "As long as you give me what I want."

She poised herself over him, holding his stiff rod at the perfect angle to sink right down onto him. He seized her waist, holding her still. "Let me get you ready."

"I am ready," she said. "And I need you, inside me. *Now.*"

"But it'll be better for you if I—"

"Listen to me, Noah Gallagher." Her voice had a commanding ring. "You can't always call the shots if you want to be with me. We will alternate. Understand? One day, maybe it's your turn. The next day, it's my turn. I've been meaning to clarify that for a while now, and this seems like the right time. Is that perfectly clear?"

"Uh . . . yeah. Sure." The heat in her eyes made his dick throb. He trailed his hand down her belly, toying with the pendant. "Damn, you're beautiful in this thing."

"If you're trying to distract me, it won't work." She preened, lifting her hair. "But I'm glad that you like it."

He gathered up a thick lock of her hair, pressed it to his face and inhaled. "Your scent has a color too," he told her. "My mods translate all sensory input into visual data. Just for the pure fucking hell of it."

"Noah," she murmured, a shiver rippling down her back at his touch.

"Sounds, too," he said. "Everything. Your voice is a violet blue. Like the evening sky. I'm so strung out on it, I can't even breathe without you. I am so screwed."

She slid her fingers into his short, glossy hair. "Noah," she whispered again.

He pressed his face to her breasts. The glittering chain that plunged from collar to waist stroked his face, warm from the heat of her body. Her taut nipple caressed his cheek.

"You sneaky bastard," she said. "I was trying to be tough with you, and you go over-the-top romantic on me. Not fair. Goddamnit."

"Didn't do it on purpose." He made a choked, keening sound as she slid the head of his cock along her moist slit, and then nudged it tenderly inside. Her hips pulsed, kissing his blunt tip with her slick entrance. Wet, licking, teasing promises of all the slick heaving and plunging to come.

That was it. The last bit of his resistance gave way. He jackknifed up, catching her in his arms. Kissing her with frenzied intensity, no holding back.

He wasn't going to hurt her, scare her. She was divinely powerful, a goddess, a rippling flame in his arms.

He groaned as she took his cock slowly inside herself. The clutch of her body yielding to him was a caressing agony of pleasure. Loved, licked, enveloped by heat, by wet. Painted by the hot colors of her body's snug clasp.

So . . . fucking . . . perfect. It was killing him.

She sank her fingers into his shoulders. Their eyes locked. The look on her face pierced right through him. Her naked soul blazing out.

"I love when you're wide open to me," he said.

"Same here. I wanted you the second I laid eyes on you."

"Me too," he told her raggedly. "Like I want to breathe."

Her slender body rode him, light and lithe. Each hot clench branded him with pleasure. Each gliding, rhythmic stroke satisfied him to the core of his being and stoked a frantic need for the next.

He clutched her, riding the rising swell of power, surging, cresting.

Crashing through them.

When he opened his eyes, it was a moment before he recognized himself.

Inside, he felt different. She did that to him somehow. The mystery was sweeter when he didn't try to figure it out. Which was totally unlike him. But he needed what she offered. Had to have it. More, please.

He pressed his hot face to her hair, which was damp. A tang of salt overlaid the scent of honey and flowers. He breathed her in, trailing his fingertips through her hair, motionless otherwise. Could have stayed that way for hours.

But she sat up, and gazed down at him. "Noah," she said.

He braced himself. He knew what she was going to say. Her mind was wide open to him now.

"Do you trust me?" she asked.

"Yes," he said. "Say what you need to say. Don't try to trap me with words."

"I'm coming with you tomorrow," she said.

His whole body clenched up. Pain flared in his jaw. "We've been through this," he growled. "We've got multiple plans in place to track Mark if he doesn't get close enough. You don't have to risk it."

"But if he sees that I'm there, he'll come for me," she said. "He can't help it. And you can finish this. Otherwise it's going to drag out into a long, ugly war."

"He wants war, he'll get war."

"I'm the one who doesn't want it," Caro said forcefully. "I want a future with you. I want my man. I want our life. That can only happen if I'm there with you tomorrow to meet Mark. You know that I'm right."

He shook his head. His voice felt trapped, like a rock blocked his throat.

"No," he forced out. "You can't be there."

She pressed her hand to his heart, as if she knew somehow exactly how to chill his combat program. His data scroll started to slow down instantly.

"It's not up to you anymore," she told him. "It never really was to begin with."

Their eyes locked, and she read his mind as effortlessly as he could read hers.

"And no, you can't lock me up," she said. "Mark Olund does evil shit like that, but people who love and trust and respect each other don't. I won't be stupid. I'm not volunteering for actual combat, believe me. But I'm taking my chances tomorrow."

He hung onto himself until he could speak normally. "Caro, I just want to keep you safe."

"You gave me what I need to stay safe," she said. "It's an incredible gift. I'll always be grateful. Now trust me. The way I trust you."

He closed his eyes. The combat program made his body tense, buzzing with desperate urgency. Kill plans winking and flashing, fountains of scrolling data, all tinted hot red. And her hand pressing his heart. Keeping him steady.

She was right, that her presence made their odds better. And he fucking *hated* it.

"You'll follow orders," he said harshly. "Do as I say. Show yourself when I say, disappear when I say. Go where I tell you. On the double."

Her smile was radiant. "Of course." She bent to press a soft kiss to his jaw. "Just one more thing."

"Spare me."

"Sleep," she said.

That took him entirely by surprise. "What? Huh?"

"I mean real sleep," she said. "Not that fake soldier sentinel bullshit. I'm talking real, normal, human sleep. That's what you need."

He was baffled. "I don't remember how. It's been years."

Caro tugged the covers down from the bed, nudging him until he rolled off them. She slid between the sheets and held out her arms. "It's easy. Come on, try it. I'll hold you."

He wasted no time taking her up on that offer, settling her lithe body over his non-dominant arm. She snuggled close, petting his chest, easing her smooth thigh over his. Felt great. He wasn't sleepy. Nor was he likely to be, ever. But who gave a shit? This was right where he wanted to be. He'd fake it if it made her happy. Forever.

But eventually, he actually did synch himself to the slow, hypnotic pulse of Caro's colors. If he focused on that, he almost succeeded in not thinking about what he was risking tomorrow.

Almost.

Chapter 32

MARK SPOKE INTO his wrist com. "How many thermals can you see?"

Static buzzed until Ty responded. "Four, inside. Three men, from the size of them. There's a smaller one with them who could be a woman."

Mark pondered that. The possibility that Asa Stone had actually kept to the terms of their bargain made him even more suspicious than an obvious betrayal. Stone was playing a deeper game. That fact stood out. Mark had studied the man exhaustively in the past few days.

He tracked the multiple images on the monitors that came from the vidcams of the slave soldiers, as well as the images from the brain-linked drones that the slave soldiers controlled. Brenner was on his way to verify that Caroline Bishop was physically at the meeting place. The others he had outfitted with cloaking gear and sent out into the forest to encircle the ruined, abandoned nineteenth century mansion.

Mark hated the place. It was a bizarre choice. Parts of it had collapsed and been taken over by invasive trees, or covered with a strangling ivy. Too big, too rambling. Full of potential hiding spots.

The drones were equipped with cutting edge visual tech, but watching the scenes through inferior mechanical eyes irritated the hell out of Mark. The drones and the slave soldiers could both detect heat signatures, but no one besides Mark could read and analyze an energy sig. The Eyes Guys had been anomalous, developing that unique skill amongst themselves in the Midlands hellhole. Brain training by brute necessity.

He saw no human thermals other than those Ty had already specified in the crumbling building or in the woods. Just small woodland animals. Still, he was uneasy.

Brenner careened toward the main entrance on a motorcycle. He'd been the obvious choice of canary for this coal mine. His annoying verbal glitch made him Mark's least favorite slave soldier. Thirty million dollar investment or not, Mark was hoping Brenner would die on this mission. It would save Mark the hassle of killing him.

Brenner slowed to a stop. His vidcam image jerked and bobbed as he dismounted, but it soon steadied, allowing Mark to see the man who walked out the front entrance. His appearance matched the sketches and descriptions that Mark had unearthed about the mysterious Asa Stone. Mark had found no obvious explanation for Stone's connection with Obsidian, though, and the blank spot bothered him.

Stone was subtle, arrogant, and fearless. A bad combo. He did not give a fuck how many crime bosses he inconvenienced. He appeared to have a death wish.

Today was his lucky day. He'd come to just the place to get it granted.

Stone was a big, thick-muscled brute. Buzzed-off dark hair and cold gray eyes. Mark was sure he'd never met him before, but something about his face was naggingly familiar. He would need to see Stone's sig to pinpoint it. But he'd satisfy his curiosity soon enough.

Stone gave Brenner a once-over, dismissed him, and focused on the vidcam attached to Brenner's coat. "Who's this clown?" Stone said, addressing Mark directly.

"Olund wants to see the girl before he comes in himself," Brenner said stolidly.

Again, Stone's level gaze reminded Mark of something, or someone. The way he was so absolutely convinced that he had the upper hand.

Mark looked forward to teaching him how things really stood. Guys like that were always so surprised.

Stone jerked his chin toward the entrance. Brenner followed him into what had once been a grand entrance hall with a vaulted ceiling and tall windows, most of them broken, letting the weather in. Drifted leaves, dirt and moss were scattered across a filthy floor barely recognizable as marble. Birds swooped and fluttered in the ceiling and a snake slithered into a pile of smashed masonry. Brenner walked alongside the man down a long gallery with broken windows. Mark could hear glass crunch rhythmically beneath the two men's boots.

"We'll talk in the chapel," Stone said. "It still has a roof." He pushed open a creaking door.

Mark surveyed the room with distaste as Brenner followed Stone into the room. He hated churches. He had childhood memories of extreme unpleasantness in churches. Life on the streets, with all its squalor and danger, had been preferable to that. And then came the Midlands freak parade. He never caught a break.

Unless he carved it for himself. With a bloody knife.

Many more broken windows encircled the base of the domed roof. A bolt of bright winter sunlight poured through the remnants of a red stained glass window, spotlighting a metal cage protected by clear bulletproof panels and casting the rest of the room into ominous shadow.

The place was a shambles. Dirty, piled with rotten wood, broken furniture, upended pews and garbage. Its moldy walls were covered with scrawled graffiti, in stark contrast to the jewel-like perfection of the glass cage.

Mark smiled thinly as he looked at it. So they thought they could protect her with a bulletproof box.

Stone lifted his wrist to his mouth. "Bring her out," he said into the comm.

A door in the back of the glass box opened. A slender figure emerged. A big, helmeted man in heavy armor stood behind her, loaded down with lethal weapons.

Mark's body tensed with raw excitement at the sight of her. She wore some black, skin-tight thing, stretched to the max over every curve and hollow of her body. Her hair hung loose, a mane of ringlets framing her face, flowing down to her ass. Her shadowy green eyes stared straight ahead. Her mouth was tight with tension.

She stood as if awaiting the firing squad.

Mark swallowed a rush of saliva. He ached to see her beautiful sig again. And then gobble it up, after he taught her what a bad girl she had been. He was so hungry.

"Why the box?" Mark waited, teeth grinding, as Brenner repeated his question.

"Just protecting my property," Asa Stone said. "The brainwaves should work just fine right through the glass. That's all we need her to do. Then she disappears. Happy now? She's real and she's here. Just like I promised."

Rage made Mark's combat program surge. He almost smashed the instrument panel. "I'm on my way. With my security."

Mark waited, teeth grinding, as Brenner mechanically relayed the message.

"Two for you and two for me, as we agreed," Stone said. "If he stays here to monitor her, you come in with one more."

Caroline was disappearing from Mark's field of vision as Brenner followed Stone with his eyes. "Turn so I can see the girl!" he snarled into the comm. "Don't look away from her for one single fucking second until I'm in the room with her!"

Brenner spun obediently back to face Caroline again, and Mark feasted his eyes on her. He was burning with eagerness to see her, smell her. Touch her.

Maybe he shouldn't have brought the safe. He had every intention of taking Caroline back for himself, but shit happened. It would be better to get the safe opened and take possession of its contents now. They could discuss who got to fuck the girl after the other issue was settled. He was a practical man, not a slave to his impulses.

Three clueless unmods and a helpless girl against himself, five slave soldiers, and a truck full of space-age killing toys that he could not wait to play with. Yeah.

Finally, this was starting to be fun.

*   *   *

"Hey. Spotted three surveillance drones circling up there." It was Hannah's voice in his earpiece. "Flying low, probably armed. Do I block the frequencies now?"

"No," Noah said. "Let him get closer. I'll signal when it's time."

Noah peered through the screen of his thermal shield helmet. He hated having to look through mechanical eyes, particularly in a combat situation, but the drones were sure to have good imaging tech, and their team had to stay hidden.

Mark's truck sped closer. Two distinct heat signatures were visible in the cab.

"No one in the woods?" Hannah asked.

"Haven't seen anyone yet," Noah said. "Doesn't mean they're not there."

"My brother, the optimist," Hannah murmured.

"You're ready to pull Caro out the second I tell you?"

Hannah made an exasperated sound. "As promised. Relax."

Right. Sure. He watched as Mark's truck rumbled past the marker.

"Now," he said. "Jam all frequencies except for this one."

"Done," Hannah said, with satisfaction.

He recognized Mark as he got out of the truck. Tall, dirty blond hair, hawk nose, ice blue eyes. Dead heart.

Mark stood, arms folded, while some musclebound dude in a helmet and body armor hoisted a huge silver box out of the back of the vehicle. The GodsEye safe. Asa came out, as he had done before, and exchanged words Noah could not hear.

The three men went inside. Their heat signatures were soon lost to sight.

Noah risked lifting the faceplate on the shield, and peered bare-eyed at Zade and Sisko's positions. "He's in," he said into the comm. "Get into position." He scanned one last time for heat or energy sigs—

And saw a ripple of movement in the leaves. Not wind. He searched again. Close to Zade, too close. *There.* Animal?

No. The fucking tree wasn't swaying back and forth, it was moving forward. Zade couldn't hear it because of the protective headphones he'd wired into his helmet to block his stun and kill codes. *Shit.*

"Zade! Behind you!" he shouted into the comm, as the attacker sprang.

Zade spun around and went down in a flurry of thrashing foliage.

"Hannah!" he shouted. "We're under attack! Get Caro out! Now!"

Trees bent and branches cracked. Zade was still fighting. Which meant that the attacker hadn't used the code. And Zade could fight like a demon straight out of hell.

Noah sprinted toward Caro.

* * *

Caro shivered. That beam of bright, blood-tinged light made her feel like a witch doll on display in a glass case. But she was still alive, and Noah's final, searing kiss still tingled and burned on her lips.

Asa had left. So strange, to just stand there and wait, offering herself up. She stared down at the man Mark had sent to monitor her. Big and strong, weapons slung all over him, but his eyes looked dull. Lost.

Familiar, too. She studied his face as recognition dawned. The TV interview she'd seen online. This was Brenner Jameson, father of two-year-old Callie.

The door into the box behind her crashed open. Hannah beckoned. "Come on!"

She whipped her head around. "What happened?"

"We're under attack!" Hannah grabbed her hand. "Noah said to pull you now!"

Caro sprinted after her, and even so Hannah practically yanked her arm from its socket, dragging her faster. Hannah dragged a camo tarp off a massive motorcycle, and straddled it, revving the engine. "Get on!"

Caro obeyed, clutching Hannah's body as the bike took off, banging and thudding over the rough terrain.

A flickering shadow, and the sky fell. The ground swung up and smacked her hard, knocking her breathless.

When she focused again, she saw a woman in dark camo shoving a hypodermic needle into Hannah's throat.

Caro lunged to stop her. The woman held her back with startling ease, barely reacting to Caro's frantic clawing. She was supernaturally strong. A modified supersoldier.

Useless to struggle, but Caro couldn't stop. The woman jerked her around and slammed her to the ground, fastening her arms behind her with zip ties.

The she-beast dragged her backwards toward the house by her arms, wrenching brutally hard. Caro scrambled to keep her feet beneath herself.

Noah burst out of the trees. His visor was up, showing the glowing amber of his eyes. That split second that their eyes met pierced through her panic, and touched her depths. She knew he'd do anything to save her. Sacrifice anything. Everything.

She felt it, with a wild, screaming intensity. Everything that they were about to lose. How beautiful it was, how precious. How fragile.

He raised his gun, and took aim.

Caro lurched to the side as the gunshot sounded. The woman who held her jerked sharply, but didn't release her grip. She kept moving. Noah slowed to aim again—and two flashing silver things swooped into her vision, hovering.

Noah swung his gun up and shot one of them right out of the sky. Small, shining pieces flew—

Suddenly, Noah stopped, staggered . . . and then collapsed.

Caro screamed, twisting in the woman's hard grip. She could just barely see another man running toward the spot where Noah had fallen before she was dragged around the corner of the house. Noah was lost to sight.

She went wild, screaming, flailing. Something hit her head. Darkness. Excruciating pain.

She came to on a floor somewhere . . . and she wished she hadn't.

Asa lay on his belly near her on a bloodsmeared floor. The cords in his neck strained as he lifted his head. His hands were cuffed behind him, and the slave soldier she'd identified as Brenner sat on top of him.

Both of Asa's security men lay still and silent. One lay just a few feet from them, a dart piercing his chest. Another one lay close to the entrance.

Another man, maybe Mark's, was sprawled on the ground, a bullet hole between his eyes. Brain tissue was spread out on the floor behind his head in a splattered pinkish fan.

Asa's eyes met hers asking a silent question. She replied with a tiny shake of her head, still half deaf from the blow to her head.

His lips pulled back from his teeth in a hiss of dismay. No help on the way.

The toe of a heavy black boot nudged her face, forcing her to look up.

Mark's unshielded eyes had an eerie glow, like arctic ice.

He grinned. His teeth seemed unnaturally white and sharp.

"Caroline," he said. "Finally."

Chapter 33

NOAH HEARD SOUNDS in the vast emptiness. Faraway, tinny. He latched onto the faint stimulus, using it to drag himself up. Toward consciousness.

Closer. His battlefield processor assessed his condition while random images and thoughts pinged wildly around like an insane pinball machine.

Caro, Hannah, Zade, Asa, Sisko. Counting on you. Wake . . . the fuck . . . up!

Couldn't do it. Sedated. Massive dose.

He forced his brain to rev up, enduring the pain. Neuron by neuron. Hurt like a bastard. He kept his eyes closed, hoping nobody was measuring his brain waves, or looking at his sig.

His own fault, thinking he could outwit Mark. The guy had more than a decade of evil deeds on him. Dickbrain stupid to assume that Mark had only unmods to back him up. He'd dug up some slave soldiers even without Lydia's safe.

He tried to move a little, willing whoever was watching not to notice. His hand tried to obey. Nothing. Like shoving a truckload of bricks.

Noah felt himself hoisted, then dragged. His legs trailed behind him, limp and helpless, scraping over rocks, dirt, dead branches. *Caro. Hannah.*

Hannah, lying still on the ground. Caro, dragged away screaming. No. *Stop.*

He pushed the terrifying images away, reminding himself of what he had to do.

Remember how to fucking *move.*

The slave soldier heaved Noah into the back of the truck and started to pull Noah's body armor and weapons off. All of it, right down to the briefs.

OK. Robots had their reasons.

He was hoisted into a black case lined with metal, chilly against his bare skin. They used cases like that at Midlands. Designed for the transport of modified humans. The flat, dead-eyed face of the slave soldier gazed down at him without curiosity.

The heavy lid thudded shut, swallowing him and the light.

But darkness was relative for him. He could still see with his infrared. He used his combat program to reassess his physical condition. He was metabolizing the drug quickly, but not fast enough.

Thinking of Caro and Hannah in Mark's grip made his numbed body twitch. That was a start. Anything to change the cards on the table.

He closed his eyes. Seized onto his last analog, imbed and all. Volcanic crater with his father's murder festering inside it? Bring that shit on. Very intense, very toxic.

The details appeared one by one: The hot fissure, the steam, the smells.

But it had changed. The fissure was larger now. Tracks led out of it, like an old-time mine. Battered ore carts waited to be filled.

He packed the carts with every memory he could think of that carried a punishing, gland-jolting kick, transforming each one into a visual analog. Dynamite, Semtex, C-4. There were plenty. Hannah, head shaved, skull drilled and sawed open for experimental surgery. His friends, suffering and afraid. Rebellion Day filled two carts. Leon bleeding out, eyes open to the sky. Kane on the ground in a pool of blood, a bullet lodged in his leg. Devon screaming as Noah cut a geotagged tracer out of her back.

Mom, gone without a note or a word. That was a ton of ANFO blasting agent, right there.

Caro tied to that bed, blood trickling down her naked chest, was his detonator.

By now the whole mental mountain rumbled in anticipation of what was coming.

Might kill him. Who gave a fuck. Living could be worse. Depending on how things went.

The loaded carts began to move down the tracks, picking up speed and momentum. He followed along, right into the hot red glow of the ominous fissure as the tracks curved . . . and then led straight into the glowing yellow light of his imbed.

Noah heaved the train forward, sending the loaded carts rattling straight into that image of the strip mall parking lot, where the grizzled man loomed over Noah's father's corpse with his bloody baseball bat. He squeezed the detonator.

He must have had a seizure. He came to with his feet drumming the inside of the carrying case. Warping it, then breaking it open.

A blaze of light assaulted his eyes. He leaped out with a shout, and stood, fists clenched, ready to do battle.

The slave soldier was gone. His body armor, clothing, guns and knives were gone. The truck was full of crates. He wrenched one open. Stared blankly at the contents. Weaponry, but he had no clue how that crazy shit worked and no time to figure it out. Back to basics.

The space-age cyborg freak had devolved into a howling cave man armed with sticks and stones.

* * *

Mark gestured at the grisly corpse with the hole in his forehead that lay behind him. "That's thirty million dollars, lying right there," he said. "Too bad your fuckboy has such good aim."

Caro was mute. She just kept seeing Noah, shot with that dart. Endlessly falling to the ground, over and over.

"Open the safe," Mark said. "Then we'll have a talk about the money and trouble you've cost me, and what's to be done with the fuckboy. Where did you find him? And how did you pay him? Never mind. Stupid question. Obvious answer."

Asa lay pinned beneath one of the slave soldiers, who held a gun to his head. Blood oozed from a gunshot wound in his upper arm, but his clear gray gaze never wavered, even when Mark sauntered over and kicked him viciously in the back.

Asa huffed out air, but made no other sound.

"I'll open the safe," she burst out. "Just don't hurt him."

"But I want to," Mark said. "He's going to die. Today. Though how loud he screams and how long it takes will be up to you."

He seized a battered old chair that lay on the floor, and placed it in front of the safe, positioning both in the ruddy shaft of sunlight.

"Lights. Camera. Action. Ready for your closeup?" He indicated the chair. "Sit."

Caro dragged herself up to her feet, fighting for balance with her hands fastened behind her. Her footsteps sounded eerily loud in the echoing room. The rickety chair wobbled as she sat.

Mark opened the aluminum carrying case and looked at the GodsEye helmet, cradled in its nest of molded foam. "Proud of yourself? Inconveniencing me like this is a real accomplishment."

For a moment, Caro searched her mind for something to say that might influence him one way or the other. The urge drained away into nothing.

398

No point. He meant to hurt them. His hint that she could change the outcome was just another kind of psychological torture. No reason on earth to play along.

She shook her head. "I just wanted to live," she said.

He slid his fingers into her hair, digging in deep. "I wouldn't have hurt you. Not if you'd been a good girl, and did as you were told."

"You killed Dex Boyd," she said. "I saw you do it."

His fingers twisted in her hair, tightening until she gasped with pain. "Yes, but that was your choice," he said. "If you'd agreed to open that safe when I asked you to, I wouldn't have been forced to kill Boyd. Or Tim Wheaton. Those deaths are on you."

"No," she said. "No, they are not on me."

"Are you arguing with me, Caroline?" Mark's voice was poisonously soft.

Huh. Dead end question if she ever heard one. "Can we just get on with it?"

He shoved her chin up, and poked at the scabbed wounds she'd gotten from Metalmouth's knife. "So Carrerra tickled you before Stone showed up? I didn't authorize him to do that. I would have punished him, but Fuckboy here beat me to it."

The door opened, and the female slave soldier entered, maneuvering herself through the door with Hannah's limp body loaded on her shoulder.

She walked over to them, and let Hannah slide to the floor in a crumpled heap.

Asa jerked his head around to look, dislodging the slave soldier. The guy whacked him with the gun butt. Once again, Asa made no sound.

Mark used his foot to turn Hannah's limp body onto her back, studying her before he turned back to Caro.

"Midlanders," he said, in a tone of discovery. "I'll be damned. How the hell did they find you?" He stared down at Asa. "And you. Noah's brother?

I thought you looked familiar." He laughed. "Bonus! When she wakes up, it'll be playtime!" His laughter cut off suddenly, as if he'd flicked a switch. "But first, the safe."

He placed the helmet on Caro's head, positioning the sensors over her forehead and temples, and stroked her hair tenderly off her cheek. "It's decorative, on you," he said. "An empress with her crown. A high priestess with her headdress. Beautiful."

She recoiled from his caressing touch. "Stop it."

Mark's hot blue AVP gaze looked right through her, but the effect was the exact opposite of when Noah did it. It reduced her, made her feel shivering and small. She wondered if he were reading her sig, like Noah did.

He had to be. He had the same mods. She had to keep her thoughts and plans small and emotionless, floating on the outskirts of her mind. Nothing happening in there but fear. Fear blanked out everything.

No need to fake it.

She felt the tickling hum in her ears as the helmet was activated. Mark loomed over her, hungrily. "Step back," she told him. "I can concentrate better if you do."

Mark chuckled. "Nothing doing, bitch. Make an effort."

It felt strange, to work with the GodsEye interface after eight long months. She struggled to compose her mind to the necessary initial stillness, and closed her eyes, trying to reduce sensory input. The blazing red light, the rancid smell of Mark's sweat. Her own rapid breathing and quick, thudding heartbeat.

"Zero the mechanism for me, please," she said quietly. "Green button on the bottom of the control rod."

"It's zeroed." Mark sounded peeved. "It's ready for the sequence. Do it." His voice vibrated with anticipation.

Caro pulled Lydia's training sequence out of her memory. Ten years of intensive practice had made her an expert in manipulating the Inner Vision software. She could control the shape of her brainwaves with more sureness and accuracy than anyone alive. She also knew how to exceed program parameters, trip the security, and blow up the safe, completely incinerating the contents.

Theoretically.

She'd never actually done it, since GodsEye equipment cost in the millions. She might well be committing suicide. But there were worse ways to go.

There were five images in the training sequence. The GodsEye's recommendation for a permanent combination was ten images. One, a snowy field with a knobbed and ancient oak tree in the middle. Two, a red half open rose. Three, a school of silvery tropical fish. Four, an eagle diving for its prey. Five, a mushroom cloud.

She blasted emotional energy into the last image. Her terror, her crushed hopes, her love for Noah, goosing that witch-hat brainwave spike up, up, *up*, off the chart—

Boom.

The blast wave flung her halfway across the room. When she struggled up to look, Mark was sitting up too, his face blackened and bloodied. His expression was empty with shock, which quickly turned to fury. He got up, swaying, and stared at the safe, which now hung open. Stinking black smoke billowed out of it.

Whatever had been inside it was nothing but ash and cinders now.

"You lying bitch," he said hoarsely. "I will rip your heart out for that!" He reached for her, hauling her to her feet.

"No, you won't." A voice from the door. Something flashed through the air—

Mark shouted hoarsely. He twisted, and pulled a long shard of bloodied glass out of his shoulder. Noah barrelled at him, from across the room. Barefoot. Nearly naked.

Mark flung her away. The two men charged each other with a guttural roar.

Caro hit the floor. Something massive landed on top of her. The woman slave soldier shifted on Caro, pinning her. She could barely breathe. She heard thuds, grunts, chunks of falling plaster and primal howls, but all she could see were billowing clouds of plaster dust.

She heaved and bucked, finally shoving off the slave soldier, who suddenly relinquished her grip. The woman stared at the two men fighting, her irises white-rimmed dark brown circles. Her mouth hung open. She'd forgotten that Caro existed.

Caro shoved sweat-matted hair out of her eyes, and saw Noah flung through the air, crashing high up against the wall with bone-shattering force. Her scream of denial froze in her throat as he fell out of the jagged hole in the plaster and landed in a catlike crouch on his bare feet, spattering bright red blood against the snow-white plaster dust.

He ran at Mark again.

Mark met him, slashing low with a knife he'd hidden. Noah blocked the stabs, his moves too swift for her to see. He caught Mark's knife hand. Mark flipped sideways and out of the hold, landing upright and spinning around. His back kick slammed Noah against the wall, punching him through the plaster and deep into the wall framing.

Mark seized the end of an old church pew from the furniture heap and hurled the heavy thing like a spear. It smashed through the wall above Noah, and the whole wall collapsed onto him, frame, bricks, plaster. Caro screamed when she saw Mark grab a heavy brass altar lamp for a lethal swing at Noah, still partly trapped under the rubble.

Noah caught the lamp mid-swing, and jerked Mark off his feet.

In seconds the men were a grunting, writhing knot. Noah kicked his legs free and flipped over, on top of his assailant. Mark's legs scrabbled and drummed against the ground, making choking sounds. Caro finally saw why. Noah had the rotten lamp cord wrapped around Mark's neck.

Mark clawed at his throat, legs flailing. The stained glass window tinted the clouds of pale, swirling dust a lurid red. The filthy floor was smeared with blood, both Noah's and the blood and brain tissue of the dead slave soldier next to them.

Mark reared up, attempting eye contact with his slave soldiers. "Controller . . . commands!" he coughed out. "Commands . . . you! Shoot . . . my enemy!"

The man lying on top of Asa slowly raised his pistol, taking aim at Noah.

"Brenner!" Caro yelled. "Don't do it! Callie needs you! Remember Callie!"

"Callie?" Brenner's gaze jerked over to her, startled. "Callie?" Blood trickled from his nostrils. His gun hand sagged, as if he'd forgotten about the weapon.

Caro looked at the woman slave soldier. Tears streamed down the woman's sweaty face. Her mouth hung open. She didn't respond to Mark's command.

Her breaths were harsh, gasping rasps of pain.

Noah would not yield. Mark's legs slowed, trembled. And finally stopped.

The silence was absolute.

Still, Noah maintained his grip with resolute patience, his expression unreadable. Waiting for some signal that only he could perceive.

Silent moments passed. No one moved, or spoke, or even breathed.

Finally, Noah let go. He crouched on one knee before his fallen adversary, and slowly rose to his feet. The bloodied cord dangled from his hand like a whip.

He stood there, a terrifying vision, spotlit in the blazing column of light, like a creature from myth or legend, his massive chest whitened and blood-smeared as if painted for combat. His eyes burned with a hot predator glow as they fastened onto her.

It had been like watching gods do battle.

Chapter 34

NOAH'S GAZE SWEPT around the room, assessing everyone. Despite her unconscious state, Hannah's sig showed strong vital energy. Close to waking. Caro seemed fine, though her face was pale and her eyes shimmering with tears.

"You OK?" he asked. His voice was hoarse and cracked.

Tears streaked down her face. She wiped them away with grubby hands, nodding quickly.

Asa had pushed the slave soldier off himself. Strangely, the man offered no resistance at all anymore. He lurched clumsily to the side and sat on his ass, swaying. Blood streamed from his nose. His gun dangled in his hand, evidently forgotten.

Asa scrambled across the floor, and crouched by Hannah. "She's blinking," he said. "I think she's coming to. Gotta get her pulse. Cut me loose, for Christ's sake!"

"She's all right." Noah scooped up Mark's bloodied knife, and snapped through Asa's restraints. "Her sig looks fine."

Asa pressed his fingers to her throat, exhaled slowly, and met his brother's eyes. His expression was somber.

"Holy shit, Noah." His voice was tight, vibrating. "I had no fucking idea."

Noah's jaw clenched. "Yeah, I know. It's a lot to take in."

"Remind me never to piss you off," Asa said.

"No point," Noah told him. "Lost cause."

Asa looked at the stupefied soldier, who sat limply, mouth gaping.

"Dude looks messed up," he said.

Noah assessed him, then the female. "Yeah. Both of them are."

"Better get their weapons."

"Yeah." It was a good thought. Noah tried to move. He stumbled, almost fell.

So he just stood and watched as Asa deftly twitched the gun from the limp hand of the male soldier, and then did the same to the woman who had been restraining Caro.

The female soldier looked lost and confused. Her nose bled heavily, and her eyes were beginning to roll back in her head, her breath coming short and sharp.

Here it came. Noah braced himself. He'd watched this scene play out many times at Midlands. It was all over for these two. They'd opted for freedom and now they paid the price. He respected them for it, but it still sucked to watch.

Asa yanked a knife from his boot and cut Caro's bonds. She pulled the strange metal helmet off her head, and started rubbing her wrists.

Noah realized, with a jolt, that he had not thought to do that for her. In fact, he had not thought at all. Thick headed lug. Couldn't seem to think. Or move.

"Who the hell is Callie?" Asa asked her, as he kneeled at the side of his employee and felt that man's pulse as well.

Caro tried to speak, coughed, and tried again. "His two year old daughter," she said. "I saw a newsclip about them on the Internet. Recognized him."

Asa nodded, moving to check his other man who lay near Mark and the dead soldier. Noah noticed that Asa's fingers were dripping blood. He'd taken a bullet to his upper arm. "You're shot," he said sharply.

His brother wiped his hand on his jacket with a shrug. "Not a problem," he said, as he peered under the unconscious guy's eyelids with a frown of concentration.

By that time, the two slave soldiers were in full crisis. The process was swift and horrible, and took less than a minute. They convulsed, gasped, struggled for breath as if drowning in their own blood. Then slowly they went still.

Asa stared at them, horrified. "What the fuck is wrong with them?"

"They resisted their programming," Noah said wearily. "That set off the auto-destruct brain implant. It makes the brain dissolve. Just turns to slop."

"Jesus." Asa looked appalled. "That is some ugly, twisted shit."

"Yeah." He stared bleakly at Mark's two prototypes, arched in agony on the ground, faces contorted. He'd witnessed that scene too many times to be shocked, but it was still depressing. Knocked him even further underground.

He was just so fucking tired. He wanted to fall at Caro's feet, put his head in her lap, close his eyes. Make it all go away.

But she wasn't coming to him. And she was giving him that look. Those shocked, scared eyes. Like she was afraid of him. Sickened by what she'd seen.

Right. Like any sane person would be.

Noise from the door sent them into guard mode again, but Noah sighed in relief to see first Sisko and then Zade stumble in. They were bruised and bloodied, but both on their feet. That was all that mattered.

"Situation outside?" he asked.

"Quiet now," Sisko said wearily. "There were only two of them out there, but it took us a while. Tough bastards. They almost won."

"Both of them are down?"

"Yeah. Gone." Sisko sounded unhappy about it. "They fought real hard. Wouldn't give up. But we finished them."

Zade took his headphones off as he walked over to Mark, staring down.

"Put those back on, you idiot!" Noah snapped. "He's not dead!"

"He looks pretty far gone." Zade crouched down. His hands were clenched into enormous fists, but his voice was carefully casual as he peered into Mark's face. "How do you want to transport him?"

"There are dedicated carrying cases out there in his truck," Noah said. "We should dose him with his own sedative, if we can find some of it. The stuff is potent."

"Help me get my men to the van first," Asa said. "They need medical attention. I have somebody on call. He's good, and discreet, if any of you need to get checked out."

"Nah, we're good," Noah said. Mark's sig still showed the slow, dull pulse of unconsciousness when he checked, so he turned to help lift one of Asa's guys.

"Noah!" Caro shrieked.

Mark's sig flashed, blinding white like lighting bolt. He jack-knifed to yank a compact pistol from his ankle holster.

Asa threw himself in front of Noah, shielding his brother as Mark emptied his gun.

Every bullet made Asa's body jerk. He crashed to the ground, breaking a rotten chair into splinters on his way down.

Then three more shots jarred her ears, from a different direction.

Mark's head disintegrated.

"Callie." The thick, garbled voice of the slave soldier that Caro had called Brenner. He'd dragged himself back to consciousness. Now he slumped to the floor, the Ruger 9mm he'd pulled out falling from his hand, blood streaming from nose, mouth, ears.

Noah dropped down next to Asa, and touched his brother with a shaking hand.

Asa's sig flashed, and his eyes opened. His grin answered his brother's unspoken question. "Nah. Dragon skin." He spoke with effort as he thumped his body armor. "This shit works."

"You still got hit," Noah said.

"No big deal," Asa rasped. "Only five bullets."

Noah's breath eased. "Fuck you. Stay down."

Asa just snorted. Someone was cursing viciously behind him. He turned to look. It was Zade, standing over Mark's body, his face a mask of grief and fury.

Noah wished he could get up. "Zade. Listen to me. We'll find Luke."

"Mark was the only one who knew where he was, and his brain is smeared all over the fucking room! Even his slaves are dead! How can we find him now?"

"Calm down," Noah said. "We'll keep at it. And we'll find him."

Zade spun around and punched his fist through the nearest wall, spraying a fresh cloud of plaster powder everywhere.

Sisko hissed, in sympathy. "Ouch."

"Fuck it," Zade mumbled. "It's only my left hand. Feels good. For a couple of seconds, anyhow."

Sisko flung his arm around Zade's shoulders. "Let's get Hannah to your place. Then we park Mark's truck in your garage and get blind drunk somewhere."

"Do not draw attention to yourselves," Noah said, out of force of habit.

"Piss off, Grandpa," Sisko retorted.

Hannah was sitting up now. Caro made encouraging murmurs as she helped his younger sister onto her feet. Hannah staggered drunkenly, but her sig still looked steady. Pallid and raggedy, but already getting stronger.

Hannah swept the room with her bleary gaze. Her eyes went back to Asa after she'd accounted for them all. "You got shot?" she demanded. "I heard gunfire."

"I'm OK," Asa said. "Wore body armor. Just bruises."

"Bruises," Hannah repeated suspiciously, seeing the blood on his face. She saw the bodies of the slave soldiers, and turned sharply away. "Oh, God. I gotta get out of here right now." She lurched forward.

Caro caught her before she fell. "Wait. I'll help you. Hang onto me."

Noah watched uneasily as the two women made their careful way out of the room. He knew that he could trust Sisko and Zade's assessment of the danger level outdoors, but he still disliked having either of them out of his sight.

He tried to help Asa up. His brother shook off his hand. "I'm fine."

"Like hell, dragon boy," Noah said. "Probably cracked some ribs."

"Wouldn't be the first time." Asa's breathing was labored.

"You need a doctor, too," Noah said.

Asa grunted impatiently. "My men need one more."

Noah looked around the room. Dust hung in the air, blurring the smeared and spattered blood, the sprawled bodies. "How are we going to clean this mess up?"

"I can send a clean-up team," Asa said. "Crime scene techs. Very competent."

"The ones that come in after detectives and coroners are done? Don't think so."

"They're not affiliated with law enforcement," Asa said calmly. "Private cases only. Discretion assured. Expensive as all fuck."

"I'm rich, you're rich," Noah said. "Do it. But I don't want the slave soldiers wrapped in plastic and thrown in a muddy hole. Those two did the impossible. They're heroes."

"They'll be handled with respect. I'll get you their ashes to spread. Will somebody help me get my men out to the van? Or do I have to hold you guys at gunpoint to get that done?"

Sisko and Zade obliged. Fortunately for Noah, since his body did not respond to his brain's commands. He stood there, empty and hollow. Alone with the corpses.

Caro came back after a few minutes, and found him there. She took his arm and towed him around the cadavers, through the rotting, crumbling house, circling around garbage and tumbled bricks. He left a trail of bloody prints in the dust behind him.

Then she drew him out in to the cold, sweet air of a new day.

Chapter 35

HE WAS SO beautiful, it broke her heart. Even ghostly white with plaster dust and smeared with blood. She'd never seen that look on his face. Raw, open and unguarded. The sapling firs that had grown up around the front entrance bent and swayed in the gusts of raw wind. He had to be so cold, wearing nothing but those stretchy boxers.

Then she clutched his arm to steady him on the broken, uneven steps, and realized that he wasn't cold in the least. He radiated roaring, bonfire heat.

Asa's van braked abruptly in front of them. His window hummed down.

"I'll be in touch about the confession," Asa said. "Give me a day or so."

Caro looked at him blankly. "Huh?"

Asa's voice was impatient. "For the police, remember? Four different vantage points, audio and video. We both heard Mark say loud and clear that he killed Dex Boyd. And Tim Wheaton. Now the police can hear him say it, too. Didn't you want to clear your name? Wasn't that a thing for you?"

"I forgot all about it," she said. "In all the excitement."

"Lucky for you, I didn't," Asa said. "Anyway, do what you want with it. I imagine you don't want the cops to see everything on it, especially that weird shit with the slave soldiers, but you guys can work that out for yourselves. I'm gone."

The van surged forward. The red taillights retreated into the dripping greenery.

Zade's van pulled out next. She glimpsed Hannah's pale, exhausted face in the window of the passenger seat as they exchanged weary waves. Then Mark's big truck rolled away, driven by Sisko.

"Do you have a vehicle here?" she asked Noah.

He squinted against the light. "No," he said. "We came with Sisko and Zade. And they all just left."

They gazed after the disappearing taillights, and Caro began to laugh. "Oh, man," she said. "That is funny. We do battle with the forces of evil, avoid death by a hair, ransom our lives back from the pits of hell . . . and forget to arrange a ride home."

"My fault."

"Don't apologize," she said quickly, before he could. "Why is it your job to think of everything?"

He shrugged. "I don't know. Because it is?"

"Not anymore. Welcome to the new world order." She tugged his arm. "The emergency getaway car you guys hid for me is thataway." She pointed. "I'd say maybe less than a mile if we cut straight through the woods."

He stared at the thick forest. "And if we take the road?"

"Much longer. Obviously, we can't hitchhike. No cars."

"And if there were . . ." He looked down at his briefs like he just realized that's all he was wearing. "I wouldn't stop for myself."

"What happened to your clothes?"

He coughed, rackingly. "The soldier who picked me up after the drone shot me took them. He was packing me up for transport." He stumbled again.

414

She hurried to wrap her arm around him. "Can you walk? Where are you hurt?"

"I'm fine. Just sore. And having an adrenaline crash. Food would help. Or lying around in bed for a few weeks with you. Naked."

"Do you ever not think along those lines, Noah? I mean, you're barefoot, and your feet are bleeding. Stop. Sit down."

"I'm not going back in that place," he said.

"Then go sit over there, by those birches. You can sit on that big one that fell. I'll hike to the car and come back for you."

"No," he said forcefully. "I'm not taking my eyes off you ever again. For the rest of my life. My feet will be fine."

Her face went so hot, the cold, misty rain against her face felt good.

He probably didn't really need her to hold onto him. Still, she had no way of knowing if he was injured internally. He wouldn't admit to so much as a twinge of pain.

So she walked with him to the clump of birches, taking everything she saw, from the dark gray clouds that hung heavy and swollen to the rustling patter of rain and the earthy sweetness that it released from the forest floor. The swish and murmur of wind in the firs, the raindrops glittering on every leaf, twig and pine needle, each detail was jewel sharp and clear. The forest around them was infinitely deep, growing deeper every second as her senses opened and merged with it. And Noah's eyes had that thrilling amber glow that made her heart quicken and her thighs quiver.

Amber? Suddenly, it dawned on her. "Noah. You're outside in daylight, with no shield lenses or even any shield specs on."

"Yeah," he said simply. "I know."

"And are you—I mean, is the AVP—"

"It's running hot, but I'm OK. It's not driving me crazy, for some reason. I'm fine. I still can't believe it. You're alive. We're all alive. We did it.

Holy shit, Caro." His voice cracked, and he pulled her into his arms "That was so fucking close."

God, it felt so good to hold him. Pleasure and relief shuddered through her body. He was so warm and strong, and his tender grip was just what she craved. The love, the care, the belonging.

She cupped the back of his head and kissed him. He tasted coppery and hot. And beneath that, there was the essence of him, the feel of him. Lithe and vital and strong. Still here. Still hers.

She realized that she was crying only when Noah began kissing the tears from her cheeks. He rested his forehead against hers, swaying slightly. Unsteady on his feet.

"You're hurting," she said.

He flinched as he dragged in a painful breath. "It's nothing."

"I don't believe you," she said. "Just let me take care of you for once. Please."

"I'm fine, and I don't want to stop kissing you," he said stubbornly. He ignored her outstretched hand as he lowered himself onto the fallen birch.

She sat down beside him, resting a hand on the white bark stippled with black. He covered it with his, adjusting his position with another subtle flinch of pain.

He stared blankly at the birch trees for a few moments. He looked exhausted. "You know, when I was a kid, I used to think those black lines were writing that I couldn't read."

"Maybe it is," she said. "And you know what? I thought the same thing."

"Yeah. Well . . . Caro," he began. "Guess this is as good a time as any for us to talk. I have to say something to you. Before I lose my nerve."

Her belly clenched. "Go ahead." Here it comes, she thought miserably. *It's not you, it's me. I'll always be a loner. What happened between us was just one of those*

416

things. Which would he pick? And did it matter? Male rationales were more alike than not.

"I saw the look on your face, after my fight with Mark," he said. "It looked like you were scared of me."

Apprehension gripped her. "I was in shock. That was all."

"You had reason to be," he said. "Because this shit is scary."

"Noah . . ." She cut herself off. Didn't want to relive any of it.

"Just listen." He lifted his head, and stared into her eyes. "You know, you could have your life back. Your old life. As Caro Bishop."

"I suppose I could, thanks to you. So? What's your point?"

Noah sighed. "This isn't easy to say. I did a lot of chest beating the other night. How you're mine, mine, mine. But now that we're here, I can't ask you to stay. It was different before. My mods protected you from Mark before. But that's all over. And everything that I am just puts you in more danger. Again."

She lifted her chin. "Are you done yet?"

"You'd never have a normal life with me," he persisted. "There will always be life-or-death secrets to keep. You have a chance to walk away. Have a real life."

"I tried that, Noah. Somehow I never got the hang of it. Maybe I'm not cut out for normal, whatever that means."

"Caro." He sighed raggedly. "I love you. But I can't keep you safe. No matter how much I want to. Walk away. Send one of the guys back for me. Go to the car. I won't try to stop you."

She stroked his cheek. "No," she said simply.

"Why not?" His eyes blazed with fiercely controlled emotion.

"Because it's too late," she said. "You've changed me. I can't go back to being who I was before you came along. Maybe we are too different . . . but I've never wanted anything the way I want you."

"You sure about that?"

She thumped the solid tree they sat on. "Yes."

"What if you change your mind?"

She shook her head. "About you? Never."

He grinned. His big, wide grin that didn't fade away. "OK, then. We're on."

She was too rattled and exhausted to decode that. "What the hell are you talking about now?"

"Isn't it obvious? I wanted to do this before all hell broke loose. Just in case we didn't make it. But here we are."

"Do what?"

"We belong together, Caro."

She couldn't quite believe he'd said the words. "And that means . . ."

"I have to improvise. Can't kneel right now, though. Sorry." Noah peeled off a strip of birch bark and took her hand, curling the speckled white shred of papery bark around her finger. "Caro," he said. "My goddess. My warrior woman. Mistress of my bedchamber. Keeper of my heart and soul. Please, marry me. Eventually, or as soon as we get back to Seattle. I don't care. Just so long as you say yes."

She gulped. Dumbstruck.

His beautiful amber eyes searched hers.

The smile started in the depths of her being and radiated out from there.

"Yes." The single word held so much she couldn't say. "I love you."

"And I love you, Caro," he whispered. "I love you."

* * *

He held her for the longest time. It still seemed too short.

They kissed with desperate tenderness. Talked too, rushing the words, then falling silent. Then kissed again. He was too injured to make love, though it pained him most of all to admit it.

Only when fat raindrops began pattering down in earnest did they come to their senses and start moving.

They headed ever deeper into the lush, tangled woods hand in hand, slipping and sliding on wet leaves and mud and pine needles as the rain beat down on them.

Laughing and crying. Heading home.

THE END

About the Author

Shannon McKenna is the NYT bestselling author of fifteen action packed, turbocharged romantic thrillers. She loves tough and heroic alpha males, heroines with the brains and guts to match them, villains who challenge them to their utmost, adventure, scorching sensuality, and most of all, the redemptive power of true love. Since she was small she has loved abandoning herself to the magic of a good book, and her fond childhood fantasy was that writing would be just like that but with the added benefit of being able to take credit for the story at the end. The alchemy of writing turned out to be messier than she'd ever dreamed, but what the hell, she loves it anyway and hopes that readers enjoy the results of her experiments. She loves to hear from her readers. Contact her at her website, http://shannonmckenna.com and find her on Facebook at https://www.facebook.com/AuthorShannonMckenna/ to keep up with all her news!

Please consider writing a review. Reviews don't just help authors; they help readers find the books they love!

If you'd like to know when new installments of The Obsidian Files are released, join the newsletter by signing up here: http://shannonmckenna.com/connect.php.

CPSIA information can be obtained
at www.ICGtesting.com
Printed in the USA
LVOW12s1141050217
523244LV00004BA/791/P